To my sister Nancy and brother Kevin for so many hours of pleasurable company.

To my family each and every one of you.

To Mick, Peggy, and Noreen the remnants of the '58 circle of friends for the great times.

A special word of thanks for Daragh and Declan for once again routing the gremlins that plague my world of modern technology.

Thanks to my daughter-in-law Connie and my friend Nuala Campion for reading the then almost illegible manuscript and saying – yes – yes.

And not forgetting Ambrose Cassells who helped greatly with his recollections of Kuwait.

A Different Kind of Loving

Also by Kathleen Sheehan O'Connor

By Shannon's Way
Silver Harvest
Hold Back the Tide
The Son of a Nobody

KATHLEEN SHEEHAN O'CONNOR

Different Kinds of Loving

A Brandon Original Paperback

Published in 2000 by
Mount Eagle Publications
Dingle, Co. Kerry, Ireland

10 9 8 7 6 5 4 3 2 1

Copyright © Kathleen Sheehan O'Connor, 2000

ISBN 1 902011 14 7
(original paperback)

The author has asserted her moral rights

Cover design by Justin King, Clifden, Co. Galway
Typesetting by Red Barn Publishing, Skeagh, Skibbereen
Printed by ColourBooks Ltd, Dublin

CHAPTER ONE

Tɪᴍ Dᴜɴɴᴇ sɪɢʜᴇᴅ and put down the newspaper. He always knew when he had lost the battle. If his wife Eileen wanted to talk about the wedding again, he knew he'd have to show an all-consuming interest, as if he cared what flowers would be perfect with the bridesmaid's dresses and not detract in any way from the bride's bouquet. As if he cared what co-ordinated with what.

"Honestly," she complained, "sometimes I think you only want to charge up the church with her and have it all over as soon as possible."

"Don't see much wrong with that. Even Sarah would like it all over at this stage. Too much panic, too much fuss. Wouldn't it be great if we woke up tomorrow and saw a little note saying that the two of them had dashed off to Las Vegas or somewhere?"

"I knew it! All you want to do when you come home from work is bury your head in that stupid paper. Who cares about the arms trial? Sure who cares about Charlie Haughey?"

Looking at her now he could see how exasperated she was becoming. He decided he'd better mollify her before she really became upset.

"Yes, yes, white rose buds would go lovely with freesias, or was it sweet peas?" Looking at his pleading, almost boyish look, her exasperation dissipated.

"Oh, it's all right – it doesn't matter. Sure, you'd hardly know a rosebud from a freesia anyway. Go back to your old paper."

Men, she thought ruefully, *simply don't want to know about weddings*. They weren't interested in the trappings, the clothes, the guests, who must be invited and who they might get away without inviting.

When her eldest daughter, twenty-one-year-old Sarah, had

got engaged to Alan Beirne six months previously, she could see herself getting through the whole procedure with a calm, almost professional efficiency. A foolish notion far removed from the present panic. She woke up every morning with a dry mouth and a thumping heart. When the fog of broken sleep evaporated, bringing the knowledge that the wedding was only two weeks away, she felt like getting sick. It was only yesterday that Sarah had told her to calm down.

"For God's sake, Mam, it's only me and Alan getting married. Sure, you know him like the back of your hand. Relax or you'll have a heart attack."

Eileen Dunne sighed. She had liked Alan the day Sarah had brought him to the house and proudly introduced him to herself and Tim. As time went by she simply couldn't imagine life without Alan Beirne. He was almost like the son she never had. She looked up and spoke to the back of the paper.

"Would you have liked a son? You know – would you have liked Patsy to have been a boy?"

He put down the paper, sighed, and then, raising his eyes to heaven, he addressed the ceiling. "What is she on about now? A boy! I couldn't have handled a boy plus Patsy. She's worse than three boys rolled into one. Who nearly drowned when she was seven because she wanted to swim to England? Who fell off the cliff because she wanted to climb Mount Everest? Who stole five pounds from my wallet to feed the poor of Waterford after she saw Robin Hood? On second thoughts, any boy would have been easier than Patsy." About to escape behind his beloved paper again, he suddenly said gently, "You know what, this wedding is getting you down. Will you relax."

"You're right," she told him. "Go back to your paper."

It was true. Tim had never shown the slightest sign of disappointment that they didn't have a boy. He was very proud of his daughters, indulging and spoiling them ridiculously. But she herself would have liked to have had a son. It would have been nice to have a lad around the place, nice for Tim to know that his name would carry on, nice for the girls to have a brother they could argue and fight with, a sort of masculine mix that would round off the family.

She supposed she felt like this because she was a farmer's daughter, and sure the birds in the bushes knew that farmers wanted a son, almost like they wanted air to breathe.

She glanced at her spouse who had gone back to his paper, now clutching it rather tensely, obviously hoping that he wouldn't be disturbed again. Sitting there in the quiet their own wedding day came back. The reception had been in the Majestic in Tramore with forty guests, her parents happy with her choice, a young trainee accountant with good prospects, although he was only earning buttons at that time. She remembered telling her older brother Seamus that Tim's wages were only four pounds a week. He had collapsed laughing against a hay rick he was forking saying, "Jasus, sure you won't be able to buy a bag of Liquorice All Sorts with that kind of money."

He was right in a way, and it had been tough in the beginning in a small damp flat over a shop on the quay in Waterford with a baby after ten months and dripping napkins on a clothes dryer in front of the fire. Tim patiently studying silent hour on silent hour hoping to get his final exam. Eventual success and an appointment with a good accountancy firm in Waterford and a semi-detached house in a lovely little crescent in the suburbs. Then, with carefully hoarded savings and a friendly bank manager, opening his own firm and seeing it grow over the years. Then buying a bigger, better house eight miles outside the city because Tim knew she had always wanted to live in the country, a bright sunlit place with a little land which made it possible to keep a pony, a Christmas present which their daughter Patsy had cajoled, begged and beseeched them to buy her.

She sighed, wondering why she was letting her thoughts ramble down through the years when she had so much to do. Sarah was only weeks away from walking up the aisle with Tim, followed by her bridesmaids, her two younger sisters, Emma and Patsy. Emma so dark, different from the others; Patsy long since outgrown her puppy flesh and her pony; Sarah blonde, calm and elegant. She sighed a long and drawn-out sigh that made her husband glance up again – a glance that was slightly tinged with guilt.

"Look, girl," he said gently, "did you ever hear the saying – it'll be all right on the night?"

After a windy, wet June the sun came out on the first of July and continued to shine from a cloudless sky. The day before the wedding there was a stoic calmness in the Dunne household as they persuaded each other that the show was on the road, with only small final arrangements to be made: the cake to be brought to the hotel in Dunmore East in the evening; the last minute calls to the florist to see that the bouquets would be delivered on time; a visit to the church to see that the altar flowers were just right. After an early tea Sarah Dunne surprisingly found herself with time on her hands. There was all of two hours before Alan would call for a last date before they would be man and wife. *Man and wife,* she thought with an unexpected jolt of surprised amazement. Although why she should feel like that about someone she had known and loved for so long was a bit ridiculous.

She wandered down to the small garden. It had always been known as the small garden, because there and only there they could do exactly what they liked when they were young. They could mess and dig. They could play and invite their friends to play. They could swing on the swing, digging their feet in so that they could soar high and higher, even glimpse the blue sea over the trees tops before they crashed back to earth again.

This warm summer evening it drowsed in the golden light and bore little sign of the years of frenzied play. The sunken sand pit was long since gone and Emma's enthusiastic efforts to turn it into a swimming pool were a memory. Sarah smiled remembering the heavy-duty plastic she had lugged to the pit, the perspiring efforts of their friends to put big stones in place to secure it, the anticipation in a dozen pairs of excited happy eyes as the water was hosed in. They had taken their turns and had romped in the home-made pool for a couple of days until the novelty wore off. The swing was still there. The grass had long since grown underneath. She walked over and sat on the swing, gently propelling herself to and fro. Her movements stirred the still summer air and the coolness it brought refreshed her.

This time tomorrow, she thought, *the wedding will be well under way.* This time the following day they would be in Rome on their honeymoon and the first night, the much talked and much thought about wedding night, would be over. She and Alan had never slept together; God knows they had wanted to but had always held back. She used to remind him they were going to be married and why not wait because it would be far more exciting if they did.

"Hey, bet you're thinking of tomorrow night?"

She looked around surprised because she had thought she was alone. Sure enough there was Patsy, sitting in the fork of the old oak tree, her long legs swinging and a look of intense misery stamped on her lightly freckled face.

"What in God's name are you doing up there? You could break a leg and then you'd have to come up the aisle on a crutch. Get down."

Sarah watched as her sister jumped down, landing with ease beside her.

"Well, answer me – bet you're thinking of tomorrow night?"

"Why would a seventeen year old who has just finished her leaving cert want to know such things?"

"I know so much about everything I'd leave you gasping. It's 1970 – everyone knows everything. And I was just wondering – not that you'd tell me anyway."

Sarah was grinning now. She knew that Alan and Patsy were the greatest of friends. Alan had spend so much time with her young sister trying to give her a maths grind for her leaving cert. He had done everything possible to break the persistent fog that shrouded the leggy, auburn-haired girl when it came to the mystery of mathematics. Patsy dropped to the lawn and started plucking the grass, tearing it into shreds.

"When you're gone it'll be different. Lonelier sort of, and then Emma will go back to bloody London and then I'll be left and I'll probably be an old maid and go mad."

Sarah laughed loudly, looking at the puckered, discontented face of her younger sister. "Old maid? Weren't you only saying a minute ago that you know everything that's to be known about fellows and don't you get more phone calls from lovesick guys that any of us ever got? So, I don't think you'll be an old maid."

"I might. I'm not beautiful like you or attractive like Emma. I'm just a tall gawk with red hair and freckles."

"Auburn hair and a sprinkling of freckles." Sarah, wallowing in her own happiness, felt generous. "Anyway I must go in, Alan will be calling and we must collect the cake and bring it to the hotel and – Oh God – I have a feeling I'm forgetting a thousand things."

"Wait a minute. I still want to know how you feel about living with Alan for ever and ever? I can't ask Mam about leaving one's father and mother and cleaving to one's partner, two in one flesh – you know the sort of stuff in the Bible?"

"Yeah, I sorta know the stuff in the Bible. You're quite crazy, but I'll tell you. It'll be easy because I love him."

Afterwards Sarah Dunne's friends said it was the most beautiful wedding of the year. She looked exquisite, tall and fair, and the dress clung in all the right places and then flowed like a gossamer cloud. Patsy and Emma looked beautiful, too. It was hard to imagine that wild tomboyish Patsy could look so good, her unruly auburn hair subdued, her beloved jeans discarded and the dress highlighting those long legs that seemed to go on for ever.

Tim Dunne had looked so proud as he walked up the aisle with his daughter. He still had no idea about rosebuds and freesias and what coordinated with what or who had been invited or who hadn't. He simply knew he was content with Sarah's choice. But it was the expression on Alan Beirne's face as he looked at Sarah that had moistened many an eye. His look of love seemed to be tinged with a sort of wonder that this girl was going to be his wife. Somehow there were no shuffles, no clearing of throats, no coughs or whispers when the priest said the timeless words for better or worse, richer or poorer, in sickness or in health. The proverbial pin could have been heard as they both clearly announced, "I do."

After that everything was right. The sherry reception loosened tongues, the meal was superb, the dance floor was crowded. Even the staid aunts, Tim Dunne's sisters, went wild when the band played "The Birdy Song" and "Put Another Nickel In". Eileen Dunne had even managed to stifle her tears when Sarah hugged her before dashing off to the festooned car. Surprisingly it was Patsy who had unashamedly let hers flow, as she told them to have a wonderful, wonderful time.

When they were gone the void was so obvious that the band made an extra effort, the lead singer clapping his hands as he shouted, "Everyone on the floor for a Paul Jones." As Eileen Dunne stood amongst the smiling circle of women, she too smiled, trying to lift her heart, telling herself that she hadn't lost a daughter she had gained a son: the sort of thing people always told themselves at weddings.

CHAPTER TWO

IT WAS ONLY seven-thirty, yet the sun was so hot that the room was stifling. Sarah lay there and listened to the noise down in the street below: loud shouts and ribald laughter, the foreign voices rising and falling in almost musical nuances. She could hear the clatter of refuse bins, the sound of a large truck revving and the horns of other cars blaring at what seemed an ungodly hour. She looked at Alan and could see that he was still sleeping soundly. The sun's rays seemed to highlight everything about that face she loved so much: the black hair, the dark lashes, the strong bone structure and a small scar near at the side of his mouth. She had never noticed it before. She traced her finger across it very gently so as not to wake him. She would ask him about it later.

Listening to the racket in the street below, she wondered how he could sleep through so much din. As she lay wide awake in the rumpled bed, she thought that maybe it was true – lovemaking took more out of men than women. It had happened last night. They had made love – frenzied, passionate love – not just once, but again and again. They had failed the first night. They had tried but it had been a fumbling, hurtful thing, and after their failure they had collapsed laughing, telling each other it didn't matter, they would try again when they weren't as exhausted. They would try when they were in Rome, the eternal city, the ancient place that had entranced them when they had studied the brochures during the wet, windy months of winter. After all, they loved each other and it should come easy, very easy. Isn't that what they had been led to believe?

She slipped out of the bed and went to the window. Down in the street below she could see the huge refuse truck stopping and starting, as the noisy, garrulous men emptied the large bins outside the modest guest houses. She looked in amazement at the flow of traffic. It went by in a bumper to bumper stream. To add to the confusion it looked as if half the population of Rome were on scooters or small motorbikes flying like huge moths amongst the cars and buses. She leaned further out the window and noticed that all the windows had shutters, faded and peeling as if the paintwork couldn't stand a chance against the merciless sun.

"I see Mrs Beirne is entranced with the view." Alan had come up behind her and, circling her with his arms, he too looked down at the unfamiliar frenzied scene. "They're sure in a hurry," he whispered in her ear.

She turned round, pulling him into her arms. "Hey, I thought you'd never wake up. I was going to lash off and get me an Italian. You'd want to see the bin men, they're pure hunks, dark, handsome, fierce virile looking."

"Am I not virile enough for you?" She hadn't a chance to answer because he smothered her mouth with a deep, hungry kiss, and as he led her back to the bed she was already weak with wanting him. When it was over they lay back, breathless and exhausted. Suddenly he laughed. "Remember the old joke about the fellow going up with the blinds after his honeymoon? Well, Sarah Dunne, you'll have me as weak as him."

Then they both laughed and their laughter became louder as they playfully wrestled and fought until they collapsed once again on the rumpled bed. Then with a lightening movement she jumped out of the bed and ran towards the door. She grabbed her lacy dressing gown and gasped, "I'm first for the bathroom."

The landing was empty except for a small, dark-eyed girl who was pushing a trolley laden with linen and towels. Sarah smiled and the young Italian flashed a dark, liquid smile in return.

The bathroom was spacious but devoid of any modern influence. The large enamelled bath was free-standing with elaborate curved legs, and the wash basin was so big it looked like a small bathtub. The tiled floor was cold under her bare feet, and the window was so high it seemed the sun

15

never touched the place to warm it. For some unknown reason she started to tremble and fleetingly wondered why. Only minutes before she had been basking in the arms of her husband, making wild, uncontrollable love. She shook away the unwanted stab of fear and concentrated on what she was doing. Turning on the taps, looking at the hot steamy water gushing into the old bath, she told herself that, maybe, marriage and lovemaking did that to you: soaring euphoric joy and then a cold chill in case anything would take it away.

She got a glimpse of herself in the mirror as she was about to step into the bath. She looked the same, the very same and *Why wouldn't I?* she told herself. *All that has happened since yesterday is that Alan, the man I love more than anyone or anything, has made love to me, has become part of me.* As she lowered herself into the hot soapy depths, another peculiar thought came, a notion that maybe right now, this very minute, in an old-fashioned guest house in the middle of the eternal city, cells and molecules and chromosomes were forming, starting a baby. She certainly hoped not – she didn't want to share Alan with anyone yet. She felt he didn't want to share her with anyone else either. They wanted time for themselves, some months of freedom.

She lay there with her eyes closed, thinking of the village where they would live, seven miles from Waterford, less than six from her own house, with a two-teacher school where Alan had recently been appointed principal. There had been some talk because of his youth, but the canon had given him the job, and when the canon had made up his mind there was no further questioning.

Their rented cottage about a half mile from the school was small but had a spectacular view of rolling hinterland and down below through the woods a view of the sea. Lying in the soapy depths she indulged in all sorts of fanciful thoughts about how they'd spend their lives there.

After breakfast they decided they'd go sightseeing. Alan

16

insisted she wear a large-brimmed sun hat. "All right for me – my thick hide will take it, but your fair skin will peel like an orange."

"Yes, master," she mockingly grinned.

They walked out from the shady hallway into the bright hard sunshine. Hand in hand they walked down the narrow cobbled street where tall buildings, all with wrought-iron balconies and shuttered windows, slumbered in the sun. She noticed that red geraniums blazed everywhere. They filled window boxes, they filled tubs on the small balconies, they spilled down through railings, their pungent odour filling the air.

"Isn't it like a painting?" Sarah murmured, her blue eyes sweeping the scene. "You know, the ones that make you feel warm in November?"

Alan tightened his grip. "As Al Jolson said, you ain't seen nothing yet. But if the new and most beautiful Mrs Beirne has no objection, I would like to leave the real sightseeing until tomorrow. Places like Saint Peter's, the Sistine Chapel, the National Gallery, the Pantheon."

"Heavens, you'd think you were here before, rattling off names like that."

"That's the teacher in me," he grinned, "the ability to assimilate. Anyway, wife, today we'll just mess around and drink coffee under awnings and I'll let the dark, virile Italians you admire, admire you. But I won't worry because I own you now." He leaned over and turning around kissed her on the mouth. An elderly Italian woman sitting outside her house looked at them, her dark eyes embedded in brown leathery skin filled with curiosity. Suddenly she smiled and mumbled something in Italian. They returned her smile.

"I wonder what she said?"

Sarah whispered, "I'm not sure, but I heard the word *buono* and that means good. I wonder would she think us good if she saw us this morning?"

"Of course she would. Aren't we married?" His eyes held hers and she could see the contentment and fulfilment in their depths.

"Funny how a marriage cert, a mere slip of paper, makes everything right. All the things that were a huge mortal sin up to then," said Sarah.

"Not a mortal sin for everyone, just girls like you. What you'd call good girls up to their necks in inhibitions instilled by the nuns and priests."

"Hey, I'm not that bad. Would you like me to be different – doing outrageous things or even saying outrageous things, a bit like Patsy?"

"No, you nut. I love you. As for Patsy, well, all I can say is she's different. She gets away with things."

Suddenly they were out of the narrow street and into the brilliant sunshine. The heat of the July sun had a furnace-like quality about it. They strode down the wide street, taking in the speeding traffic, smelling smells from wayside cafes, looking at black-dressed old ladies sitting behind blazing, dazzling flower stalls.

"Oh, I'm glad we came, I'm so glad we came," Sarah whispered, her eyes sparkling like a child.

"And you wanted to go to Kerry," he grinned.

"No imagination, master," she laughed. "You know that's what you'll be called now. The master. The master said this, the master said that. Oh God!" she exclaimed as if the thought had only come to her, "I suppose I'll be called the master's wife. Maybe they'll want me to go around in tweed skirts and brogue shoes."

He looked at her, tightening his grip on her hand. "Can't for the life of me see Sarah Dunne going around in tweed skirts and brown brogue shoes."

Six wonder-filled days later they were sitting at a street-side cafe eating delicious ice cream after yet another sightseeing tour. "You'd want six months in this city," Alan told her; "you mightn't even see it all in six months. Did you know that Napoleon said the history of Rome is the history of the world?"

"You're showing off now. But you're right – it's incredible. I can understand it being called the eternal city and all roads leading to Rome and stuff." She ate her ice cream, remembering her absolute wonder as she tried to grapple with the sights of the city. They had seen so much. The Coliseum, where Alan filled her in on everything he knew about the gladiatorial games and the massacre of Christians. In Saint Peter's Basilica with hundreds of other tourists, he bent down and whispered, "This, missus, is the largest and most famous Catholic church in the world. Look up there at the dome. See those crawling specks? They're tourists just like us and we're going up there now." Sitting there in the warm sunshine she recalled what he had said looking at the enormous fresco of the "Last Judgement" in the Sistine Chapel: "Men die before women, so wife, I'll be up there beside the hot seat before you."

"Don't you dare say things like that." His lightly tossed words had brought another stab of stupid fear. "We'll make a pact. A Roman pact that we'll both go together." As she said it she crossed her fingers, silently offering up an aspiration that she wouldn't be left in a world without him. As they strolled down the Via De! Forum Imperiali, he told her that the city owed a lot to Mussolini, who had enormous vision where the capital of his country was concerned. As they sat on the Spanish Steps in the burning heat, he told her he wanted to make love to her there and then. As they stood hand in hand looking at the illuminated ruins at night, he told her they would come back when they were old and grey and do it all over again.

Two days later they met Sean and Breda Curran.

CHAPTER THREE

THEY HAD ONE week left of their stay in Rome when they met them. As they were sitting outside their favourite street cafe, it was Sarah who noticed them first. She decided they were Irish, and not alone that, but they were on their honeymoon as well.

"But, of course, they won't think we're Irish," Sarah whispered. "You're so black with the sun already they'll think you're an Italian and I'm your English-born mistress."

"Let me wallow in that role until you undoubtedly enlighten them." Alan was still laughing when the young women exchanged smiles, and when a minute later the Currans invited them over they agreed readily. After the initial introduction, Alan asked, "Tell me, did you think that I was an Italian Romeo with a blonde English mistress? That new wife of mine thought you'd think on those lines."

They laughed and the ice was broken and soon there was more laughter and gladness that they had met. As the sunbeams slanted and the shadows lengthened, they sat and talked for what seemed like hours. They discovered that the Currans were from Blackrock in Dublin. They, too, had been married a week before and they, too, had seven more days of their honeymoon left. Like Alan and Sarah, they had most of their sightseeing finished. It was Sean Curran who suggested they hire a car for the remainder of their stay and share the cost.

"It's reasonable enough here," he told them. "We could go to places we wouldn't normally see. We could get to the coast, see remote villages untouched by the twentieth century, maybe see the real Italy. There's an English fellow in our hotel who told me one could rent a Fiat for buttons. Look, I hope you don't think we're barging in. It was just an idea."

He sounded a bit sheepish, as if his enthusiasm for the idea had carried him away. Alan looked at Sarah, her face propped on one hand, the other with the unfamiliar gold wedding band stirring the remnants of her now cold coffee.

"What do you think?"

"I'm on," she grinned. "See Naples and die."

"I don't know about Naples in a Fiat," Breda Curran laughed. "I've already given thumbs up. I agree with Sean, don't let us influence you – but if you're interested it would be cheaper to share."

"Naples!" Alan turned to the Currans. "My new wife has no sense of distances. We were in Dungarvan once and she wanted to know was Enniscorthy the next stop."

They all laughed, and with the stifling air a little cooler they decided they'd meet and have dinner later and then make plans for the collection of the car the following day.

"What'll I wear?" Sarah, standing in her slip, looked at her four new dresses. She had just finished her bath, and her face was scrubbed and shiny, her long hair dripping on to her shoulders. "I've worn all these already and I'm sick of them. Did you notice the cut on Breda's shorts? Bang on – up-to-the-minute Grafton Street chic."

"No, I didn't. I never notice anyone when you're around." He had come from the bathroom and had the bath towel hastily wrapped around his waist. Coming up behind her he put his arms around her and kissed the nape of her neck, murmuring, "Why didn't you dry your hair? You'll get your death of cold."

"In July in Rome? I don't think so." She turned around and he held her close, tilting her head, looking into her deep blue eyes.

"God, I love you, Sarah Dunne."

She returned his look, her eyes steadily holding his. "Ditto, Alan Beirne."

Then they were in each others arms and she couldn't care what dress she'd wear; she couldn't care if Breda Curran's shorts were straight from the House of Dior; she couldn't care if they never went out to dinner, never hired a car, never saw all the little unknown hamlets of rural Italy. She only knew she wanted him with a feverish desperation. When he carried her to the bed she helped him pull down the straps of her slip, and though their union was rushed and uncontrollable, they lay there afterwards fulfilled and content.

"I've become wanton, Alan," she murmured, "and you always thought I was a Holy Jo."

"No, I didn't," he whispered into her ear, noting that her hair was still damp. "I knew when this schoolmaster taught you all his wily ways there'd be no stopping you." He turned his head and his dark eyes held hers. "I'll never forget this evening: this room, our happiness, the feeling that there's a storm brewing, the eternal city out there and our whole life ahead of us."

She reached up and removed the lock of hair that had fallen over his forehead. "I know exactly what you mean. I feel the same." She turned to her locker and picked up her watch. "Hey, we must get moving. And, Alan Beirne, as a result of you wandering around in your pelt, like Tarzan, we have to bathe again."

"All in a good cause – all in a good cause." He was grinning as he grabbed the offending towel and made his way back to the bathroom.

That night lying in bed, surfeited with good food and wine, they were unanimous that their chance meeting with the Currans was fortunate. They both agreed that they were good company and that their suggestion of the rented car was a good one.

"Sean and I will collect it at the crack of dawn," Alan told her. "Seemingly the car hire companies do business at that unseemly hour. We might as well get the value of our weighty lira and have a full day tomorrow. You can languish in bed until I return, and then we'll have wheels and there'll be no stopping us."

She murmured something incoherently and he could see that she was already asleep. He kissed her briefly on the warm lips and he, too, fell into a deep sleep.

Sitting on the small, wrought-iron balcony, she noticed that the sun was obscured with a slight fog. It was still extremely warm and the pungent smell of the now familiar geraniums was everywhere. She knew the warm humid air, the delicious smell of coffee and freshly baked bread, mingled with the peculiar smell of decay, would for ever bring back memories of Rome.

She glanced at her navy shorts and blue and white striped T-shirt and felt they would be right for a day's touring in the heat. Her small watch, a present from Alan, told her it was already ten-thirty. He had told her that he'd be collecting the car at the crack of dawn and when she woke up he was already gone. There was a note on the locker accompanied by a snip of unopened buds of the multifarious geraniums. He had written:

> Looking at you lying there, your blonde hair all over the place, your mouth slightly open, your face scrubbed like a child, I said to myself, damn the car, I'll stay here and make love to my woman all day. Then I thought you'd be disappointed and reluctantly tore myself away. I love you. Alan.

She looked at her watch again and decided that they were lost, that maybe the Fiat had broken down, that Breda Curran was probably as impatient as she was, wondering what happened. Behind her in the landing she could hear Maria clattering the buckets as she mopped the floor. She had found out that Maria had five sisters and that her father was dead and her mother had to work in a clothing factory to make ends meet. Maria was the eldest and was hoping that someday she would save up enough to go to America. She had heard that there were plenty of good jobs and plenty of dollars. Sarah glanced down the street and thought she heard the blaring of a car horn below the balcony. She peered at the moving traffic trying to see a Fiat with a smiling Alan waving, but no – the horn was yet another irate Italian driver, and God knows they were legion. They seemed the most impatient race on earth when it came to traffic snarls.

Then there was more noise and more voices, but this time the noise was in the landing behind her. She could hear Maria and words rising and falling in the musical nuances that were now so familiar. There was another voice and she was surprised to hear that it was Breda Curran who spoke. So Breda had gone with them. *Obviously not as lazy as I am,* she thought. She was waiting to hear Alan making some laughing comment, but her straining ears didn't hear him. She turned and walked in from the balcony just as Breda Curran burst into the room. Sarah could see that her face was deadly white. The tan seemed to have faded, leaving the contours of her pretty face etched and stark.

"Sarah, there's been an accident – Sean and Alan have been taken to the hospital. Seemingly some bus or other ran into them – some question of fog or something. We must go to the hospital immediately. There's a guy from our hotel down below – he'll take us."

Sarah's heart stopped, and yet somewhere inside the thought came that she would always remember this moment. A moment of fear when the air was thick with the sharp pungent smell of geraniums. The perfume seemed to choke her, and fighting against a rising tide of blackness she silently followed Breda out the door. As they ran down the length of the landing, she noticed that she had picked up the spray of unopened buds that Alan had left that morning. Like someone in a dream, she was aware that her shaking hands were tearing it to shreds.

There was confusion and voices and heat. Strange, she hadn't felt the heat unbearable up to now. The short ride to the hospital had been in silence, the driver, an English tourist, seeming to know that conversation would be pointless. There was so much noise as they waited in a cool tiled area of the hospital waiting room.

Sarah sat in silence and prayed. As a child she used to pray for what she wanted, persuading herself that if she totally concentrated on the Sacred Heart or the Blessed Virgin to the exclusion of everything, her prayer would be answered. She did this now. *Dear Sacred Heart of Jesus, let him be all right. Let him be all right. Don't let anything happen to him in this foreign place. Please, please let him be all right.*

In silence Breda Curran put her arm around her shoulder, as if the human contact would somehow help them as they waited for some news. Sarah reached out to squeeze her hand, reminding herself that this girl from Dublin was suffering, too. This girl who had impressed with the well-cut shorts, who spoke with a south Dublin accent, whose husband had suggested that they hire a car – the terrible thing that had happened bonded them now.

After all, it might be nothing, a slight concussion. She remembered he had been concussed after a football match and he had been taken to Ardkeen hospital in Waterford. She had been demented then, just like she was demented now. But the next day he had been left home and he had called for her that evening in his old rusty banger, grinning at the door saying, "Hey, it's me – hard to kill a bad thing." She remembered the small scar that the strong sun had shown on the first morning of their honeymoon. Maybe that had been caused by another little accident like this one. She was going to ask him what had caused it but she must have forgotten. Suddenly Breda nudged her into the present.

"I think they're coming to tell us something."

Sarah lips were so dry, but the feeble attempt to lick them

brought no relief. The doctor was grey haired with an aquiline nose and had the same dark liquid eyes as Maria, the housemaid back at the guest house. He held out his hand and shook both their hands formally.

"I am Doctor Cellerino and this is Doctor Morella and we are very regret about this accident. Perhaps you would tell me who is who and which of you young women belongs to who?"

Another time Sarah might have found his broken English and his stiltedly phrased question amusing, but not now – not now.

Breda spoke first. "I'm married to the fellow with the reddish hair and Sarah here is married to the dark guy."

Sarah noticed that Breda also had trouble with her dry mouth. Dr Cellerino spoke to Breda first.

"We do not know now the exact position, but he has many lacerations and a bad leg fracture, also the broken collarbone, but he will make a good recovery."

Sarah's heart lifted momentarily as she heard his comforting words. She prepared herself to hear something similar. As he turned to look at her the unwanted thought flashed that there was something different, some fleeting expression, was it pity, was it sympathy in the depths of those dark liquid eyes? *Calf's eyes, bloody calf's eyes,* she thought hysterically, *that's what they all have in this godforsaken place.* Like someone in a dream, someone looking on from the outside, she heard the word "spine". When she focused and listened there were more words, but the words didn't mention full recovery, didn't say the things she wanted to hear.

"We are not, shall we say, certain. It will take much time and much tests and x-rays. There are all many bruises and lacerations and some chest injury, but the extent we are not sure. But," he smiled and his smile embraced the two of them, "it is – what do you English say? – early days yet."

"Irish," she heard Breda correcting him, and Sarah wondered why she bothered.

"Ah, *Irlandese* – beautiful green island, so I hear. So nice to meet someone from Ireland. So nice if the circumcisions were different."

Then he was gone with his liquid brown eyes and his dark foreign face, maybe gone to tell other people that it was early days yet. The nurse led them into another room where there were tables and chairs and some other people, many of them calmly reading magazines. She smiled at them and said something in Italian. Then seeing their vague faces she translated, "Coffee will be brung soon."

As they waited, sitting on the blue tubular chairs at a small white Formica-topped table, the words tumbled out. Words they had bottled up until now. Breda got in first.

"I know they'll be fine. They have to be, for God's sake. I mean, we're all just married. Nothing serious can happen, we're all only starting out. It doesn't sound too bad. Fractures, bruising, lacerations. Oh! God, Sarah, they're alive, thank God they're alive."

"Spinal injuries, he was talking about spinal injuries," Sarah whispered. "Could that be serious?"

"No, backs give out very easy. My father had a bad back for months. Now after physio he's fit as a fiddle. Don't worry."

CHAPTER FOUR

THE STRIDENT SOUND of the phone stopped the argument momentarily. Eileen was glad of the interruption. Patsy and Emma were having one of their endless tirades about clothes, the current row being about a white mini-skirt that had belonged to Sarah.

"She gave it to me," Patsy declared hotly. "I remember the actual minute she said I could have it. You remember, Mam? You were here."

"No, Mam wasn't, because she gave it to me in her bedroom just before the wedding. She also gave me a matching top. You know you hate Sarah's clothes – you always said they were frippery and feminine." Emma was quite worked up.

"Maybe they are, but I want that because I have nothing else to wear going to the tennis dance – so it's mine and . . ." Her voice trailed away as she heard her mother exclaim, "Oh no! Oh God, no."

They both rushed into the hall and saw their mother's white, shocked face.

"Something's happened to Dad," Patsy whispered, all thoughts of who owned the white mini-skirt fading rapidly. They sat on the stairs looking at their mother, try to gauge her reaction. She glanced at them and putting her hand over the mouthpiece whispered, 'It's from Rome – it's Alan – some sort of car accident." They could hear Sarah's voice now and the cackle and interruption. Their mother was making an effort to have a calming influence.

"No, love, it won't be like that. They can do wonderful things now. Six weeks in traction – he won't feel it – right as rain. Maybe Dad should go out and be with you? I'll call Dad now. Try not to worry, love, you'll see, he'll be fine. I'll light a candle every day. God spared him and that's the way to look on it. Goodbye, love. You'll phone again tonight, eight o'clock our time. Dad will be here. Don't worry too much. God spoke before the doctors. My mother used always to say God spoke first. Remember that."

They watched as she put down the receiver. She looked at them and they could see the pallor and the shocked look in her eyes.

"It's Alan. He's in hospital in Rome. Seemingly they met another couple of honeymooners from Dublin and they hired a car. Alan and the other lad went to collect it and they were hit by a tourist bus. Alan has possible spinal injuries and a lot of abrasions and things. Sarah is distraught."

"Will he be all right? What did the doctors say? God, imagine that happening to you on your honeymoon. Poor Sarah." Emma still sitting in the stairs closed her eyes in an effort to shut out the unthinkable.

"Poor Alan." Patsy's voice shook noticeably. "When are they coming home? What is this traction business all about?"

"Seemingly he's in traction until they see the extent of his injuries. They won't know until he's out of it. Sarah sounded frantic, poor lamb." Eileen blinked the moisture from her eyes. "She said the other girl whose husband was also injured was with her. She'll phone again this evening when Dad will be here."

"Maybe we should go out there." Patsy looked at the two of them. "Maybe we could help?"

"No, love, not much point," her mother told her. "There's nothing we can do now only pray. She tells me they're very good in the hospital and that he's sort of semi-conscious. Your Dad will be very upset. And think of his parents and that lovely old lady, his grandmother. God grant that he'll be all right."

They watched their mother wander into the kitchen, heard her open the cupboard, and they both knew she was taking out her mixing bowl. They had learned over the years that if ever she was in bad humour or very upset she worked like a mad thing, hoovering, mopping floors or making scones. This time it was obviously the scones.

Patsy, getting up, looked at her sister. "You can have the white skirt. I haven't the heart for the dance now." She wandered up the stairs and into her room.

Emma could hear her locking the door. She knew that Patsy had her own way of dealing with upset. Their mother occupied herself to try and shut out the unthinkable and Patsy locked herself into the room and wallowed in it. Whenever she had a row or was in trouble at school or had such a bad school report that it infuriated their father, she would disappear into her room. If they tried to prise her from its chaos, she would yell at them and tell them to drop dead. Emma knew it wasn't like that today. Alan had been like a brother to Patsy. In the earlier years she had followed him around like a gangling puppy after Sarah first introduced them.

Over the years they seemed to have enjoyed each other's company immensely. She had declared to all and sundry that she would have absolutely and categorically failed her inter cert without him. Only days before she had announced that she was certain of at least three honours in her leaving due to Alan's help, but that without him she would have been a gonner.

Patsy looked unseeingly around her untidy room. She forgot that she had intended to tidy it up and surprise her mother. She forgot that she had intended going to the tennis hop with Gavin Power, who only last week had told her that he had been trying to pluck up courage for a whole month to ask her. They had met at a disco in Tramore, and after he danced with her three times he got around to asking her. She had agreed because she liked him and thought she might as well go out with the fellow and maybe a miracle would happen and she might fall for him. She had forced herself to try and like fellows she met at the tennis club or at dances and parties in Tramore. She even tried to like the bespectacled young clerk with the stammer who worked in her father's office where she was doing a bit of summer work. But she was failing miserably, and no one, not anyone in her family, not any of her friends, not even her best friend Anne Marie Richards, not one single living soul except herself knew why. She was in love. Hopelessly and irrevocably in love with her sister's husband, Alan Beirne. Her feeling wasn't just a childish crush, wasn't because he had helped her with her ghastly homework, wasn't because he seemed the only one interested in her as a person. And it wasn't because they had spent so much time together.

When Sarah was working in the bank he had called during his long summer holidays. He had taught her how to dive in the deep waters at the back of the harbour; he had told her how to hold her breath and open her eyes and see all the movement and life and wonder under the water. And it wasn't because he had taken her in his arms at her seventeenth birthday and kissed her lightly on the mouth. Now, that was a shaky, unforgettable minute, but it wasn't even that. She had loved him almost from the first time she had seen him.

She could recall the evening down to the minutest detail. It was Sunday and it was April, because she remembered that Sarah and Alan had been caught out in a heavy shower before they burst into the hall. Sarah had told them a little about him, but he was just a name until then. She remembered thinking that he wasn't as tall as she had imagined. In fact he was only a few inches taller than Sarah. He was dark with black hair and very dark eyes, but it was his mouth she really noticed, because Anne Marie was going out with a fellow and she kept saying he was quite all right but for his mouth. His lips were too full, she insisted, quite slobbery in fact, and because of it she was definitely going to end it. She told Patsy she would even have settled for a fellow with thin lips, a bit like the fellows in the novels, lips in a straight almost cruel line, but full slobbery lips were out. So when Alan Beirne stood in the hall, his hair and face positively glittering with rain drops, she ran down the stairs and shook his hand.

She pummelled it up and down far longer than was normal and he said something funny about feeling like a politician. She hardly heard because her eyes were glued to his mouth. His mouth was perfect. She wondered was it what the writers of romantic novels described as firm and strong. She wasn't sure, but whatever it was it won hands down. In fact everything about Alan Beirne won hands down. In her estimation he was pretty perfect.

She wasn't even remotely jealous of Sarah. After all, Sarah was pretty perfect, too: tall with silvery blonde hair and deep blue eyes. She never had to worry about her figure because as far as Patsy knew she could eat like a horse and never put on weight. She was even all right for a sister. Not like Emma, who could be selfish and full of herself, going around as if the world owed her a favour. Sarah was different, and for the time she was going with Alan, Patsy had got to know him more and more. And the awful terrible tragedy was, the more she got to know him the more she got to love him. She looked out the window at what her father often boasted had to be the loveliest view in the south-east of Ireland.

The back windows of the house faced the back strands of Tramore, a spot known as Sauleen, a lonely deserted place rarely frequented by summer trippers. Then again it was considered dangerous for swimmers. But the Dunnes knew the area like the back of their hands and they knew the safe swimming places. When the tide was out, the pristine golden beach was dotted here and there with small pools and wandering rivulets. Out there she and her sisters had spent endless summer hours collecting crabs and cockles when they were small. They knew which rippled pool was the warmest, they knew where the big crabs were, and they knew where to dig in the firm wavy golden sand to unearth the biggest, whitest cockles. But it was the oyster bed that gave them most pleasure. When the tide was out, it was it was like a lagoon. Under the watchful eye of their father, they could swim its full length, their noisy shouts disturbing the gulls and the black divers who frequented the place.

Across from them were the tall whispering sand hills at the far end of Tramore beach, and way over there, shimmering in the distance, the town of Tramore itself, with its church spires and its great cliff-top houses.

Today she didn't even see the view because a thousand thoughts were churning through her head. He had been in an accident. He had suffered terrible injuries and was stretched on a bed in Rome and was in traction, whatever that meant. She wasn't quite sure, but she knew a bit about spinal damage. Two years before a sixteen-year-old boy had misjudged the tide in Newtown Cove over in Tramore and had broken his neck. There had been talk of spinal cords and spinal damage, and he had ended in a wheelchair paralysed from the neck down. Someone had said later that only his head worked. That simply couldn't happen to Alan. It was unthinkable. Unthinkable. Dear Jesus, if love could protect, her love would protect him from a fate like that. Staring unseeingly out the window she recalled the romping days after she had met him. When they all had played football on the beach. When he had beaten her by two lengths at the baths in Newtown Cove. She was so furious that she had challenged him again. When he let her win that time she had been twice as furious. She had stormed away yelling that she knew why she had won – did he think she was a right cretin?

The ringing of the doorbell downstairs brought her back and she wondered who it could be. When the impatient ringing got no response from below, she ran down the stairs and, opening the door, saw that it was Alan's parents. She saw the terrible concern on their faces and knew that they had received the bad news, too. She ushered them in, wondering where on earth her mother and Emma had gone.

"What have you heard, Patsy? Do your parents know? Is it as bad as we think?"

She was spared trying to think up comforting answers when her mother came in from the back garden. Eileen Dunne went over to the distressed couple and put her arms around them. "We're not sure of anything yet. Please God, he'll be all right."

"To think the last time we all met was their wonderful wedding day," Alan's mother sobbed as her husband Frank tried to console her

"He'll be all right," he gruffly told her. "They can do great things these days. Stop worrying, girl. People always imagine the worst."

They didn't waste too much time in the hospital in Rome. Ten days after the accident Sarah Beirne was told that the long-term prognosis wasn't good, that her husband's spinal cord had been damaged in the accident. He would possibly be paraplegic, paralysed from the waist down. Whether it was the suffocating heat of the Roman weather or the agonising days she had been through, the meaning didn't sink in. She looked at the doctor, her deep blue eyes questioning.

"But he will get better? I mean, not today or tomorrow but in time?"

The dark liquid eyes were filled with sympathy as the doctor gently tried to let her off lightly. "Yes, he will recover from his other injurious and, yes, he will get strength back. It is hard to say, as we cannot be certain, but it is possible that he will not walk again."

"But he will in time?" Her voice rose, and looking at the agony and the terror in their blue depths he would have given so much to say, "Yes, in time – in time all will be well," but he couldn't. He believed in not fobbing the relatives off with false hope, that it was right to tell them exactly where they stood and what the future held for the patient.

"No. When the spinal cord is severed, it does not mend."

"Does he know? When will you tell him?"

"We think it advisable to wait until the shock is lessened. We find that is better."

Her mother brought no consolation when she phoned to say that her father was coming to Rome to be with her and that Alan was in everyone's prayers. The days crept by, days of shock and anguish. Days when she hardly realised what was happening. Days when the heat was unbearable, the air so lifeless, the traffic so noisy, the smell of the geraniums so overpowering that she thought she would go mad. Days when the only semblance of normality she experienced was when she was with him. He had recovered consciousness and with the exception of a dressing on his head and contusions on his chest he looked so normal. He was lying flat on his back and weights and pulleys and all sorts of contraptions were hanging from the bottom of the bed. But when he regained consciousness and smiled the old smile, and it lit up his dark eyes like it always had done, and lit up her heart like it always had done, she persuaded herself that there was nothing serious wrong with him.

"Hello, love. The bridegroom is a bit of a wreck."

"Yeah," she tried to infuse warmth into her answering smile, "I can see that."

"Nothing I can't handle."

"Yeah, nothing you can't handle."

He reached out his hand and took hers in his strong grasp. His hand felt the very same as it always felt and his warm touch filled her with need and longing.

He didn't know yet; they said they would tell him when the time was right. He didn't know that the legs under the light white cover were useless. He didn't know that never again would he stride with his purposeful stride as if time were rationed and he had to get to his destination very quickly. He didn't know that his back was broken and that he might spend the rest of his life in a wheelchair. He knew nothing on that hot, suffocating evening when even the crazy traffic outside seemed to have quietened.

35

"How is Sean? Did he fare better or worse than I did?"

She smiled and intertwined her fingers in his. "He looks worse but will live to tell the tale. I see a lot of Breda; we're keeping each other company till the men in our lives are better."

She didn't tell him that she was jealous of Breda Curran's good news. She didn't tell him that she felt it was wrong to be jealous of such a thing.

He nodded. "It was so unfortunate. Sean was driving quite slow, right side of the road. He works in the car business, so driving here in this mad city came easy. The coach came round the bend at sixty and skidded. We hadn't a chance. I suppose, love, I'm lucky I'm not going home in a box."

"Don't say things like that. You'll be fine." She tightened her grip on his hand and her smile was warm as she leaned over to kiss him on the mouth. As she did so she tried to console herself, telling herself she, too, should be grateful he wasn't going home in a box.

CHAPTER FIVE

Doctor James Gillen was relieved that he had finally made the decision to take on a partner. The practice in Tramore didn't quite warrant it, but as he would be sixty next birthday, his wife Kit was all for it.

"You're not getting any younger," she pointed out. "You've been tied hand in glove to that practice all your life. Why you pay a golf fee for a game you rarely play is a mystery to me. And I do think we'll be dead long enough. Did it ever strike you it might be nice to have a little time to ourselves?"

He sighed. "I suppose you're right, and if I wait long enough you'll trot out your father's favourite, 'no pockets in a shroud'."

She could see he was relaxed now and the look of strain and tension had eased since he had agreed to take on Conor McElroy. They were sitting in their modest conservatory reading the papers, soaking up the last of the summer sun, sipping a liqueur, an after dinner treat they enjoyed when possible.

"Well, what did you think of young Conor? By the way, I'm glad you asked him to dinner. He says the only time he was ever in the south-east before was when his crewed on a yacht in Dunmore East as a student."

"I think he's a fine fellow. Handsome chap. I suppose all the young women in the place will go down like ninepins, seeing that he's unattached."

Her husband sighed. "Women for you, always talking about a fellow's looks. 'Tisn't his looks I'm interested in but his dedication. I hope he knows that this place is a bit of a backwater. I heard great reports about his internship. Seemingly he's the kind of fellow who gives as much time to the aged and the chronic as he does to the more interesting cases. And of course I knew his father, God be good to him, a great surgeon and a great loss when he went. They had a fine spread in County Meath beyond Athboy. His father inherited the place when his father died, although young Conor won't be rolling in the stuff down here." He finished his drink, only then remembering that he had something he hadn't wanted to tell her over dinner, knowing how the news would upset her.

"I heard bad news about young Sarah Dunne's new husband."

She looked up sharply from her daily battle with the crossword. "What happened? Sure, their wedding picture was only in the paper last week. Lovely young couple, take the sight from your eyes."

"Seemingly the bridegroom was in a car crash in Rome. Word has it that Alan Beirne has broken his back. From what I hear the break is midway, so it looks like he'll be paraplegic."

"Oh, my God," his wife's eyes were filled with horror, "that's terrible. Terrible. Are you sure? Who told you?"

"Why don't you believe anything I tell you? Do I have to get verification from the pope? I heard it and sadly it's true." He sounded exasperated.

"I'm sure the Dunnes are devastated," his wife answered, ignoring his sarcasm. "He was like a son to them. Maybe it's exaggerated – you know the way they put legs on everything here. With the help of God, it's not as bad as that. Is he home yet?"

"I believe he's back from hospital in Rome. He's in the National Rehab in Dublin. At least it's one of the best in Europe. If there's anything that can be done, it will be done there."

She was silent as she bent her head and went back to her crossword, but somehow she had lost interest in five across. She thought of young Sarah Dunne who was such a lovely girl. She had met her several times with her mother in Waterford shopping before the wedding. At the ICA meeting Eileen Dunne had been so happy about everything. Alan was an only son, too, according to Eileen. She thought of his parents and how they must be levelled by such a cruel blow. She sat there in the warm rays of the sinking sun, thinking life was such a bitch at times. Sailing along everything fine one day and then out of the blue a kick in the teeth to pull you up.

"By the way," her husband scattered her negative thoughts, "as young Conor hasn't fixed himself up with accommodation, I was wondering could he stay in the granny flat? Since Sadie went it's such a waste having it unoccupied. What do you think?"

Sadie had been James's mother, a vibrant, colourful character, who played golf, bridge, swore and drank Scotch whisky with gusto. When she died suddenly at eighty-two she had left a terrible void. Mother-in-laws weren't supposed to be friends, but Kit's mother-in-law had been her best friend. In fact it was Sadie who had suggested to James that they take over the house.

"Too bloody big for me now. You could do with the space what with three young fellows. Sure they'll need space when they're young men, bringing home their friends to stay and maybe their women, too."

Kit had pointed out that they were all under ten at the time and they wouldn't be bringing women home yet, but her mother-in-law had snorted. "Listen, my girl, the years go like that." She had clicked her fingers with a resounding snap. "After fifty you look around you and you're seventy. And you can't even remember what you did in between. Oh, they'll be men too soon – believe me."

So Sadie and James had come to a financial agreement where he had bought the fine house overlooking Tramore Bay for way below market price and they had built a granny flat where Sadie had lived comfortably for twenty years. She had been too busy to intrude on their lives. Their three sons adored their outlandish grandmother and never seemed to tire of her company. Sadie had been so right. Like a click of the fingers, three rowdy fellows had indeed been bringing home hordes of friends and eventually girlfriends for inspection. Then came the Trinity College years and their smiling faces at graduation. Two of them were doctors living in Canada now. The youngest, Noel, who had surprised them by becoming an actor, was living in London, married with two little girls and a zany, hippy wife with whom he seemed quite happy.

Her husband again brought her back to earth. "I think I'll have to prescribe something that will keep you with me. You're daydreaming more and more, Kit."

"I was just remembering Sadie and the boys and the way it used to be, and I got sad the way things all pass away."

"Haven't you me? Aren't we both above the ground?"

"You're right. We are," she sighed. "Of course, we'll take Conor McElroy. He'll keep the place aired and it'll be company to have him coming and going."

Conor McElroy proved to be a godsend. James Gillen's burden was so lightened by the young doctor, he told Kit, that he felt he was on a perpetual holiday. At first the old timers in the town, who had seen Doctor James grow from a young energetic doctor to an elderly caring one, were reluctant to unburden themselves to a young new whippersnapper from God knows where, but his easy unhurried manner and his genuine ability to listen soon won them. The new lad was a fine-looking fellow, too: tall and broad shouldered, as if the God above had fitted him out to carry other people's burdens, and nothing seemed to escape those light grey eyes.

On this humid summer-like day in early September the waiting room was full. Sarah Beirne, sitting in a pool of isolation, could hear two elderly women who knew each other discussing him.

"Do you know what, Molly? He has eyes like x-rays. I told him about my terrible crampy pains last time, and he didn't just give me a prescription but examined thoroughly as if he really cared. I thank the Blessed Virgin I had my new vest on me. Anyway, he suggested an x-ray and that showed I had polyps on my ovarian tubes. Sure, I didn't think I had an ovarian tube in the world left. Anyway, he thought I should have them removed, telling me I would be far healthier without them. God bless Doctor James and all that, but I don't think he'd have bothered. He'd have said, 'Tessie, sure you're going to have pains and aches. You're not as young as you were; none of us are as young as we were.' So now I'm here for a check-up before I go in for the operation."

Sarah, looking at her, felt slightly envious that a woman could be almost happy because her doctor cared enough to search for polyps. Looking around her she could see that she'd be second last to go into the surgery. The day was humid and dark, almost stifling. She even felt too warm in her cotton dress. It was a nice dress – white background with tiny rosebuds. Glancing down at the full skirt, her eyes strayed to the flat-heeled sandals. Honeymoon clothes bought when she was filled with anticipation and swamped with happiness. It seemed a hundred years, yet the calendar told her that that bright spring day her feet were so light that she almost skipped round town looking for light bright things for her honeymoon in Rome was a mere couple of months ago. She even remembered meeting Doctor Gillen's wife Kit as she and her mother walked up the Quay in Waterford laden with parcels.

In the weeks since she had come home from Rome, she refused to accept what had happened there. She had angrily questioned God and had stormed high heaven wondering why Alan, her beloved Alan, was lain so low. What had he done to be burdened with such an appalling cross? Possibly crippled and bound to a wheelchair for ever. Her lithe, physical Alan who had revelled in all sorts of sports. How proud his mother Mary had been when she shyly showed Sarah the trophies and medals he had won at school sports and on the playing field. In the photograph albums she had taken down

41

the first time Sarah had been invited to tea, most of the black and white pictures had shown him as a grinning, white-toothed youngster holding aloft various cups he had won. There was one picture in a prominent place in the album. He was in the back line of the Kilkenny hurling team which had won the All-Ireland minors that year. She knew now that he would never again be photographed standing proudly holding anything aloft: no cups, no trophies, no babies.

Admittedly the doctors in the Dublin hospital had told her that it wasn't all over. Far from it. People went on to live full, happy, fulfilled lives although they were bound to wheelchairs. In fact her husband Alan would be considered luckier than some. He could have broken his neck and been a quadriplegic with both arms and legs paralysed. During the long spell of rehabilitation, he would see at first hand people who had learned to cope with injuries far greater than his. They went on to tell her that up to the fifties people who were paralysed usually died within a year of their injury with kidney failure. Things were different now. They spoke of new techniques and catheters and tubes where the bladder would drain into a bag. On that day in the Dublin hospital she had listened in growing horror, knowing that somewhere in that vast hospital her beloved Alan was lying, probably terrified at the prospect of what lay ahead.

"Next, please."

She glanced up and realised that it was her turn. As she followed the new doctor into the consulting room, she wildly wondered what she was doing there. *Why did I bother coming? Soon enough I'll know and will it matter now that our lives are over in a way?*

When Doctor McElroy reached his desk he sat down and motioned for her to sit down also. She glanced up and saw that the woman was right: his eyes were extraordinary. Light grey, but it was the black lashes that framed them were responsible for the penetrating look. She could see that they were kind, too. He didn't have a white coat on – just a blue shirt with grey flannels. Somehow he didn't look like a doctor and she was glad. She was sick of white coats.

She cleared her throat and met his gaze.

"Well," a slight smile played around his mouth, "what can I do for you?"

Sarah cleared her throat again and nervously fiddled with the buckle of her dress. For a wild second she wondered should she run out and keep her worries to herself instead of telling them to this grey-eyed stranger whom she didn't know from Adam. Maybe she should have waited for the benevolent Doctor James. But Doctor McElroy was there and he was waiting and suddenly the words came in a breathless rush.

"Doctor, I was married six weeks ago." Her eyes met his and he thought that if she hadn't looked so ravaged with whatever was troubling her she would have been positively beautiful. The deep blue in her eyes was such an extraordinary blue that memories of his mother's delphiniums came back, massed strong and upright against the old red-bricked wall at the back of her much loved herbaceous border that was the pride of her garden. Conor McElroy checked his racing thoughts, telling himself that he was here to listen and maybe find out what was it that made her look so desperately unhappy.

"We were merely married ten days when it happened. It's six weeks ago now and the doctors say that in all probability, he'll never walk again. They tell me he'll be paraplegic. He knows now, but I honestly don't think he realises the extent of the damage. He's a very physical person and maybe somewhere inside he has a hope that he can beat this."

Conor tried to keep the sympathy from showing, to look professional and attentive to what this lovely young woman was telling him. Looking at the unhappiness in her blue eyes and the pallor of her oval face, he, who prided himself on his ability to listen, didn't want to listen any more. He wanted to walk to other side of the desk and maybe hold her and console her and wipe away some of the misery from those eyes. *Christ*, he thought to himself, *this is a first. I must be losing it. Losing it completely.* She was now fiddling with the buckle of her belt, her long slender fingers plucking and pulling.

"I just thought I should see you and maybe confirm what I think. Is it possible I could be pregnant? As I said, we were only married ten days before the car crash."

He was back now in the listening pose. *Pregnant*, he thought. *It would be a good thing if she was, because the poor bastard with the broken back won't be able to make her pregnant ever again.* He resumed his professional approach now and dismissed the unfamiliar tumultuous thoughts that were assailing him.

"How long is it since your last period?"

"Since before I was married. I haven't seen anything since."

So she had been in the middle of her fertile period when they were on their honeymoon. He noticed that she wore no nail varnish, in fact little or no make-up. He reached into his filing cabinet and pulled out a card.

"May I have your name?"

Looking at him with his head bent over the reference card, the pen poised, she felt relief that she had come. It would be good to know one way or the other. She had kept the possibility of her pregnancy to herself. She couldn't possibly talk about it when everyone were so distraught about Alan. Talk of a baby would be almost ironic – ridiculous – crazy – a bit like a blue joke.

"Sarah Dunne – no, no, Sarah Beirne. I haven't got used to it yet."

"Age?"

"Twenty-two."

"Have you ever missed periods before? Maybe during stress or due to physical illnesses?"

"No."

"To be certain, I'll need a sample of urine. The cycle can go haywire at a time like this." The grey eyes held hers, and for some reason she couldn't understand, she was the first to break away.

"I know. I brought it." He could plainly see she was pink with embarrassment, if anything highlighting the extraordinary blue of her eyes. "I know how busy you are, but I would be grateful if you could test this as soon as possible. I just want to know. They haven't told me, but I've been reading up on spinal injuries." She looked at him again and her gaze was direct, as if she wanted no messing, no fobbing off this time. "I believe my husband will be incapable of fathering a child from now on. Is that so?"

Sarah Dunne – no, Sarah Beirne – wanted to know exactly where she stood. Strange, but it was his turn to clear his throat. "Yes, I'm afraid that's so. When the spinal cord is broken there is no sensation below the damage. So if your presumptions are correct and you are pregnant after such a short while, you should consider yourself very lucky. How do you feel about it yourself?"

His eyes held her and she remembered the women with the polyps and the new vest who said he had x-ray eyes. Maybe he had – maybe he could see inside her head. Maybe he could even know that she was thinking that living with Alan and unable to express their love would be hell. Living with Alan and he tied to bags, pads and catheters would be hell for him.

"I feel that I should be glad. Should I?"

Her voice shook slightly, and he could see she was battling against tears that had suddenly sprung to her eyes. The stupid, ridiculous, crazed desire to go over to her and take her into his arms and console her came again. This girl who was linked for ever to her crippled husband, whose seed she probably carried inside her but who could never make love again. They used have a handyman at home who, when things went against him, used to mutter, "Ah, sure, 'tis all a balls." Now sitting in the surgery where the sun had come out from behind the clouds silvering the blonde of her hair, he remembered old Jack's words.

"Phone me tomorrow and I'll have the result of the pregnancy test." He stood up and held out his hand. Hers felt cold and thin inside his warm grip. "Take care and try not to worry too much."

He knew even as he uttered the words that they were empty and would bring no consolation. He knew that the life that lay ahead for this young woman would be very difficult. As he stood there in the sun, briefly holding her hand, he wondered if he would have any part to play in it.

CHAPTER SIX

Patsy had her eyes glued to her book as the train sped to Dublin. She tried to concentrate because the book, *Strumpet City*, the best-seller by James Plunket, was the talk of the place, but she couldn't wallow in the Ireland of the early twentieth century. She couldn't identify with the striking workers, couldn't identify with people whose main diet was tea and dry bread. She couldn't lose herself in the world of Jim Larkin, their charismatic leader fighting for their betterment. In the past when she came across thorn-filled passages in a book, she was always reduced to tears, but not now. The words danced before her unheeding eyes because her thoughts were already up in the hospital in Dublin with Alan Beirne.

She wondered how she'd greet him. She always tried to be breezy and funny with him. She had to, because he could never know how she felt about him, but she would have to adopt new tactics now. She couldn't say, "Hi, so there you are on the broad of your back," because it looked like he'd be spending the rest of his life on the broad of his back. She couldn't rant to high heaven and sob and cry under a pillow, as she had in her bedroom at home, because he belonged to Sarah, who was sitting opposite her now, looking terrible.

Sarah hadn't talked at all about the honeymoon. Normally honeymooners came home all aglow, full of stories and funny incidents and souvenirs and loads of photos about the most important holiday of their lives. But of course there hadn't been anything like that, only a dry-mouthed girl whose eyes were filled with a mixture of desperation and puzzlement.

In the quiet grey hours when Patsy couldn't sleep, she wondered how the honeymoon had gone for the first ten days. She was used to her own friends boasting about getting off with guys who knew every trick of the trade. She firmly believed that most of it was bravado and that a lot of couples kept themselves for each other until the wedding night. She knew that's what she'd like to do – that is, if she ever met anyone she could love like Alan Beirne. Had Sarah and Alan waited until their wedding night, and if so, was it wonderful and heaven and all the things girls were led to believe? The very thought of the handsome young couple making love made her feel so peculiar and wobbly that she ran her hand through her short thick hair distractedly.

"Next stop, Kilkenny."

The announcement jolted her from her chaotic thinking and was a welcome interruption, even if it was only a train stopping in a station with people alighting and departing, voices and carriage doors banging. Far better than losing oneself in a dream world yearning for something you could never ever have. Maybe she should go away. Maybe she could get around her father and tell him that she didn't want to go to university, that she would like a year off to see the world. When you were gazing at the walls of China or romping in the eternal sunlight on golden beaches in Australia or trekking through the hamlets of Spain, could you be thinking of someone you shouldn't be thinking about? If only she could get advice from some soul who could look at her problem objectively and see things clearly and then be in a position to help her. Or if she lived in America she could go into therapy. She thought of all the films she had seen where people reclined on couches and bared their souls to an impersonal grey-suited man who listened and then delved into the subconscious and started untangling the web of the troubled. But in her case there was no web to untangle – she was simply in love with the wrong man. Anyway, that was America and here she was in a train speeding to Dublin with her sister whose husband was more than likely crippled for life. And when she saw what she thought he'd

48

be like, she wouldn't have a word to say because she'd be frozen in misery she loved him so much.

She glanced up at Sarah and saw that she was looking out the window at the flashing hedgerows and the grazing cattle, munching contentedly in the autumn sunshine.

"How is Alan looking? Will we recognise him?" Her question was stupid, but was better than the silence that had almost enveloped them since they left Waterford.

"Of course we'll recognise him. He's still Alan. Most of his injuries were superficial except his back, and if anything he looks well. He still has the look of the Italian sun. At least he had when I saw him last week."

"How is he? You know what I mean, is he demented or what?"

Sarah looked at her as if her thoughts, too, were a million miles away. Then she focused on Patsy, her tone gentle. "You'll miss all the fun and games you had with him. He used to say you were like the young sister he never had." She glanced out at the flashing greenery again, and when she looked at her sister again Patsy could see the fear in her eyes. "Jesus, what'll I do, looking at him like that?" she spoke in an undertone, because the woman near Patsy was pretending to be reading the *Irish Press* but Sarah could see she was all ears.

"Maybe things won't be so bad," Patsy said softly. "Miracles do happen, you know. Look at all those things that happen in Lourdes and in Knock. Mam keeps saying that the doctors don't know everything. She's always saying that God spoke first, whatever that means."

She was rewarded with a ghost of a smile and then they lapsed into silence.

The hospital was sprawling and huge and it looked as if it housed the population of a small town as they walked the long length of the corridors. The nurses were chatting, and one nurse cheerfully directed them to Saint Gabriel's ward, showing no great interest or sympathy. The encounter made Patsy realise that Alan was only one of many patients, maybe some with far worse injuries than he had. As they made their way she tried to avoid the eyes of the many patients she saw in wheelchairs, but when their eyes met, she returned their smiles, feeling humbled, almost ashamed that she was striding on two long strong legs and maybe they would never walk again.

Alan was propped up in bed with a book in his hands, and seemed to be reading it. Patsy's mouth went dry and her heart started to thump unevenly against her ribs, making her feel faint. The last time she had seen him, he was bending down getting into the car to sit beside Sarah on the way to the airport. The car had been sprayed with shaving cream, and she had flung handfuls of confetti on to it until it looked like a cake coloured with hundreds and thousands. She had caught his eye and he had winked, maybe a forgiving wink, knowing that she had been the chief culprit in the defacing of his car. Now he was propped up in bed with a back support and there were weights and pulleys and wires supporting his legs. His face hadn't changed. With the exception of a scar under his eye and a greenish tinge on his chin where a bruise was healing, he looked the same.

Glancing up he saw them coming, and his dark eyes roamed over Sarah. Patsy felt like a total intruder because his eyes held so much love.

"Hi."

His voice sounded husky to her ears and she wanted to run and run down the polished acres of corridor, out through the door, out on to the busy road and down all the way to Dún Laoghaire where they were staying. But she didn't get the chance because he held out his hand and her cold, shaky one was held in his firm, warm one. For a fleeting second she felt that it had all been a nightmare. He looked so like himself and his hand felt so strong that it couldn't be true that the two outlines of his legs under the white spread were the outlines of legs that would never walk again.

"Hi, Patsy." His eyes held hers, and she could see that he was making an effort to be normal.

"Hi, yourself." She hoped she sounded someway right on the surface because inside she was a screaming ball of pain.

"How are things in your neck of the woods? How is life after the schooling?"

He was looking at her as if he wanted her to rabbit away about mundane things, as if to keep at bay the tragic thing.

"Nothing great happening, now that the leaving cert results are a thing of the past. Everyone's running around like blue-arsed flies wondering what'll they do. Will they go to college? Will they do secretarial courses? Will they try and get a rich man to marry them?" She warmed to her subject, even injecting some animation into her voice, telling him things like she had a thousand times before. "I was just wondering when I was on the train: if I put off going to college and travelled for a year, maybe work my way around the world washing dishes and stuff, wouldn't it be great? A sort of education in itself. And next year I could go to university. Think of how interesting I'd be instead of a dull old teacher who hadn't lived at all." *And I'd do all that*, she told herself silently, *not because I want to see the bloody world but because I want to get away from you and the effect you have on me.*

He grinned. "I'll tell you what, I didn't think I was that dull. I'll put in the good word for you with your dad, but I'd say your chances are slim. What do you think, Sarah?" His eyes seemed to devour Sarah and Patsy could clearly see he was just filling time talking to her. It was Sarah he wanted to be with.

"Look," Patsy's glance took in both of them, "I know you two have oodles to say to each other. I'll take myself off for a bit and you can talk."

She airily waved at both of them as if taking herself off was exactly what she had planned. She walked down the ward, passing three other beds all with young men and all with pulleys and weights and one unfortunate with a neck brace as well. Again she felt ashamed of her long striding legs as they took her outside into the warm autumn sunshine.

"Well, love, how are you? You look pale."

Sarah leaned over and kissed him. As his lips hungrily pressed hers, she felt the old fire and longing wash over her.

"I'm fine, I'm very fine."

Her eyes held his and she wanted to reach out and take away the pain, the worry and the fear that she could clearly see in their dark depths. For a second she wondered should she tell him – was the time right? She had spoken to no one except the grey-eyed doctor about herself.

"Alan, I'm pregnant," the words came in a torrent. "We're going to have a baby. Hey, what do you think of that? Will we call him Guisseppe? I wanted you to be the first to know."

She saw that her news had taken him completely unawares. Then the shock faded and she could see a sort of wonder replacing it. "My God, that's something." He reached up and tried to pull her down to him. "Together a mere ten days. It must be easy to make babies."

She leaned over and he ran his hand through her hair and touched her lips and her eyelids. Then she kissed him again and his lips moved as he tried to haul her closer, but the equipment and the tubes and the weights were in the way. They broke away, completely oblivious of the glances of the visitors at the other beds.

"You know, we can't call him Guisseppe. Think how the lads would treat a Guisseppe in our part of the world."

His voice was husky now. She noticed a nerve throb near his eye and she knew he was very moved. Then she thought how imprisoned he was. If she was telling him her momentous news at home, maybe after tea, when the work of the day was over, how different his reaction might have been.

Knowing him he would in all probability have jumped up and taken her in his arms and swung her around shouting with excitement. He had once told her he wanted ten children because no child should be an only child. She had laughed and said they would have ten if they won the Hospital Sweepstakes. He was saying something and his words brought her back to the present.

"And, love, another reason we can't call him Guisseppe is – he will be the only one." His voice was low, his gaze steady. Suddenly tears sprang into her eyes and though she tried to blink them away one escaped and ran down her face. He reached up and gently brushed her cheek.

"Who knows what's ahead for anyone." She tried to keep the sob from her voice by swallowing hard. "When I get you home I'll work wonders on you." She looked at him, expecting him to say something funny, witty, like he would have in those happy carefree days before the accident. He didn't. As she stood there it was only then she saw that his dark eyes were full of tears, too.

They stayed a week in Dún Laoghaire in a fine house overlooking the harbour. The house belonged to a Kerry woman, Hannah Tobin, an old school friend of their mother's. Widowed a few years previously she had converted her large home into a guest house. She was warm and welcoming and couldn't do enough for them. When Sarah suggested that they would only have breakfast there, she was horrified.

"Breakfast and then you'd be out roaming the streets, wondering where you would get a decent bit. If you think I'll let Eileen O'Connor's girls out like that, then you have another guess coming. Tell me, alannah," her lined hazel eyes were full of sympathy as she questioned Sarah, "how is that poor lad of yours? Wasn't it a fierce that your young husband should have such a thing happen?"

Sarah nodded, warming to her. She thought the Kerry accent was like music with its up and down nuances. "Yes, it was terrible. The doctors are not one hundred per cent certain, but the prognosis is bad."

Hannah Tobin looked at the young woman and sympathy welled from within her; it should have been so different. She knew anything she would say would be inadequate, but all she could do was try to console Eileen's lovely girl. She remembered her disappointment that she couldn't attend the wedding because the guest house was booked out due to an international sailing event held in Dún Laoghaire that weekend.

"Sure, you can't tell – those doctors can do wonderful things. Only the other day I was reading about the new hearts that chap Christian Barnard is putting into people in South Africa. And if they can put in a new heart they can fix an oul back. Look, love, leave it in God's hands. You can't do more than that."

She looked at Patsy then, her warm brown eyes taking in the young lines of her boyish figure, the high cheek bones, the wide mouth, the same deep blue eyes as her sister. The short mop of auburn hair was rich and curly, cut short and close in the newfangled razor cut.

"You have a great look of your mother, even more so than Sarah. And I believe Emma is the spit of your father." She walked over and plugged in the copper kettle. "Nice to have three girls all different. Now your mother was no saint, I can tell ye. She was a bit of a tomboy, always in trouble with the nuns. She was always at me to run away from that boarding school, but sure I couldn't, my father would kill me. I think your father Tim tamed her, although I'd say he has his work cut out."

They both laughed, and for the first time Sarah felt the terrible knot that was a fixture inside her chest ease a little.

"After a hot cuppa, up the two of ye and have a wash or a bath and," her eyes again looked at Sarah, "you look tired, love. Why don't you have a bit of a rest? Dinner will be on the table at six o'clock, so there's plenty of time."

The room was wide and spacious with two large windows overlooking Dublin Bay. They could see the harbour and the long jutting pier where people looked small and toy-like as they walked with their dogs or small children. Yachts and small sailing craft dotted the bay, and way out there they could see that a race was in progress, with dozens of small sailing boats sitting on the water motionless due to the lack of wind. The bedroom suite was mahogany with delicate inlay, and the two matching single beds were covered with thick white candlewick bedspreads. Hannah Tobin turned down the spreads with the quick movement of constant practice.

"Now as I said, a little rest. I don't want Eileen's lovely girls looking like two washed out jumpers." Her smile enveloped both of them as she went out the door. They could hear her humming as she ran down the stairs.

"Isn't she great?" Sarah was already yawning, kicking off her sandals and getting into bed.

"Well, you're taking her advice to the letter," Patsy added looking at her sister in surprise. "I certainly don't feel like crawling into bed like an old-age pensioner at four o'clock on a lovely sunny day. Maybe we should go out an see the sights of Dún Laoghaire. Isn't this where the Top Hat Ballroom is? You know all those pain-in-the-arse types that are always talking about going up to town and dropping out to the Top Hat. Well, maybe, we should have look at the place anyway."

She glanced away from the magnificent view and saw that her sister was already asleep. Patsy, surprised that she had crashed out so soon, could see that she was pale and exhausted. There were dark shadows under her eyes and even the shiny blonde hair looked limp and out of condition. She could only guess the extent of her sister's suffering. After all, she was Alan's wife. She had loved him for yonks and God knows how much they had shared together. Patsy sighed, turning to look out the window again.

The sun was starting to descend, the rosy glow brushing the sea as its rays lit up a passing ship and seemed to set it on fire. It touched the houses on the summit in Howth, brushing them with the same blaze. As a child, she had read a story about a man who had set out to search for the golden window, only to discover when he got there that the rays of the setting sun had moved on and had turned his own windows into flaming gold. She remembered the English teacher preaching rather primly that the moral of the story was that happiness is found in your own backyard.

Standing there as motionless as the little sailing boats perched like coloured butterflies on the still water, she recalled her own excited but short-lived enthusiasm for sailing. The two weeks' sailing course over in Dunmore East had been fun, all the young crowd noisy and boisterous, thinking that they were old salts after a few days. She hadn't minded the wet and the cold when the light craft went over and they were tossed, shouting excitedly, into the water. What she did mind were the endless hours of boredom when they were marooned and motionless in a dead calm sea. She lost interest after one season.

Turning back into the room she could hear Sarah's steady breathing and decided she'd go for a walk and see the sights. She went quietly down the stairs and let herself out without disturbing Hannah Tobin. There was a delicious aroma emanating from the kitchen, so she presumed that dinner was being prepared. She decided she'd stroll towards the sea. She thought the town looked well. The narrow main street was in shadow, and people bustled on the pavements, obviously doing some last-minute shopping. She wandered down to the seafront where a huge crane was lifting giant slabs of concrete, joining a small crowd which had gathered to look at the work. One small elderly woman gazed at the proceedings with a look of utter disdain in her eye.

"They tell us that they're building upmarket apartments – whatever they are. And they tore down a magnificent old building to do this. Did the powers that be ask us, the people of Dún Laoghaire, do we want them? Not at all. Who are these people who can come along and destroy a town? A town with the finest Georgian architecture in the country, built by the British who knew their business. Did they tell us what they were at? I'll tell you who they are – faceless developers with money and no imagination. My little Jessie here," she pointed to her little Yorkshire terrier who was tugging impatiently at a lead, "has more imagination and brains then these ignorant men with no vision. They'll rue the day that they built these cheap monstrosities in this old town. Thank God my poor mother didn't live to see this destruction."

Before the bemused Patsy could respond to the very small, very articulate woman's obvious frustration, she snorted and moved away. A fellow in overalls, wearing a helmet and clutching a sheaf of papers who was standing near by winked at her. She found herself blushing self-consciously but it didn't deter him.

He leaned over and whispered, "The remnants of the ascendancy classes, here every day, giving out about the development, the builders, the destruction and the vanishing skyline. Not a word about employment and bread on the table. Anyway, I haven't seen you before. Did you come in on the boat?"

"The boat? Oh, the boat." She nodded towards the sea, realising that the B & I ferry might be responsible for bringing a lot of strangers into the port town. "No – I'm just here for a few days."

Embarrassed by his overtures she made to move away. He caught her lightly on the arm leaving a faint mud mark on her new, navy cardigan. He looked at it ruefully.

"I'm sorry. I really am. I'll buy you a new one. The name is Rory O'Driscoll, and I'm one of the people responsible for changing the face of Dún Laoghaire. Where are you staying?"

Patsy looked at him in amazement. "Do all the guys in

Dún Laoghaire just stop girls in the street, put mud on their clothes and ask them where they're staying?"

He grinned and she could see that he was good looking in a rugged sort of way. He pushed back his helmet and she could see that his hair was fairish and his teeth were the whitest teeth she had ever seen. She even noticed that there was a small chip off one of them.

"No, it's just that this poor Joe Bloggs is sick to the teeth of elderly spinsters with dogs that look like cats standing here sniffing disdainfully. Then out of the blue someone comes along just like you and I'm gobsmacked with surprise."

She returned his grin. "Yeah. I believe you. But I'm off, I promised I'd be back for dinner at six. Bye."

She made to move off but he shouted after her, "Hey, where are you staying?"

"Corrig Avenue, I think."

"What number?"

"Not sure – a red door. Three doors down." She waved her hand and walked away feeling all legs and arms, aware that his eyes were following her every step.

She saw a church and decided she'd go in and say a prayer. First glance showed that it was the most unusual church she'd ever seen. The pale grey granite walls were broken by narrow stained glass depicting nothing in partic-ular, and yet the brilliant colour relieved the grey to such an extent that the effect was very beautiful. She could see that the altar was a large polished granite boulder, the mica chips gleaming silver and bright, and she thought that it was far lovelier than all the stuffy altars laden with embroidered cloths and bits and pieces like the ones in her part of the world. She knelt down, wondering was she all right in the head to be in a church gawking around like a tourist when she should be on her knees praying. The thought brought all the terrible troubles back. Alan lying there trying to be bright and positive when his life was over – at least the life that he knew.

She knelt down and prayed as she never prayed before. She remembered the timeless words of the gospel: "Ask for anything in My name and it will be granted." Well, if there was a word of truth in it, she wouldn't fail for lack of trying. She put her hands over her face and prayed with an intensity she hardly knew she possessed. She prayed that God would work a miracle and cure him – make him whole again. After all, Christ did work miracles here on earth two thousand years ago and what was wrong with the odd one now? So she prayed for a miracle. She also prayed that her sister would be happy again, and then she realised that would take as big a miracle as having Alan walking again. And last but not least she prayed that God would change the way she felt about her brother-in-law. She prayed that she could go back to a more carefree time, a sort of romping time when the sun seemed to be always shining, when she could talk and laugh untroubled and unfettered by this emotional secret love that was so wrong, almost incestuous, and definitely misplaced.

When she left the church to try and find her way back to Hannah Tobin's house, she could still hear the diggers and the heavy machinery at the building site. Glancing at her watch, she saw that it was almost six o'clock. Then the bells of the Angelus peeled out and the din from the heavy machinery stopped abruptly.

CHAPTER SEVEN

Rory O'Driscoll looked around at the shrinking band of onlookers, wondering would he see her again. As the giant crane lifted and positioned the huge slab of precast concrete into place, he wondered, not for the first time, why there was such huge interest in this apartment complex. Dún Laoghaire, once named Kingstown, was a town heavily influenced by British architecture with its Georgian houses and Georgian facades, a town inhabited with what were commonly referred to as West Brits. These people didn't want any change, particularly late twentieth century, streamlined apartments. The natives of this town firmly believed they owned the spectacular harbour, the finest in the country, where the monument to Queen Victoria was prominently placed. He was indifferent to the inhabitants' objections. He went where the company sent him. "You go where the living is," his father used to say. "You follow the money." He smiled thinking of his father, retired now, living in a refurbished cottage on the shores of Lough Derg.

Where was the beautiful bird who had wandered into his life yesterday? She was only visiting, she had told him, red door, three houses down in Corrig Avenue. He knew the place well. Big houses now honeycombed with flats, guest houses or B and B's. Yesterday evening after he had soaked in his bath, removing the grime of the day, he had made a quick decision he might call and try and ferret her out. Then he thought he'd look like a right idiot. He decided he'd wait and see if she'd come along again.

There was no sign of her. The woman with the squeaky accent and the small dog was back, still objecting to all and sundry about the destruction of Dún Laoghaire. Rory presumed she was one of the band of the lonely people the Beatles sang about: "Where do they all come from?" The bloody town was riddled with old ladies who walked their dogs and bought their few messages and talked to anyone who would stop and listen. He had never seen so many elderly people in his life. He had discussed it with Jack Murphy, the overseer, and he had been told that it was a sort of retirement town.

"Moneyed old folks come to live here," Jack had said. "They just wander around the town, or walk down the pier and then go home to their flats at night, waiting for the next day to go wandering around again."

Jesus, he hadn't painted much of a picture of this harbour town, which according to the small excitable woman had the finest Georgian architecture in the British Isles.

But where was she? Staying for a few days, she had said. She was hardly on holidays – a bit young to holiday in Dún Laoghaire. Still the Top Hat Ballroom attracted a lot of people to the town, although somehow she hadn't seemed the ballroom type. He had pretended to be studying the plans, but under his eyebrows he had followed her movements, and he had noticed her go into the church. She didn't look like a Holy Mary either, but then again you'd never know. Admittedly, newly built after a disastrous fire had gutted the old one, the new granite church was considered an architectural wonder and was attracting a lot of sightseers.

"Rory, come over have a look at this."

Jack Murphy was calling him. As he walked through the rubble he glanced up the street and thought he saw her. If it wasn't an hallucination she was with another girl and they were both walking fast. He watched them until the crowd swallowed them up. Could it have been her? Could he want to see her so much he was seeing her everywhere? On the way to the foreman, as he passed the woman with the little terrier, he caught her eye and winked. He must have shocked her because her glasses slipped down her nose.

He grinned to himself as he heard her lament, "The types coming to the town certainly aren't gentlemen any more."

"Patsy, love, would you open the door? I can hear the bell ringing." Hannah Tobin was kneading her brown bread on the floured board. "I don't want flour marks all over the hall."

Patsy jumped up, putting the evening paper aside. She almost ran down the long hall to open the door.

She had decided not to go to visit Alan this evening, for all sorts of reasons. Sarah might want to be with him on their own. After all they were still honeymooners in a way. She had put her size six foot in it, with her stupid talk about wanting to travel, knowing only too well that his travelling days were over. Mostly she didn't want to see him because looking at him lying there so helpless was breaking her heart.

She reached out to open the door as the bell rang again. When she opened it wide she saw a young man standing outside. He was grinning and he looked slightly familiar and yet she couldn't place him.

"Yes, may I help you?" She found herself uncomfortable under his scrutiny and thought she sounded like someone in a shop embarking on the hard sell.

"Yes, you may. I wonder would you do me the honour of coming out with me and I'll show you the sights of Dún Laoghaire."

She looked at him, her mouth hanging open in amazement. Then it came. God almighty, he was the guy on the building site who had put mud on her arm. The guy with the helmet. She would never have recognised him but for the voice, deep and masculine with a definite country accent. He wasn't tall, but he was tall enough to guarantee that she wouldn't tower over him. Then, of course, she noticed his mouth. This guy's mouth was pretty all right, too.

She could hear Hannah Tobin coming down the hall. "Who is it, love?"

Patsy swung around still clutching the red painted door and shouted, "I'm not sure."

"The name is Rory O'Driscoll, ma'am. I met this girl downtown and I suppose it's crazy and intrusive, but I was

62

wondering would she come out with me this evening? I'm working on the new apartment complex."

Hannah Tobin, looking at the young man, decided there and then he was a decent looking chap, and that accent was Tipperary if ever an accent was. Her mother was one of a large family from Tipperary, and they all spoke with the same overtones as that young man who stood at her door.

"Come in will you? Not much point standing there."

He grinned as he walked passed Patsy who was still standing, holding the door, in amazement. As he passed she noticed that his hair was fair and his shoulders very broad and that he wore a black leather jacket over jeans that were faded the exact colour that she had wanted for her own. They followed Hannah Tobin into her big wide kitchen. The dough was still there but now kneaded into two round cakes.

Patsy stood there, uncertain and confused, wondering was this sort of thing common in Dublin, that a fellow could walk in off the street and seem suddenly right and almost at home. He glanced at the dough and the black gleaming range.

"I think that's what I miss most," he said to no one in particular.

"What do you miss most?" Patsy asked, her blue eyes meeting his for the first time.

I won't blush, she thought frantically. She had been tortured all her young life with this appalling affliction, so much so that she constantly told her friends that if she didn't get rid of the misery she'd throw herself into the river. To her joy the dreaded blush stayed wherever blushes stay, as he answered simply, "The dough. The smell of the range. It was great."

"Your mother bakes?" Hannah inquired.

"Used to bake," he told her. "She died some time ago."

"I see," she said gently. "Well, lad, I'm not sure I can let this girl go out just like that. I'm supposed to be keeping an eye on her and her sister for a few days."

She glanced out the window and she could see the lights down at the pier. She looked over at Patsy, reminding herself that she, too, was very upset about Sarah's husband. This young man had a look of decency about him. Maybe it would be a bit of distraction for her to go out and take her mind off the terrible trouble in the family.

"Patsy, a lot of people come to Dún Laoghaire just to walk down the harbour – to look at all the boats and all the lights across the bay. Looking at the harbour lights they call it."

Patsy looked at her and something prompted her to say, "I suppose I should have some say in this. Do I want to go strolling down by the harbour lights?"

Rory O'Driscoll suddenly laughed, and the sound was warm and genuine. "I didn't mention harbour lights – it was this good woman's suggestion – but the idea is growing on me." He turned to Hannah. "I'll give you my word she'll be safe with me."

"God, you'd think we lived in Victorian times or in the ghettos of New York," Patsy told them. "I'll go out till my sister comes back – it'll kill an hour. I'll get my jacket."

They could hear her running down the long hall and up the stairs until her footsteps faded away. Hannah broke the silence in the kitchen: "You're from County Tipperary, I'd say."

"That's right. How did you guess that now?"

"The accent. I spent all my summer holidays on my uncle's farm in County Tipp, although I was born and bred in Kerry myself."

"Yeah, I guessed that."

"How did you know?"

"The accent."

Suddenly they both burst out laughing, and when Patsy walked back into the kitchen they were still smiling broadly at each other as if they had known each other all their lives.

Rory and Patsy didn't speak until they were down the steps of the house and out on the pavement. Then they both spoke together and then laughed together and the laughter eased the tension.

"Why did you call?" Patsy asked, zipping up her jacket.

"Because I wanted to. I'll tell you what, I had a squint in me eye looking out for you all day yesterday and today. I couldn't bear it any more so I just took a chance and called."

She was silent, a thousand thoughts clamouring through her head. He was nice. He had a very deep voice. He was older than most of the fellows she knew, except Alan of course. Alan again. Always Alan.

"Are you usually as quiet as this?" he wanted to know.

"No, I'm not a bit quiet. I'm a terrible talker. I drive people mad I talk so much. But I must say, where I come from guys don't wander in off the street and knock at doors looking for girls to go out with them. We're sort of civilised where I come from."

"And where would that be now?"

"Waterford."

"Ah, *Urba Intacta* – the unconquered city."

"Well, I'm from the country really." They were in the town now, in fact, opposite the building site where she had first seen him. She could see the enormous crane and the diggers and the red lights where the traffic was being diverted. "Hey, can't you keep away from the office?" she giggled and she was rewarded with a shout of laughter.

"Come on." He grabbed her arm and led her across the road. "There's a little pub here. We'll sit and you can tell me the story of your life."

"I don't go to pubs," she told him. "My father would do his nut and anyway I don't drink so I don't see the point."

"All right. The Marine Hotel is down there – right posh, right old fashioned, probably full of genteel old ladies. Would you like a pot of tea in a place like that?" She could see he was disappointed.

"No, I would loathe a pot of tea in a place like that. I'll go to the pub and sip a lemonade like a good girl and you can tell me the story of your life."

They went to the dark and cosy pub. As she looked around, it struck her that it was nice to be with Rory O'Driscoll. As he helped her take off her jacket, she surreptitiously glanced at him. He definitely looked older than the fellows she knew. Was he an architect or an engineer? If he was, he must have done four years in college. At the building site he had carried sheaves of paper, and she presumed he wasn't a labourer or a tradesman. Then again, she didn't care what he was.

"Well, what do you think?" He was sitting down and there was laughter in his eyes and she couldn't make out what colour they were because he had a habit of crinkling them up when he smiled.

"I was thinking it must be great to be working. I have to go college and get an old degree, and then after I get it I'll have to do my H. Dip., and then get a job as a boring old teacher, and the whole thing makes me sick."

"So, I have a schoolgirl on my hands."

"Remember, I didn't want to be on your hands – you called me and positively hijacked me out on the town. And I'm not a schoolgirl. If you want to know, I feel as old as time."

"I'm sorry I highjacked you, but you shouldn't go around Dún Laoghaire with a lost look and then stand a breath away from me and excite me. Anyway, what'll you have to drink? Will you change your mind about the lemonade?"

Not wanting to appear gauche and stupid and a little schoolgirl all moon eyes in a pub in Dún Laoghaire, she remembered that a shandy was acceptable – a sort of in-between drink. "I'll have an ale shandy."

"A pint?"

"Yeah, a pint." Patsy casually yawned, hoping to appear a woman of the world looking for a daring pint. She thought she saw a look of amusement in his eyes. She still wasn't sure what colour they were, but she came to the conclusion they were a mixture of blue and grey. Watching Rory O'Driscoll go up to the bar to order the drinks, she saw that the pub was full of young people. Over at the far end they were noisy, and one girl was telling what might have been a funny story because her audience had that expectant look tinged with worry in case they wouldn't laugh at the punchline. She had the most peculiar drawl, but it certainly didn't affect her ability to tell a joke. The punchline was obviously timed perfectly because there was an absolute explosion of laughter when she finished.

Patsy sighed, wishing for the millionth time that Alan hadn't had the accident, because it had made things worse instead of better. If anything it had heightened her feeling for him. She had heard talk at home that his job was certainly safe, even if he was permanently tied to a wheelchair. The canon would have ramps built in the school. The cottage they had rented was all on the flat making the building of ramps an easy option. Ramps – ramps – there had been so much talk of bloody ramps. Things she had hardly ever heard of before. She could see him now, even in this dark, dimly lit, noisy pub, standing up at the altar. She remembered even then she had wanted him for herself – not for her sister who was walking up the aisle looking so absolutely radiant. She sighed again.

"A penny for them?" Rory was back with the drinks placing them carefully on the small mats.

Embarrassed that he had caught her in the throes of her daydreams, she pointed to the beer mats, "I was wondering what was so great about this new drink they're advertising."

"You weren't, you know. You looked too downcast to be worrying about a new brand of drink, seeing that you don't drink. Anyway, if you want to know, it's a new rum." He sat down beside her, easing himself into a comfortable position as if he spent many hours in many bars. "And if you're worry was about me, I'll tell you all about myself. I'm an architect, twenty-four, free, unfettered, an unspoiled only son and healthy. Now, what do you think of that?"

"I think you're a bit mad," she said as she looked at her pint of shandy. She could see all the little bubbles rising to the top and the pink indentation on the froth where the lemonade had been added. "If my father saw me now sitting in a pub I never heard of, in a town I don't know, with a fellow I certainly don't know, he'd do his nut."

"Maybe you'll get to know me?"

"Hardly, because we're going home in two days."

"Who are we?"

"My sister Sarah and I. We're here because her husband is in hospital. He's in bits – it's terrible. We're devastated."

"Would you like to talk about it?" Her glance showed that he seemed genuinely interested. Then she thought it would be wonderful if she could talk. If she could tell him everything. Imagine. Tell everything to this comparative stranger whom she would never see again. Strangers in the night, wasn't that how the Frank Sinatra song went? The comfort it would be to unload this thing inside her, this feeling she had for someone she could never have. Way back she had wondered was it incest and had looked up the word in the dictionary: "incestuous commerce between two blood relatives". She had been relieved that at least she wasn't guilty of that. He certainly wasn't a blood relation.

"Sarah was married last July. All the usual fanfare and excitement. My poor mother nearly went off her head with the worry of it all. Sarah is – well – well, she's beautiful."

"Like you."

"God, no, not like me. I'm sort of red headed and freckled and tall and all bones. She's blonde and has the most amazing blue eyes and she's sort of everything."

"Like you."

"If you're going to keep saying that, I won't tell you anything."

Patsy picked up her pint and hurriedly gulped down a

mouthful, her blue eyes glaring at him over the rim of the glass.

"All right, I promise. Not a word will escape me. Tell me."

She put down the glass and the words came, hesitant and slow at first and then in an unstoppable flood as if she were glad to unburden herself to this stranger. She told him of the wedding, the excitement, the build-up. She told him of her closeness to Alan. The way he was always around, helping her with a thousand and one things, particularly her wretched homework when she was doing her exams. The way he had patiently brought her through the minefield that was the new honours maths. She told him of the sharing days when they had gone swimming together, when they had gone blackberry picking together, when they had gone cycling together. Then she told him of the honeymoon and the terrible, unforgettable phone call.

"I couldn't believe it. And he's now crippled in a wheel-chair."

With no warning the lump came and then her throat constricted and to her horror she started to cry. She sought wildly to control her sobs, but they came, shaking her shoulders, bringing the wretched tears coursing down her face. She was hardly aware of his comforting arm around her and the fact that he was wiping her tears with his hand.

The noisy crowd in the corner had become suspiciously quiet. The girl with the drawl looked over, nudging her partner. "I bet the guy who looks like Robert Redford is breaking it off and she's heartbroken."

Her companion muttered, "No, she's just told him she's pregnant and is so relieved that he didn't run for his life she burst into tears."

Six pairs of eyes watched as the fair-headed guy helped her on with her jacket. Six pairs of eyes watched as the couple walked away from two pints hardly touched, and all agreed they'd love to know what had caused the copious tears.

Out in the cold with the wind gusting from the sea, Rory O'Driscoll wondered also. There was no doubt what she had told him through her sobs was pretty awful: her brother-in-law in hospital, possibly crippled for life, young with everything ahead of him and a decent bloke to boot as far as he could gather. Yet there was something, the unspoken words between the lines, the sheer misery that had flooded her eyes, the way she had torn up the mat that had lauded the praises of the new drink . . . The way she had completely and uncontrollably broken down. Was there more to it than that? They headed for the sea in silence, she striding ahead as if to escape something that stalked her.

Suddenly he caught her hand and held it in a firm grip. "Hey, take it easy – it's all right, you know."

"No, it isn't." Her voice still shook uncontrollably. "I've made a bloody fool of myself. I've probably made a show of you and you working in this place. I'm sorry, it's just that – it's just that . . ."

"I know, I know. It was a terrible thing to happen. But maybe it's not as bad at it seems."

They had reached the seafront and he continued to hold her hand as they strode along the promenade. They came to a seat under some trees, where he sat down and pulled her down beside him. Putting his arm around her he drew her to him and kissed her gently on the lips. He could taste the salt of her tears. He wouldn't mind spending more time with this girl. She didn't try to pull away, just sat there with her head on his shoulder. She had never felt so drained in all her life. He broke the silence.

"Hey, Patsy, what sent you along to my building site to torture me – tell me that?" His tone was gentle and he was rewarded with a watery smile as she rubbed her eyes with the back of her hand.

"I won't be torturing you much longer. I'll be going home." She sounded so young and so uncertain.

"Sure, won't I come along and knock on your door? I'm good at knocking on doors."

"No, you won't. There's no building activity where I live, no big apartment blocks driving old women mad. Just sea and sand and sand hills and the only excitement is the tide going in and out."

"Sounds good." Reluctantly he removed his arm and got up. "Come on, I'd better bring you back to Hannah Tobin. She might be afraid we took the boat. And talking about the boat – there it is."

Patsy looked over towards the wharf and she could see the brightly lit ship just pulling away. The wind carried the sound of the throbbing engines and she could see some tiny figures standing on the deck.

"I wouldn't mind being on that," she said softly.

"Why don't we go over?" He was almost talking to himself. Then turning around and putting his hand under her chin, he sounded absurdly serious. "I wouldn't mind a stint across the water myself. I might do well in England. They tell me the money is huge. Tomorrow night when I knock at the red door, have your bags packed."

He grinned at her. With all traces of tears dried, she looked more like the lovely girl who had rambled into the circle of onlookers at the site. Was it possible it was only the day before yesterday? He already felt he had known her all her life. Walking up to the town he made a silent promise that though he knew little or nothing about her now, he would make every possible effort to know her more.

The next day when Patsy and Sarah went to visit Alan again, they were amazed to see his bed empty and him sitting in a wheelchair over at the window. Secretly Sarah had dreaded the day he would sit in one of those contraptions, feeling that it meant the end of all hope, that nothing more could be done for him. They were surprised to see he was smiling, his eyes alighting on the two of them.

"Tell you something, this thing has gears and brakes and good tyres, not like my banger at home." He looked for Sarah then. "Mrs Beirne, this is the beginning of your husband's rehabilitation, and who knows where it will end? I might make the Great Wall of China in this thing."

Sarah bent down and kissed him. "Bet you will," she smiled.

Whether it was the sight of him in the wheelchair or the wonderful way he seemed to accept it, Patsy wasn't sure. All she knew was that she was bending and kissing him, too. It was the first time she had ever kissed him like that, and the feel of his lips on hers caused her stupid heart to thump so wildly and her knees to get so wobbly that she felt she needed a wheelchair.

Patsy didn't go to see him that evening. She decided she couldn't take much more of the hurt, and she also knew that Sarah and Alan would in all probability want to be alone. Sarah didn't insist.

The bus journey to the hospital wasn't pleasant. It was crowded with workers going home, many of whom were smoking, and the stifling air caused Sarah's nausea to return. As she walked down the long corridor to Saint Gabriel's ward, she thought there was something familiar about the man who strode ahead of her. To her amazement she saw it was Conor McElroy. What on God's earth was he doing here in the National Rehabilitation Hospital in Dublin? A nurse wheeling a trolley was coming from the opposite direction. When she saw him she stopped dead in her tracks.

"Conor," she almost shrieked, "what are you doing here? I heard you were working down the country."

He stopped and greeted the nurse and they stood talking. Sarah felt suffused with embarrassment as she prepared to pass them. Just when she hoped she could creep by unnoticed, he glanced up. His eyes met hers and the dizziness and nausea that had swamped her on the bus surged back.

"Hi," she managed.

"Hi yourself," he smiled. "I was actually dropping in to see your husband. Doctor James told me to call, introduce myself."

He introduced her to the nurse who was obviously an old friend from his part of the country. She laughingly told Sarah that they had been in love when they were three. Sarah tried to smile and say something polite. From a distance she heard Conor say that he would accompany her to the ward. They walked away from the nurse who was still saying something in farewell to Conor but Sarah didn't hear. The bilious acid came welling up in her throat, and she looked around wildly for a toilet. She felt a strong arm propelling her to a large litter bin, and the same strong arm bent her head, calmly holding her as she got violently sick. The terrible sound of her retching filled her ears and made her want to die. When it was over, she leaned against a windowsill with streaming eyes. His face came and went and she gratefully took his proffered handkerchief and wiped her mouth and the beads of perspiration from her forehead.

"What can I say? "she gasped. "I was never so embarrassed in my life."

"Don't be. This is a hospital and I'm a medical man and used to things like that." He could see her pallor and was aware that she was trembling. He tried to lighten things. "But I will say that it was handy to have the old bin right where we needed it."

Alan was back in bed, staring straight ahead, indifferent to the open book in his hand. Sarah knew just by looking at him that the joviality he had pretended when he was showing off the wheelchair was just a performance of desperation. He glanced up when he saw them, his eyes puzzled and questioning at the sight of Conor McElroy.

"Alan, this is Conor McElroy, Doctor James's new partner. He was coming in to see you when I bumped into him in the corridor."

The two men exchanged greetings, shaking hands, both

of them sizing up each other in their thoughts. *The poor unfortunate bastard*, Conor thought, *everything to live for a few brief months ago: handsome, fit looking, a beautiful wife and now a child on the way, and ahead of him life as a paraplegic.*

Alan thought, *Another doctor. Christ above, I've seen enough of them to last me a lifetime, with their calm reassurance and avoiding my eye because they know I'm completely shagged. But at least this one is from home and won't go probing and shoving, tapping and lifting. Sick to the teeth of doctors – so sick, in fact, if I ever get out of this place I'll stay out.* He looked at Sarah, noting the pallor, the shadows under her eyes, the film of perspiration on her forehead.

"Are you all right?" he asked.

"No, I'm not." Her smile was shaky. "I've just made a total show of myself. If Doctor McElroy wasn't here I would have gotten sick all over the polished corridor. He saw what was coming and hauled me to a litter bin."

Conor laughed. "It couldn't have been handier, just where we wanted it." He looked at both of them. "Call me Conor. We might be seeing a fair bit of each other so first names would be easier."

Alan smiled. "If you saved the polished corridor, I'll have to call you Conor." He looked at Sarah again and saw that the colour was creeping back into her cheeks, making her look like her old self. "I thought all this nausea was a morning thing."

"So did I," she nodded, "but things trigger it off. There were geraniums on the windowsills and I've got a thing about geraniums now. They remind me of Rome."

There was a silence and Conor McElroy could see the swift glance between them, both obviously swamped with memories. He cleared his throat, breaking the spell.

"Look, I'll push along. Glad to have met you, Alan." He glanced at Sarah. "Forget what happened. It's part of the process. I'm glad I was handy." He smiled at them and waved and was gone.

That evening Rory O'Driscoll called again and he and Patsy went to the pictures in the Pavilion. It was *Ryan's Daughter*, the David Lean epic that had been filmed in the Dingle peninsula in Kerry. Rory held her hand throughout the three hours of the film, and she didn't object. If anything she found his strong, slightly calloused hands comforting. Anything to forget the searing thrill that had ripped through her body when she had kissed Alan – a kiss that wasn't brotherly or casual or meaningless.

Later, outside the red door, she bade Rory goodbye, as they were going back to Waterford the next day. They swapped phone numbers and addresses, "Because there's no doubt I'll be down to design some of those sand castles." He kissed her gently on the mouth. She felt he was holding back and she was grateful, as if he understood that she wasn't prepared for anything more.

The next morning Patsy heard Sarah getting sick in adjoining bathroom, so violently sick that Patsy rushed out and hammered on the door. Sarah came out white and drained and, sitting on the bed, told Patsy she was pregnant.

CHAPTER EIGHT

Eileen Dunne STOOD with her back to the window of the parlour and breathed a sigh of satisfaction. "I don't care what you say, Mary, but I think we've done a great job."

Mary Beirne nodded in agreement. "I think so, too. Sarah won't know it. And wasn't that carpenter really good, making everything easy for him? You'd hardly notice the ramps. And in the school, too." Suddenly her eyes shadowed as she studied the carpenter's handiwork. "Lord above us, Eileen, if anyone told me last July that we'd be talking about ramps in October, I wouldn't have believed it."

"No, you wouldn't and neither would I," Eileen said gently, "but, Mary, it happened and it could be worse now. Alan seems to have taken this terrible thing in his stride. I'm not pretending it's not bad, but it could be worse. Sarah says he can do so much. That Rehabilitation Hospital must be marvellous. He can manage the toilet end of things and that's marvellous for his sense of dignity. I also believe he can fly around in that wheelchair and, Mary, think of how marvellous it is that they're having a baby so soon. That's a miracle surely. Look at how long some people wait to have a child." Eileen walked over to the other woman and put a comforting arm around her. "Now think of the fun we'll have buying things for our grandchild. Come on into the kitchen and we'll have a cup of tea. I brought some queen cakes."

They moved into the kitchen and sat at the pine kitchen table. Tired now from their efforts, they were content to wait in silence for the friendly hum of the kettle. Everything was ready now. The walls of the kitchen had been painted a warm yellow on Tim Dunne's advice, as the kitchen was north facing. The paint was cheerful, as were the blue gingham curtains that Mary Beirne had made and had lined with warm heavy lining to keep the winter draughts at bay. The kitchen presses were new, but Sarah had tinted them antique pine so as not to clash with the pride of her eye, an old dresser she had picked up at an auction for little or nothing. It was there now, laden with the willow-patterned dinner service she had got from her godmother as a wedding present.

The rest of the cottage was also ready and waiting. The parlour with its white-painted walls was the perfect background for some bright cheerful prints that Sarah had bought. The old knotted floorboards had been sanded and varnished. Alan's mother had given Sarah a bright, cheerful handmade rug that toned perfectly with the Victorian fireplace, picking up the tones of the old tiles. The two women had made the bedroom as attractive and as comfortable as possible. They had vigorously polished the old brass bed ends until they shone brightly. They had settled for the pale primrose coloured sheets and the blue blankets. Both were agreeable that the patchwork quilt made by Eileen at the ICA was just perfect.

As they sipped the hot tea they were both silent, a companionable sort of silence with both sunk in thought. Eileen had a fair idea that Alan's accident and subsequent paralysis affected his ability to carry out what her generation called the marriage act. She didn't want to think too much about sexual pleasure and fulfilment. She hadn't been brought up to think of these things.

Mary was remembering how Alan's father, on hearing the doctors prognosis, had muttered, "God be good to him, but he'll have the sort of problems no man would want." Mary remembered the first two years of her marriage, when the longing for a baby was so great that she felt almost sick. When the weeks became months and the months became years, she tried to offer up her failure to conceive. She had read somewhere that the menstrual flow was like the tears of disappointment from a frustrated womb. After she read that she had gone to her doctor and she had died a thousand deaths telling him about her anxiety and her inability to conceive. She had died a thousand deaths again as the doctor examined her, telling her a minor operation might help. She had been delighted and had almost romped into hospital to have the minor surgery. Two months after the simple procedure she was pregnant.

No couple were as happy – she must have knitted a dozen matinee coats and even more baby blankets. The hard traumatic labour of three days' duration was instantly forgotten when she saw her newborn son. She simply couldn't believe she had produced such a baby. The dark unblinking eyes seemed to stare right at her as if he could see her the way she could see him. The nurses in the nursing home in Waterford laughed at her, telling her that babies couldn't really see for weeks. But she knew better – her son was looking at her and he saw her. She was sure of that. And now after a short and vigorous life he would come home to this cottage tomorrow in a wheelchair.

Eileen Dunne was thinking on somewhat similar lines. Sarah, though spoiled and demanding as a youngster, had grown up to be pleasant and reasonable, enabling them to become quite close. They, like most mothers and daughter of her generation, had never discussed sex or the physical relationships between sexes. Eileen had been over the moon when she heard about the baby. She was so excited about it she couldn't sleep one wink the night Sarah had told her. She kept Tim awake all night, talking about it.

"Imagine! Isn't it wonderful, a baby so soon? I can't get over it."

She repeated it so often that Tim had shut her up by muttering, "He was on the job quick enough. He knew what he got it for."

She had turned on him in the bed telling him he was the crudest man she ever knew, that she was from the heart of the country and they were crude enough there, God knows, but he took the biscuit. But before falling asleep she broke out laughing, and when he asked her what was wrong with her she giggled, "Thank God, he knew what to do – not like you – fustering for a fortnight before you got the hang of it."

It all came back in the bright, scrubbed kitchen, and she thought if Mary knew what she was thinking she'd die from the shame of it. To dispel her thoughts she said, "Anyway, isn't it wonderful that he's coming home tomorrow? And Conor McElroy has taken a right interest in everything. He has become rather friendly with Sarah, even though he is her doctor. I think he'll be a great help."

"Yes," Alan's mother agreed. "When all is said and done, they're going to need great help. Anyway, Eileen, tell me, how are your two other girls?"

"Well, Emma is in London working in a bank and she loves it. I think she likes big city life. Patsy was due to start in the university but she put it off for a year. She had a big argument with Tim, telling him she wasn't ready. I think she won the argument when she told him that she was too young and innocent to be plunged into the university rat race. Imagine giving up an opportunity like that. She keeps talking about finding herself. All that stuff you hear these days about young people finding themselves," she sighed, "sure we didn't know if we found ourselves or not. We just got married and hoped for the best. Anyway, Tim will take her into the office for a year – at least she'll know about work and she'll earn a few bob. In a way, Mary, I'm glad. Patsy isn't herself lately. She was always a bit of a tomboy. You wouldn't know what she'd be up to for a minute. Wild as a March hare, I used say. Now there's some fellow phoning her from Dublin, someone she met up there when she was staying with my friend Hannah Tobin. He keeps phoning and wants to come down and visit her. She keeps putting him off, but he's so tenacious he'll wear her down. It might be good for her. I think Alan's accident took more out of her than we knew. They were great friends."

"I know," Mary sighed. "He often talked about her and I used to love to listen. I'll miss all that now. The place will be dead without him. I was reading in a book recently that you never really own your children, you only borrow them for a few years. Still, you feel you own them and it's lonely when they go."

"Yes, it's very lonely when they go."

James and Kit Gillen were happy with the arrangement they had made concerning Conor McElroy and the granny flat. Sometimes sitting in their conservatory they could hear his music player and smiled, noting his taste swung between Buddy Holly and the soaring magnificence of Maria Callas. Maria Callas seemed to have an edge on Buddy Holly, because he played "One Fine Day" from *Madame Butterfly* again and again. Sometimes they sat and listened until the final note faded away, leaving a tangible silence until they were jerked back to reality with "If I Didn't Have a Dime".

"He's settling in well," Kit commented squinting indifferently at the crossword in her newspaper.

"He's such a hit with the patients I might soon be out of a job," her husband commented wryly.

"I don't think so," she said. "You've given a lifetime of caring to the people in this town. When I think of all those wakeful nights, wondering would you ever come home. . ."

The music stopped in the granny flat and they could hear the sound of the front door closing and of Conor's Volkswagen as he drove away.

"Alan Beirne came home today, and I think Conor said he was going to look in on them," James told her. "He was doing duty on the day young Sarah came in wondering if she was pregnant or not. Had some idea that stress might be the cause of her symptoms."

"She could be forgiven that," his wife added, "but isn't it wonderful about the baby? Eileen Dunne is over the moon about it. It's almost a miracle. It lessens the tragedy of the young man in a way."

"Don't know what's so miraculous about it," her husband

muttered. "After all, they were a young, healthy couple who probably couldn't wait to get their hands on each other, and what's the miracle in that? Babies are easy to come by – the trouble is that the world is overflowing with babies. But I suppose the birth rate will drop even here in holy Ireland. The pill will see to that."

"Nonsense," she said dryly. "No girl worth her salt should swallow pills so that a man can enjoy himself without the responsibility. Certainly no one will catch me taking a pill."

He laughed heartily. "You are sixty, love, so I don't think it'll be necessary."

Her answering laugh was spontaneous. "I forgot. I feel seventeen inside my head." Still smiling, she returned to her original subject. "I don't care what you say, I still think it's great about Sarah Dunne's baby. After all, we were waiting six months before anything happened, so don't make too light of it."

Her husband didn't comment as he returned to bury his head in the newspaper. "So Charlie Haughey and the boys escaped the net," he commented. "He was acquitted in the High Court today – a bit of embarrassment there for Jack Lynch."

"Isn't the radio full of it all day? Cheers and jubilant scenes outside the Four Courts. I wouldn't be surprised if he'll lead the Fianna Fáil party some day," his wife told him.

"Doubt it. I'll say Jack'll keep him festering on the back benches for years."

Kit decided to change the subject; she knew her husband would talk politics till the cows came home. If he had no one else to discuss current affairs with, she would be bombarded, not alone with the Irish political scene, but with the politics of most countries in the world.

"I think we'll ask Conor McElroy in to for dinner tomorrow evening – he might like the change. It's sad in a way, listening to him banging around the pots and pans at times."

"He won't be banging them around if some of the birds

up in the golf club have their way, but if you want to ask him in that's fine. Maybe he could do with a bit of home cooking."

"Well, it'll be a change from the two of us looking at each other."

He took the pipe out of his mouth and hit it off the ashtray, a familiar repetitive sound when he was smoking his beloved pipe. Looking at her his expression was thoughtful. "I suppose you miss the boys. Pity that they didn't settle here in these parts."

"Yes, it would have been nice to have a bit of a rumpus with the grandchildren. Nice to have had a daughter, too." Her tone was so low he gathered she didn't want him to hear.

"Sure, haven't you me? Sure I'm not six feet under yet."

"God forbid, James Gillen – you shouldn't be flying in the face of God talking like that. So I'll ask Conor to dinner?

"A deal," he said contentedly.

She was silent then, letting him to enjoy his paper, but it was funny the way men went on. They were so different from women. If anything they were more content when their children left home. No more decisions, hurdles, arguments or taking sides. No more hurt, no more jealousies, no more stupid sulks. They were their own men again with the woman of the house was back in their possession, just like she was before she ever had a child. Strange the way life went full circle. Two people starting off together and two people ending up together. She often sat there in the twilight hours thinking it would be great if two people who had shared a lifetime together could die together. It seemed a fair arrangement. Not to have one struggling on alone, almost like an amputee, as if half of the whole had been taken away. When thoughts like that flooded in she tried to dismiss them, reminding herself that she had reached a time of life when she should live a day at a time.

Conor McElroy drove down the narrow lane that lead on to the cliff road and then decided he wouldn't bother with the golf club. On Wednesday night the competition would be over, and he would have to listen to post-mortems about every shot, every bunker, the state the greens were in and if they didn't cut back the rough soon the bloody course would be unplayable. He had joined the club shortly after taking up the partnership on the advice of Doctor James. He enjoyed the odd round of golf and was no mean player, having served a hard apprenticeship with his addicted father, but he could take it or leave it, something his father couldn't understand.

He was soon in the deserted centre of the town. All the amusement arcades were closed and it had that dejected air of all seaside towns when summer went away. The prom was empty with the exception of one lone man walking a red setter. He parked his car facing the sea, switched off the engine and turned on the car radio. The sound of the Doc Hamilton singing "Sylvia's Mother" filled the car. He turned the volume down. It was dusk now but he could see that the tide was full in. Huge waves were lashing off the pier wall, sending spray heavenwards. He pulled out a packet of cigarettes and lit one, inhaling deeply, idly wondering would the nicotine ease some of his restlessness. Suddenly he heard the sound of an engine as another car pulled up a few parking spaces away. If the occupants, a young couple, were aware of him, they showed no embarrassment. They were already devouring each other, kissing and courting frenziedly. Suddenly they disappeared out of sight. Not wanting to appear too curious, he looked towards the sea again, inhaling deeply. Whether it was the effect of the cigarette or the frenzied fumblings of the young lovers, he wasn't sure, but suddenly, as clear as day, as clear as the full moon breaking from behind the clouds, he knew what was causing his restlessness.

He hadn't seen her since the evening in the Rehabilitation Hospital. She had been in with him today for a routine visit. After the check-up they had talked about mundane things, like the weather and the advancing winter. Had she settled in her new home? Did she miss her work in the bank? Then he asked her about Alan. She had told him that Alan was home from hospital and coping well under the circumstances. He asked her had the nausea eased and she told him it had eased a bit. A quick glance showed him that her pregnancy didn't show. She was tall and slim and it probably wouldn't for months yet. As he smoked his cigarette, oblivious of the goings on in the car two spaces away, he even recalled what she had worn: jeans, faded and well worn, a white blouse and a long black cardigan with pockets. She was the sort his mother used to say could wear anything.

Before leaving she had asked him to call out sometime – that Alan would like it. She had said, "I think he's weary of being mollycoddled by too many women." She had smiled then, but the smile didn't reach her eyes. He had told her he would like very much to call out and she had given him directions to Grove Cottage, telling him it was five miles from Tramore, seven miles from Waterford. Sitting there he wanted to call now. He wanted to go to her and take away the shadows from her eyes. He wanted to make everything right. He wondered, with a stab of fear, was it because he wanted her, too?

The moon had come out again silvering the tossing waves. Out of the corner of his eye he would see that the couple in the car were now sitting up, passion spent, smoking cigarettes. The girl's head was resting on the young man's shoulder. They put him in mind of Sarah and Alan Beirne and how good life must have been a mere few months ago – all excited about the imminent wedding and their honeymoon in Rome.

He had been to Rome once with some student friends from university. They had stayed in a youth hostel. At the time he thought he was hopelessly in love with a fellow student, also doing medicine. Sitting there, the faded terracotta ancientness of Rome came back to him. The small, narrow, cobbled back streets where brown-eyed youngsters shouted and played. The six-storied apartments with the geranium-strewn balconies. Had Sarah mentioned geraniums to him the evening she got sick? He lit another cigarette and wondered if they had been as impressed with the wonders of the city of the Caesers as he had. He remembered the Pantheon with it's wonderful dome and the magnificence of its marble floor. It had rained cats and dogs when they were there and the monsoon-like rain had come through the roof. Maeve, his girlfriend, had look entranced and said that the raindrops looked like miniature ballerinas. He had laughed and kissed the raindrops from her lips, telling her she was very imaginative.

They had gone to the Forum the next day and he recalled how Peter Connolly, who was studying architecture, stood in awed silence. Maeve had nudged him into the present, quipping, "Take a few drawings, Peter. You might built a Forum in your own backyard." Outside the Coliseum an American couple had asked them to take some pictures, and he had clicked them from what seemed like a dozen different angles with the Temple of Castor in the background.

The car near him throbbed into life but he still sat there thinking. He had proposed to Maeve Carey in Rome and she had accepted. They had nearly lost their virginity there but something held them back. Maybe because it was the seat of Christianity and at every corner you bumped into a priest or a nun. Maybe because they had a public audience with Pope Paul VI. They had been deeply affected with his presence. Maeve had later said he looked as if his dark searing eyes had glimpsed eternity. Whatever it was, they had come home with their souls unsullied and their virginity intact. Some months later she had fallen in love with someone else. Since then he had put many girls through his hands and had long since lost the youthful innocence that had been part of his make-up in Rome.

He sighed briefly, looking at the moon-dappled sea, realising with clarity that he had never really been in love since those innocent days. He had been involved, but not in love. That is until now. Now he was in love with a young women he could never have. He rolled down the window and flung out the half-smoked cigarette, feeling the cold gust of air from the sea. He put the key into the ignition at the same time, making up his mind he would visit Alan and Sarah Beirne when convention would allow.

CHAPTER NINE

IF SHE DIDN'T let her imagination run riot, it would seem like normal. The cottage was lovely, showing the wonderful effort both mothers had put into it. It was cosy, too. When the range in the kitchen was going well, the heat was sometimes overpowering. On days like that Sarah would open the window and let the salt sea air flow in. She loved the little parlour. In the evenings when she and Alan sat there in front of the fire, he told her about his day at school. She would tell him all the little titbits of news: who called and whom she met on her walk and how they referred to her as the master's wife and how shy they seemed but how inquisitive they somehow looked. Only last evening he laughed and told her, "They are cute hoors in the place and inquisitive isn't the word." It was almost like normal, that is, if you didn't see the wheelchair and if you didn't see the beads of perspiration on his forehead as he heaved himself out of it into the armchair. She had wanted to help so much at first, but he had insisted he could do it. "Look, love," he had told her, "I must. I bloody must. And anyway you can't lift heavy things – so leave me to it."

She had. Sometimes it tore at her heart to see him struggling to do things that had been such an accepted part of his life. Sometimes she averted her gaze as he struggled. Now three weeks after his homecoming, three months since the accident, things were becoming easier. He could now manage the catheter and his bowel function, saving him the humiliation of needing help. Nancy Ryan, a friend of her mother and a retired physiotherapist, called to see him. Her manner was so matter of fact with Alan that he agreed to undergo physiotherapy with her in the weeks ahead. Before leaving she called Sarah aside, telling her how lucky they were.

"If the paralysis had been from the neck down, you'd

know about it then. As it is, he's doing fine – I'm telling you, girl, things could have been much worse."

Only yesterday evening Doctor James had called also to tell Alan that he had got a full report from the Rehabilitation Hospital. Coming straight to the point he told him, "I was talking to your spine man. He seems to have taken more than the usual interest in your case. He told me things were a bit inconclusive, not all that cut and dried."

"What does that mean?" Alan had asked wearily.

"Simply that the x-rays weren't too clear. It had been difficult to pinpoint the exact spot of the breakage. There was some question of a small deposit of fatty tissue on the spinal cord that was making it difficult to locate the point of severance."

Alan had listened politely and had thanked the doctor for taking such an interest and going to so much trouble. He didn't question him further, a fact that had surprised Doctor James who had expected to be bombarded from someone so questioning, so young, so obviously athletic and who had been felled like a tree.

The calm front he put on for others ended when they were in bed. There Sarah knew that things would never be the same again. They could never fulfill their love like most young couples. They would lie beside each other and hold each other and they would kiss passionately and their kisses would bruise and hurt in their desire for each other, but it would end there.

When they broke away it was only too clear that the paralysis had totally incapacitated him when it came to sexual intercourse. She would lie beside him and pretend to herself that it was a temporary setback. A bit like the flu. That he would be fine soon. That the weekly sessions of physiotherapy would put life and feeling back into him some day. It helped to keep her in a state of denial.

On one occasion she woke up and was instantly aware that he, too, was wide awake. A sideward glance show that he staring ahead, and even in the half light she could see how desperately unhappy he looked. She turned over and took him in her arms and tried to kiss the shadows away. At first he seemed unaware of her efforts and then, looking at her, he took her face in his hands.

"This, Sarah, is sheer, fucking hell – absolute, total, fucking hell. Have you any idea what it's really like to be a half a person? Have you any idea what it's like to have half yourself dead?"

"Stop." She tried to sound positive. "Everyone said it could be worse – that you were lucky in a way."

"Lucky, God! Not that nonsense from you of all people. Do you know what it's like to have no control of your own body – messing around with goddam bags, tubes and pads. Christ, I'd put up with that, and that believe me is sheer humiliating hell, but I'd put up with it if I could have you. But I can't. Sarah, you know and I certainly know I'd be better off dead. I'd be out of it and you could have a life."

She had propped herself up on her elbow, her blue eyes blazing. "Don't say that. For God's sake, don't say that. We have a lot going for us. We love each other, we are expecting a baby, it's very good. Maybe you'll get better, who knows what's ahead."

"No, it's not good, in fact it couldn't be worse. And I know what's ahead. I know that I won't get better. I know that I'll want to make love to you and make more love and all I have is this dead part and what will it be like? Tell me what will it be like? You'll lie there beside me, and I'm not fancying myself, but you'll want me and you'll desire me and I won't be able to do a goddam thing about it. How do you think, Sarah, I'll feel about that?" He turned and looked at her and she could see the despair and the hopelessness in the dark depths of his eyes. "You could get an annulment, you know. I know you could. I have a leg of the canon."

He sounded bitter as he turned away. She was glad that she could no longer see the hell and the despair in his eyes.

She sat up and put her arms around him, pressing his head against her breasts.

"Hey, you. Do you know what I want?" she whispered.

"No." He sounded so tired. "But tell me?"

"I want you to shut bloody, fucking up, and I don't ever ever want to hear talk like that again. I also think we'll have to go to confession because of our filthy language. And listen – listen, I don't ever want you to think like that again. You didn't marry a red hot Jezebel panting for sex. If you did, I wouldn't have been able to hold you off like I did. Remember the night in the sand hills, remember the night in the park, remember the night when your parents were away and we had the house to ourselves? I had to cool your ardour all those times, so there!"

"Remember Rome?" he said quietly. "Remember how good it was? And I'm still the same as I was in Rome. This broken spine didn't break the feeling, the desires – I wish it had."

"I'll always remember Rome," she whispered, her lips buried in his black hair.

He sat up and taking her in his arms he held her so tight it hurt. "Rome did it in more ways than one. You were aroused in Rome, and that arousal and desire won't go away, Sarah. I know that."

"Shut up. No more such talk or I'll arouse you with a clout on the head." She was rewarded with a fleeting smile as she snuggled down into his arms. "Come on, we'll go to sleep," she whispered. "It'll soon be tomorrow."

They lay in each other's arms, and it seemed hours before she heard by his steady breathing that he had fallen asleep. Then and only then did she allow herself to think that sadly everything he said was only too true.

Conor McElroy didn't give the impression that mere politeness made him accept the dinner invitation readily, no hint that James Gillen was the senior partner and he was accepting out of duty. They had their pre-dinner drinks in the conservatory.

"I know you think this is mad – summer a memory and here we are amongst the greenery – but I have the heat on so we won't perish. I do so love the view." Kit explained.

Conor, drink in hand, looked out the wide window. "I know what you mean – it's some view all right."

The Gillen house was built on an elevated site, and way down below one could see the lights of the town and almost the whole of Tramore Bay. Dark now, the only sign of the ocean was the white frothy breakers crashing on the shore-line. He stifled the memory of last evening spent looking at the same breakers and thinking of Sarah Beirne.

"Well, are you settling in?" Kit asked.

"Very much. I'm beginning to like the sunny south-east. It's certainly easier than Dublin."

"I hope you won't be too bored in the winter here. A curtain of silence comes down after all the summer activity, but then the locals hate all the hurdy gurdies and all the mobs from Waterford."

"Don't you believe a bit of it – she loves all the common masses," her husband chuckled. "When the kids were small she used to treat them to all the amusements. I think she was the addict and the boys only went with her to keep her happy. She was even casting a longing eye on the one-armed bandits, only I told her it mightn't be too good for a doctor's wife to get the habit."

Kit Gillen laughed heartily, telling him not to mind her imaginative husband. Conor relaxed, thinking what good company they were and how well they communicated with each other after all the years.

"You're having roast beef whether you like it or not," Kit told him. "It's my favourite dish and I hope you like it."

"Reared I was on it – reared. It was my father's favourite dish also."

When she went into the kitchen, Doctor James asked him

how the clinic had gone. "Had you the usual chronics or was there anything dramatic?"

"Nothing much. A few elderly patients looking for the flu jab. One man after a wedding had a touch of alcoholic poisoning. A few routine pregnancy check-ups, including Sarah Beirne." Her name was out. He liked the sound of it on his tongue: Sarah Beirne – Sarah Beirne.

"I suppose she knows the worst now," Doctor James said. "She knows what it's like to be living with such a handicapped husband." He sighed. "Every day she'll be aware more and more. Still, they seem to be coping some way, and the baby will be a great interest."

"I can't get them out of my head." Kit had returned from her culinary efforts in the kitchen. "I've known Sarah since she was a child. Remember our Noel?" she turned to Conor. "Noel is our youngest," she explained. "He had a fierce crush on her even though she was years younger than he was. He was always ringing her on any old pretext, but she had no interest. He was heartbroken for all of three months and then met someone else. Is it possible," she looked at the two men sitting on each side of the table, both doctors, both knowledgeable, "that she might have more children?"

"It's possible, but highly improbable." Conor found himself answering Kit's question. Since he had met Sarah Beirne he had brushed up on his knowledge of spinal injuries. He had told himself that he was doing it so that he could be helpful when the questions came, and they undoubtedly would come. "It would be a complex process and very technical. It would involve extraordinary invasion of the patient's privacy, but who knows? In the future things could be vastly improved. There is ongoing research all over the world concerning spinal injuries and hopefully someday there could be a breakthrough."

"Anyway, young Sarah will have her hands full with one child and her disabled husband," James sighed. Conor was relieved when they want on to other subjects.

They discussed the arms trial and the exoneration of the three defendants: Haughey, Blaney and Kelly. They discussed books and music and whether the Russians would let Alexander Solzhenitsyn go to Stockholm to receive the Nobel prize. All three of them had read *Cancer Ward* and *The First Circle* and Kit admitted she found them heavy going, but as he was the writer in the news she had stuck it out. She grinned at Conor.

"When they get going on all that stuff at the odd dinner party, I like to hold my own."

She smilingly told him they were aware of his taste in music, that they could hear it through the wall. He was all contrite, telling them he'd keep the volume much lower in future. No, she didn't want that; she like to think there was someone near – it made her feel less lonely.

Before he left he told them he intended to visit Sarah and Alan Beirne, possibly the next evening. Maybe he thought by telling them the intended visit would appear like a routine thing, a friendly gesture to a young couple in a crisis situation.

It looked very normal to Conor McElroy also. Sarah opened the door and welcomed him to Grove Cottage. He told her he had quite a time finding the place. "But when I found the school, I knew things were warming up."

They were standing so near each other in the small hall he could smell her shampoo or her soap, something clean, pleasant and light, not cloying or sweet like the perfume he disliked.

"Grove Cottage, a bit of a misnomer seeing that the place is windswept and not near the green groves." She smiled, and it was only then he noticed that her eye teeth slightly overlapped giving her smile a gamine, even mischievous look.

Alan Beirne was sitting in an armchair, and when Conor came in he held out his hand and grasped it firmly. Conor hoped his glance was the glance of a friend, casual and interested, and not that of a probing physician. Conor thought Alan looked very well. His good physique seemed no way impaired. Sarah told him to remove his jacket; Alan offered him a drink. "A short or a beer?" He settled for a beer and he was pleased to see that both of them settled for beer also. In fact Sarah was drinking stout and he noticed the slight grimace as her eyes met his over the rim of her glass.

"Alan's mother told me it was good for me – build me up, sort of thing. Is that an old wives' tale or is it a fact?"

"A fact." He laughed at both of them. "It's a well-known fact that stout will put hair on a young fella's chest, so it has to be good for women."

The ice was broken then and they sat in the lamplit room like, a bit like, friends discussing all sorts of things. Conor was relieved that Alan had no inhibitions when it came to talking sport. They argued the merits of the two teams that had clashed in the All-Ireland football final, Kerry and Meath. Alan thought that the Kerry team had a great future ahead of them: "I think they'll dominate in the next few years." Conor thought that Dublin's day had finally come. Conor told them he had joined the golf club in Tramore. He couldn't see himself playing that much, but being a member might be handy.

Alan surprised him by discussing his job and the changes his handicap brought to the situation. He smiled as he told them, "You should have seen the wide-open astonishment on the faces of the youngsters when they saw me in the wheelchair. I don't tower over them any more, but maybe it's good for a teacher to be on the same level as the kids he's trying to teach. Easy to get carried away with one's power."

His comment moved Conor. It was easy to know why Sarah Beirne was so much in love with her husband. There was something about Alan, a strength, even a great strength. It was only a matter of months since the accident and he seemed good humoured and almost jovial, as if everything were perfectly normal. He left early because he didn't want to wear out his welcome.

"Come again," Alan invited as Sarah helped him on with his jacket.

"I will."

They stood in the narrow hall and Sarah opened the door. She still smelt like a summer's day, and as he moved to the door his arm accidentally brushed off her breast. The brief touch sent electric shocks through him and for mere seconds their eyes met and held.

"Bye. Take care of yourself," he told her.

"I will. Don't have quite a time finding your way home." She was smiling but the smile still didn't reach her eyes.

CHAPTER TEN

THE PHONE RANG and Eileen Dunne picked it up. The male voice at the other end was becoming familiar.

"Patsy? One moment please and I'll get her. I think she's up in her room."

Going up the stairs she hoped that Patsy was in her room, but there was no sign of her. Jumpers and jeans were scattered on the bed as if she had changed her clothes to go somewhere, yet she hadn't shouted her casual, "I'm off," as she usually did. She tried the sitting room and saw that Tim was snoring gently in front of the fire. The television was flickering on unattended and his favourite programme, "Seven Days", was going out unwatched. When he heard her his eyes flickered open and he looked around in that half-awake condition.

"What's wrong?" He sounded so tired she was sorry that she had woken him up.

"I was looking for Patsy. That chap is on the phone again."

"She's gone to Sarah's. She asked for the car. She said she wouldn't be too long, just to look in on them."

"I see. I wish someone would tell me an odd thing or two," Eileen commented wryly as she walked back to the phone.

Patsy is spending too much time in Sarah's, she thought. *Maybe it isn't good for her.* She was young and had many friends, but since Alan's accident she seemed to have lost interest in so many of her former activities. Eileen supposed it was good of her to care so much. She went back to the hall and picked up the phone. "I'm sorry, I thought she was around somewhere but she's gone to visit Sarah. It's Rory O'Driscoll, isn't it?

"Yes, ma'am, it's Rory O'Driscoll. Tell her I phoned."

"I'll tell her you called and she'll phone back if she's not too late." He seemed to hesitate, as if he wanted to prolong the conversation. Eileen, curious about this young man who was showing more than a keen interest in her daughter, was only too glad to chat. "I know you met both my girls in Hannah's when they were up in Dún Laoghaire. I don't suppose you ever see Hannah now?"

"Would you believe, I see a lot of Hannah. She's my new landlady. I moved in last week. The last digs I had weren't great, so she asked me would I be interested in moving in? I asked her, 'Would a duck like to swim?' So there was mutual agreement and here I am. She's a great woman, I'm telling you."

"She is that. Are you phoning from Hannah's?"

"No, I'm at the payphone, but I'm going back there in case that daughter of yours will take pity on a lonely devil up in the big bad city." He sounded so pleasant and she could hear the laughter in his deep voice. Then again, if Hannah had taken him in he must be all right. Hannah was no fool when it came to assessing people. Maybe he'd be the very distraction Patsy needed – she was so moody and so up and down of late.

"I'll see that she phones you. You know she's still upset about the trouble we had – Sarah's husband and that. Patsy took it so much to heart it nearly killed her."

"I know, I know," Rory O'Driscoll was saying. "Wasn't I there to mop up her tears?" She didn't answer, thinking that if Patsy had wept tears over Alan when she was with a comparative stranger, she must have been greatly affected. Rory O'Driscoll's voice scattered her thoughts as he said goodbye, but she was still thoughtful as she walked into the sitting room to join her husband.

Patsy drove the six miles to Grove Cottage without passing a single car on the narrow potholed roads. The night was dark and a slight wind was rising, yet she had to come. Whenever she was there in the room with him and he looking as good as ever, sitting in the armchair, sometimes reading papers, sometimes correcting homework, she felt as if he were the very same Alan. When she came in his smile was always as warm as ever, dispelling all her nervousness.

This evening he was alone. When she knocked at the door she heard him shout, "Come in." The very act of lifting the latch and letting herself in highlighted how helpless he must feel at times. She went into the tiny hall and heard his voice call, "In here." He was sitting in front of a blazing fire and he had been correcting homework. She could see pile of copies on a table near him and the red pen poised in his hand.

"Where's Sarah?" she asked.

"She's gone to visit Niamh O'Toole in Waterford. She didn't want to go – had all sorts of worries about leaving me here all alone." He sighed and she could see he looked tired. "That's my new problem. She thinks she has to stay with me all the time. Maybe she thinks I'll do a wheeler into the sea." He laughed then and he was so his old self her heart turned over.

"Look, if you're busy doing homework and stuff I'll go."

"Over my dead body. I'm delighted to see you. Sit down, young Patsy, and talk to me. Tell me all the news."

"There's no news. The only news is the baby. I'm thrilled, Alan, I really am. It must be a great feeling."

"It's great. Great for Sarah, too. It'll keep her mind off me and that's something." He closed his eyes briefly and it was then she noticed the shadows beneath them. "It's good that it happened so fast. Normally we would have preferred a bit more time. Anyway, what's happening in your life?"

"Nothing."

"Now don't tell me that. I know you. You make things happen."

"Do I?" She sat opposite him and looked into the fire. It was banked up with slack so that it would burn slowly and he'd have no need to replenish it, a small thing that made her realise how Sarah had to think ahead and make things easier for him. She thought of the thousand and one things her own father did about the place even though her mother laughingly told people that Tim couldn't put a nail in the wall. The room looked cheerful and cosy. Their wedding presents like the new brass fire irons and the lovely brass framed mirror above the fireplace and the Waterford cut glass vase on the sideboard filled with bronze chrysanthemums had brought extra comfort and brightness. They were coping very well. She realised what she felt was envy. More envy. And yet how could she be envious where such tragedy had struck?

"Does Sarah still get sick? She told me about Conor McElroy rushing her to the litter bin in the hospital."

"She doesn't get that sick any more, and yeah, it was well he came at the vital moment. Actually he was here visiting last evening. He's an okay kind of fellow. Hey, Patsy," he looked at her and the old sparkle flashed for one moment in the depths of his eyes, "you could do worse than capture the young doctor. He's single, unattached, obviously on the lookout, and you're young, available and very attractive. Just a bit of advice from big brother."

"You're not my big brother."

"I feel I am."

"I know you do, but you're not." *Oh, you're not,* her thoughts clamoured, *you're not. Because if you were I wouldn't be like this. I wouldn't love you so much that I'd give the sight from my eyes to spend the rest of my life with you. Yes, even though you're crippled and wrecked and in a bloody wheelchair and I believe you can't make love any more. And just say, Alan Beirne, that it was I that was having your baby, and, and – Jesus, I'd better stop thinking or I'll cry or do something crazy or go mad or something.* "I don't think that Conor McElroy would be remotely interested in me and I wouldn't be interested in him. He's too old. Anyway, I believe he's caused quite a stir with all the women around the place, not to mention my own crowd that think he's the bee's knees. And if you want to know, I don't need him. There's a fellow phoning me non-stop, maybe Sarah told you."

"She did, but you tell me."

"He's an architect. I met him in Dún Laoghaire when I was gawking at a big crane lifting slabs of concrete like a curious kid. He sort of put his talk on me and then he called to Hannah Tobin's and I went out with him a few times."

"How did it go?

"Okay." She didn't tell Alan that they had sat in a dark pub in Dún Laoghaire and she had made a show of herself, and it was because of him, sitting there now asking her brotherly questions.

"Maybe you should invite him down and show him the sights?"

"What sights, in a godforsaken kip like this?"

"Oh, I dunno. There's Tramore and Waterford, and the view from your father's place is something else. Sauleen with the tide out and all the little pools reflecting the moonlight and the whispering sand of the dunes and all the lights of Tramore over across the bay. What could be more romantic?" He was smiling now. "Sure 'twould drive the poor fellow mad."

She wondered how he could smile when he knew he would never run across the sand into the oyster bed where they had swum and shouted, telling each other the water was bloody freezing. He would never stand near the fast-flowing channel to cast a line in the hope of catching a fish. He would never chase her with a large dead crab, pretending he was going to stick it down her swimsuit. She used to lie screaming and shouting in the small warm pools, kicking at him and protesting violently. Sarah had never shown one iota of possessiveness or jealousy at all the time they spent messing. She didn't because she was so sure of him – so sure. Suddenly a flash of light came through the windows and lit up the room as Sarah drove to the gate.

"She's back."

Patsy could almost feel the relief in Alan's tone that Sarah had returned safely.

Sarah came in and seemed happy to see her. "You came. I was going to ring you to tell you to drop over. Niamh was having a sort of hens' party and asked me over."

"What did I tell you, Patsy? She thinks I need a babysitter. Will you put some sense in your sister's head?"

Patsy didn't answer, just watched in silence as her sister walked over and hunched down beside him, dropping a light kiss on his mouth.

"Complaining as usual," she said, her eyes holding his as if there were no one else in the room.

Patsy stood up and picked her jacket off the floor behind the chair where she had flung it. "I'm off. I'll see ye again."

Alan looked up at her. "Bye, take care of yourself. Seeing that I'm incapable of seeing you to the door, give me a brotherly goodnight kiss.

She walked over, and bent down and was about on kiss him on the cheek, and then for some inexplicable reason kissed him lightly on the mouth, the mouth that had passed her raking examination a hundred years ago. Once again she was unprepared for the shock that speared through her, but she hid it – she was expert at hiding things. She had years of practice now.

Patsy had hardly had the key in the lock of the front door when her mother told her that Rory O'Driscoll had phoned yet again.

"You should ring him. He's staying at Hannah's now. It's polite to return a fellow's call," her mother advised.

"Oh, all right, I'll phone him."

Patsy flung her jacket into the cloakroom and reached to pick up the phone. Her mother had returned to the sitting room. Patsy could hear the sound of the television quite clearly and remembered her father had mentioned that *Shane*, his favourite western, was on the box that evening. Seemingly way back he had taken her mother to it and on the way home she had told him she was pregnant, and the pregnancy was Patsy. Patsy didn't quite remember how her mother had told her that, but she had.

As she dialled the Dún Laoghaire number she could hear the boy calling, "Shane . . . S-h-a-n-e . . . S-h-a-n-e!" and the sound reverberating off the surrounding mountains and echoing back.

Rory O'Driscoll answered the phone as if he had been standing there.

"Hi," she said, "I believe you phoned."

"Oh, I phoned all right, Patsy Dunne. I believe you were visiting the newly-weds?"

"Yeah, I was."

"How are they now? Are you still demented?"

"They're coping, but it's still bloody awful."

"Because of Sarah?"

"Because of Sarah. Also because of Alan and because of the baby. What other reason would there be?"

"Oh I dunno – maybe because you love him."

"What in God's name are you on about – love who?" He was over a hundred miles away so he couldn't see that her hands were now trembling. Surely to God a fellow she had only met a while back couldn't possibly guess what was torturing her for so long.

"Joke – joke. Are Waterford girls not able to take a little joke? The story is, I'm thinking of going to Waterford for a weekend. I'm going to stay with a mate of mine and maybe you'd deign to meet me."

"You never mentioned a mate in Waterford. What's his name? Why didn't you tell me about him?"

"I couldn't. You were bawling most of the time." He was glad when she laughed and he thought she sounded so young.

"God, was I that bad? Tell me more about your mate?"

"He's just a guy I was in college with and he's working in your neck of the woods."

He didn't tell her that he'd had a lot of trouble running

Tony Dwyer to ground to inveigle an invitation to stay with him. Tony had told him he was welcome, more than welcome, but the place was a bloody kip. Rory had told him not to worry, that he was used to bloody kips.

"Have you a car?" she wanted to know.

"Yeah, I have a banger. Where will I meet you?"

"Why not call here? My folks won't eat you. They'll be glad of the diversion."

"Tell me where to find you."

She gave him directions: a house named Summerville Lodge built in a townsland called Carbarry about a mile from Sauleen beach which was facing the back strand of Tramore opposite the sand hills.

"Wait till I get a bit of paper. It sounds like a maze."

She could hear his footsteps going down Hannah Tobin's tiled hall; she waited, shutting out all thoughts, until he came back. When he had taken down the directions, he told her if he didn't turn up at seven-thirty on Saturday it would be her fault and the fault of her vague directions.

"I'll have to have a word with your father, burying you alive in a place like that."

When she put the phone down, she walked into her bedroom, switched on the light and pulled the curtains, shutting out the lonely world outside. Somewhere out there a curlew rose and screamed. The cry was so full of desolation that she was momentarily filled with gratitude that Rory O'Driscoll had phoned and that he was coming to see her. She sat at her mirror and, leaning over, she examined her face. Never one to ladle on the make-up, she wondered now if she could do a cover-up on her freckles. They weren't that bad, mostly across the bridge of her nose and scattered on the cheek bones. Her hair was more red than auburn. She recalled someone in school telling her it was Titian red and she lucky that it wasn't carroty. When she had it cut short and close to her head, the hairdresser had told her it was perfect with her bone structure. She wasn't sure of her bone structure – she wasn't sure of anything. She would have liked blonde hair like Sarah's, but wasn't that her problem. She liked too much that Sarah had, including her husband.

She glanced at her mouth and ran her fingers across her lips, thinking of the goodnight kiss from Alan. She knew her mouth was wider than Sarah's, maybe too wide, but her teeth were white and even. She looked at her breasts and thought they were too small. She would have loved big breasts. Clare Kelly in the tennis club was only saying last week that men loved big breasts. If they did they could whistle for them when it came to Patsy Dunne. When they would lie on the golden sand after a swim in the oyster bed, Sarah and Emma would still have some outline of breasts, but hers would have completely disappeared. When she'd sit up they'd come back, so she supposed that was all right.

Sarah's breasts were bigger now – she supposed that was the baby, conceived in the sultry heat of Rome. What had it been like, lying in Alan's arms making love? She closed her eyes briefly, not wanting to think about it. When she opened them she saw her reflection in the mirror, the pallor and the obvious yearning in her eyes. Only this very evening she had wanted to take him in her arms and console him. Then she remembered the look he had given Sarah when she came in, a look that said everything. *You're home safe and I love you.*

She reached for a dark red lipstick that had belonged to Emma and drew bold red lines again and again across the mirror so that she could no longer see the look in her stupid eyes. Then through the bold red lines she saw the picture of the Sacred Heart in the mirror. Her mother had announced that she didn't mind the posters of hairy pop singers and half-naked film stars, but they wouldn't take precedence over the Sacred Heart in her house. He must be there also. Patsy rarely looked at the picture but she looked now, and from somewhere deep down inside her silent, prayers came. She prayed that her feeling for Alan would change from her hopeless love to something sane and normal. She prayed that Sarah would have the baby safely and that the baby would be perfect. That Alan Beirne, whom she loved more than life itself, would recover in time. She knew it would be a miracle, but miracles did happen now and then. And last but not least she prayed that she would fall for Rory O'Driscoll, maybe even love him as much as she loved Alan. She knew, as she looked over at the reflection of the Sacred Heart, that if that prayer were answered it would be nearly as big a miracle as Alan's recovery would be.

"Tell me a little more about this Rory O'Driscoll?" her mother asked. It was Saturday afternoon and Patsy had just told her mother that he might be calling that evening and she might be going out with him.

"Maybe to Waterford to see a film or somewhere."

"I'm not talking about going to Waterford to see a film or whatever, I'm talking about Rory O'Driscoll."

"Oh, Mam, sure you know everything that I know. I met him in Dún Laoghaire. He's nice and sort of easy and is from Tipperary. He certainly passed Hannah Tobin – she thought he was great. They were like old buddies after minutes. And I know you probably really want to know what he does for bread." Patsy couldn't keep the sarcasm out of her voice. "He's an architect, works with a building company – sometimes in an office, sometimes on site. He's twenty-four, an only child, and his mother is dead and his father is retired, and you'd probably like to know he was an architect, too. That's it."

"Well, you don't have to be so narky. And I don't know if that's it. Maybe your father mightn't think that's it."

"You know, Mam, that Dad will go along with you, and anyway I'm nearly eighteen, I'm almost a spinster, and weren't you the one at me lately to me to go out more? Telling me that I've become a right moose around the place?"

"You always have an answer," her mother said dryly. "By

the way, Sarah and Alan called today when you were getting your hair trimmed."

"They called here! How did he manage? Why didn't you tell me?"

"I didn't tell you because we want things to look normal. If he wasn't in that contraption a brief visit wouldn't warrant telling, would it?"

"I suppose not."

"And he managed by going round the back door. It was sad in a way to see him the way he is, but he certainly can get himself out of that car and into that wheelchair very well. He wouldn't even let Sarah or me help him. It was so different seeing him sitting there drinking coffee in that yoke, instead of bounding around like he always did." Patsy's mother sighed. "We must accept God's will – they say he has a plan for everyone."

"That wasn't much of a plan he had for Alan. How could there be any justice in crippling a fellow like Alan? Sometimes you'd wonder if there is a God at all." Patsy sounded bitter.

"Patsy Dunne, don't speak like that. That sort of remark is wrong coming from a young girl. That's the sort of thing you'd hear from a Communist. Who knows what was in God's plan? Maybe a tragedy like that will make Alan a stronger and better person. Not to mention Sarah. She's married to him and I don't hear her questioning God."

"You don't know who or what she's questioning," Patsy sighed. "It must be hell for them, Mam, watching him and remembering the way it was. God, it must be hell."

Eileen Dunne looked at her daughter and saw her terrible upset and the blue, dangerous flash in her eyes that always heralded a row or a fierce tantrum. She could also see how unhappy and miserable the girl was talking about Alan.

"I know, I know, it isn't easy. But what can we do but make the best of it and turn the bright side out?"

Suddenly Patsy surprised her mother by bursting into

tears. Her mother stood there not quite sure how to react. Then she went over and put her arms around her youngest daughter.

"I know, love, I know. You loved him like a brother. Sure we all love him . . ." She was fighting to keep the tears from her own eyes. "But we must think of Sarah and we mustn't show how depressed we are. If she looses heart it will be so much worse for him."

"I know, Mam, I know." Patsy desperately tried to regain some control. "And I do think of Sarah – I actually prayed for a miracle."

Eileen walked over to the sink and started to fill the kettle from the tap for what was undoubtedly one of her healing cups of herbal tea. She had a firm belief in concoctions that Patsy loathed. Patsy drummed up a watery smile.

"Not now, Mam – I'll take deep breaths or something, but spare me from that terrible camomile."

"All right, so, but you're missing out, believe me."

Patsy wondered was she an idiot to have encouraged Rory O'Driscoll to come visiting. She wasn't interested in him really. Still she idly wondered what she'd wear. If he was coming all the way from Dublin, she'd want to make some sort of effort. Maybe she'd wear her grey trouser suit and stick a polo jumper under it . . .

". . . and as she's retired and with loads of time on her hands she'd be ideal." Patsy realised that her mother was talking away as she sipped her herbal concoction.

"Sorry, Mam, I wasn't listening. Who's retired with loads of time on her hands?"

"Nancy Ryan. You know, Nancy in the ICA. She's a wonderful physiotherapist. She was trained in London and worked in an army hospital during the last war. She also knows Alan's mother and has asked Alan if she could come to the cottage and start physiotherapy with him. She a marvellous character, and sure if it does him no good it might help him psychologically."

"But what good would putting him through all those endless exercises do? She can't put all those nerve endings together again."

Eileen, looking at her daughter, could still see the traces of tears. She was glad that this Rory fellow was coming.

"When did you become an expert on spinal injuries?" She looked at Patsy over the gold rim of her favourite china cup.

"Oh, I read all about them in the medical tome Dad has upstairs. I honestly think that Nancy Ryan will be wasting her time."

"At least she'll keep his muscles from deteriorating – that's something."

"Yes, I suppose that's something." She stood up and wearily thought she had better poke out the trouser suit. She hoped it was clean. She hadn't worn it for ages, sometime way before the wedding when she went shopping with her mother and Sarah. She realised she hadn't dressed up for a long time.

When the bell rang Eileen and Tim Dunne were in the sitting room looking at "The Man from U.N.C.L.E." on the television. They could hear Patsy at the door and the murmur of voices, one deep and masculine. They glanced at each other.

"At least he found the place – that's something in his favour," Tim muttered, taking out his beloved pipe and shaking it into the fire.

Suddenly the sitting room door was opened and Patsy came in with a young man in tow. The first impression Eileen got was that he was a bit too old for her youngest daughter, more like a man of the world, fair haired and broad shouldered. When Patsy introduced them she could see that the faint traces of laughter lines as if laughter came easily to Rory O'Driscoll. She liked his smile and the firm handshake. When the introductions were over, Tim offered him a drink, which he refused. She offered him a cup of tea to refresh him after his journey.

"Don't jump at it," Patsy warned. "She might be trying to calm you with her camomile tea."

He laughed and Eileen could see that he had even, strong white teeth and, as she had guessed, a ready laugh. Suddenly there was an ease in the room and she thought that maybe they were going to see a lot of Rory O'Driscoll.

"Tell me, how is Hannah?" she asked.

"Healthy as a mountain goat. Spoiling us all rotten. By the way, she'll kill me if I don't tell all of you that she sends her love. There's an open invitation for you to come and stay with her and visit the capital any time. Now," he gave an exaggerated sigh, "that's out of the way."

As the Volkswagen clattered down the drive, Patsy and Rory were silent. When he got on to the road he looked at her. "Well, where will we go? I'm at your mercy."

"Tramore. There's a lovely pub with a thatched roof and fierce atmosphere. I know you like pubs."

"I won't deny that. We'll have a look at your pub with the thatched roof and the fierce atmosphere, and then what?"

"We might go to a disco. There's one on in the Majestic Hotel. Then again we mightn't. I'm not in great disco mood."

"I know."

"How do you know?"

"I just do."

They lapsed into silence again as they drove through the darkness. When they got to the top of the hill before branching off to the road to Tramore, Patsy asked him to stop. He glanced at her, surprised. She laughed and as she did so she could feel the knot inside her ease and she was glad that Rory O'Driscoll had come down from Dublin to be with her.

"I'm not going to assault you – I only want you to see the view."

She was still laughing as they got out of the car. They stood on the hill and below them in the moonlight was

Sauleen Strand. Alan's description had been accurate: the tide was out and all the rivulets and pools glimmered in the pale light. Across the way, past the dark, deep, swift-moving channel they could see the outline of the sand dunes and the distant lights of Tramore.

"It's beautiful in the daylight, particularly on a bright summer's day. My dad thinks it one of the loveliest views in the country. That's probably why we live where we live. We live nowhere really – we're neither in Tramore nor Dunmore nor Waterford."

Rory looking down at the desolate yet beautiful scene, murmured, "It is beautiful – not everyone's cup of tea, but I know what you mean."

Putting his arm casually over her shoulders, he glanced up at the sky and pointed out the Milky Way. "The stars are much bigger and brighter in a place like this. I can't even see them in Dublin, what with the city lights and smog."

As he pointed out the great stars in the constellation, Patsy noticed how boyish and enthusiastic he sounded. Looking up at his pointing, she almost whispered the words: "Could this be a prayer to stop and stare at a million stars?"

"God, that's lovely. Did you make it up?"

"No, I read it in a book – I think it was a prayer book." She glanced up again at a sky that seemed almost boastful in its flamboyance, showing off everything it had. The giant black canopy over their heads was crammed with limitless stars. For good measure one of them streaked across the firmament and then plummeted with a cascade of light.

"A falling star. And it's November, so we must pray for the holy souls."

He dropped his gaze and looked into her eyes. "I don't know about the holy souls, although my mother, God be good to her, used to have me exhausted about the holy souls come November. I just think that a little planet out there has ended its billion years of existence."

Suddenly he bent down and kissed her on the lips. His

kiss was gentle and undemanding. She didn't pull away, and as they got into the car she felt good about the brief kiss so lightly given under a million stars.

"Tell me, how is the work going? Do the people still gather and look at the cranes and stuff?" Patsy was sipping a glass of beer in a cosy corner near the fire in the thatched roofed pub.

"No, that's all over. The place is nearly finished. The population of Dún Laoghaire are now used to the fact that they'll have an up-to-the-minute apartment block instead of crumbling Georgian mansions. I believe there's a new indoor shopping centre planned for the centre of the town. Won't the little old lady with the dog do her nut then? Thank God, I won't be there. My next job will probably be in Drogheda. I'll miss Hannah Tobin – she's ruined me."

He was lifting his pint. Over the rim his eyes met hers and she couldn't read what was in them, but they seemed to have a message of sorts. He put his pint glass down on the table.

"I'm thinking of moving to England. There's a great opportunity there for fellas in my business. What do you think of London?"

"I hardly know the place. I was there once when I was small, but my sister Emma is there now working in a bank. She's over there a year and keeps whinging because we haven't gone to visit her yet. All I remember were the big black taxis, millions of coloured people and everyone rushing around like blue-arsed flies."

He laughed, and meeting her eyes again, said, "Blue-arsed flies is it? Would you like to live over there and rush around like the said blue-arsed flies?"

"Why would I be doing that, for God's sake? Haven't I to get my life together? Haven't I to go to college? Haven't I to get a blooming education? Anyway, I could never see myself leaving here, although this year I'd love to have blown but I

111

couldn't. After the accident I feel I might be needed." She looked at her glass and swirled the beer around. "Although, maybe I'm more of a hindrance than a help. Anyway back to London – why London?"

"Because you'd be living there."

"Why in the name of all that's holy would I be living there?"

"Because you'd be living with me. Married to me." She looked at him in astonishment.

"Are you gone cracked altogether? Sure I don't even know you."

"Ah, but you will, Patsy Dunne. And I'm nice. So what about it? Will you marry me and we'll go to London and have a big Catholic family? We'll show the two-kid Brit families what life is all about."

He was grinning at her now, but there was a quizzical expression in the depths of his blue-grey eyes. She found herself laughing for the second time that night.

"Oh God, if things get really bad here I'll phone you in Drogheda and tell you I'm on."

"All right, so that's out of the way, too. Now, how are the newly-weds getting along and how is Alan?"

He seemed really interested. She glanced down at the fresh glass of beer he had ordered. Looking at the tiny bubbles rising in the golden liquid, the urge came, as it had come when she was with him the very first time, to unburden herself to this guy who was still a comparative stranger and yet had asked her to marry him. She knew he didn't mean it for one second – still it would be nice to tell her friends.

"They're fine. Sarah is going to have a baby."

"That's great. So you'll be an aunt."

"I never even thought of that, but they're both obviously thrilled. Alan is confined to a wheelchair now but gets around all right. He still teaches." She closed her eyes briefly. "I still can't believe it. Jesus, it's incredible to think that Alan Beirne will never walk again."

"You were very close to him?" The question was lightly asked.

"Yeah. They all tell me he was the brother I never had."

"And was he?" She looked up at him, her heart missing a beat, wondering could this guy with the casual, breezy way, with the laughter-filled eyes, have guessed what no one else on the whole planet knew.

"Yeah, I suppose he is the brother I never had."

Later they went to a disco, where she met all her friends and introduced them to Rory. Laura Madigan told her when they were in the Ladies that he was the nearest thing to a younger addition of Robert Redford that she had ever seen. Anne Marie Richards whispered, "For God's sake, Patsy Dunne, don't let him slip through your hands. If you do there'll be loads of takers, believe me."

Patsy laughed, thinking that it would be great if she was attracted sexually to Rory O'Driscoll, seeing that all the girls thought he was really something. She danced with verve with him, and as they jived she felt hopeful that maybe things weren't all that awful. Things happened all the time to change one's way of thinking.

CHAPTER ELEVEN

T HE DAYS SHORTENED as the winter advanced, and the fog came. Sarah had always loathed the coastal fog which drifted in and tenaciously hung around, reducing visibility for days on end. Before her marriage she could escape into the brightness of Waterford and her job in the bank and forget it. Returning home with her father, he would drive with his face only inches from the windscreen, saying, "I wish I could follow the sun like Churchill and Onassis and that lot."

He would make her laugh and she would tell him, "Who knows, Dad, you might win the Sweep and you and Mum can go cavorting with that lot."

Looking out the kitchen at the pale grey, dripping world, she recalled that she used to laugh a lot in those days. Not so much now, although for Alan's sake she tried. She would relate any funny thing she could drum up, like when the egg woman, Mrs Taylor, who was well known as a money-grubber, owed her ninepence change. She had found it impossible to get the ninepence. Instead she got a cabbage or a turnip. On one occasion she was even offered a hen because her laying days were over and she'd make good soup.

Another time she met Father Kennedy on one of her walks and told him that she heard there had been a bank raid in Waterford. He had stopped in his tracks and said, "Jasus, isn't that fierce? What is the world coming to when little bastards like that can do such things? It's now like the cowboy films." He then apologised profusely for his language, telling her he was doing everything in his power to clean it up. If he didn't he would never see the face of God.

Alan enjoyed hearing her accounts of her day. He tried, too. He told her about the kids in the school and about his religious instruction classes. He had asked one of the ten year olds what sin was. The boy had looked at him and without any hesitation said, "Shit, Master." She had laughed and

Alan had laughed and then they had sobered and their eyes had met, and she wasn't sure if he was thinking the same thing: that laughter between them was a scarce enough commodity now.

Last night in bed had brought a certain fulfilment, though, when she felt the baby move. He had put his hand on her abdomen and had waited and waited, and sure enough the small flicker of life came again. He got so excited it was nearly possible to forget the accident. He had kissed her tenderly and then not so tenderly, and then the passion that was always only a whisper away flared, and desire and need consumed her, and she wanted him so badly she clung on to him and pulled him close and closer, bruising him with her kisses until he pulled away whispering, "I'm sorry, love – it's out of action, like everything else down there." She had been left there every nerve in her body wanting and needing him, but she covered up her desire and kissed him gently, brushing back the black hair from his brow and kissing his eyes, glad that she couldn't see the torture in their depths. She lay there in the dark, his arm around her, his hand on her stomach, waiting for another flicker of life – maybe thinking that it was tangible evidence that his child would be born and his life would have some purpose after all.

Still staring unseeing at the grey, wet, enveloping fog, she remembered the first time she had seen him. It had been February, at Elaine O'Neill's eighteenth birthday party in the Tower Hotel in Waterford. It was a rather grand affair. For weeks before all the crowd had been wondering what they'd wear and what they'd give her. Elaine's father was a successful bookmaker with a chain of betting shops and trying to buy for her was virtually impossible. Patsy had been sitting at the kitchen table battling with an English essay when she asked her mother for suggestions. Patsy had looked up and said, "Get her a half dozen interlock knickers – can't go wrong there." Even her mother had exploded with laughter.

She did, in fact, buy her a lovely matching set of delicate lacy underwear. She had gone clutching the gift never knowing that that particular party would change her life.

She was introduced to him by one of Elaine's friends, and her first impression was that he was too handsome, his hair almost blue black. She had been reading a novel at the time, and the writer had described the male character as handsome, dark, with eyes put in place with sooty fingers. Alan Beirne had those sort of eyes. The dance had been a slow one, and when he held her close she had felt no need for the usual small talk. Afterwards she had learned that he was a friend of Elaine's brother and that he was a teacher. She danced with him again and again, and before the party was over he asked her would she see him again, maybe go to a film or out for a bite to eat. They went to *Lawrence of Arabia*, which was long and tedious, and she wondered, sitting there beside him, would he hold her hand? He didn't, and afterwards they went to a small restaurant on the quay. He wanted her to have a big steak, but she was so tense in his presence she had lost all appetite and settled for tea and cakes. She was eighteen and he was twenty-three and she knew that she was in love.

It had been a wonderful heady time. The first time he had kissed her, his kiss reduced her to a quivering jelly.

After that she was with him every possible available hour of every week, month and year until they married. Weeks, months and years that were filled with such happiness she was sometimes afraid. She had some notion that happiness wasn't doled out that generously.

Sarah remembered the first day she invited him home. It was April and her mother had invited him to tea.

"We must see this wonder man," Eileen had laughed.

Her father had entered into the mood and had added, "To let him see that he's walking out with a spoilt brat."

She had met him outside the old Atlantic Ballroom in Tramore. It was a dark, sultry day with storm clouds piled high over the Metal Man. They drove the six miles to her house in his old rattling Ford Prefect. Before turning off the narrow road to go up the drive of her house, he had said, "Hey, maybe I should have left this old jalopy down the road. Your father won't be impressed."

When they got to the gateway to her house, the storm had broken and the rain was lashing down. He opened the gate, grabbing her hand, saying something about a monsoon. They ran up the steps and, before the door opened, he dropped a kiss on her rain-moistened lips, whispering, "I adore you."

Suddenly the phone shrilled into life and woke her from her reverie. It was her mother, reminding her that she had an appointment with her doctor that afternoon

"I know, Mam, I know. Yes, yes, I'll tell him everything. Maybe you're right, maybe I should make a list."

Sarah sighed and then felt guilty, hoping that the sigh wouldn't be heard over the line.

It was only to be expected that her mother and indeed Alan's mother would be fanatically interested in their first grandchild. They both phoned almost every day, the advice pouring in like a river. Maybe Alan's mother knew that it would be her only grandchild. She wasn't sure how much they knew.

"Yes, Mam, I'll mention that I'm tired and that the nausea has returned. Don't worry. I won't forget things. Don't worry. Bye – I'll be in touch soon."

At times she regretted that she had gone to Conor McElroy for confirmation of her pregnancy. She was sorry now that she hadn't gone to the new man in Waterford, a Dublin gynaecologist who in a very short time had a large practice. She was aware that her relationship with Doctor McElroy was no longer strictly a doctor-patient one.

Over the weeks he had called, and Alan valued the calls, but she felt uncomfortable with Conor McElroy. Uncomfortable when those light grey eyes bore into hers. Now she had to see him this evening and she had to discuss her pregnancy. If her mother had her way she'd be talking about all sorts of symptoms, things you would never tell a fellow like Conor McElroy – that is, if he wasn't a doctor.

There were only men in the waiting room. One was elderly with a tickling cough that he couldn't control. He coughed so incessantly that she wanted to run out and get him a glass of water. She looked at him in sympathy as he gasped between the coughs.

"The fog, miss – it kills me so it does – right kills me."

"I know, I know – I hate the fog," Sarah answered.

"And the weatherman's giving it for the next three days," the other man intervened. He was a younger man, dressed in a heavy sweater and a navy duffel coat. Looking at his weather-beaten face and the premature lines around his mouth, she guessed he was a fisherman over from Dunmore East. "With weather like this there's no living to be made," he added, confirming her assumption. She nodded and he nodded back, his glance drifting to her waistline. "Sure, they come and life goes on, no matter what the weather."

She smiled and didn't answer, hoping for a few minutes peace before she faced Conor McElroy.

Suddenly he opened the door and nodded to the old man with the cough and then saw her sitting there and smiled. His smile seemed warm and genuine as if he were glad she was there. Then her own turn came all too quickly and she was sitting in front of him, her mother's advice ringing in her ears. *Tell him everything – tell him everything.*

"How are you keeping?" he asked, his eyes taking in her pallor and straying briefly to her waistline. He checked the urine sample at the sink, commenting, "That's fine." He came back and put his forefinger under her eyes, gently pulling. "Iron for you from now on." He pulled out a prescription pad and scribbled something which she knew would be indecipherable to her but would obviously make sense to Dermot Keane, the family chemist. "Hop up there." He nodded towards the couch and her heart started to beat uncomfortably and she felt the blush flooding her cheeks. "Don't worry, Sarah." He sounded so matter-of-fact she felt a right fool, reminding herself that he was her doctor and she was his patient and the whole damn thing was pure routine. She lay on the couch and remembered that she had put a large safety pin in her jeans and that the undone zip was hidden by her loose sweater. He walked over and she could feel her heart beat so heavily that she knew he must hear it, too.

He pulled her sweater up gently, laughing when he saw the safety pin. "Funny how some women stave off the inevitable – particularly on the first." He removed the pin with a quick gesture, handing it to her, his eyes meeting hers. "Relax, will you? This will take exactly ten seconds." His hands felt cold as he felt her bared stomach. She could feel the pressure of his fingers here and there, kneading a bit like her mother kneaded dough before making soda bread. Leaving her there in her total humiliation, he walked away, coming back with a small instrument which he put to his ear, at the same time pressing gently on her stomach. Then he glanced up, the grey eyes registering satisfaction. "Relax now. You'll be glad to hear this little fellow has a strong heartbeat and is doing fine."

With a quick movement she fixed her clothes, swung her long legs and jumped off the couch to the floor. "If I'd known I had to have this examination, I'd have bought the smocks. My mother keeps telling me about them – seemingly every woman wore them in her day."

He was sitting down at his desk again. "Handy things, smocks." He smiled at her before glancing down at her chart. She was aware that the thudding heart had eased and she told herself she was ridiculous. She wondered fleetingly what her reaction would have been if it had been Doctor James who had carried out the routine examination.

"How is Alan?"

It was as if the business part of their meeting were over and he was no longer the doctor – more of a friend genuinely wanting to know.

"Alan goes on."

She looked at him and he remembered again his mother's delphiniums. Her eyes looked the same today, as if the grey fog outside and the grey paintwork inside enhanced them, like the old brick wall enhanced the blooms in his mother's garden. She was talking and he told himself to get his act together and listen, as she was the very last women in the entire world he should want.

"He more often than not gives the impression that he has accepted things. Doesn't want me to do anything for him. He can manage most things, but there's the odd time he must call on me. He gets so frustrated then that I feel sorry for him, but I can never show it. Sympathy is out. But he's thrilled about the baby."

Her smile was shaky and he felt his heartbeat quicken. Once again he fought the urge to walk over to her side of his desk and take her in his arms and change that small shaky smile into a big, wide happy one. He briefly wondered what she had been like before the accident, before the shadows had taken away the glow. In an effort to dismiss his madness he got up and they both walked to the door. Before letting her out into the murky fog, he put his hand under her chin and meeting her eyes he said, "Keep your courage up. Tell Alan I will call over soon, if that's all right with you?"

"Of course it is." She sounded irritated. "As for the courage, I dunno. I don't think I'm too great at the courage stakes."

Two weeks later he called. When he knocked at the door he heard Alan call, "Come in – just push the door." Alan was sitting at the table with a pile of copies in front of him. The kitchen was warm and snug, the red coals glowing in the small black range. Alan nodded at the copies, "Remember what it was like getting your copy back with three out of six sums wrong? And you felt like Einstein because they weren't all wrong. Memories like that keep me from throwing the whole lot into the bin. Anyway," he looked up at the other man, "the woman in my life is gone for a walk. She loves walking on that beach when the tide is out. She tells me she needs exercises – good for her condition."

He glanced back at the mountain of copies and Conor was aware that his unexpected visit was disrupting a routine.

"Look, Alan, I'll toddle off – you're very busy."

"No, don't do that. I'll be finished in half an hour. Why don't you go down and meet Sarah? She could do with the company, and when you come back we'll have a spot of supper."

"Maybe. Do you think she'd mind?".

"Devil a mind. See you in a half an hour." Alan picked up his pen, his eyes already returning to his task.

Conor opening the door to the tiny porch, glanced back and could see that Alan Beirne was already absorbed in his work. The light from the table lamp highlighted the black hair and the handsome profile. The hands that held the red pen were brown and strong. Once again he felt that life was cruel to fell such a fine guy in the prime of life.

The night was still and the east wind that had blown for the last week had eased. The sky was dark with piled clouds obscuring the moon. As Conor turned down the narrow, rutted road that lead to the beach, he could smell the sea, and when he rounded the corner he could see that the beach stretched for miles. As far as he could make out it was deserted. The tide was out and the dark narrow channel glinted as the moon made a brief appearance from behind the clouds. He walked past the drifts of seaweed piled high and uneven at the edge of the unmarked sand, but further up he could barely make out footprints nearer the dunes.

He followed then and saw that they ended abruptly, as if the walker had decided to go up into the dunes to rest or maybe to shelter from the cold. He stood there uncertainly, wondering would he follow or would it be intrusive, or indeed what right in the world had he to be there at all? As he wrested with his uncertainty he saw her and he knew that she saw him. She was sitting in a sheltered spot by a large clump of tufted grass.

"Hi," was all he could say.

"Hi, yourself. I suppose I should follow this by saying what brings you here?"

He laughed as he bounded up to sit beside her. "I'm here because I called to the cottage, nice and friendly like. Your husband was up to his neck correcting copies and I, being the nice guy I am, was going to go home to my nice bachelor flat. But he, being the nice guy he is, told me you were walking and he suggested that I go and meet you. If I was successful I could accompany you home and I might be rewarded with a cup of tea."

She laughed, pulling up the collar of her coat, but made no effort to get up and go. "Put that way I'll have to get you the cup of tea." She glanced at him and he could plainly see what looked like traces of tears on her cheeks.

"Is it the wind," he said gently, "or would you like to talk? I'm a listener. I'm good at it."

"As well as that you have x-ray eyes. A woman in the waiting room told another woman that." Suddenly without any warning, she started to cry, and like a child she made a valiant effort to hide her tears by putting her hands over her eyes. He reached out and took them away and her eyes met his and he gently took her in his arms.

"Cry, Sarah – cry for Christ's sake. Maybe you haven't cried enough."

She lay against his chest and sobbed, great wracking sobs that seemed uncontrollable. He made no effort to restrain her, just held her close, hoping that in her trauma she wouldn't feel the thumping of his heart. When her sobs started to subside, he rocked her gently, and when she broke away, searching in her coat for a tissue or a handkerchief, he came to the rescue and gave her one.

"God, Conor, you must think I'm a fool. Sitting in the dunes in the middle of winter crying like a banshee." She met his eyes and tried to smile.

"It's unusual," he smiled, "and I can think of better things to do. As for the x-ray eyes, maybe the woman was right. I could see you wanted to cry."

Suddenly she was aware of him – aware of his masculinity – his physical presence. She looked at him and her eyes met his and held, and whether the tears that she'd shed gave them a greater clarity he wasn't sure, but in their clear depths and in the palpable silence he was aware of her terrible need. Suddenly they were in each others arms and he was kissing her, at first gently and tenderly. Then their kisses became desperate and demanding. He could feel his rising passion and he was unable to check it and it came strong, overpowering, like an unstoppable flood. He was clearly aware now that her desire was as great as his. He gently pushed her down amongst the dunes and hurriedly opened her jacket. Pushing up her sweater he kissed the tops of her breasts and kissed her neck and then searched for her mouth again. She pulled him so close he could feel the slight mound of her pregnancy.

Suddenly he stopped. From inside realisation flooded that this would be a terrible wrong. He drew back, taking her face in his hands, kissing her on the cheeks, kissing her on the mouth, tasting the salt of her tears.

"I can't, darling – I can't. I want to. I want to more than you'll ever know – but I can't. We can't."

She sat up slowly, pulling down her sweater, her hands trembling. She looked at him and he knew he would never see such sadness in a human glance again.

"I know, I know – dear God, I know. What must you think?" she whispered. "What must you think?"

In the silence that followed a curlew rose and its cry filled the night sky with the solitary, despairing sound. He waited until the sound had subsided and then took her in his arms again, this time as you'd gather a hurt child.

"I think that you are a beautiful young woman and that the tragedy of your husband's accident has left a void. I can only imagine how you need him physically. It's understandable, you had so little time together. I know your hunger, Sarah, and there's nothing to be ashamed of. And I know something else. And I can't afford to know it . . ."

"What?" she whispered.

"I know that I love you and you're the last woman on earth I should love."

She looked at him and it was her turn to see agony and desire in his eyes. The restless bird rose again and if anything its cry was more agonising than before.

"Oh God, what have I done?" she sobbed. "I've given you the wrong impression by acting like a – like a – whore. You see, Conor, I love him. I always have. I don't know what happened to me – I don't know. Don't love me. It would be all wrong for you to want someone like me." Her gaze was unwavering and there was such despair in her face he could hardly look. Tearing her eyes away she glanced towards the dark heaving sea and she spoke as if she was speaking to herself. "But what am I saying? Of course you could have me. I wanted you to have me. Even though I'm carrying my husband's child, I wanted you to have me." She looked at him again and then got up on her knees in the sand. "Conor, what happened here tonight – what didn't happen – what we said to each other – what you said to me – must never, ever be spoken of again. I will see you as my doctor, you will visit us, and we will go on. I'm sure you will be with me when my baby is born. We must put out of our minds what happened here tonight. We'll just wipe it away like the tide will wipe our footprints away. Promise me, Conor. Please promise me."

Leaning over he brushed the sand from her jacket and

jeans. "I promise. No one will ever know except that bloody insomniac bird."

They walked up the strand in silence. Before they reached the small lane that lead them up the hill to the cottage, she looked back at the two sets of footprints in the sand. "The tide will come in and obliterate those, and in a hundred years time it will come in and obliterate someone else's footprints. Doesn't it make you feel very unimportant?"

He nodded, quoting, "'We have not here a lasting city.' God, we're getting very melancholy. If you weren't in that interesting condition, I'd race you to the end of the strand."

He sounded so boyish she found herself smiling. He looked at her, his light grey eyes raking her face, "Great – you look fifteen when you smile. And I'm taking Alan up on that spot of supper – I think we could do with it."

They walked on in silence. Sarah wondered, could the momentous and terrible failing that happened, and didn't happen, be dismissed so easily? Would she be forgiven because she was already suffering so much? She glanced over at the whispering sand hills, at the fast flowing channel, at the flickering distant lights of Tramore. There was no answer anywhere.

When they came into the kitchen they saw that Alan's eyes were closed and his breath was steady. Sarah looked at him and turning to Conor she whispered, "He gets so tired. All that effort, physical and mental." She silently gestured to Conor to sit down as she went to fill the kettle. Walking back she saw that Alan's dark eyes were looking at her, their expression unreadable. For one wild, heart-jolting, terrifying minute she wondered if he could possibly have guessed what had happened in the sand dunes, but suddenly he smiled and all fear evaporated completely.

"You were a long time." He looked at Conor. "I told you this woman covers miles."

"I know," Conor replied. "I'm back for the cup of tea to recover."

"Patsy was here," Alan told Sarah. "She just dropped over in your mother's car."

"Why didn't she stay?" Sarah sounded surprised.

"She was here for quite a bit. Anyway, the company wasn't great. She propped herself there, and I think she was reading 'Hy Brasil' with that husky voice she has when I fell asleep. I'd say she left in high dudgeon." He smiled at Sarah.

Conor sitting there could see the love he felt for her – see it in his eyes, could nearly feel it like a tangible thing in the small warm kitchen. Reaching out for his cup of tea his heart bled for them. It also bled for himself.

Later when Conor had gone, when Alan had gone to bed, Sarah cleaned up the supper things. She never felt less like sleep in her life. She didn't want to think of what had happened on the beach, didn't want to dwell on what might have happened if Conor hadn't restrained himself. She didn't want to think, not for one second, that she would have let him take her. *Christ*, her thoughts screamed, *if you would you're no better than a whore. Even worse than a whore because of your condition.* Stilling her thoughts she tiptoed into the bedroom and saw that Alan was asleep.

Back in the kitchen she searched in the drawer of the dresser for her diary, which she had only yesterday found in a box of books. A girl in the bank had given it to her, advising her to keep an record of the most important year of her life – the year of her marriage. It had seemed a good idea at first, but she saw flicking through it that, with the exception of the few enthusiastic entries in the early months, she had obviously tired of the exercise. Now 1970 was nearly over, the year that had seemed to hold so much promise and joy before it all evaporated on a hot humid day on a busy highway in Rome.

She read the hurried entry on the fourth of January:

> Today was the usual dull, boring, awful day in
> the bank. The boss was cranky as hell, trying to

find fault with everyone or anyone. As I counted the notes before balancing I caught a glimpse of my engagement ring. The diamond looked so pure and beautiful amongst the dirty money. I twisted it and it caught the light, sending out spears of blue and red. I can't wait until I'm married – I can't wait until tonight when I see Alan – I can't wait to leave this dull, boring bank.

There were other entries describing days of shopping, days of planning, days when they looked at the cottage that was to be their future home. The cottage she lived in now and where her sleeping husband lay paralysed.

She decided she would keep the diary from now on, a diary that no one would ever read but herself. Maybe putting down things she couldn't relate to a single soul would be therapeutic, lessening the pain and the guilt. She searched in the drawer for a pen, went to the table and started at the top of the page:

27th November 1970. The fog was gone today and it was good to see the world again without the grey curtain. I've made a resolution that I will become a diary fanatic, recording everything that happens. Right now it's late, but I feel so restless I couldn't consider bed yet. Alan is sleeping – the guy I love with all my soul and who I nearly betrayed tonight. Am I mad? I'm pregnant and according to all I've heard and read, pregnant women are like blancmanges of contentment, only interested in nesting and producing. So I must be mad or maybe Conor's explanation was right.

The pen effortlessly filled the page as she described the scene amongst the sand dunes, as she tried to analyse her emotions.

But tonight, looking at Alan when he woke after we came in, I felt a love for him that I didn't think possible. Looking at Conor as we lay in the dunes I felt need. Love and need are obviously two totally different things.

Sarah put the pen down and wondered where she'd keep the diary, away from the possibility of its ever being found. She glanced up at the top of the dresser at the old blue dinner plates that Alan's mother had given them. Mary had told them that they had belonged to her grandmother and had pointed out the old method of wire stitching that had been used to mend them. Sarah stood up on her toes and carefully placed the diary behind them. Sadly, Alan would be physically unable to find it. Already she was forgetting what it was like to be in his arms with the top of her head reaching his eyebrows, or so he used tell her. Sighing she tiptoed into the bedroom and slid in beside him; he put his arm around her, sleepily telling her she was cold. He was right; she was cold, but the coldness wasn't merely physical – it was a coldness of fear, of confusion.

CHAPTER TWELVE

THREE TIMES A week, Nancy Ryan's old rusty Mini rattled down the narrow road to the cottage at four o'clock. At first Sarah thought the physiotherapy might be very disruptive, but as the weeks went on she quickly changed her mind. Nancy's only demand was that they procure a sheet of plywood and a thick blanket, "because," she advised, "that bed is as soft as a kitten."

After one week of her visits Alan found himself looking forward to her company and seemed eager for her ministrations. As he lay face downwards on the bed, she massaged and manipulated, her nimble fingers pushing, circling and pinching where she thought the spinal cord was broken. As she worked she talked about England in the forties when she worked in a military hospital during the war.

"They came in droves, the poor lads, some only youngsters. Some were back from the front, back from the desert, others shot down from the skies – crippled, injured, and would you believe, they were still cheerful. The Brits are like that – keep the sunny side up. I was there the day they told one fellow he'd never walk again. When the doctors had swept away, he just lay there stunned and speechless with the shock of it. I was working with another lad at the time, but I went over and sat with him and told him that sure enough the doctors knew what they were at, mostly, but there was a God over our heads and He spoke first. He told me he hadn't given God much thought, but maybe he'd do something about that now. Then he asked what part of Ireland did I come from and I told him Waterford – known the length and breath of Ireland as the unconquered city. He smiled for the first time and told me his grandmother was Irish from a place called Cloughjordan in Tipperary."

Alan listened to her, almost mesmerised by her soft voice as she gently worked on his spine. If she wanted to come and practise her expertise, instead of "weeding the bloody onion beds", he was happy to comply.

"What happened to him?" Alan asked.

"He walked again after a gruelling three years. At times when the sensation came back he used to scream at me, saying he'd prefer to be back at the front. But would I listen? Not at all. He told me once that I was worse than Hitler. He even told me to fuck off a few times." Alan laughed so much she had to stop her work. "He's in his fifties now and a grandfather."

"That must make you very happy," Alan chuckled.

"Ah, it's all so long ago. Yet at times it's like yesterday. Do you know I'm facing seventy myself, and you know what, you never get old inside your head. Sometimes I feel I might meet a nice fellow who'd have me – a sort of pensioner Prince Charming." He was laughing again and making him relaxed was part of her programme. Every day before she left she worked at the muscles of his legs. "Can't have those fine legs wasting."

"You're the expert, Nancy."

Sometimes she could hear the hopelessness in his tone and knew he felt it was a waste of time. Days like that she'd have liked to take him in her arms and mother him, but of course she couldn't. She wanted their relationship to be friendly, casual: no emotions, no pity, no tears, just one hour's work three times a week, and if the lad wanted to talk about anything on earth she'd listen.

There was no doubt that his wife was a lovely girl. Four and a half months gone and she hardly showing, still wearing those jeans. Nancy Ryan had been up in Blackrock in Dublin visiting her youngest brother in September, and there was a sort of concert affair with one of those mad, noisy rock bands in the park. She had gone for a walk and had strolled into the park, and there was nothing to be seen anywhere only the blue denim stuff, as if all the little rolling hills there were blue instead of green. When she went home and mentioned it to her brother at teatime, her nieces had burst out laughing, telling her that she was fierce old fashioned. They couldn't be good for a young expectant mother, tight things like a board rubbing off your groin.

There is a terrible restlessness about Sarah Dunne, she thought, as she rubbed Alan's skin up and down, round and round, pressing gently, probing, holding and hoping. *Those blue eyes have a sad, unhappy look. There is no doubt young Sarah is finding it hard. But if God is good, maybe the little baby will make up for all the their misfortunes.* Looking at him lying there, still physically a fine young man, she thought how lucky they were that she had conceived before he was paralysed. *Jesus love him, he was lucky in that respect.*

When the sessions were over he would sit up and manipulate himself into his wheelchair. She noticed how easy his movements were becoming. Her experienced eye told her that the physio was helping there. In the early days the sweat used to break out in beads on his face.

This evening sitting in the cosy kitchen drinking a cup of tea and eating a buttered scone before leaving, she asked Sarah, "Is it old Doctor James you're having for the baby?"

"No, it's Doctor McElroy. He was on duty the first time I went and I'm sort of stuck with him now. I don't know if that's a good thing, maybe I should change or something?" Her blue eyes held the kind, faded eyes of the older woman.

"No, girl, stay with the young man. Whenever a young doctor is on duty and doing his job, he doesn't see a body like you think he does. It's a job like any job and there's no such thing as embarrassment. And yet poor young mothers die a thousand deaths lying there with their legs strapped and those fellows peering in, casually talking to the nurse about two centimetres and three centimetres."

"Stop, Nancy," Sarah laughed. "I was enjoying my scone." All three of them laughed heartily, and in the warm cosy kitchen they relaxed and drank their tea almost unaware of the bond that united them: they wanted Alan to get the use of his limbs again. They wanted to see him walk again. In short they wanted a miracle.

Patsy lay in bed, her book lying unread in her hand, the golden pool of from her bedside lamp falling on the letter on her locker. The letter was from Rory O'Driscoll. Since he went to Drogheda he had phoned several times and on one occasion he had asked her to write.

"Letters are better," he had argued. "You can put more into them than the few words on the phone. Anyway, be nice and pity a poor, lonely bloke up in Drogheda pining for company."

So she had written a bright sparkling account of her day at work in her father's office, telling him about how the old-est clerk there had been courting a woman for twenty-five years and now out of the blue they were getting married, and he was fifty-five and she was fifty-two. "You certainly couldn't call it a shotgun marriage," she had written. She wrote about the discos she had gone to and told him he had made a lasting impression on some of her friends when he was down. They were constantly asking when he was coming down again. She told him that Sarah was well and that Alan was coping. She told him that Christmas was coming and she'd have to get her head together about presents, but the bright spot was Emma coming back from London. She wrote that they would in all probability spend all their time fighting. Still it would be better than the quietness.

She told him that, yes, if he kept asking her to go to Dublin for a weekend she might, providing that they stay in Hannah Tobin's. He had written by return.

Dear Patsy,

I got your letter yesterday and here I am like a good guy replying to it today. I liked getting all your bits of news. It made me feel I belonged somehow. Now don't go walloping your head off the wall wondering what the dope means – it just means it felt good. Okay. Regarding the couple finally tottering off to the altar – at least one of the telegrams won't hope that all their troubles will be little ones. I'm glad that Sarah and Alan are managing. Regarding the possibility of you visiting Dublin – sure I'd settle for Hannah's if you won't come to a more exotic dwelling with me.

Yeah, Christmas is coming. Regarding a present, would you like a lovely engagement ring from me? You know, the kind of ring that tells every other guy to back off? I still think we should go to England after we marry – heaps of dough there. Think of coming home to County Waterford and romping down that beach you call Sauleen with a horde of little kids with British accents.

I know you must go to college and get your degree. A decree from your father, Now isn't that a good word – decree – a sort of biblical word. But who knows, you might change your mind and even he might change his mind when he sees what a fine fellow you captured.

Ah, Patsy, don't be furious with me for writing this rubbish – then maybe it isn't rubbish. Maybe I'm dead serious. Anyway, think – think and let me know exactly when you're coming up. Superfluous to say I want you to come, Hannah wants you to come. We might have a night on the tiles and take in Zhivago's afterwards. It's a night club and all the heads go there. If your mother knew what goes on in Zhivago's she'd be up the wall but – anyway, I promise I'll keep all the wolves away.

Love, Rory

She had read the letter and reread it and was happy she'd gotten it. It somehow made her feel normal. It didn't make her heart beat rapidly or her mouth go dry or fill her with a strange hungry longing. It didn't swamp her with the sort of emotions that had swamped her last evening. Alan had been alone when she called, and looking at him sitting at the table, the light from the lamp highlighting his darkness, highlighting the shadows under his eyes, highlighting the black stubble on his chin, she knew she should leave. He looked so alone, separated in a way by the accident that had taken away so much. Seeing the copybooks and the school books on the table, Patsy knew she had come at a bad time.

"You're working, you don't want me wasting your time." He looked at her almost as if he had seen her for the first time. His dark eyes roamed over her face, her cropped hair cut, the long slim lines of her figure.

"No, Patsy, you're not going to waste my time. Stay until Sarah and Conor come back. It gets quiet at times, makes me think too much. Stay and talk to me."

"Okay – what'll I talk about?" The mad notion assailed her that the look in his dark eyes had some sort of message – or was it some sort of longing? Whatever it was, it made her uncomfortable and fidgety. She sat near him and picked up a poetry book off the table. Flicking through it saw "Hy Brasil", a poem she had learned at school.

"I remember that. It used fire my imagination and I'd sit drooling in my desk gazing out the window at the sea and persuade myself that I could see my own private Hy Brasil," she said. She was prattling because she thought there was a sense of something different between them as they sat in the quiet kitchen. The man who was her brother-in-law, whom she loved with an unreasonable love, was a mere whisper away, and no matter what she did or said there he'd stay because there was no way he could walk away from her.

"Hey, read it to me," he asked.

134

"Okay – if that's what you want." She threw the large ging-ham cushion in the armchair by the fire on the floor and got down on her knees and, sitting back on her heels, cleared her throat.

"Come over here." Alan gestured to a spot near him. "You're so far away I won't hear you." She placed the cush-ion near him and resumed her position.

"Okay – is the curtain up?" she joked.

"It's up," he smiled. She cleared her throat and read from the book because she didn't want to look at him.

On the ocean that hollows the rocks where ye dwell,
A beautiful land has appeared, so they tell.
Men thought it a region of sunshine and rest
So they called it Hy Brasil, the isle of the blessed.

From year unto year on the ocean's blue rim,
The beautiful spectre showed lovely and dim,
The golden clouds curtained the deep where it lay
And it looked like an Eden away far away.

As she read the second verse she felt him touch her hair, and his touch sent her heart thumping and a longing shoot-ing down through her body. She didn't comment but con-tinued to read. The poem on the next page was another one that brought back childish memories: "The Old Woman of the Road". As his hand continued to rub her hair, maybe a bit like you'd rub your favourite puppy, she continued to read. As she sat on the cushion leaning against his leg read-ing the childish poems, she was suffused with a contentment she had never felt in her life. Then his hand was still, and glancing up at him she could see that he had fallen asleep. She sat there quietly for a while and then she reached up and gently removed his hand and placed it on his thigh. She stood up quietly, her eyes never leaving his face. His mouth was slightly open and she could see the glimmer of his white teeth. She reached out and quietly picked up her jacket.

Some time later, lying in bed unable to go to sleep, she wondered why she did it, what had prompted her to get down on her knees in front of him and kiss him on the mouth, slightly touching his teeth with her tongue. He had moved slightly and said something – what it was, she wasn't sure. She was only sure she did seventy in her mother's reliable old car as she belted home. She touched her lips and recalled the sensation that the stolen kiss had brought. She had experienced it before, but now she knew it was wrong, crazy, maybe even sick. She decided there and then that she'd write to Rory and that she's go to Dún Laoghaire and that she's do a steady line with him. Maybe she might even marry him and go to England with him. Maybe if she did all that she would get rid of her sick obsession.

The big Christmas tree in Heuston railway station looked festive and bright, and the milling crowds that thronged the station added to the air of festivity. Patsy walked through the mad throng of people rushing to get the trains out of the capital. Her mother had warned her it would be chaotic – the eighth of December in Dublin was always chaotic with most of the country people up for their Christmas shopping. Her father had advised, "Maybe you should put it off until the following week." No, she was adamant. After all, she told them, when she was arriving all the country people would be leaving. She wanted to see Rory, to have a trial run on what it might be like to do a strong line with him, to see if what he said in his letters was genuine. After all she had only been with him a few times.

When the crowd thinned out she saw him standing near the Christmas tree. He didn't see her at first but was scanning the crowd with an anxious look on his face. She weaved a little amongst the throng to escape his searching glance until she could touch him on the shoulder.

"Hey, I'm here."

He looked so relieved when he spun round and grabbed

her. "Did you ever see such a mob?" he laughed. "I said to myself, Rory boy, if she comes at all, that gang will whisk her back to where she came from. God, I'm glad you're here."

He held both her hands looking at her and his eyes told her he was definitely glad she was there.

He had his Volkswagen parked outside the station. Driving through the heavy traffic he pointed out places that might interest her. When they were stopped at the red lights she got a glimpse of swans at the far side of the canal.

"Look at the poor swans," she pointed. "Wouldn't you pity them, living out their lives in an old canal with the fumes of all that traffic?"

"They know nothing else, probably as happy as Larry. Not for them the wind-tossed lakes or the unpolluted river. They'd probably die away from the smell of Dublin. Anyway, enough about swans. How are you?"

"I'm great, so I am. And you?"

"I'm great, too, so I am."

She could hear the smile in his tone and she snuggled down in her seat, glad that she had come away from all the traumatic happenings at home. Sitting beside him she remembered dinner the previous Sunday. She wanted to forget it but it wasn't easy.

Her mother had asked Alan and Sarah to dinner, as she did most Sundays. It was the first time that Patsy had seen Alan since the evening she had visited. If he was aware that their position had changed slightly on that evening she read the poems, lulled him to sleep and kissed him goodnight, there was no sign of it then. He seemed in good form; the terrible exhaustion that had been apparent then seemed to have lessened. At the dinner table the talk was general. Her father and Alan touched on world events like the death of General de Gaulle, how it would affect the French economy, and the way he had requested a simple humble funeral, wishing the ordinary men and women of France to accompany his body to the grave. Then they had got on to the awful tragedy of Lilian Board, the British Olympic runner who was dying of cancer. She had joined in, telling them about the unorthodox doctor in the Bavarian clinic who had taken out her teeth in an effort to save her life.

"A last-ditch, gimmicky exercise." Alan's look was warm and brotherly. "I suppose when you run out of time, you'll agree to anything."

"Enough about death and sadness," her mother said. "Can we get on to something cheerful?" She looked at her eldest daughter whose pregnancy was now apparent. "How are you now, Sarah – are you still troubled with the nausea?"

"No, not much," Sarah had smiled. "It seems to have eased off."

"And do you know something," Alan laughed, "this child will be another Georgie Best – kicking like a trooper." He looked at Sarah and Patsy could plainly see the adoration in his dark eyes.

"Alan," Sarah nudged him, "you don't talk about things like that."

"You do, you do, when it's the most important thing in the world to you." It was as if there were no one else in the room but the two of them. The naked love blazed in his eyes as he looked at Sarah. Patsy sat there, a lump rising in her throat, a lump she tried to swallow. Suddenly she could feel the moisture in her eyes and she prayed that no one would notice. What a stupid nut she had been to think that her feeling for Alan was even slightly reciprocated. That night, lying in bed, she vowed that things would change because things had to change. She was eighteen now and it was over three long years since Alan Beirne came into her life.

"A penny for them." Rory's glance was teasing.

"They're not worth a penny," she smiled back. "I was thinking of how nice it is to be away from home – to be free from the family – that's all," she lied.

Then there wasn't much time to be thinking because he was driving through the main street in Dún Laoghaire.

When they reached Hannah Tobin's, he reached out, took her cold hand and gave it a warm squeeze. His touch was comforting and made her feel good. As he switched off the ignition, she decided there and then she'd settle for feeling good. It was far and away better that been sick to the heart with love for someone who looked on you as a sister.

After a sumptuous tea of chips and steak followed by homemade apple tart and cream, they sat in Hannah Tobin's warm kitchen. Hannah's questions came fast.

"Patsy, I'm dying to know all the news. How is Sarah, and she expecting and everything? How is that poor boy, her husband, and he so bad? How is he managing? Do the doctors give any hope that he'll walk again? How is poor Eileen taking it at all?"

"Wow, Hannah," Rory laughed. "She'll be here all night if she's to answer all that. I was hopeful I could show her the bright lights."

Patsy sighed, realising that there would be no escape, and smiled at Hannah. "I'll start at the beginning," she said, and answered all Hannah's questions.

"Poor boy," Hannah shook her head, "it must be hard. Are the doctors giving any hope? I read in the paper about a young girl who broke her back in a skiing accident and she was told she'd never walk again, but she did. Sometimes the doctors are wrong."

"Nancy says that, too."

"Who's Nancy?" Hannah was decidedly curious.

"Nancy is a friend of Mam's, a physiotherapist who comes to Alan and Sarah's house three times a week." Glancing at Rory, Patsy saw a slight imperceptible nod towards the door and knew he was anxious to go.

Hannah aware that she mustn't keep them agreed, "Yes, maybe it will help him – poor lamb, maybe it will."

Rory pulled out all the stops to please her. They had two drinks in the same pub where he had taken her before, "just to exorcise the last visit". Then they drove into the city and

139

they danced the night away in the dimly lit Zhivago's. It was crowded and she could see that Rory was an enthusiastic dancer. He bopped and gyrated happily, the revolving light turning his teeth luminous purple as they undoubtedly did the same for hers. She was glad she was wearing her newest mini and was glad that her long legs were encased in tights that fitted her perfectly and hadn't the wretched gusset halfway down her thighs. During the slow waltzes he held her close. The last dance was another slow haunting number, and as they moved in perfect unison, he whispered, "Do you know what they say about this place?"

"No? How could I?"

"It's where love stories begin. All the ads on all the buses say 'Zhivago's – where love stories begin'."

"Interesting," she said. Rory O'Driscoll made her feel very good, and feeling very good was something she was beginning to like.

"Well, will it?"

"Will what?"

"Will our love story begin here?"

"Not here. Not now. Maybe next year."

She laughed and her white teeth and her white blouse caught the revolving light and turned purple. "I've got to get something out of the way first."

The words were out before she realised. Suddenly he pulled her in so close and held her in such a tight grip she could hear the pounding of his heart.

"I know, I know," he whispered into her ear.

Her own heart pounded. "You know what?"

He pushed her away and looked at her. She couldn't read what was in his eyes. He couldn't possibly know her innermost secret – her ongoing obsession.

"I know that young flighty girls can't make their minds up about anything. They feel they want to travel, want to live, want to find themselves."

She laughed, her luminous purple teeth flashing, and he

bent his head and kissed her. It was a tender kiss, and like the touch of his hand, she welcomed it because it had made her feel good.

CHAPTER THIRTEEN

SARAH GLANCED AT the calendar and the little circle of red surrounding the date, 16 December. She had glanced at it every day for the past week. Even Alan had noticed, asking, "What's so big about the sixteenth? You look like someone going to the electric chair."

She had laughed and had gone over to him and dropped a kiss on his head, noticing with a shock of surprise one or two grey hairs amongst the black. If things had been normal – if he weren't so vulnerable – she might have said, "Hey, you're getting old; you're going grey." But she didn't. You didn't say things like that any more, joke like you did before. Instead she merely told him that the circle of red on the sixteenth was her appointment with the doctor.

There was no doubt she felt decidedly uncomfortable now with Conor McElroy. Ever since the night on Sauleen Strand, whenever she recalled his declaration of love and her need and hunger for him, she felt so devastated with guilt that she felt physically sick. She dreaded her continuing visits, the wretched urine sample, the way he tried to put her at her ease when he briefly examined her.

During the long days when Alan was at school, she tried to keep busy – sometimes to the point of distraction. She walked for miles when the weather was fine and when the fog lifted. At night when she was alone in the kitchen after Alan had retired, the written word brought ease as she tried to assuage her guilt and she would take down her diary, sometimes filling in the events of her day, sometimes trying to untangle her thoughts.

> I console myself by telling myself that the way I responded to Conor's advances was because I miss Alan's lovemaking so much. As the weeks go by all physical contact between us ends in his deep

frustration. I keep telling him it doesn't matter. I tell him that sex is overrated anyway. He reminds me of what we had in Rome and tells me if that was overrated he'd go for overrated sex anytime. That is, if he wasn't half a man. I try to joke and say that it would be old hat now and undoubtedly the novelty would have worn off. Mostly he's asleep when I go to be bed or maybe he pretends to be. At times I'm so bitter about his accident I ask God why did he do it to us? Why Alan? Such a fine person. Caring and good living. Doing his utmost at work to make decent citizens out of that unimaginative bunch of rural hicks. That sounds awful but that's the way I've become – bitter and awful.

The highlight of our life is the baby. I can't wait to see if he or she looks like me or Alan. And of course he or she moves all the time now. Alan gets enormous pleasure feeling his child moving. God, I'm sometimes terrified that things mightn't work out. If anything happens that baby he'll die. So, I must go to Conor McElroy for my visits for my baby's sake. Of course I would prefer to change to Doctor James but it might appear peculiar.

Then there's Patsy. I worry about Patsy. She's so restless that it's hard to pin her down about anything. She's still seeing Rory O'Driscoll, in fact was up visiting him last week. But I don't know if she's that gone on him – there's something bothering her as far as I can see. She even says she might go back to London with Emma after Christmas. I hope she doesn't – I'd sorely miss her.

Suddenly her flow was distracted as she heard Alan calling, "Sarah come to bed. It's late – you must rest."

"All right, I'm coming now. Just clearing up." She closed the diary and put it away in its hiding place.

The two other pregnant women in the waiting room

stopped talking when Sarah was ushered in by the receptionist. As she walked over to the brown leatherette-covered chair, she supposed, like waiting rooms the world over, the already ensconced were curious every time a new patient entered. They smiled reassuring smiles and their eyes noted her thickening waistline. They were both in an advanced state of pregnancy, so huge in fact that she wondered how they managed to carry on propelling such massive bulks around. Was it possible, she wondered, that she would get as enormous as they were?

"Not bad for the time of year."

"No, it isn't," she smiled back.

"Still, it's too mild for Christmas," the dark-haired women said. Then unable to hide her curiosity she looked at the blonde girl in the soft fawn coat – still belted, mind you – but despite that there was no denying she was in the family way. Beautiful, too, a face like a film star, but she could do with a bit of colour, so she could.

"My kids are always praying for snow for the Christmas," she nodded, "but I don't want it, bad enough trying to keep the place warm as it is. What would it be like with snow?"

Sarah smiled, "This is my first so I haven't anyone praying for snow."

Two pairs of eyes raked her waistline and the quieter one commented, "Just started, are you?"

"No, I'm more than halfway there."

Then their conversation was interrupted as Conor opened the door and nodded. The dark women rose to her feet heavily and heaved her body toward the door. Sarah's heart thudded and her mouth went dry. She felt a wave of the old familiar nausea sweep over her.

"I wonder," the other woman commented, "does Doctor James mind that all the women want to go to Doctor Conor now? He's something, isn't he? Makes you feel you're the only person in the world. I hope he'll be with us for a long time."

Maybe that's all he was doing. Maybe that was his speciality, making patients feel that they were the only people in the world. But he had told her he loved her. Did he? Did he really or was it a dream of her fevered imagination on that terrible night? She hadn't seen him alone since, only when he had called to Alan with some books he had promised to lend him. It had been a very brief visit.

Sarah tried to drag her thoughts back to the pleasant looking women who was looking at her, waiting for some sort of response. "Yes, he is nice," she smiled. She didn't want him around and she didn't not want him around – she didn't know what she wanted. There had been a golden time when she knew exactly what she wanted, but the accident in Rome had taken away all that.

"And she said that when she went into the last stage of labour he was there. Never left her side – told her when to push and when to stop."

She didn't have to answer because the door opened and Conor stood there, white coated now. The woman got up and, wishing Sarah luck, walked heavily towards him. Before he closed the door his eyes met hers, and as she sat staring blindly at a magazine, her heart thudded so heavily she was glad she was alone, because if she was certain it could be heard. Then it was her turn.

Walking into the consulting room ahead of him, she was so conscious of his presence, of his eyes drilling into her back, that she wanted to be anywhere else. Inside it was easier. His smile was reassuring as he held out his hand for the urine sample, nodding at the chair, telling her to sit down. He walked to the sink and said that her kidneys were doing the job at any rate. Then he was back at his desk, pulling out her record from his filing system. His head was bent studying the card and she could read it upside down: "Sarah Beirne, aged 22, date of last period 16 June", then lots of small print. He glanced up then and she thought his glance was more professional than it had been as he nodded toward the couch telling her, "Hop up there."

"For God's sake, Conor, is this really necessary?" she blurted out.

"Yes, I'm afraid it is," he answered, gently.

Sarah stood at the side of the couch, and stepping out of her flat-heeled walking shoes, she eased out of her coat. Shrugging away his helping hand, she hopped up with as much agility as she could muster. Lying down, her eyes glued to the white stippled ceiling, she recalled Nancy Ryan's comments, "When a doctor is on duty and doing his job, he doesn't see a body like you think he does." But it was no good. Conor McElroy mightn't be aware, but she, Sarah Beirne, was, as he stood near her, his hands gently feeling her swollen stomach, his grey eyes staring ahead and the look in their depths almost cold and definitely professional. The scene might be commonplace in any doctor's consulting rooms, but she felt it was unreal in this one.

Did this man tell me he loved me? Did he? He could never have told me something like that. He's there beside me touching and probing and listening to the heartbeat of another man's child. Maybe it was a pregnancy hallucination.

"Good," he commented as he helped her down from the couch. "Heartbeat strong, baby developing, everything on course." He sat at his desk and wrote something on a prescription pad. Looking up his grey eyes met hers and he saw the question in their blue depths. "Are you taking your iron?" he asked.

"Yes," she sighed, "I'm taking my iron."

He closed his eyes briefly and then glanced at his almost illegible scrawl. *Christ,* he thought, *Why? Why couldn't it have been anyone else?* Anyone. Even one of the very pleasant young women in the golf club. Or the brown haired, cheerful girl he had met at a hooley in Waterford three weeks before who had phoned him twice since on some pretext or other. Only last evening she had asked him to a party and he had told he would be delighted to go. When he had put down the phone he hoped he had injected enough enthusiasm into his tone.

146

Even it he had, it was all so false, because he wanted this girl who sat so uneasily in front of him. The girl who was the talk of the town. The girl whose husband had been crippled on their honeymoon. The girl who was considered lucky that she had become pregnant so soon.

"Thanks," she said, as she reached out for the prescription, worry in her eyes and a slight tremor in her hand. He wished as he had often wished that he could prescribe some sort of potion that would take all her unhappiness away, but all he could think of saying was, "Don't forget to give Alan my regards."

"I'll do that."

He helped he into her coat and he watched as she tied the belt. She was one of those pregnant women who didn't like to show off her condition. He remembered when he had worked in Holles Street Hospital in Dublin, a colleague had remarked, "Funny about some women, they waddle when they're two weeks over." He remembered her long stride as she walked beside him on the beach and when she had walked the length of the corridor in the National Rehabilitation Hospital before her embarrassing bout of vomiting. He remembered too much about this beautiful woman who had stumbled into his life.

"Don't forget your next appointment in a month's time, January the sixteenth."

"I won't. Christmas will be a memory then. I suppose you're going home?"

"Yeah, my mother wants us all around her like chickens at that time. Maybe mothers are like that."

"I suppose. Alan and I are going to my mother's and of course Patsy will be there and Emma is coming home from London, so maybe it won't be too bad. We'll try and forget the way it used to be."

"I believe Alan is having physio from Nancy Ryan. It might help, you know."

She was at the front door now, standing on the lower step.

She looked pale, frail and very vulnerable. He didn't want her to go. He wanted to hang on to her – to drum up some stupid thing that would do just that.

"You of all people know it won't help," she said, before running lightly down the steps into the grey, foggy December day.

Later that night she wrote in her diary describing her feelings during her routine visit to her doctor. She wrote about the two women she met and about her wonder at their enormous girths. She went on to write:

> This is my first baby and obviously is going to be my last, so maybe I should wallow in my condition. Record every single little change in my body. But it's difficult and almost impossible to be that interested because of Alan. Sometimes I lie beside him in the dark room listening to his breathing and I remember the better times. I remember our honeymoon, the heat and the steady rolling of the traffic. I remember the happy noisy Italians shouting to each other in the markets. I remember the smell of real coffee and, of course, the geraniums, and I remember our lovemaking. I remember when we really got the knack – maybe I shouldn't call it that – I should call it the art of love. That's what it's called in magazines. Anyway, whatever it is, I know that we were crazy for each other – crazy. We couldn't want each other more. We couldn't love each other more. It's hard to believe that a broken spine could make such a change and render him so incapable.
>
> Last night we kissed and hugged and did more to show our love for each other, but at the end I saw the desperation in his eyes and he might have seen the unfulfilment in mine. I wonder is there some drug that Doctor Conor McElroy could give me to

take away the longing – the loss – the pain. This is the first time I've given him his full title Doctor Conor McElroy. Mrs Conor McElroy – oh God! Maybe I'm going crazy. When I think of what nearly happened on the beach that night, I must be.

Dear God, I simply can't write what I wanted to do. Virgin Mary, please help me. Please. Because if you don't I'll go stark raving mad. It's funny though, I do get a bit of ease from writing all this down. I remember Sharon White, the girl who sat beside me that last year at school, telling me that whenever she had a bitter row with anyone she'd go home and write to them. She'd pour out her fury, letting them know exactly how she felt, and then she'd burn the letter and feel great. I won't burn this – I'll tuck it away where no one will ever ever see it – but I don't feel great, I'll never feel great again, but it does bring a sort of ease.

As Christmas inched nearer the fog evaporated and the temperature dropped. The lanes and hedgerows glittered with frost and the surrounding fields were covered with a lacy broken white. Eileen Dunne was looking forward to her daughter Emma's homecoming.

She knew having her home would be a great diversion for everyone. She could already visualise Emma sitting on the kitchen table swinging her legs, a childhood habit that drove Tim mad. Yes, she felt a glow of anticipation. Maybe it would help them all forget the troubles of the past year.

Patsy was looking forward to Emma's return even more than her mother. She had never felt so isolated as she had this winter. It was the very first winter that she resented where she lived. Carbarry, despite its natural loveliness, was merely a backwater lying between the desolation of the Tramore back strands and the fishing village of Dunmore East. She would like to be in the thick of things with crowds and traffic, shops, markets and hawkers. Then she would be distracted.

If anything Rory O'Driscoll was even more enthusiastic about her than ever. On the phone only last evening he had told her in that half jocose way that he was crazy about her and that he knew he was a fool.

"But dammit, Patsy," he had said, "there's not a goddamn thing I can do about it. I bloody want you and I'm hoping."

Yes, it would be great to tell Emma all about him, but of course she couldn't tell her what was troubling her most. She could never tell anyone. Patsy had been over in Sarah's only last evening evening while Sarah was writing her Christmas cards and Alan was correcting the Christmas tests. Sarah had been so glad to see her, maybe a little too glad. For a while they sat in the warm glow of the range talking about Christmas, the rush and hassle it was and the difficulties of what to get for parents and aunts. Alan made them laugh by saying that his grandmother of eighty-three loved Christmas, nearly believed in Santa, so he liked to make a special effort to please her. It had been almost normal, even a bit like old times. Then Sarah jumped up.

"Would either of you mind if I went for a short walk. It's the restless legs driving me crazy." She looked at Alan. "Do you mind, love? I think this baby had aggravated my condition."

Patsy could see Sarah was smiling that special smile that always made her feel she was on the outside looking in.

"No, I don't mind," Alan's dark eyes were unreadable, "because I have Patsy to keep me company." They were silent as Sarah grabbed her coat off the hook of the door and they were still silent as they heard her light footsteps fade away down the narrow path. Alan looked over at Patsy.

"She does that. She walks down those lonely lanes without an iota of fear. The other night old Bill Lynch, the retired master, dropped in and told us of all the weird and strange things that happen in this area. Talk about ghost stories! He told us all about the glowing light that has been seen hovering around the old places up at Brownstown Head when people are going to die. He swears by it. I thought it pretty stupid, but I hoped it might put a stop to her gallop. But she was off up around the head the next evening and you couldn't see your fist with the fog."

It was the very first time that he had confided or hinted that things about Sarah bothered him. Suddenly he smiled and he looked like himself again. "Anyway when she comes back all the restlessness is gone."

Looking at him sitting there so helpless and vulnerable, Patsy wanted to run over and put her arms around him and pull his dark head on to her breast and console him like you'd console a child. Instead she remarked primly, "Walking is good for her – they say exercise is great when her time comes."

She felt the stupid blush suffuse her face as she held his eyes. There was no doubt now that the shadows under his were no trick of the firelight. His mouth, his lovely mouth that she had examined on that rainy summer day a thousand years ago, had fine lines now. But his glance was warm and enveloping.

"Do you know what, Patsy Dunne?" he grinned.

"What?"

"You're a sight for sore eyes."

"Gee, thanks," she laughed, and then grabbed the cushion like she had done before and sat back on her heels. "Alan, don't have a heart attack or anything like that, but there's something I want to tell you."

"Fire away."

"I'm thinking of getting married. I wanted you to be the first to know." His look was so incredulous it was nearly funny. In fact she had shocked him so much he seemed to have lost his voice.

"Jesus." She didn't even try to hide the exasperation. "Don't look like that. I suppose it's possible that a fellow

151

might want to marry me. I'm not that bad, Alan Beirne. You look like a fellow going to take flight." Then realising what she had said, she got up from her kneeling position and went over to him and held his hand – still brown, still strong. "Wasn't that the most stupid fucking thing to say? I'm sorry."

Suddenly she started crying uncontrollably, the tears rolling down her cheeks. He leaned out and took her in his arms, pulling her head on to his chest.

"It's okay – it's okay. I wouldn't want to take flight when I hear news like that." Brushing her tears away with his hand, he spoke softly as if she were a child, "Mop up and tell me all about this extraordinary news of an impending marriage."

She knelt so near him she could feel the heat from his body. She had no idea that his mind was now full of her as realisation came of how much she meant to him. She was always there. Tall, boyish Patsy, with the deep blue in her eyes, just like Sarah's – but after that she was so different. Coltish, awkward, young like a young creature not yet tamed. But there was nothing boyish about the wide, almost sensuous mouth.

Like flashbacks in a film he recalled all the time he had spent with her: helping her with her Irish, helping to pierce the fog when it came to honours maths. Then when the school holidays came, easing away the summer hours with her when they were both on holidays whilst Sarah worked in the bank. One year he taught her to dive. Though she was a capable, strong swimmer she couldn't master the art of diving. She was openly jealous of the lissome youngsters who could dive like swallows into the clear blue sea. He had spent hours standing in his swimming trunks patiently explaining how to jump, how to bend her body, how to cut the water with her hands.

She used to give out, saying, "All right, all right, I hear you, but why do I drop like a bullock and nearly rip my stomach open?"

When she eventually got the hang of it, there was no stopping her. She must have dived hundreds of times every single day. One time she couldn't go, telling him she had a terrible cold coming. Since she didn't have any symptoms and she wouldn't meet his eyes, he guessed that she had got her period and was excruciatingly shy about the whole business.

Now here in the warm room with the wind rising outside and the ash falling into the grate, she was telling him she was getting married.

"It's Rory O'Driscoll, isn't it?"

"Yeah," she sighed, "who else? He has me sort of pestered."

"Do you love him?"

"I wouldn't say I love him."

"So what are you talking about?" His voice was rough, his eyes puzzled as they held hers. "Christ, are you all right?"

"Of course, I'm all right. I'm not pregnant, if that's what you mean."

He reached out and firmly putting his hand under her chin lifted her face until it was mere inches from his.

"Well, Patsy, you don't – you simply don't – marry someone you don't love. You don't even think of it. Love, at least the sort that lasts, is easy enough to define. If you can have any sort of life without the person you're supposed to love, then you don't love them – you don't marry them. That's it."

"I know all about it." Suddenly she sounded very tired. "I really do. But I can't marry the person I love."

He looked bewildered and then it was his turn to sigh. "Will you please tell me what's happening? When did all this excitement come into your life and not a word about it to anyone."

"The excitement, as you call it, came in dribs and drabs." She didn't look at him but fiddled with the fringes of the rug in front of the range.

"And why, you most complex girl, can't you marry the guy you love?"

"Because he's married already."

"Does Sarah know anything of all this?"

"No." She sounded impatient. "Didn't I tell you, you are the very first to know."

They heard the key in the door and Patsy jumped up. Putting her fingers to her mouth she whispered, "Mum's the word – I don't want a soul to know. I'll drop the bombshell after Christmas. And you're to look more surprised than anyone else. Promise?"

"I promise," he told her, shaking his head, his tone indicating his disapproval.

Sarah came in bringing in a gust of icy air. She wondered why Patsy and Alan, who were always so happy in each other's company, were sitting in such strained silence, and why he looked so puzzled, so peculiar, almost grim.

CHAPTER FOURTEEN

NANCY RYAN WAS never late. She appeared at four on the dot three afternoons a week and went about her business cheerfully and competently. Alan felt he was merely humouring her, but he played the game, maybe propelled by her cheerfulness and certainly impressed by her ability. He stretched out on the bed as she pummelled and massaged, gently probing his spine, lifting and lowering his legs endlessly, all the time talking cheerfully.

"Christmas is all right for people with families, but what about poor lonely souls like myself?" Then she laughed and added, "But when all is said and done 'tis a great rest. Lounge all day and treat yourself, too. Now don't get me wrong, Alan, I could go to a dozen houses, including the home of your good mother-in-law, but why would I do that – sticking out at people's tables like a sore thumb?"

He listened, nodding and commenting vaguely, his thoughts wandering. Lulled by her manipulations, he wondered if he were losing his mind because he'd thought he felt something: a sort of warmth, a vague sensation in his legs, in the paralysed groin, as if he could feel the blood flowing again. He derided himself for being a fool. He presumed it was a bit like an amputee feeling for a phantom limb.

A week before he had thought he could feel those capable strong fingers of hers on his leg. He turned his head and glanced up at her small nut-brown eyes behind the glasses, but her eyes were expressionless as with pursed lips she worked on and on. When she left he felt more confused than ever. *Now, as well as being disabled, my mind is playing tricks.* He knew that there was no hope he would ever walk again, and yet – goddam it – what was happening? Why was he being persecuted, thinking he felt life where there was deadness? It had to be a trick of his mind brought on by desperate false hope.

He dismissed the crazy notion and thought of Sarah. When it came to his wife, his mind knew no rest. She was different now, different from the girl he had married. They were on an equal footing then, with so much to give, so much to share, in tune to each other's needs, desires, moods. He sometimes recalled their lovemaking on their honeymoon in Rome. They had waited so long for each other because it was the right thing. It was the Church teaching: no carnal knowledge before the marriage. God, it was ironic now – they had bided their time, keeping themselves in check for a lifetime of bliss ahead only to have it snatched away after a few brief days.

Now almost six months later there was a different message in her eyes. Love – yes. Tenderness – yes. But that look, that special eye to eye contact that meant one thing, was gone. Sometimes he persuaded himself he saw pity. *Jesus Christ, anything but pity.* But last night, lying beside her, listening to her steady breathing, his arm encircling her, he felt his child move and he felt then there was purpose to his life.

Lying wide awake beside Sarah, his thoughts eventually turned to Patsy, his young sister-in-law who had astonished him with news of a possible marriage to this chap he hardly knew – Rory O'Driscoll. The coltish tomboy, who had seemed a child just the other day, was now talking of marriage. And then the bombshell that she really loved someone else, someone married. Of course she was the most imaginative, impressionable girl he had ever known. Maybe in the cold light of dawn she would have a rethink. He hoped so.

Then Sarah murmured and turned and he took her in his arms, kissing her gently on the warm lips. She murmured something in her sleep and he thought he heard the name Conor. Of course, her doctor played an important part in her life now. It was he who would be with her in the long traumatic hours of labour, he who would deliver her child, he who would guide her through the early postnatal period.

Just before oblivion came, in the grey world between sleep and wakefulness, when reality merged with fantasy, it came to him why Patsy might be embarking on this premature marriage: in short, the possible identity of Patsy's married man. The knowledge left him quite shaken and then slowly filled him with sadness.

The seasonal weather held. The fields and hedgerows were covered with a white glittering coat. Sarah, looking out her kitchen window, decided she'd go for a walk, maybe her last long beach walk for a while. The school was closing for the Christmas holidays tomorrow, and she didn't like to leave Alan too much alone, although she found the confines of the small cottage suffocating at times. If things had been different they could have shared all the waiting months together, going for long walks along the beach and through the woods, or shopping together for the things they needed to decorate the tiny room they had decided would be perfect for the baby. This morning she had had a letter from Breda Curran who wrote that her husband Sean had made a complete recovery from his physical injuries. She hoped that Alan was making some progress. She wrote saying they should never give up hope. She congratulated Sarah on her pregnancy, telling her it was the most wonderful thing, that she was quite jealous in fact. Breda had thought she was pregnant two months earlier.

> We had reached the stage where we were looking at baby things. But alas, it was a false alarm so we must keep on trying. But keeping on trying takes the excitement away from the whole business. I sometimes feel we're like two mathematicians counting the days to the fertile period, taking a rest when it's safe.

Putting the letter away Sarah realised she had forgiven the couple who had stumbled into their lives and in their friendliness and enthusiasm unwittingly caused disaster for Alan.

As she walked along the beach the tide was going out. All that was left were the pools, the blue, choppy oyster bed and the deep channel between the beach and the sand hills which was flowing swiftly to the open bay. From where she walked she could see the dangerous currents and whirlpools. She remembered her father's warnings down through the years: "Don't attempt to swim in the channel when the tide is going out. If you don't drown you'll end up on the Welsh coast."

One day when she was sixteen, she had come down along to the beach. Emma was having a music lesson and Patsy's dog Tilly had just given birth to pups the evening before. There was no question of prising Patsy away; in fact she had slept beside Tilly and the pups the night before. Sarah was as alone then as she was now. She had undressed and waded into the oyster bed. The water was warm as she swam and floated, looking up at the sun and the small puffs of cotton-wool clouds. After a while the tide turned, and the oyster bed lost its distinct outline as the incoming tide came swiftly in. Wading ashore she saw something swirling in with the tide, and at first guess she thought it was a sack or some long-lost fishing nets. The gulls knew better. They accompanied whatever it was with strident excited cries. The bundle swept near her and she could see that it was the decomposed body of a man. She knew exactly who it was. A young fisherman had been lost six weeks previously out on the lobster grounds whose family had been devastated at their terrible loss. She knew they had a perpetual candle lighting in the window, hoping that his body would be found. She remember feeling almost privileged that she would be the one who would bring the news.

She had been interviewed by the local paper, had her picture on the front page and had been extremely embarrassed about the unwanted publicity. At the funeral the young man's mother had hugged her, telling her that they now would have a grave to visit and wouldn't have to think of his bones bleaching in that terrible sea. She shivered as she looked at the deep channel where the body of the young fisherman had been washed in all those years ago.

The screaming gulls were flying higher today. They looked like silver specks floating against the blue, wintry sky. She glanced at the dunes near by and could see that the tufts of grass were fringed with white, every blade identical as if the hand that touched them was meticulous, wanting order and perfection. Even the long golden beach was covered with a broken lacy veil of frost. For the first time the loneliness and the isolation didn't appeal, and she decided to turn back. As she did so, she got a glimpse of someone in the distance. Closing her eyes she offered up a silent prayer that it wasn't who she thought it was. Her silent prayer was unanswered as Conor McElroy came nearer, not wearing a white coat now, but just a zipped casual jacket and faded jeans. His long stride shortened the distance between them and as he approached she could see his breath was visible in the icy air.

"Hi." He was smiling and the dark-lashed grey eyes were red rimmed with the cold or maybe fatigue. "I called to wish you a happy Christmas, but the place was deserted so I guessed where you'd be." He looked around, his glance taking in the lonely desolation of Sauleen, the dunes and the frost-fringed blades of grass. "You love it here, don't you?"

"Yes, I love it here. That's why I was happy when Alan got the job in the school. I love it specially in winter. I always thought it was the most peaceful place on God's earth then, the channel ebbing and flowing, the sand whispering and moving through the dunes.

Conor McElroy looking at her standing there, her white oval face now slightly tinged with blue, the tossed blonde hair, the eyes the colour of his mother's delphiniums, the casually belted coat over her slightly swollen stomach. He felt the hopeless and unwanted desire flood him, but her gaze was towards the sand hills, giving him some respite.

"You're in a profound mood again. Perhaps, Mrs Beirne, you should be in town with all the bustling Christmas shoppers. Maybe right now this isn't the place to be."

"Maybe you're right. Maybe I am a nutty melancholic." She gave him the full blast of her beautiful blue eyes and once again the hopelessness of his situation assailed him. "I hope you have a very happy Christmas." The familiar wish broke his chain of thought.

"I'll try. At least it will be a rest. No more calls in the middle of the night, no more hysterical women thinking that their husbands are dying when they're merely overdosed on pints."

She laughed and it occurred to him that she rarely laughed. They retraced their footsteps, both walking briskly because of the intense cold. They were silent until they got to the gateway of her house where they stopped.

"Would you like some tea, coffee? Perhaps a drink – something to warm you up?"

"No, thanks all the same. I promised my mother I would make it home before dark. She worries about things like that. I think she thinks we're all still kids."

"I suppose all mothers are like that." She saw his glance fall to her abdomen and suddenly she was filled with embarrassment. It was all wrong, too intimate, to be standing with a man who was her doctor, who in an impulsive moment had told her he loved her. But thankfully, since there had never again been a whisper or a hint, it was in all probability a temporary aberration.

"I want you to take care of yourself. Don't forget the iron and do take it easy," Conor said.

"Yes, Doctor, I will." Standing by the old gate pillar she didn't meet his eyes, yet she made no effort to turn away. She pulled off her sheepskin glove and pushed the glittering frost that showed no sign of thawing into little piles. She wasn't sure why she stood there not wanting him to go.

"What will Christmas be like on your farm at home? Will you still have to milk the cows? Still have to feed the chickens, pigs and things?"

His laugh rang out spontaneous and warm. "We will Sarah, we will, but I hope it won't be me this year, I did it though, till I milked cows in my dreams. So, when you're over with your folks on Christmas Day, don't think poor Conor is up to his neck in cows' you-know-what."

"I won't. Anyway, I couldn't imagine you up to your neck in you-know-what."

"I'd better get going – there are things I should be doing." He leaned over and kissed her gently, saying, "Try and have a good time, for Alan's sake, your baby's sake – for all our sakes."

Suddenly the wretched moisture filled her eyes but she could see through the blur that he was already walking away. He waved as he got into his car, and she stood there watching it go down the road past the school house, John Flynn's thatched cottage and the edge of the brooding woods before it disappeared around the corner.

> I woke up today almost unaware that it was Christmas week. If things had been different you can imagine how excited we'd be. Shopping together. Maybe having a good-humoured argument about what we'd get for our new in-laws, maybe hiding things we bought for each other, laughing over our greetings cards with our new signatures, Alan and Sarah. Thrilled our first baby is on the way. But it's not like that – it's not like that at all. This morning he was very frustrated; he had some trouble with the catheter and I helped him out. I could see he was impatient and annoyed that I had to do it. His self-respect and

his dignity and goddam independence was hurt. He positively infuriated me, and I told him I was his wife and I loved him and who else would help him if it wasn't me? I shouted at him that he seemed happy shut up for hours with Nancy Ryan, letting her do all sorts of things to him and not a complaint out of him. He looked at me with such disdain that I felt a fool and decided there was nothing for it but a long walk on the beach. It was so cold and white and beautiful, just like Christmas card, but instead of robins there were seagulls. They were soaring and free and unfettered. I decided I'd walk to the far end of the beach to the breakers, but halfway up the cold got right inside me and I turned back.

I saw someone coming towards me and I saw to my horror that it was Conor McElroy.

She went on to describe their meeting in detail and the emotional effect it had on her.

When Sarah finished writing, she stretched up to her full height and put the diary in its safe hiding place. When she slid in beside Alan, he turned and put his arms around her, murmuring that she should have come to bed earlier.

"And another thing," he whispered.

"What's that?" she whispered back.

You're getting as big as an elephant. He'll be a ten pounder at least."

Her heart lifted as she snuggled into his arms. "You're absolutely wrong. I look like a sylph. Only yesterday Mrs Flynn told me I didn't look as if I was expecting at all. So there."

"Everyone knows that Mrs Flynn," he nibbled her ear, "is a complete lick-arse."

"Whether she's a lick-arse or not, go asleep," she said muzzily. "I'm exhausted. I walked miles today."

He was silent, and her last thought before sleep claimed her was that she shouldn't emphasise her walks so much, because it was one of the many things they could never do together again.

CHAPTER FIFTEEN

"**H**EY, YOU'VE CHANGED beyond recognition," Patsy gasped, looking at Emma with disbelief tinged with envy. "How'd you manage that? How did you straighten your hair? Where did you get that brown eye shadow? God, would you look at the brown lipstick."

"London, my dear child," Emma laughed. "London, the capital of the fashion world – Mary Quant's the name, Mary Quant's the game."

Emma sat on the bed, surrounded by cases and bags, the contents spilling out of most of them. She looked at her sister almost as if she were seeing her for the first time. Her brown impish eyes took in the long legs, the intense blue of her eyes and the auburn red of her curly cropped hair style.

"I know, I know, I'm old hat," Patsy complained, "and I know little or nothing about Mary Quant, so don't be looking at me like that. Anyway, you'd never know, I just might end up in London myself."

"You might? That'd be great. You'd have no bother getting a job what with the experience you have in Dad's office. The bank would take you on. Loads of banks there." Emma trailed away as she appraised her sister, noting once again the short brown skirt and the yellow polo neck sweater outlining her small firm breasts and the never-ending length of her legs in the high zipped platform boots. "Maybe you could train as a model. You'd make a fortune. Think of Jean Shrimpton and Twiggy – you're tall enough, skinny enough and you have the hungry bony look in your face. You're different from Sarah and me – we have the boring curves – they're old hat now, went out with Marilyn Monroe. Talking about Sarah, God, how is she? How is Alan?"

Patsy had forgotten how her ebullient sister could spew out so many words, swinging from one subject to another, talking about a hundred things in so many seconds. Before she got a chance to answer, Emma was off again.

"I knock around with a crowd in London and a few of the guys are studying medicine. I told them all about Alan's accident and he being a paraplegic and what have you. They knew all about such accidents and stuff. They said he'd be a gonner when it came to making love. Everything dead below the waist. God, isn't it tough on Sarah. Great about the baby. Thank God, he did the job when he could."

"Jesus, that sounds crude," Patsy retorted.

"It might, but it's a fact," Emma answered, "and don't you think I'm over there forgetting all that happened. In fact I think of them all the time. Mam said they'll be coming over tomorrow for Christmas." Her eyes suddenly clouded as the animation drained from her face. "I saw the ramps and saw that Dad's study is turned into a temporary bedroom for them. It's tough. Does he still look as dishy as ever?"

"Yep," Patsy answered. Then getting up from the window seat she joined her sister on the bed, pushing the bags and suitcases aside. She touched a large PVC shopping bag on the floor with a map of the London underground on the outside with the toe of her boot, only half aware of the Christmas-wrapped boxes inside.

"When I mentioned London I didn't necessarily mean work. I meant to live there. I'm actually thinking of getting married."

"You bloody what!" Emma shouted abruptly, jumping off the bed, her eyes wide with astonishment. "You secretive bee. You never mentioned anything." Then her brown eyes widened in horror. "Oh dear Jesus, I hope you're not pregnant." Her astonished gaze slowly raked her sister. "You know, you do look a bit haggish."

"No, I'm not pregnant,". Patsy said irritably. "Funny how someone young getting married is always accused of that. You remember the guy I met in Dún Laoghaire when I was up with Sarah after Alan's accident? Well, I've seen him a lot and he came and stayed in Waterford with a friend. I was up in Dublin seeing him not so long ago. He has asked me to marry him and do you know what? I probably will."

"What about college? What about the notion that you'd go backpacking all over Europe? Married and you only eighteen. Are you mad? "

"No, I'm not mad."

"You must be. Or are you so mad about him you can't wait? You don't have to marry him, you know." Emma adopted her worldly air.

"I know I don't. I know some things. But he's great, real nice," Patsy sounded defiant.

"Nice," Emma almost shouted. "Nice! What a bloody, awful word. You can't marry someone that's nice. You must absolutely adore him. Marriage is for ever. Sickness and in health sort of stuff. Look at Sarah, stuck with Alan for ever."

Patsy turned around her eyes blazing with fury. "Don't talk about Alan like that. Don't you dare talk of him as if he's a has-been. Jesus Christ, just because of the one thing he's a has-been, is he?"

Suddenly she further astonished Emma by breaking down. Putting her hands over her eyes, she turned over on the bed and buried her face in the pillow, which shook with the intensity of her sobs. Emma, completely taken aback, looked at her sister's heaving shoulders. Then she reached out and shook her gently.

"Look, I'm sorry, I really am. I just blather away without thinking. Tell me, Patsy," she asked, "what's up? What's really up?"

Patsy took quite a while to regain her control, and when she did Emma was waiting quietly. The only sound outside was the moaning of the wind and the sound of a lone curlew. Patsy, wiping the tears and blowing her nose, looked at Emma with her tear-stained face. If she had to tell someone, it had to be Emma. Emma a mere two years older than she was, the second child, the strong one.

"What's really up, as you put it, is. . ." She cleared her throat as if searching for words that were reluctant to come. Emma sat still and unmoving. Glancing in the mirror she could see their reflection – Patsy troubled and confused with red-rimmed eyes, she with her new image forgotten, sur-rounded by bags and luggage patiently waiting for Patsy to speak. "You haven't a notion what my problem is, have you?"

"No, Patsy, I honestly haven't," Emma told her.

"It's simple, really. I'm in love with my sister's husband. In fact, I love him so much I would die for him. Dear Jesus, isn't that crazy? I love Alan so much it has filled my whole life. Don't laugh," she pleaded, "please, don't laugh. And I am very aware that it's a wrong sort of loving." Suddenly she started to cry again.

Emma sitting there dumbfounded, looking at the tears that were flowing down the face that only a half hour before she had imagined on the catwalks of London, now distorted and crumbled with obvious heartbreak. She felt awkward try-ing to comfort Patsy because it was years since they had shown any physical affection.

"It's all right, Patsy – it's all right. Sure, it's not the end of the world. Girls get crushes, fierce terrible crushes. Patsy," she shook her sister, "listen to me. That's all it is, a crush. Alan came into your life when you were a kid – the most impressionable age, all hormonal and stuff. He was with you so much and you followed him around like a pup. Remember?"

"I remember," Patsy sobbed. "I remember every single day I was with him. I remember the very first time I saw him. I was weak then and years later I'm still weak. So don't talk about crushes. Or hormones. I honestly think," she sobbed, "that even Rory has copped on to the way I feel about Alan and he still wants to marry me."

As Emma listened, pictures flashed into her mind of all the times they had fought like tigers. All the noisy inter-minable rows screaming at each other, until their mother had intervened and brought some measure of peace. Now her young sister was madly in love with Alan, a love undiminished with her sister's marriage or with the car accident that had crippled him and according to the know-alls had made him impotent. That in itself was peculiar because when she recalled her own crushes it seemed to her that she always thought of the object of her desires in bed with her, making passionate love.

She shook her head in an effort to concentrate on what Patsy was saying. "I go over to them a lot. He's always so alone. Sarah goes to Sauleen Strand and walks for miles and miles."

Patsy told Emma about the evening Alan had fallen asleep as she read poetry to him, and how she had kissed him as he slept.

"I just bent down and I kissed him on the mouth. I know I've kissed loads of fellows, and Rory of course, and it can be great. But when I kissed Alan – and remember he wasn't even a participant – it turned me inside out." She looked at Emma and her sister could see the absolute misery in her eyes. "So he's crippled and he's bunched and incapable and he's married to my sister who is going to have his baby and I worship him. It's all so wrong I'm going to have to get him out of my system, so I'm going to have to marry Rory O'Driscoll. So there. God, Emma! Why is life such a shit at times?"

Emma Dunne was rarely without words, but tonight, looking at her younger sister, she found it difficult to say anything, even to apprehend what she was told. Patsy in love for years with Alan Beirne? Looking at the tear-stained face she knew that it would be insulting now to waffle on about crushes or mere phases or being carried away at an impressionable age, but to go to the extent of marrying a fellow to end an unwanted situation was so extreme as to be ridiculous. And from what she could gather, this Rory O'Driscoll was a bit of all right.

"Just tell me," she asked gently, "do you love Rory at all – in any sort of way?

168

"In ways I think he's great, but I don't love him the way he'd like me to. I just told you why."

"Well, if that's the way, it would be crazy to cheat the poor sucker like you intend to do. But I think London would be the answer. You don't have to get married to escape your love for Alan. Three weeks over in that mad place and you'd be well on the road to recovery. Believe me, you'd perk up. You could be swept off your feet. The guys that I know can give you such a good, mad, crazy time that there's not a minute to even think. Distraction, change – that's what you need, a time away from this misty, parochial country where sin is the name of the game. Look, I'll introduce you to everyone. The English fellows are something else. The edu-cated fellows with the BBC accents are divine. They're so, so – minimalist, that's it; a few clipped words and you're a gonner."

Emma got off the bed, looked in the mirror and ran her hands over her Mary Quant hair style. She could see Patsy's reflection, too, and meeting her eyes fleetingly thought that maybe it would take more than a few English fellows with BBC accents, maybe even more than a marriage to Rory O'Driscoll, to eradicate the love she had for Alan. Patsy had always got what she wanted – a kitten, a pup, a pony. She never nagged to death when she looked for things; she just had a way with her and she ended up with what she wanted. Emma shivered.

"Come on, it's getting cold here. We'd better go down to the old dears or they'll think we've taken to the bottle on the beds."

CHAPTER SIXTEEN

IT WAS ON the table in the hall: a square parcel with the address in bold black marker. Emma could see the address, to Patsy, even before she jumped the last few steps of the stairs. She wandered into the kitchen, her hair wet from the shower but already combed and plastered to her cheeks. Her mother, in the process of making mince pies, looked up from her task and shook her floury hands.

"Why don't you use the hair dryer? You'll get your death of cold wandering around with a wet head."

"Can't, Mam, ruin the look. If I have one stray hair or a whisper of bounce the whole concept is gone. This cut cost me a fortune."

Her mother raised her eyebrows to indicate how unimpressed she was with a sleek, cheek-length bob that could somehow cost a fortune and returned to the task of the moment with relish. She usually made the mince pies after she had put up the holly, put the final touches to the tree and had put up the all-important crib. Only that morning she had put fresh straw into the shadowy depths of the crib to steady the cradle for the infant Jesus. She wanted everything done by this evening before Sarah and Alan arrived. Tomorrow was Christmas Eve and she liked being organised by then. She always liked to think of Christmas Eve as sort of waiting day with just the last few straggling cards to open and the few odds and ends to do. In fact, for the last few years she and Tim had driven over to Tramore and gone for a walk down the long deserted beach.

As she thumped and rolled the pastry, she remembered last year and the excitement after midnight mass when Sarah and Alan had come in, their happiness and joy palpable as Sarah held out her hand to show off her beautiful diamond-cluster ring. The hugs and congratulation all around. And now everything so changed. Yet it was almost miraculous the way that

Alan seemed to have accepted his fate, without bitterness. If anything, Sarah was the one showing the strain, with her moody restlessness at times and at other times a brightness that was too brittle and somehow not right. But then again, even at the best of times, pregnancy brought its own problems. Having Alan the way he was must be a terrible strain.

"I wonder what's in the box?" Emma's question diverted her.

"Oh yes, The postman brought that after Patsy had gone to work with Dad. It looks interesting. Maybe it's from Rory O'Driscoll. She sees quite a bit of him and he phones a lot. I think he fancies her."

Emma, looking at the bent head of her mother, thought, *If you knew how much he really fancies her. If you knew that this Rory O'Driscoll is going to be tricked into marriage because Patsy is obsessed with Alan whom she absolutely loves. She might even love him more than Sarah ever did. Would you believe, she's thinking of going to England to lead a new life because that might take her mind off her problem?* As her mother expertly cut out the serrated circles she felt sorry for her. How little mothers, even good mothers like hers, knew of what went on in their children's heads. *When I have children,* Emma thought, *we'll be mates, talking mates, and hopefully they won't live secret lives inside their heads and suffer the torture of the damned. At least they can share their problems with me.*

Her mother's voice broke into her thoughts. "You'd better get dressed, Emma – it's after eleven." Glancing into the hall she sighed, "I suppose we'll have to contain our curiosity until Patsy comes home."

The parcel was nearly forgotten in the flurry of Sarah and Alan's arrival. They heard the car on the gravel drive and Emma started to the front door, forgetting that they had to come in the back. Patsy and her father had come in minutes earlier and, just like that, the kitchen seemed crowded. Emma could see that Alan hadn't changed that much. His pallor emphasised his darkness and there were shadows under his eyes now, but his smile and his greeting as she bent down for a welcoming hug was warm and genuine. Sarah looked as beautiful as ever, her blonde hair washed and gleaming and thrust into the collar of her travel coat, now belted over a decided bump.

"Congrats," she smiled at Sarah, glancing at the bump. "Will it be a boy or a child?"

Her parents seemed embarrassed at her question and once again she had to remind herself that she was back in Ireland, where pregnancy and sex were sort of taboo subjects. Girls got married and then had bumps and no one ever discussed how it all had come about. She remembered the parcel with relief.

"By the way, Patsy, you have a big box of something in the hall – we're dying all day with curiosity to see what's in it – come on, open it." Patsy, leaning against the work top where the mince pies were now on trays, their egg-brushed tops gleaming golden, didn't appear to hear. Emma sighed. "The present, Patsy – will you blooming well open it or Mam and I will die of curiousity."

"After tea – I'm starving. We're probably all starving. Mam, after you give us a few of those pies to gobble up, I'll open the parcel. I know the idle rich one from London will blow up if I don't." Everyone laughed and the strain of seeing Alan in the wheelchair eased.

After devouring tea and mince pies, Patsy, as promised, ripped open the brown-papered parcel. Inside there was festive wrapping. She tore off the sellotape and glancing up she saw them all up waiting in good humoured silence. "God! Look at you – you'd imagine you never got a present in your lives. I sure hope it's not a bomb."

"Patsy, this is Christmas – don't say that, not even in a joke," her mother scolded.

Patsy removed the tissue paper, drew out the gift and held it up: a black dress, simple, soft, beautifully uncluttered and

172

obviously very expensive. It had a scooped neckline, the fashionable three-quarter length sleeve and a short hemline. Emma gazed with open envy.

"Who in the name of God has that sort of taste? I'd die for it."

Patsy was reading the inside of the Christmas card that had fallen to the floor. They could see the front of the card with two bobble-hatted, red-cheeked kids riding on a sleigh through the snow. "It's from Rory and I suppose it's nice – even though it's not me, is it?" Her eyes strayed round the table.

"Nice?" Emma exploded. "Nice? Imagine having a guy who knows exactly what's right. Hey, if you don't think it's you, I'm waiting in the wings."

"And so am I," Sarah laughed, "when I get back to normal."

"Put it on," Alan suggested. "Let's see what the best-dressed girl is wearing this season."

"I couldn't possibly. I'd have to haul off all these jumpers and my hair is like Mam's mop and I have a rake of pimples and I'm a wreck."

"Well, let's see what a wreck look likes in a classy black dress." Emma yawned.

"Humour them, Patsy," her father said, taking refuge in his beloved pipe.

Up in her room Patsy hauled off the bulky, chunky jumper. Looking at herself in the mirror in her bra and black tights, she wondered why she had been such a stupid fool to go along with their ridiculous suggestion. Then she remembered it was Alan who had suggested it first. She wondered wearily as she slipped into silk-lined dress if she had agreed just so he'd see her not just as his young sister-in-law who had been the plague of his life. *Be honest,* a little inner voice whispered. *That's why you're here shivering in this dress, so that he will see you that bit differently.*

When she slipped it over her neck and patted it into

place, even she was impressed. It was so soft, it clung perfectly in the right places. She had never looked slimmer and her neck had never looked whiter. She could just see the top of her breasts and she gave it a slight tug so that they'd disappear. It was short and yet not too short. The hemline came down to two inches above her knees. She was glad she had on her black tights and on an impulse she reached out and put on a slight trace of lipstick.

"Well," she walked into the brightly lit kitchen, "will I do?" They must have forgotten her because they were all chatting and suddenly her entrance made them look up. She felt a self-conscious fool as they all looked up together. Emma's opinion came first.

"God, it's fabulous! Makes even you look something."

"Thanks," Patsy retorted.

"It's gorgeous, Patsy, and it's perfect on you." Sarah was generous in her praise.

"A bit on the low side," her mother commented, looking at the glimpse of cleavage.

"Well, if that's the in thing," her father puffed his pipe, "I'm all for it."

Alan looked at her as she shyly stood in the black moulded dress, her hand lightly resting on the laden dresser, so different from the young Patsy he felt he knew. He cleared his throat as his dark eyes met hers. "You look beautiful. And you know what I think?"

"No. How could I?"

"I think this Rory O'Driscoll has great taste, not alone in clothes, but in girls, too." His words were spoken softly.

Later that night Emma recalled his words and the look in his eyes and she wondered if it were possible that he might have guessed how Patsy felt about him. Was he telling her gently to appreciate what she had and not to be seeking the impossible? And yet had there been more than understanding and admiration in his eyes? No, definitely not. He had always adored Sarah – always. Ah, God, it was all so confusing.

There was no doubt it was great to be home with all of them, but it was all quite complex, confusing and emotional. That was Ireland for you. In London with its seething, fast-moving populace there was no time to think, no time to agonise and let your imagination run away with you.

She fell into an uneasy sleep and in a fragmented dream she saw Patsy with Alan. She was wearing the black dress and it looked so ridiculous because they were running across the beach to the oyster bed, and as they ran through the silver rivulets their feet sent up a shower of sparkling drops. They were hand in hand and she had never seen Patsy look so radiantly happy. Emma woke up with a start and the room was cold and shadowy. She realised that there was no sign of Sarah in the dream and she shivered. She hauled the bed-clothes up around her, telling herself that she eaten too many of her mother's mince pies.

CHAPTER SEVENTEEN

Looking at his mother sitting at the top of the laden table, Conor thought she looked a little absurd. There was a solemnity about her as she sat there with her freshly set hair covered with a red Santa hat as she peered through her bifocals at the names on the tags. After she read out the name she would hand over the present to the recipient, who would duly open it with oohs and aahs of admiration, even though the gift might be the very last thing on God's earth that he or she would want. It was different with the grand-children. They usually ripped open the paper with energetic verve, and no matter what the wrapping yielded they were enthusiastic and happy. Conor wondered if they had been warned in advance to show appreciation. It was tradition in the McElroy household that the head of the house would hand out the presents after dinner. His father had sat at the head of the table as long as he could remember and when he died two years previously Conor thought his mother might abandon the whole business, but no. Everyone was invited to Christmas dinner and everyone came: his two married sisters, his three brothers, and their children. The youngest son, Paul, was still living at home but not for long. He had become engaged the night before and that was an added reason for celebration.

The McElroy home was a fine Georgian house set comfortably back amongst sheltered trees surrounded by two hundred acres. It was the sort of house that beckoned. Conor had never been away for Christmas and couldn't imagine spending it anywhere else. Now, at long last, all the Christmas presents were opened, duly admired and tucked away. The children had gone into the old playroom to examine their festive loot, and their disappearance brought momentary peace.

Their elders sat there sipping the brandies, the huge fire now settled down to a quiet red glow, the conversation easy now after the two hectic hours of dinner and gift opening. Carol, his eldest sister, looked at him.

"Well, Conor, what do you think of Paul getting there first?"

"Getting where first?"

"Engaged – married. We all thought it might be you. Why no stir? Is there no one down in County Waterford that would fit the bill?"

"No, not a soul. I'll have to come back up to get me a wife."

"But you must have met someone. You joined the golf club, always a good place to meet women."

"Women that are desperate to find men, usually getting a bit long in the tooth and past their prime. Mad to have kids before the sun goes down," Michael the eldest butted in.

"That is ridiculous," Carol said heatedly. "Believe me, women don't join golf clubs to get men. They care about the game as much as any man. As for the mad to have children bit – you'd want to cop on. Big changes coming. This women's liberation movement will put you all in your place, mark my words. Anyway, Michael," she asked sweetly, "what is your handicap now?"

Michael's ability as a golfer was questionable. Despite many hours spent on the fairway, he had never settled to the game, never controlled his wild, erratic swing. He was a long hitter, sending the ball out of sight, so far away in fact that it was rarely if ever found. Carol was good. Despite having three children she had continued to play and to play with excellence. She had won all the major competitions in her club and now boasted a handicap of four.

"Listen, children," their mother clapped her hands. "I don't want any rows today. Today should be a time of peace and goodwill – remember? And anyway, Conor will meet a nice girl in due course. Won't you, Conor?"

"I will, Mother," he laughed, "any day now."

Later when his sisters were helping with the wash up, he

decided he'd go for a stroll. It was already dark but the weather was exceptionally mild. He could hear Paul and old Davy talking and laughing in the milking parlour, which reminded him of the last conversation he had had with Sarah. He wondered what she was doing at this very hour. He glanced at his watch and could see the luminous face telling him it was after five. He presumed they'd be over dinner now, relaxed and possibly relieved. Or would the restless legs she complained of trouble her to such an extent that she'd want to go walking? He wondered was she even now striding along the road, maybe with her sisters, looking at the sea glimmering through the black winter trees? Or was she content and happy to be with Alan on their first Christmas together? Or was she doing the sort of thing you wouldn't do at any other time of year, like playing cards or Monopoly or Scrabble?

He strode down the drive, the unseasonable warm breeze clearing his head, noticing that his mother's pride and joy, her herbaceous border, was sad and dormant now. As long as he could remember the herbaceous border had looked the same. As a child it used to intrigue him how, ablaze with colour in summer, things that would completely vanish in the grey winter, coming back almost overnight. He remembered mentally comparing Sarah Beirne's eyes to his mother's delphiniums. Crazy what a feeling for a woman did to you. At least what it was doing to him. Bringing back the adolescent torment of longing that he had long since put aside. He had reached the gate now and he found himself turning to the left. The narrow road was long and winding there, with low ditches, few trees, a brighter place to be on Christmas night than near the dark, gloomy woods. He was alone; few would leave the comfort of their homes on Christmas evening.

Conor thought that maybe he had made a wrong decision in taking on the partnership with James Gillen. He had turned down the offer of a good partnership in England, but at the time Bamber, in the north of England, didn't appeal as much as Tramore in the south-east of Ireland. If he had gone there he wouldn't have the dilemma he had now. When he got back after Christmas their relationship would have to be put back on a more professional level, strictly doctor-patient. It was the only way. Just the routine visits, the routine check-ups, no question of seeing her outside the clinic. He could drum up some excuse to terminate his visits to Alan. And definitely no more intercepted meetings with her during her beach walks. The only way to exorcise her from his life was to leave Tramore. However, he had promised Doctor James that two years was the minimum length of time he would stay if things didn't work out to his satisfaction.

When he reached the bottom of the hill he turned back. Returning up the drive he looked at the house. For a fleeting minute he saw it through the eyes of a stranger with all its familiar lines erased. It was undoubtedly a lovely place, old, mellowed and timeless in the perfect setting. He even liked the name, Redfern. Glancing at the facade he thought it was the sort of house you'd draw as a child. A big square with a big door and two big windows at floor level and three on top, with three chimneys jutting to the swaying trees at the back. Like a lovelorn adolescent he wondered what it would be like to live down through the years there with Sarah Beirne at his side, having his children, sharing his life, all the shadows, all the restlessness, all the unhappiness erased from her lovely face. Just when he became convinced that he was absolutely losing it, Carol called him as he entered the hall.

"Come on, Doctor, we're about to play poker. About to clean you out."

"Coming," he shouted.

As he opened the living room door they were sitting there, looking very serious about this poker game that was about to start. Carol was shuffling the cards, Michael and his wife Mary had already stacked the money in sizeable piles in front of them, his sister Joan and her husband were in the process of doing the same. He walked over to join them grinning and jingling coins in his pocket. He knew that for the next three hours at least he would be at peace.

"I told you," Alan grumbled. "That woman of mine can't stay the course even on Christmas night."

Sarah knew he had no objection really. The day had gone well – full of distraction and company. Her parents had invited in some friends for a drinks session. The conversation had flowed and if there was curiosity about Alan it didn't show. His parents, Mary and Frank, had dropped by and his grandmother Alice had come also. She was eighty-three and looked sixty-three. She had knitted big roomy Aran sweaters in a deep wine colour for both Sarah and Alan. They thanked her profusely and tried them on there and then to the praise of all. Yes, it had been a good day; a day when worries were put away; a day when tomorrow hadn't come and they all lived for the minute

"A short walk," Sarah said, "just to help digest all the rich goodies." Both Emma and Patsy agreed to accompany her.

"After all," Emma informed them, "if anyone has to keep her figure it has to be me. I have to land a millionaire Londoner so I must look like Twiggy."

"I thought it was Mary Quant," Patsy asked dryly.

"Ah, you haven't a notion. It's the Mary Quant look with the Twiggy figure that's the thing," Emma retorted.

They put on their coats and left, saying they wouldn't be long, just a little trot – nothing too energetic. They would be back for the "Christmas Show" on television – they wouldn't miss Maureen Potter for anything. Walking down past Mason's woods, glimpsing the sea between the trees, they told each other it was very mild, nearly mild enough for a swim, completely unseasonable. Emma suddenly burst out laughing.

"Jesus, we're like three oul wans talking about the weather. Come on, will ye – tell me all the gossip. Since I came back I haven't heard a breath of scandal."

They all laughed and it was a bit like old times. Patsy dredged up a few titbits of news that what might come across as gossip. Sarah told her she was an old expectant married women past all temptation. Emma told Sarah that this Rory O'Driscoll might be something big on the horizon. Patsy nudged her, warning her not to say too much. They decided they'd go to the beach, just to get a breath of sea air to blow away all the indulgences of the day. Patsy got up on the stile that lead down to the beach and jumped to the ground, followed by Emma. Sarah clamoured up and jumped, landing heavily on the grass. She made an effort to follow them, but when they glanced back they saw her bent over, holding her stomach. In two strides Patsy was at her side.

"What's wrong? What ails you?"

"Oh, God," Sarah gasped, "I think I've done some damage."

Patsy grabbed her and helped her over to the ditch. "Sit down – Jesus, sit down."

Emma, unaware of what they feared, was irritated. "Maybe you sprained your ankle. You should be more careful."

"It's not her ankle, dope – she's worried that it's the baby."

Patsy's voice shook at the enormity of what might be happening. She got down on her knees in front of Sarah.

"It couldn't be the baby, could it?"

"Yeah, I feel something happening," Sarah whispered as she rocked to and fro, as if the gentle cradle-like movement might help.

"You can't," Patsy cried. "You can't lose Alan's baby. You must, for God's sake, hang on to it. It'll kill him – it'll absolutely kill him."

Across the far side of the road a rat darted out and, seeing its nocturnal foray was being observed, darted back to safety. Way down the road the headlights of a car appeared. Emma jumped the stile and, running like a hare, flew down the middle of the rutted road to flag it down, at the same time sending up a wild but silent prayer of thanks to heaven.

CHAPTER EIGHTEEN

"THAT'S FINE, DAY after tomorrow will fit the bill. How did Christmas go?"

Doctor James laughed. "Why do we always say the same thing – quiet? As if we expect it to be a brawl. No, nothing untoward happened – well, that is, with the exception of Sarah Beirne. Thought she was going to lose the baby. Started contractions but a shot and bed rest did the trick. I think she'll hang on all right. No, there's no need to come back tomorrow – as I said, all's quiet on the western front. No, I don't know exactly how it happened. Out walking on Christmas night with her sisters. Luckily a car came along and they had the sense to get her straight into hospital. Touch and go all the night as far as I can gather, but the contractions went and she's all right. Ah, that's it then. Regards to your mother and wish her a happy New Year."

Doctor James put down the phone and walked back to the breakfast table to finish off his last cup of tea, his favourite cup, the one that always got cold because of interruptions like phone calls.

"Who was that?" Kit wanted to know.

"Conor, just ringing to know how things went and to tell me that he was coming back day after tomorrow. Seemed quite floored when I told him about Sarah Beirne. She is one of his patients."

"Thank God, she hung on to it." Kit sounded exasperated. "Now, maybe she'll have the sense not to go trotting all over country lanes at all hours. Imagine, jumping off ditches on Christmas night. Wouldn't it have broken that young man's heart, not to mention Eileen and Tim and his poor parents." The phones strident ringing shattered the peace again. "Sit there and finish your cup of tea," Kit advised, rising to answer it. "It's probably a house call so you might as well be finished."

Her husband listened. He could hear his wife laughing and talking with a certain animation so he presumed it was one of her friends. When she came back he looked up from his paper.

"Well, who was it this time?"

"Conor McElroy, again. He told me to tell you he's changed his mind. He'll be driving down today. Seemed anxious to let you know. I told him it was strange that he couldn't keep away. He laughed and said he made a quick decision to get away before he that he was cleaned out by his avaricious family who were poker mad. If he stayed longer he'd lose his shirt."

"Hmm – that's strange. A few minutes ago he was quite happy to stay for another day. Young people don't know whether they're coming or going."

His wife was silent as she sipped her tea. She was looking out the window, her eyes on a cheeky robin who had perched on the lower branch of a variegated laurel bush.

"It wouldn't have anything to do with Sarah Beirne, would it?"

"Sarah Beirne? Why would the fellow want to come back because of Sarah? She's over the crisis." He looked at his wife, her gaze firmly fixed on the robin who was still perched there, his little head cocked to one side.

"I don't know. Her position is so peculiar and she's very attractive and her doctor is young and unattached and I wondered. That's all."

James Gillen took off his glasses, cleaned them with the edge of the tablecloth before putting them slowly back on again. "Maybe I'm losing my marbles or maybe you're losing yours, but if what I think you're thinking is right, all I can say is that you ate too much over the Christmas."

His wife didn't give the expected laugh. "I don't know," she said. "I hope it's the meandering of an ageing idle mind, but I did see Conor and Sarah Beirne together Christmas week. I was over near Carbarry visiting Josephine Stafford.

The bridge club made up a hamper to give her because of her arthritis. When I was there I saw the two of them passing. It looked as if they had been for a walk. And, God forgive me, I got a strange feeling."

"Forget it, my Kit. Sure the girl is distracted over her husband. Her father told me he loses sleep worrying about her. If anything he thinks that the accident has affected her even worse than it has affected her husband. She probably ran into Conor on one of his calls or maybe he was over that way and called in. No Kit, forget such a thing. This bloody town is alive with scandal mongers and I don't want you to add yourself to the bunch."

"You're right. You're absolutely right. Maybe I need a hobby, beekeeping or something." He noticed with some relief that she was smiling.

As Conor strode along the polished corridor of Airmount nursing home, the nurses greeted him warmly, wishing him a happy New Year, telling him they had missed him and that all sorts of things had happened when he was away. He smiled and ruefully shook his head.

"I know. A fellow can't turn his back but everyone falls asunder."

Then they told him that Mrs Power had had her baby, that it had been jaundiced but after the transfusion it was fine. She was very neurotic about the whole thing, though, wondering whether the baby's having someone else's blood would affect him and would he be all right.

Nurse Breen, a capable pretty nurse, smilingly advised, "You'd better drop in. She said she won't be happy until you see her and the baby."

He nodded, agreeing that he would do just that when he had a minute. He called to number six first.

Sarah was there with Alan. She was lying in bed with her knees drawn up and her husband holding her hand, just as it should be. They both looked up when he entered the room. Conor knew then he wasn't there because he was her doctor; he wasn't there to see that everything was all right with her and her baby after the threatened miscarriage. *Face it, Conor,* the inner voice hinted, *you're here because you want to be with her. You're here because it gives you a reason to talk to her, to feel her, to touch her.*

"Hi," she greeted with that half smile that was becoming so familiar.

"Conor, great to see you," Alan smiled, holding out his hand, and Conor took it, aware of the strength of the other man's grip. He also noticed other things about this man he respected greatly and in some way envied greatly. It was more than just good looks. It was a mixture of charisma and strength and maybe acceptance at the hand he had been dealt. Whatever it was, he hadn't come across it before.

"A happy New Year to you. I believe this woman of yours was falling over ditches and things." He sounded so normal he surprised himself.

"Yes, I suppose I was very stupid. I nearly gave everyone heart attacks, but I'm here now and I'm fine, and," she lightly patted her abdomen, "he's decided to stay put. So the panic is over."

"It had better be," Alan sighed. "I've had enough excitement to last me a lifetime." He looked at Conor. "Doctor James said you weren't due back until tomorrow."

"Aye – that was my intention until I heard that my patients weren't behaving. One Sarah Beirne who was falling over stiles on Christmas night and a few others who didn't behave themselves either." Nice normal words said with an ease that was becoming familiar, the sort of things you'd say to friends. He smiled and, looking at the two of them, said, "I'm glad things are fine again. I'll drop in tomorrow, Sarah, and be good till then."

Then he was gone out down the long polished length of the hospital corridor. Going out the revolving door, he bumped into two young women. He recognised Patsy

Dunne immediately and looking at her his heart jolted at the cold blue gaze in eyes that were so extraordinary similar to Sarah's.

"Hi." She was unsmiling as she introduced him to the dark glossy-haired girl. "Emma, this is Conor McElroy, the new doctor – this is my sister Emma home from London."

He smiled and shook Emma's hand, "I've heard about you."

"So that's the new doctor," he heard Emma saying before he was out of earshot.

Driving back to Tramore, his foot down hard on the accelerator, it struck him that he had utterly forgotten to visit Noreen Power and her new infant. "Fuck," he said softly to no one in particular, knowing that he had broken the cardinal rule of his profession – he had become so emotionally involved with a patient that it was coming between him and his work.

CHAPTER NINETEEN

PATSY HEARD HER mother's muffled message above the hiss of the shower as Eileen shouted through the door of the bathroom, "Patsy, it's the phone, Rory O'Driscoll phoning from Dublin. You don't want to waste the poor lad's money, so come down."

"Okay, Mam," Patsy yelled as she stepped out of the warm, comforting stream and into her dressing gown. As she ran down the stairs, she remembered she hadn't waited to dry herself. She wondered why she was so eager, and then she wondered why not. Hadn't she slotted him into her life.

"Hello, I hope I didn't get you out of bed."

"No, not out of bed – out of a shower. So, what you have to say had better be good."

"I only want to tell you that I must see you. I'm going to bum a kip off Tony for the weekend, so I'll be down. Okay?"

"It's okay, but you don't have to bum any kip, as you call it. This house has loads of room. Emma's room, Sarah's room and the guest room which is a bit of a dump. But it's probably better than Tony's floor."

"I'll take you up on that. Check it with your mother and if it's all right, I'll be there at eight and I'll be fed, watered and ready. So you be ready now and we'll paint the town that red they talk about. All right?"

"All right, and I'll wear the black dress."

"That's the only reason I'm going down – the black dress. Then again, you have to see me in the jumper. Hey, why are you whimpering?"

"I'm not whimpering, you idiot, I'm shivering – water running down on my mother's carpet. I was so eager I didn't dry myself. So, as I talk I'm mopping up."

"I wish I was there – I could do the job for you."

"Yeah, I get the message. I'll see you Saturday evening at eight."

"Okay, Patsy Dunne, and there's something I want to say."

"What's that?" She didn't hear his answer because her mother brought the blare of the television with her as she came out of the sitting room. She thought it was, "I love you," but she wasn't sure. She hoped it wasn't. Replacing the phone a drop of water fell on to her hand. It looked like a tear. Rubbing it impatiently away she wandered into the sitting room. The nine o'clock news was on, and past experience had taught them all not to open their mouths during the news. Her father, a patient man about most things, was positively obsessive about news. He had once said that the news would go by the board only if there was a bomb or a fire in the house.

Her mother's eyes told Patsy that she was very interested in what Rory O'Driscoll might have wanted, but her forefinger to her lip warned that they must bide their time. Patsy, sitting down on the old footstool, fiddled absent-mindedly with the cord of her dressing gown and gazed unseeing into the heart of the glowing coals. She heard the news announcer talk about the budget and the old reliables being taxed again. Sonny Liston, the boxer, had been buried that day and Coco Chanel, the French fashion designer, had just died. Looking into the fire she thought that it must be great to be famous. News of your death would go out on all the networks of the world, the newspapers would headline it and all sorts of people would talk about your passing. Whereas she was absolute nobody and lived in the remotest backwater – a house that overlooked the back strand of Tramore, a wide dull bay where nothing moved for nine months of the year. If it was an interesting port like Cobh in Cork, where great big liners came with multi-millionaires whose goings-on made the news on TV all over the world, it might be something. Even over in Dunmore East the fishermen made news with blockades and fish wars and demonstrations about the prices they received.

Suddenly she heard the jingle for "Seven Days", so she could say her piece.

"Is it all right if Rory O'Driscoll comes for the weekend? I thought it would be okay, what with all the empty rooms now."

"I see no reason why not," her mother said. "That's if your father feels the same."

Tim Dunne slowly took out his pipe and looked at his youngest daughter sitting huddled in front of the fire, water still dripping from her hair. "I liked that lad," he told her. "As far as I'm concerned he's welcome."

"Thanks," Patsy answered, getting abruptly off the stool and rubbing her hair impatiently. "I took it on myself to tell him he could stay. He'll be here at eight and he told me to tell you, Mam, that he'll be fed and watered."

Tim didn't speak until he heard her run up the stairs. "She's not our same Patsy, is she? She's quieter and a lot of the gizz is gone. I'm glad the lad is coming, although I shouldn't be, because to me she's only a child still."

When Rory arrived exactly at eight o'clock, Patsy opened the door still wearing her jeans and polo necked jumper. She had dabbled with the idea of wearing the black dress but had dismissed it, telling herself she didn't want to be all dressed up like a ham bone when he arrived. He grinned as he tried to tidy his windblown hair.

"Hi, I got here and I'm on time."

Her heart warmed to his casual approach and the warmth spread throng her as she brought him into the kitchen to say hello to her mother. Eileen Dunne insisted that he sit down to what she called a high tea: a plateful of home-cooked ham, a salad and her brown bread and apple tart. As he sat down without hesitation, Patsy thought that maybe he wasn't as fed and watered as he made out.

"While you're feeding your face, I'll run up and get ready." Patsy told him.

She knew it had to be the dress. Pulling off her warm jumper she shivered. A frantic search in her drawer yielded a black lacy slip. She hurriedly put it on and then slipped into the dress. There was no denying it looked good. She recalled the look of admiration in Alan's eyes the day she had tried it on in the kitchen before Christmas. Every day she recalled most things about him. Looking out the window there was nothing only blackness. She closed her eyes tight and made things blacker still. That's what she had to do: shut him out, shut him away. After all, wasn't that the very reason why Rory was here?

Looking in the mirror Patsy thought she looked pale. She found a lipstick and applied it to her mouth. That looked better, she thought. She found the new blusher that Emma had given her and brushed it on as Emma had taught her. Then she thought she looked too made up, even garish, a bit like a prostitute. She told herself she was mad, and leaving well enough alone she ran down the stairs to the kitchen.

Whatever Rory was telling her mother it had a good effect. Her mother was laughing so much there were tears in her eyes. Rory looked up, putting down his cup, and his eyes roamed all over her.

"Hey, you're a bit of all right," he told her.

"Thanks," she said, dryly, "I was waiting to hear that all day."

Then she laughed, and looking at her he thought she looked so young and yet so perfect in the dress. He noticed the hastily applied blusher and thought that when they were alone he would rub if off, because he definitely preferred her the way she was.

They drove down the narrow road with her mother's voice still ringing in their ears: "Be careful. It's stormy and the wind could fell trees."

Rory drove silently until they reached the main road and then he pulled into a lay-by and turned off the engine.

"No, Rory," she said, "we're not looking at the stars again, surely."

"No, we're not because, miss, there are no stars tonight. Or did you even notice?"

"No, I didn't. I'm too busy to be looking at the sky." She could see he was looking at her with a strange quizzical expression – or maybe a summing-up expression. "Why are you staring at me like that?"

"Because you're a sight for sore eyes, so you are." Then he took her in his arms and kissed her with a bruising intensity and she surprised herself by returning his kisses. She could hear his heart hammering away and wished that her own would hammer and fill the car with its thuds, too. But it didn't, and when he kissed her on the eyes and neck, his mouth roaming to the top of the famous dress and his lips touching the tops of her breasts, she felt a unfamiliar warmth spread right through her. As she pressed his fair head against her breast, she didn't feel she was doing anything wrong; if anything she felt she was doing everything right. When he raised his head and his eyes met hers, he lifted her chin and she thought his fingers were a little rough, a little impatient.

"Will you marry me?" he asked huskily.

"I will," she said, kissing him gently on the mouth. As she did so she hoped that Rory O'Driscoll, the guy who had stumbled into her life on a building site in Dún Laoghaire, might be happy with her and might bring the healing she so desperately wanted.

They went to the Grand Hotel in Tramore and he insisted on buying a bottle of champagne. She told him he was mad, that she had only tasted champagne once before in her life, at Sarah's wedding. He told her to forget Sarah's wedding because their wedding would be better, and that she'd taste champagne maybe ten times more when they celebrated the birth of their ten children. It was that sort of night, a bit crazy, a bit funny, as he regaled her with stories of growing

191

up in Tipperary and she in return regaled him with stories of her childhood, always steering clear of the latter years when Alan Beirne came into her world.

The lounge in the Grand Hotel was pretty full and the young couple who were obviously celebrating something got a fair share of surreptitious attention. One middle-aged couple sat near the huge fire. The woman wearing a pale blue, wrinkle-free dress with a mink coat over her shoulders whispered to her dark-suited husband, "That chap has obviously proposed and look – don't stare now – but I think he's getting something out of his pocket. He is and she's surprised – don't think she saw that coming. I think it's the ring."

Patsy looked at the diamond cluster in amazement. "Rory, I can't possibly take this now. My folks would die. They still think I've just left school and am just biding my time to go to college. They haven't a notion that we're that serious." She looked at the ring nestling in the blue velvet covered box. "It's beautiful, Rory. It must have cost a fortune."

"It did," he was smiling, "and you know what, you're wearing it and we're going back and we're telling your folks. Then we'll tell my father and then your sisters that we're getting married next summer. And I have another surprise in store for you."

"Oh, God! What would that be? I'm still reeling."

"I'm off to London next month. I've got a great job lined up there and I want everything signed, sealed and delivered before I go."

She was silent as he took the ring from its box and, holding her eyes, he slipped it on her finger. She looked at it and slowly twisted it, watching the light overhead spearing and catching the diamonds, sending out its brilliant flashes of colour. It was only then the enormity of what they were doing struck her.

"My God, my mother will have a stroke and my father will die of a heart attack," she whispered, "and everyone but everyone is watching us."

"I don't give a damn," he grinned as he bent over and kissed her.

The reaction from her parents wasn't quite as disastrous as she had predicted, but they were obviously shaken. Her mother was the first to speak.

"We had no idea," she told them with an incredulous look on her face. She then looked at the expensive ring on her youngest daughter's hand. "You should have told us," she admonished. "You're usually so outspoken. Why all the secrecy?"

"There was no secrecy. He just popped the question tonight and already had the ring and I said yes." Patsy said.

"Perhaps you could have discussed this with us," her father said dryly, his words mostly addressed to Rory.

"I know I should have, Mr Dunne. I regret I didn't now, but since the day I met her I fell for her. You see, I love her and I'll take care of her. My job is good, my prospects even better, but unfortunately it will be in London for a while. But we'll be back in a few years."

"But she's only a child," her mother told him. "She's only eighteen and we hoped she'd go to college. We had all sorts of hopes for her. How do you feel about all this yourself, Patsy?" She looked at her daughter, her eyes still troubled.

"Mam, getting married to Rory is what I want." Patsy sounded so emphatic that Eileen Dunne's racing heart eased.

"Well, well," her father cleared his throat, "what can we say but congratulations. Admittedly I'm shocked. I had no idea we'd be losing you so soon, but if you're both sure about what you want, who are we to say no?" Tim Dunne walked across the floor and stuck out his hand and shook Rory's hand warmly. He put his arm around Patsy's shoulders, hugging her close. "Well, young Patsy, so you're off, too. I thought you'd be around a bit longer. But that's life, I suppose. Fledglings leaving the nest."

His wife then surprised them all by bursting into tears. "I'm happy, I really am, but it's so sudden – so sudden," she sobbed. When she had regained some control she put her arms around her youngest daughter. "But I do love the ring, too, and Rory is a grand fellow, I know that." She then hugged Rory O'Driscoll, wishing him all the happiness in the world, telling him he had to mind her youngest daughter. "And don't stay too long in London. When you have your fortune made you're to bring her back now."

He patted her on the back and told her that of course he'd bring Patsy back – that it was only for a while, a case of making hay whilst the sun shines.

CHAPTER TWENTY

"**W**HY WEREN'T YOU shocked? I mean, it just took my breath away and you weren't even rattled. How come?" Sarah and Alan were in bed. Sarah was propped up on her pillow, a position she found more comfortable now that she was seven months pregnant. "Tell me, did you know about this? You look guilty. I bet you knew – and you didn't even bother to tell me."

"Don't get over-excited now. It mightn't be good for someone in your condition. Think of my son – he had one little jolt already. Be calm." He grinned in an effort to calm her agitation.

"Oh, stop the school-lecture stuff. Tell me, did you know that Patsy was going to get engaged to this guy we hardly know? After all, you two are as thick as thieves – she probably told you everything and left the rest of us out in the cold."

Alan, aware that she was really upset, suddenly became serious. He lay back on his pillow, his hands behind his head.

"Yes, I knew. She told me that she intended to get married. I was shocked at the time, pointing out that maybe she was rushing into something she might regret. I tried to tell her about how serious and final marriage is. I also tried to explain what love is. I even went as far as to tell her that if she could live without him not to marry him. You see, woman, I know all about love." He turned around and kissed her. "I was going by my own experience." He looked at Sarah, her blue eyes angry, her oval face flushed. "I'm an old hand at this business of loving. I love you so much I couldn't live without you."

Sarah, relenting, put her arms around him, and pulling him close whispered, "I know, I know. But you could have told me about my little sister. God, I thought she'd be around for ever. I thought she'd marry one of the Tramore guys and settle in these parts, and now she's gone mad and got engaged to a man we hardly know. And she'll be in London as well as Emma and I'll have no sisters left."

Alan was silent as he turned over and switched off the lamp. Lying together with their arms entwined, he felt his child. The movement became quite strong and he lay there wondering was it tiny legs that kicked. He thought of his own legs and their deadness. And yet at times were they so dead? Was everything as dead as it was supposed to be. He wasn't sure – oh Christ, he wasn't sure. He only knew the hell that raged through him at times could destroy him.

The calm acceptance he showed to so many was a complete act. With the exception of the few outbursts to Sarah, no one knew what he was going through. He loathed the messing around with catheters and pads, like an old incontinent man. "You'll get used to it," they had said in hospital. "You'll hardly notice, it'll all become so automatic." It didn't become automatic and he did notice. And then the flaccid deadness when it came to sex. A deadness that no fantasising or flights of erotic fancy could help. And recently the confusion and madness in his tortured mind that there was a slight improvement. And the goddam dreams. Never crippled in dreams. Always as it used to be dreams. At the peak of physical perfection in his dreams, whether he was working, walking, making love; the wheelchair had no part in his taunting dreams.

Lying beside his wife, Patsy came into his mind, her eyes holding his as she knelt in front of him telling him she was going to get married. He remembered the way she had rocked on her heels, her long slim fingers fiddling with her cropped hair. He remembered his astonishment when she told him that she was going to marry Rory O'Driscoll because she might as well – because she couldn't marry the man she really loved. Because he was married already. Then he remembered the night when he stumbled on the possible identity of who the married man might be. He sincerely hoped he was wrong.

The days lengthened as winter eased its grip. Sarah Beirne still went walking but the beach hikes were over. The threatened loss of her baby made her so careful that at times she was a nervous wreck, thinking every single pain and ache might be premature labour. The people in the sprawling townsland of Carbarry got used to the sight of the young woman walking the roads. Although everyone knew who she was, some of the women in the cottages were shy to put their talk on her at first, but as her pregnancy advanced and her footsteps weren't so brisk, they smiled and wished her well. Sometimes she stopped and spoke to them and heard all about their large families; it seemed that no woman in the area had fewer than six. One women who unabashedly smiled despite the fact that she had lost most of her front teeth told her that she had thirteen – all alive – and all in England now.

When she was safely out of earshot, they spoke about her in whispers. They told each other that she looked like a film star. And, God help us, her husband the schoolmaster would take the sight from your eyes, too, but sure what good was it and he in that wheelchair from morning till night. But it didn't take from his teaching. He was the best master the school ever had. How he could din things into some of their young fellas' absolute thick heads was a miracle, but he did, because there was some talk of a few good lads in sixth who might get scholarships to the secondary school in Waterford. Wasn't it well, they told each other, that the Beirnes had come to live in the parts because they wouldn't know what to talk about if they hadn't.

There was a whisper, just a little bit of a whisper, that the doctor in Tramore, the new Doctor McElroy, fancied her. Ellen White, who had the thirteen children, had a sister who lived in the cottage just a quarter mile from the master's house and she had seen her with the doctor a few times before she showed so much. The sister didn't see so much of them now, but sure it was only right. How could a young married woman nearly on her last legs be seen walking around with the local doctor, and her poor husband the way he was.

Then again there was the other story – the fact that her sister barely out of school had got engaged to a fellow no one ever heard of. He wasn't from Tramore or Waterford, a case of getting engaged to a black stranger, but it didn't look as if there was a problem. She was skinny as ever, even skinnier if anything.

Sarah Beirne knew that the women who lived in the scattered cottages in the surrounding area gossiped about her and gossiped about Alan and indeed anyone who came to the house. They had little else to talk about in the winter months, a time when the acre or two behind their cottages lay fallow, when their husbands had gone labouring for the big farmers, when their children had gone to school.

Today, a breezy fitful day at the end of February, made Sarah realise that spring was coming. Somehow she didn't want to talk to Ellen White or Noreen Fitzgerald as they stood smiling and waving at the gate of Whites' cottage. She just smiled and mentioned how pleasant the weather was and moved on. Tomorrow she was due for her check-up. Conor McElroy had mentioned that the visits would be twice monthly for the next six weeks until the birth of her baby. Their relationship had got back on a more professional footing, at least on the surface. When he briefly examined her he was sometimes funny, telling her bizarre little stories of happenings in the area, or sometimes casual. He always asked about Alan and how he was, and was Nancy Ryan still at the good work? She had written about him late that evening when Alan had retired.

I went for my check-up today and everything
was so normal and casual that it was like a remote

dream that anything had ever happened between us. I can understand his patients being enamoured with him because, if we had a normal doctor-patient relationship, I would just love him as my doctor. I would casually say, like the other women patients, that, "He's great – I love Doctor McElroy." They say it all the time when I meet them in the waiting room. They say it with easy smiles as they wait with their enormous bumps and their legs full of varicose veins. I can't say that – I can't say anything like that because of what happened. Of course, writing this brings back the evening on the beach. Remembering it fills me with a hunger and a longing that somehow terrifies me, because it won't go away. I looked up today when I was pulling up the zip of the wretched maternity skirt and I caught him looking at me unawares. I swear – I swear, and dear God, I hope I'm wrong, that in his eyes there was something I didn't want to see. I'd better stop and go to bed because if I don't, I don't know what I'll be writing next.

She put the diary in its hiding place, wondering would she take it down sometime in the future, maybe when she was old and all fires diminished, and smile at her foolishness in that terrible first year of her marriage.

Tomorrow was check-up time again and then a fortnight after that and then another fortnight and then she'd have it. She didn't want to think about that. She had read all about easy breathing and had practised some relaxation exercises and after that hoped for the best. She remembered Nancy Ryan laughing and saying these fellows standing looking at a woman in the last throes of labour with her legs straddled were in all probability wondering what they're going to have for dinner.

Thinking of Nancy Ryan brought her worry about Alan to the fore. It was only in the last few weeks that she had realised that he was in pain. She had been of the opinion that with paralysis there was no pain, only numbness. She was obviously wrong. She could see the pain in his eyes and in his pallor, but when she saw a large packet of painkillers on the dressing table and questioned him, he made light of it, telling her that he wasn't quite dead – that he could have a pain like anyone.

"This is crazy," she had argued. "I should know everything about you. You should go back to the specialists in Dublin – they'd know what's causing it."

She would ask Conor McElroy tomorrow what it might be. He should be able to help.

However, when Sarah went to her appointment, Conor wasn't there. The disappointment and flatness that his absence caused didn't surprise her. Since he had come he seemed as permanent as the stars, and the thought that he might move on filled her with so much panic that she had to take deep breaths to calm herself.

Doctor James greeted her warmly, telling her, "That young whippersnapper, Conor, has a doze of flu."

Flu, she thought with relief, *a week in bed – nothing – he'll be back. God,* she wondered, *What's happening – what? Why do I care? Dear Jesus, why?* But her face was calm while Doctor James gave her the briefest of examinations as he softly whistled "Don't Let the Stars Get in Your Eyes".

When he was finished he beamed. "Everything under control. You're as fit as a mountain goat. I believe you're a great one for the walking. It'll stand to you when your time comes."

Looking at the fatherly smile, she asked him, "Tell me, Doctor James, is it terrible? Childbirth, I mean?"

"For a fit youngster like you, it'll be nothing. The first one is a bit slow, so don't be impatient, but after that you'll spit them out." He must have realised then that he had put his foot in it because he sat down and reached out and took her cold hand in his. "You won't know yourself, Sarah, and neither will Alan when you have this child. You'll be wondering what filled your days up to then."

"Talking about Alan, I think he's in a lot of pain these days. Is that normal for someone like that? You know – paralysed and all that."

He didn't answer immediately. "I don't know too much about that, Sarah. Spinal injuries aren't my area, as you know, but I will talk to Patrick Dempsey, the spine man up in Dublin, and let you know."

She smiled and thanked him. After she left he had to clear his throat before he put on what Kit called his genial patient face.

They sat looking at each other, bonded by a frail wisp of hope.

"It's something, isn't it?" Alan asked quietly, as if he were almost afraid to put it into words.

"It is something. It's definitely something. But, Alan, don't be building your hopes, because it might be nothing significant. Maybe a reflex thing. I'm not sure." Nancy Ryan looked into the dark eyes that were afraid to hope. "I think it might be something more important, but we should get you back up there to the Rehabilitation Hospital and get their opinion."

"No. Absolutely not, Nancy. If it's a hopeful symptom, it's thanks to your wonderful work. We will go on as we are."

He looked at her and she thought, *God in his heaven above, I'm glad I'm sixty-nine, or who knows what my feelings would be about him.* "It could take years," she told him, "years going on like this."

"If this sensation, this feeling, continues and isn't a figment of my imagination, I will gladly put up with a year or two. If it stops and goes away, we'll know it was merely muscular reflex. Not a word to anyone. It would be cruel to

Sarah to raise false hopes. Maybe you'll say a prayer because I sort of gave up praying myself. By the way," he was smiling and the smile reached his eyes and made him look so young again.

"By the way, what?" she asked dryly.

"Did I ever tell you I love you?"

"Shut up now, you a married man with a first child on the way giving notions to an old woman." Later in the warm kitchen they drank their tea in comfortable silence. He was thinking once again how much she meant to him. Apart from the important physiotherapy she was giving him, he liked to listen to her yarns, he liked her wit, her dry rejoinders, and even if her enthusiastic efforts to make him walk again failed, he hoped that she would stay in their lives.

Nancy had a gut feeling that he would walk again. She wanted that for him more than she wanted anything on God's earth. She had nearly reached her allotted three score and ten and it was only now she knew what it was like to have a son. Oh yes, she had thumped, slapped and pummelled more human flesh than she would have thought possible and had always wanted good results from her work, but in her free time she could put it aside and live her life doing other things. But now it was different. Now she felt intrinsically linked with this small family, and she, too, was secretly hoping that she would have some part to play in their future.

CHAPTER TWENTY-ONE

"IF ANYONE HAD told me I'd be thinking of another wedding a year after the first one, I simply wouldn't have believed it." Eileen Dunne looked at her daughter who was nibbling her toast, so engrossed in the free offer of a Beatles poster on the back of the cereal box that she didn't hear her mother. She was still so much a child in so many ways. Eileen worried about her youngest daughter. Why was there such a rush on her to get married and settle in London? She had had such grandiose plans for travelling around the world, backpacking to remote and uncharted places. However, although Eileen worried about her daughter's surprise engagement, she didn't worry about her choice of partner.

"He's sound," her husband had said, "sound," and over the years she had learned that Tim Dunne's verdict was usually pretty accurate. Looking at Patsy, still engrossed in the cereal box, she repeated what she had said. Patsy heard her this time.

"Sure, you thought you'd never be rid of us – what with all the fighting and arguing – and now we're nearly gone. Anyway, it's four months away, so don't panic."

"Still, there's no doubt it'll be a lonely place when you go. I don't know what your father and I will do, rattling around in this place. Where do the years go at all, at all? It was only the other day you had us worn out looking for that pony. Then you grew a foot and the pony was too small, and now you're getting married. It isn't the same at all around here now," she sighed.

Patsy could see that her mother was near tears. She jumped up and went to the sink and filled her cup with water. With her back to her mother, she raised her voice above the running water.

"Mam, you'll be fine. You and Dad will have what you never had – time. You can travel a bit more and maybe you could take up the golf. And anyway, you'll have Sarah's baby in a month's time to drool over, so you'll be so busy you won't even notice I'm gone."

"I'll notice," her mother sniffed, "but the baby will be great – something to take our minds off our troubles. No hiring foreign cars on your honeymoon. Mind that man of yours."

"No question of foreign cars – we're going to Kerry in Rory's own banger, so we'll be safe enough."

Suddenly the phone shrilled into life and Patsy got up and went into the hall to answer it. Eileen could hear her talking and laughing and see her animated young face. *It's good,* she thought, *that her young man can make her light up like that.*

Then she heard her say, "All right, Alan, I haven't forgotten. I'll be over. Take care."

Alan, her mother thought – *Alan.* She sighed, not quite sure why. There was no doubt the menopause gave one all sorts of notions. She sighed again as she watched Patsy race up the stairs humming a snatch of a song.

Conor was in the clinic on the second of March when Sarah went for her second last visit before the birth of her child. She had already been experiencing pressure pains for a week now, which her mother had told her could be eased by hot baths. After her bath this morning, she had put on her best underwear, persuading herself that it was for her own pleasure. No other reason in the world. It made her feel good to have a touch of glamour when she felt so misshapen and positively gross.

"Well, how are things?" His eyes met hers, but she couldn't read what they said.

"Look at me – I think that tells a story." She tried to sound casual, maybe a bit witty. "I've forgotten what it's like to be half this size."

"Soon, soon," he smiled. As he studied her chart, she

noticed the downward sweep of the black lashes that were responsible for the intense look in the pale grey eyes. He looked tired, and there was a small cut on his chin from shaving. He glanced up quickly, catching her unawares.

"The baby is due April fifteenth, three weeks time. First mothers usually go over, but that's not saying it mightn't happen tomorrow."

"Is that possible?"

"Possible but a bit improbable. But you are into your ninth month, the baby is perfectly developed, and there is not much more you can do for him except have him."

"It's not that easy for me. Someone must be there with Alan. Of course he'll hotly protest this, but it can be a bit awkward for him at times."

"I understand, Sarah, but he wouldn't want too much intrusion. If it'll relieve you, I promise I'll keep an eye on him myself. 'Sufficient unto the day' isn't a bad policy, you know. Hop up there and let me have a look at you." His hands were gentle. "The head is engaged," he said, looking at the wall.

"You might not go over after all," he told her as he helped her down from the couch. Walking towards the door he put a light hand on her shoulder. "When you start and feel that the time is right to go into hospital, get Alan to phone me – I want to be there." She glanced up at him and he could see the confusion in her troubled glance. "Don't look so worried. I'll take care of you both."

"All right, I'll do that. Thank you, Conor, I'd like you to be there – I'm terrified."

"Don't be. It's a very natural business."

"Maybe it is. Nancy Ryan says while you fellows haul babies into he world that you're more than likely thinking of your dinner or your girlfriends."

"I'll have to talk to her," he laughed. He was still smiling as he opened the front door to let her out into the blustery March day.

The labour pains started about nine in the morning one week before the due date. When they came, small and insignificant at first, she thought that they were the pressure pains that had plagued her for weeks. When they persisted for three hours, she wondered should she phone her mother. Alan had the car at school. At two-thirty she phoned Eileen.

"Did you time them?" Her mother's tone was excited, yet tinged with anxiety.

"Yeah, I did. They're regular and mostly to the back."

"I'll be over as soon as possible. Maybe they're false pains and maybe they're not. We can't take any chances. Don't worry – just get your things ready."

Sarah didn't have to get much ready. Her case had been packed for two weeks now. She walked into the bedroom and took the case out of the wardrobe, opened it and checked it once more. Everything was there, all the bits and pieces on the hospital list and the two old nightdresses her mother told her to bring "for the duration of the birth and the first few hours. Your good ones would be destroyed." Her glamourous ones, purchased in high hope for her honeymoon, were there also. Looking at them she stifled the memories as another pain gripped her in an ever-tightening knot. When it eased its hold she walked towards the fireplace and looked into the mirror, noticing how pale and drained she looked. Glancing away, her eye caught a tiny corner of her neglected diary sticking out from behind the large plate on top of the dresser. She'd make a brief entry while she was waiting for her mother, put on record one of the most important days in the life of any woman – the birth of a first child.

> I have felt the pains for hours now and they're getting worse, so I suppose this is it. The day Alan and I have waited for. My mother will be here soon and it's hard to write with this knot in my

stomach. Will he be there as soon as he said he
would? Will he be there when it's ending, when,
according to everything I've read and heard, a
woman has no control. God, the thought kills me.
This man who told me he loved me will be there
at the birth of my child, seeing me without a
shred of dignity. Yes, the pains are getting worse.
I must go.

As she slipped the pen into the pocket of her coat and
reached up to put the diary in its hiding place, she felt a
gush of warm water streaming down her legs, spilling in a
pool on the kitchen floor. After a brief moment of cold
panic, she realised that the waters had broken. *Oh dear God,*
she thought, *maybe the baby is in danger now – no water to protect him.* Then she heard her mother's car coming up the
road and she was filled with a heartfelt relief.

The calmness of the efficient nurse who took her particulars
on the admission form relaxed her so much that she wondered why the pains had gone and whether it was false
labour. The dark-haired nurse assured her that there was no
question of being sent home again; the waters had broken
and the labour pains would start up again. As she was being
prepared for the birth, the nurse asked her if she'd like a
boy or a girl. Sarah told her that she didn't know why, but
that everyone presumed that it was going to be a boy. Even
her doctor always referred to the child as "that little chap".
When Sarah told her who her doctor was, the nurse
laughed, saying, "All the women are in love with him. They
all go to him now – it's crazy."

Sarah laughed and said something inane all the while
thinking, *So he has all the women crazy about him and I am a stupid idiot to attach such importance to the brief interlude on the
beach.*

"So the day has come."

Sarah looked up and he was there, and she saw to her intense relief that the nurse had finished and had pulled down her nightdress. It was obvious, though, that having a baby removed every bit of modesty because he gently pulled the nightdress up again, turning to speak to the nurse as he pulled on a pair of surgical gloves.

I'll think of something else – something beautiful like the oyster bed in full tide and Alan and me swimming and splashing and the sun turning all the splashes into gold – Oh Jesus, that hurt!

When she glanced up his head was bent and she could see the goddam black half moons of lashes again and he was probing gently inside her and she was dead. She had to be because if she wasn't how could a woman look into the face of a man who was more than a doctor and who shouldn't be more than a doctor. A terrible pain ripped through her, obliterating all thought. He was talking now and the wretch was smiling as he peeled off the rubber gloves, putting them on the nurse's trolley. He was saying something about two centimetres or four centimetres and then she got the full blast of his eyes.

"You've started, Sarah," he told her, and she could see that the use of her Christian name surprised the nurse. "I'm going to put you on a drip. It'll hurry things a bit."

"Why a drip?" she asked weakly.

"Because your membranes are broken and it's safer for the baby."

"Thanks." Her voice sounded dry and shaky.

He smiled reassuringly. "This time tomorrow you'll be holding that little fellow in your arms, all your troubles over."

Sarah looked at the nurse and saw the small conspiratorial wink at Conor's "little fellow". He gave some more orders to the nurse as she was going out the door, and then he, too, left, telling her to relax, that everything would be fine and that he would be there. She was transferred on to a trolley and moved to her own room where she would stay until she was ready for the labour room.

It was small and bright with matching curtains and screen coverings. There was a big window, and she thought she heard kids playing football on the road outside. There was an out-of-season geranium on the windowsill, and the smell brought back Rome.

"Would you mind removing the plant? I have a thing about them." She tried to smile but the pain was starting up again.

The nurse who was setting up the drip looked at the offending plant. "But it looks grand."

Sarah tried to smile, "I just have a thing about them – please take it out."

Puzzled, the nurse removed the plant out into the corridor. Sarah could hear her saying to someone, ". . . a notion she got that she didn't like geraniums." Then the nurse was back adjusting the drip with a little tug, and the next pain was so bad, so searing, it took her breath away, making her gasp.

"Good," the nurse said calmly, "a few more of those grand pains and you'll be on your way."

Grand pains, Sarah thought, but then she couldn't think because another one came. The nurse rubbed her arm, telling her to relax – relax. She closed her eyes and tried, but the pain was a constant mountain she couldn't climb, making her wonder what all this nonsense was about an interlude between pains.

Her mother had told her that between pains she might be able to sip a cup of tea. Not in this world of agony. She lay there and made an effort to think beyond the pain. Alan would know at this stage that she was in hospital. Dear Alan, who would be demented with worry and would pretend not to be – just like he pretended not to be demented about his own situation. She tried to recall when this baby who was now crashing its way into the world might have been conceived. Was it the morning before they went sightseeing? Was it the first time they succeeded in making love? Was it

209

the evening before they went for the meal with the Currans? It all seemed a thousand years ago so much had happened since. Then the pain came again and it stayed and stayed and she felt a groan from someone. When she glanced around and couldn't see anyone, she presumed the sound had come from herself. Looking out from the lonely isolated world of giving birth, she could see that the nurse had come in and Conor was with her. He had a needle in his hand and as he bent down to her outstretched arm he whispered, "Just a little jab – help you relax."

"I'm trying to relax." She tried to smile but her face was too stiff and she was sure it was more of a grimace.

"Babies take time," he said gently. "I'll be back."

He was gone again and the nurse had gone with him. Obviously some other woman was in labour, maybe one all smiles and positive, who was brave and relaxing – relaxing. *It's stupid,* she thought; *how can a body relax when gripped in a straitjacket of hell.* She felt herself dropping into a well of endless pain, and when she was about to scream out, mercifully the injection seemed to work and things became hazy and the edges of pain weren't so sharp and grinding. She even thought she was floating off into blessed unconsciousness, but the nurse and Conor were there again and they did something to the wretched drip which caused a pain that arched her back and choked the wind from her lungs and indeed made her cry out. Then another one came, and after it subsided Conor was there with his wretched gloves, probing inside her again. She resented this man doing these invasive things to her.

"I hope that part is over," she muttered.

The awful wretch actually laughed.

Then the pain came again and he didn't leave her. He helped to lift her on to a trolley and she was rolled down somewhere. She could see a few women passing, their eyes filled with sympathy. She noticed that the awful pain-inducing drip came along also. She wondered if she pulled away from it would all the pain go away just for a bit – just for a bit? The lights were so bright in the labour ward they made her eyes water and she asked someone to wipe them. It could have been Conor because she heard his voice. She tried to see if she was strapped, but the pains came again and the sweat ran into her eyes and Conor wiped it away, saying gently, "It won't be long now."

She glared at him and gasped, "Is there something you can give me – gas, air, something, Conor?"

"Not yet," he said as he put the wet strand of hair away from her forehead. Then the pains changed, and though they were equally as terrible, she felt a pushing sensation and a terrible sound like a grunting animal. He was there and he held her hand and said, "Good girl, Sarah. When the pain comes again, push – push, and when I say stop, you're to stop." It came again and she pushed and pushed. His voice was jubilant as he held her hand, head bent, obviously watching for the appearance of her baby as it made its passage into the world.

"Good girl, we're just there now. I can see the head – black hair."

She held on to him like someone drowning. She felt her nails pierce his palm and she didn't care because she knew she was going to die. The next pain was so bad that she pushed and pushed. He sharply ordered her to stop but she didn't. She pushed and pushed and the more she tried to stop the more she failed. Then she heard him order, "Once more, Sarah, once more," and she pushed again and then something tore out of her in a wet, slimy flood.

He let go of her hand and through a haze she saw Conor lift up a red bloody baby. He was smiling and the terrible pain was gone. He wiped the baby and then placed it on her breast.

"Congratulations, you have a beautiful baby girl."

She raised her sweat-drenched head and looked at what had caused all that misery. She saw a perfectly formed face, surrounded by a wet halo of black hair. She gazed at the little face, the tiny forehead a mass of wrinkles. Then the mouth opened and there was a mighty yell. Sarah laughed and her eyes blurred and she couldn't see her for a second. Then Conor came back and he was looking at her with a peculiar expression she didn't even try to fathom. He leaned over and brushed something from her cheeks and she realised she had been crying.

"Thanks," she whispered to this man who was her doctor – this man she loved but couldn't love. "Thanks for staying with me."

He didn't say anything flippant, like "It was all in the day's work" or "That's what I'm here for". He just looked at her steadily.

Back in her room, bathed and wearing a fresh nightdress, Sarah was leaning over looking at her baby when the door opened and Alan came in. He was alone and the huge bunch of bright yellow daffodils almost hid the wheels of his chair. All thoughts of Conor McElroy faded as she looked at the blazing pride in his eyes – eyes that were duplicated in the miniature little girl who was sleeping so contentedly in her cot. He leaned over and kissed Sarah, and this time his long and tender kiss didn't bring back stabs of longing for other times.

"Sarah Beirne, so you did it."

"Yeah – there she is."

Her eyes filled with tears as she nodded towards the cot. Then he handed her the flowers and she could see the wheels and the chrome, and the foolish illusion that he was the old Alan was gone. When he wheeled around and looked at his child, she could see the wonder there. He reached out and touched the tiny cheek, and the little forehead cascaded into tiny velvet wrinkles at his touch.

"God, she's beautiful," he whispered. "So small I'm positively terrified. I adore her already. Tell me, was it awful?"

"Bloody awful," she laughed. "I never knew anything could be so awful. To die would have been such a relief."

"Was Conor with you?"

"Yeah, he was great." She didn't want to talk about Conor McElroy. "If it was a boy I was going to insist on calling him Alan," Sarah told him, "but now that all the know-all's were wrong, I've decided to call her Alannah. The name has all the letters of yours and I want to do that." Alan was leaning down over his daughter to get a closer view. His blue-black hair was identical to the tiny soft hairs that covered her head.

"Alannah. That's fine with me." Sarah thought she could see tears in his eyes but she wasn't sure. "I couldn't cope with another Sarah, anyway."

The door opened and her parents, Alan's parents and Patsy all came in together. There were gasps of admiration, hugs, kisses and tears, the women shameless in their joy. Patsy hugged Sarah and bent down and dropped a light kiss on Alan's forehead. *That's all,* she thought. *That's all it will ever be from now on.*

She told them Emma was coming the following weekend and had already insisted on being godmother as she was next in line. Patsy gently lifted the baby up and Alannah opened her eyes.

"God, Alan," she told him, "she's you. I didn't think it could be done – the same eyes, mouth, shape of her face. God, it's crazy, so it is."

She was about to hand the baby to Sarah when her mother said, "Give me a hold of my first grandchild." Eileen Dunne examined the baby closely and then handed her to Mary Beirne, the two grandfathers both laughing gruffly, saying that they were glad they were as old as they were – they wouldn't be back there for any money. When the baby was handed back to Sarah, she shyly slid down the shoulder of her nightdress and the baby's mouth found her breast and started to suck vigorously.

"Well, now," said Eileen Dunne, clearing her throat in embarrassment, "we'll go now, Sarah, and leave you to it. You must be exhausted."

As Sarah and Alan sat in a pool of happy contentment, they could clearly hear Sarah's mother telling someone as they walked down the corridor, "The next big event now will be Patsy's wedding."

CHAPTER TWENTY-TWO

THE NEXT FEW weeks were hectic. Rory's father told his son in no uncertain terms that he must see this girl who was to be his daughter-in-law, as soon as possible, so Rory made arrangements to take her to stay with his father for a long weekend.

Eileen, though putting a good face on everything, was still puzzled. When they were alone, she would lightly toss out questions. "When exactly, Patsy, did you decide on getting engaged to Rory?" She gave a little between-us-girls laugh and asked, "Was it love at first sight?" Patsy told her that it was.

Two evenings later Rory phoned asking her to come to Dublin. "Can't live without you now. Must see you – we'll plot and plan. You can stay with Hannah if you don't want a practice run."

She had told him no way – that she was a convent girl and if he was expecting a practice run he could forget it. He gave an exaggerated sigh, telling her he thought as much, but despite that she'd better come up anyway.

On the train to Dublin she sat thinking about her mother's questions and her father's silent acceptance of the situation. She had dropped over to Sarah's last evening to tell them she was off for a few days and her sister had plied her with more questions. "Why didn't you let us in on the act? And why the rush to get married, you're too young, for God's sake? Are you sure you know what you're at?" She had brightly assured Sarah that she knew what she was at. It was still months away, they'd all be well used to it before she got married.

Alan had been there with Alannah on his knee. As Sarah's questions flowed, his eyes met hers over the baby's head. She had been so impulsive and stupid to have told him. If she hadn't, he would think like the rest of the family, that she was so crazy in love with Rory O'Driscoll that she was willing to give up her job, her future plans and everything that was known and familiar to live with him in England.

Patsy sighed as she looked out the window and the flashing hedgerows, the primroses peeping out with their friendly little faces, the cows munching happily after the long confinement of winter in the bright hard sunshine of the late March day. She thought about Emma's reaction when she heard the news.

"Jesus, you're mad, you're wired to the moon. You should just come over to me. Maybe you're not being fair to this Rory guy."

As the train noisily sped on a little inner voice niggled on the same lines. *Why not face it? You're deceiving a decent guy. You're marrying him because you can't have who you want.* She tried to silence the torturous little voice by reading her paper. Charles Manson had been sentenced to life imprisonment for the murder of Sharon Tate. Patsy wondered what her last thoughts had been before she was savaged to death by Manson's Satanic gang. She shuddered.

The woman sitting opposite to her said, "I was just thinking that this train is quite chilly. You wouldn't mind but they know how to charge." She told Patsy that she was going to visit her daughter in Clontarf in Dublin who had to go into hospital for a repair job, a Manchester repair. They chatted away about their different trips until an announcement came over the public address system telling them they had arrived in Heuston Station. They smilingly said their goodbyes, then they were separated by the throng, and it was just as well as Patsy got a fit of giggles. When Rory saw her she was still grinning.

"It's a long story; it's about Manchester," she told him, bursting out laughing again.

"Mad," he muttered. "I'm marrying a mad one."

He tucked her arm into his, and as they walked to his car she told him the story of the woman on the train and her daughter's Manchester repair. He laughed heartily, and she thought it was good that they both had the same sense of humour.

As usual Hannah Tobin couldn't do enough. She raved about the engagement ring and fussed around laying the table even though Patsy protested that she wasn't that hungry and a cup of tea would do.

"Who ever heard of a girl who had travelled the length and breath of the country settling for a cup of tea?"

Hannah Tobin looked at Rory. "I can't believe it. Getting married to Eileen's girl." She looked at Patsy. "Ah, sure, tell me how is Sarah and the baby and her poor husband."

"Sarah is great, Hannah. The baby is beautiful – dark and dusky with eyes as dark as they come, the absolute spit of Alan. They're over the moon and Alannah's a pet and a great distraction."

"That's good. Sure, a baby in a house makes a home. Tell me, is there any hope for him at all?"

"No." Patsy said, vaguely aware that Rory had gone quiet. "Hannah, I must freshen up. Thanks for the spread. This fellow," she nodded at Rory, "wants to take me out on the town."

Hannah Tobin laughed. "Don't I know? Can't I see he's living to lay his hands on you?"

"Now none of that, Hannah," Rory laughed. "I know Kerry people think like that all the time, but remember, I'm a good boy from Tipperary."

As she cleared her table, Hannah was thinking how peculiar life could be at times, like the way this young man had come into their lives, knocking at the door to ask Patsy to go out with him. *Strange the way God works*, she thought as she watched them go off hand in hand.

The evening was chilly but it didn't deter the many walkers who were jauntily striding down the pier to get the sea air. Patsy and Rory were silent, but the warm clasp of Rory's hand was comforting as they leaned against the railing to watch the lit-up B & I boat pull out. Patsy waved back to the waving passengers, thinking, *If I could stop the world and step off now it would be fine. Not to have to think of the time I'll be on that same boat with Rory – married and going away from so much I love. Not to have to think of all the frenzied preparation before that happens. Not to have to think of marriage and all that it entails.*

As if he could read her mind, Rory broke into her thoughts. "We'll go to the pub and talk. We must plan, Patsy. We'll be on that blooming boat ourselves soon."

"Yeah, you're right. We plan tonight."

He laughed, and despite her protestations that everyone was looking, he took her face between his hands and kissed her hard on the mouth.

"We have to visit my father in Dromineer. He's anxious to see you. He's all right – you'll like him."

They were in the same pub with the oak-beamed ceiling, and she agreed that she must see his father.

"I'm looking forward to it. He must think you're terrible running off getting engaged to someone he has never met and hasn't a notion about."

"No, my father doesn't think like that. He's got a sense of proportion. He was heartbroken after my mother's death. Even though it was staring him in the face that she was going to die, he simply didn't believe it would really happen. After her death he nearly went mad. He's a real man's man but he loved her so much. No matter how much pressure he had in his life – the job and stuff – she'd make light of it and he'd listen. She had the ability to take all his burdens away." He looked at her with the familiar wry grin. "Will you do that for me? Will you take all my burdens away?"

"Yeah, I'm an expert at that. But it's very sad about your mother. Were you demented, too?"

"Yeah – I was pretty demented, too."

It was her turn then to be indifferent to the crowd as she leaned over and kissed him, telling herself that despite the extraordinary reason for her marriage to him she would do everything in her power to make him happy.

After the pub closed they walked up through the town, past the new apartment block where she had first met him. The place was in darkness now. She remembered the day she had stood there and listened to the irate little woman.

"Remember the day you came wandering into my life?" Rory asked.

"I was just thinking of the same thing."

He removed his hand from hers and walked out on to the road. "It was just here. You stood just here, and when I saw the look in those eyes I said to myself, 'Rory boy, that's the bird for you.'" He grabbed her hand and they tore across the road when the lights went green. On the other side he stopped and hauling her into a darkened doorway he took her into his arms and kissed her with a passion that surprised her.

"Jesus, Patsy, I love you." His voice was filled with urgency. "Look, I have a mate with a flat up the road. We were in college together. He told me I can use it any time." He was holding her so close now she could feel the heavy thud of his heart and the hard urgency of his body. She tried to pull away but the space in the doorway was small and cramped.

"No, Rory, no, it's only three months. My God, we're rushing it so much anyway – we'll wait, love – we'll wait." With her eyes a mere inch from his, he tilted her chin and kissed her again, and this time it wasn't so demanding.

"I'm sorry, Patsy. It's just that I'm afraid. I feel I have you and I haven't you."

Her heart missed a beat. "Now, that's a stupid thing to say. You know you have me – haven't I this ring to prove it?" She lifted her hand, spreading out her fingers, and displaying her ring like a child.

He smiled at her gesture. "Like my ring encircles your finger," he said touching his chest, "I want my body to encircle yours, and until then I won't be happy."

"Lord, for a guy from Tipp you're very poetic." Her voice

was teasing and light. That's the way she wanted it until they were married, she told herself as they walked away and turned up the road to Hannah Tobin's. Then she wasn't sure how it would go

Watching Alan with the baby in his arms, seeing his face suffused with love and pride, filled Sarah with contentment. The knot that had settled like a hard core of stone after his accident seemed to ease. The days went by: bright spring days when the breeze blew from the sea, when she wheeled her baby along the country roads, when she put away all thought of anything outside her tiny family circle. It was easy because she never knew that a small baby could be so demanding. Feeding, winding, changing, holding – admiring. Her baby daughter had lifted everyone's spirits. Her parents and Alan's parents visited often. Patsy also came and wanted to hold Alannah all the time. She told them she'd babysit any time if they wanted to go anywhere, or if Sarah wanted to go on her long walks, "To get your figure back – that sort of thing."

"Thanks very much," Sarah said sarcastically, "but I have the figure back – the breastfeeding has seen to that. Anyway, you have your wedding preparations. You should be getting excited at this stage." Patsy sat there with Alannah in her arms telling her there was loads of time. Sarah shook her head. She'd never really known what made her young sister tick.

Sarah welcomed the baby-filled days when she didn't let thoughts of Conor McElroy intrude. Sometimes before dropping off, when she was exhausted with the interminable hours it took the baby to breastfeed, he came back. She remembered how he had stayed by her side all the time before the birth of her child. She remembered his patience, his almost boyish excitement when the baby was just there. As she was lying there exhausted after he left the labour ward, she had heard one nurse whisper to the other, "What brought that on? I never saw him so involved before."

Her check-up was due in a week's time and she dreaded it so much that she told her mother she mightn't bother.

Her mother had been horrified. "You must have your check-up to see that everything is back in place. You'd be amazed all the things that could go wrong during childbirth. You could lose your next baby if there is a misplacement."

"Mam, there won't be a next baby." She sounded weary. "You must know that."

Her mother had tightened her lips, busying herself wiping an already immaculate worktop as she said, "There's a God over our heads and we don't know what his plans for us are."

Only last night, lying beside Alan in bed, almost afraid to breathe in case they'd wake the baby up, she had whispered, "I must go for a check-up next week. But I honestly don't think it's necessary – I might let it go."

"But you should go. These things are important."

"Like all the check-ups you've had in the Rehabilitation Hospital? You've ignored at least three letters to go up."

"I have Nancy Ryan. She's good enough for me."

She smiled and, nudging him in the ribs, whispered, "Sometimes I think you're in love with her. All that time you spend with her: physiotherapy, how are you?"

"You'd be amazed what we're up to," he whispered, "and I'm definitely in love with her."

He turned over and she put her arms around him. Clasped together they fell asleep. Just before she drifted off Sarah wondered, *If he wasn't disabled, would this be about the time that we would have resumed our lovemaking?*

Patsy thought it was the most enchanting place she had ever seen. Her father could rave till the cows came home about the view from their house, but the view from Rory's father's house was to her eyes lovelier by far. He lived in an old stone house almost on the shores of Lough Derg. It had originally been a three-roomed house, but he had converted the attic, adding a new bedroom and bathroom. The stone of the two dormer windows matched so well that the extension merged perfectly. The house was old and beamed with wooden floors and old-fashioned, black iron fireplaces with richly coloured tiled sides and a dresser laden with old dinnerware.

"It's fabulous," said Patsy, looking at the older man with the wry smile and the same grey-blue eyes as Rory's, although his were heavily lined. "You've great taste."

"I see my son has inherited my taste."

"Has he?"

"Of course. To pick a girl like you."

He was laughing as he sized her up. They all relaxed and there was an ease she wouldn't have thought possible at first meeting her perspective father-in-law. He showed her to her room, a cosy one with an angled ceiling and a dormer window with the curtains drawn back so that she could see the vastness of the shimmering lake.

"It's just like the sea, it's so big. I didn't think lakes were so huge." She turned back into the room to see the two of them looking at her, wondering what her reaction might be. "But it's so different, no waves, so peaceful and still."

"That's where you're wrong, my girl; it can turn nasty and dangerous with a devil's mood at times. I know I've been on it when 'twould almost caress you and then with little or no warning 'twould turn vicious and frighten the bejasus out of you." He smiled the Rory smile at her and she warmed to him so much she quietly promised herself that she'd do everything in her power to make his only son happy. "I don't often have female company here, but I remember when Rory's mother and I went visiting, she'd want to be on her own for a while to fix things, hang up a favourite dress, shove things into drawers, so we'll leave you to it for a bit. I'll be rustling up a bit of grub for seven. The bathroom is right across the landing."

They clattered down the wooden stairs and she could hear them laughing and joking. How close they were, father and son – both with the same interests, both not so long ago lev-elled by the loss of the woman in their lives. She unpacked her bag, glad she had brought one dress that might give a sense of occasion to the meal he was preparing. As she pulled off her jeans and sweater, she noticed that he had put a bunch of bright yellow daffodils on her dressing table. Looking at them she hoped she could bring some sort of joy or some new dimension into the rather lonely life of John O'Driscoll.

The following morning they woke to a balmy spring day. After breakfast Rory's father told them they were going fish-ing. Patsy, standing at the door looking at the vast blue expanse of unruffled water, wanted to know if the lake would be in a caressing mood today or would it go mad like the devil.

"Not to worry," John assured her. "Haven't I listened to the forecast? You'll be as safe as a bug in a rug."

John and Rory were like two friends that hadn't met for a long time. Sitting away from them in the boat, she could hear them talking about their work, Rory looking for advice about some planning laws and appeals, something she hardly understood. As they talked, the engine at times drowned their words. When the tree-lined shore almost faded out of sight, John cut the engine.

"Now, Patsy, down to the serious business of catching our dinner." He bated a line expertly and placed his strong brown hands over hers. He cast the line into the water, lift-ing and testing until he seemed satisfied. Handing it to her, he advised, "If you feel a tug you might have a fish, or you might have an old boot, but haul it up anyway and we'll see."

"I know a little about fishing," she grinned. "We fish in a place we call the channel."

He smiled Rory's smile again. "Bedad, maybe you can teach this know-all something."

"No, I can't," she shook her head. "I only fished a few times. I caught a salmon bass once, but it was a long time ago."

"Listen, Dad, to that old woman of eighteen." Rory's eyes were full of her and she could see love, a love that made her struggle to dismiss the memory of the time she had fished near the channel. It had been Alan who taught her how to fish. As she stood on the shingle in her bare feet, he too had put his hands over hers as he flung the line into the fast moving current. She was going to forget all that. She was going to forget it today, tomorrow and for ever.

After an hour's patient fishing she caught the ugliest fish she had ever seen and called, "Look, maybe I have the dinner." When they looked at the fish that was struggling wildly on her line, they laughed.

"No," Rory laughed, "you haven't the dinner. That's an ancient old pike. Better let him go."

He helped to unhook the fish and she watched as the fish darted gleefully away. Rory was somewhat disgruntled that he had caught nothing. Though John O'Driscoll took some speckled trout and had talked about catching the dinner, he had booked a table for three at the Lakeside Hotel in Killaloe.

"Wear your best bib and tucker," he told her. "I want to show you off."

Her dress, Kelly green with a full skirt and a simple round neck, looked good when she slipped it over her shoulders. She added a simple strand of pearls that her mother had given her for her eighteenth birthday. When she came down the stairs, the two men waiting for her both whistled appreciatively.

Over the delicious meal and wine, Rory told his father about their plans and the good job he had landed with an up-and-coming firm of architects in London.

"It's just for a spell. We'll be back. I'll make a bit of a killing and then come home and start up here."

"You'd better," his father said: "I want to see my grandchildren."

"I want you to see your grandchildren, too," Patsy said, smiling.

"Ditto," Rory answered, lifting his glass. His eyes were on Patsy's and she held his gaze, not looking away or blinking.

They stayed long after the other diners as Rory's father told her about his wife, Ann, and how he decided after she died to retire early and live near the lake.

"But isn't it very lonely?" she asked. "I mean, maybe you wouldn't miss her so much if you were surrounded by people."

"No, Patsy. I'm as content here as I'd ever be anywhere. I sort of feel at one with the greater things – the environment, the lake, the woods. Do you know that the sky and the lake can have a hundred colours in one day? I never knew things like that. I spent too much time at a drawing board. Her death taught me how much I had missed. It's sad that we couldn't have discovered this together." He cleared his throat and she looked at him through the smoke of his cigar. "But, sure, I'll have the grandchildren."

"You'll have the grandchildren," she said quietly.

Later, she found it hard to sleep, telling herself it was too much wine and rich food. She lay there listening to the gentle soothing sound of lapping water, so different from the rolling surf that at times kept her awake at home. She could hear the strong cry of some unfamiliar bird. She'd ask John what sort of bird it might be. She eventually drifted off into a restless sleep dominated by fitful, uneasy dreams.

She was on the shore near the channel at home. Across the way were the whispering sand hills of Tramore and she was fishing. The hands that helped her cast the line were young and smooth, and when she looked up it wasn't Rory's father but Alan. He stood there, dark and smiling, his hand guiding hers, making her cast out the line in a long arch. They were happy and the sun was shining, and when the line tugged he helped her haul it in. At the end of the line was the ugliest fish imaginable, with a mouth full of sharp needle-like teeth. She told him to throw it back into the sea.

She could see that his face was covered with drops of sea water with one of the drops running down over his mouth. She dropped the line and he took her in his arms and she kissed all the drops away. They stood there so close that the lines all tangled around their feet. They kissed passionately and the dream became all jumbled and dark. She wasn't sure if they had made love, but she felt so happy, so elated, she felt they had. Then the air was filled with the mournful cry. The bird was at it again.

She opened her eyes and reality flooded in. Alan Beirne could never make love to her, and even if he could he wouldn't because he didn't love her the way she loved him. She would have to use every ounce of strength she had to cure herself of this hopeless, sick addiction. Maybe she could be exorcised, like in the Bible, and the unwanted love cast out. That would be absolutely great.

CHAPTER TWENTY-THREE

DESPITE THE SLEEPLESS nights, the all-pervading weariness that drained her energy, Sarah continued with her diary.

I went for my appointment with Conor today, but when I saw him I knew I simply couldn't hop blithely on the couch and have him stare at the wall while he examined me. Different before the baby when it was so important that everything was right. Different when I was in agony having Alannah. But sitting there in the cold light of day and looking at him so calm and so professional with that half smile that seems to say, "I know so much about you", I simply couldn't.

I just said, "I'm here because I have an appointment. And Alan and my mother thought it would be better if I came. But I don't want to be examined – I just don't."

"That's entirely up to you. If you don't want me to examine you I won't."

Then I found myself sort of spluttering like an idiot that my mother told me that the examination was mostly to see if things were back in place and it didn't really matter because I wouldn't be having any more children. He laughed then, said I looked great and we'd take a chance on things being back in place. Then he examined Alannah and it was strange to see his fine strong hands handling her so tenderly and giving his verdict. "She has everything in place, too."

Then we stood there and he asked me about Alan and I told him things were pretty much the same and there was an uncomfortable silence and

I broke it telling him to drop over sometime. He told me he would and then it was over. I was walking down the steps and instead of feeling on top of the world that I hadn't had that awful internal examination, I felt peculiarly deflated. Now writing this, waiting to give the baby her last feed, I still feel deflated. Maybe having babies makes one feel very deflated, even a bit mad at times.

There was definitely a slight change, so almost not there that Alan was afraid to think about it at all. Sometimes as Nancy Ryan concentrated on the area where the breakage was, he wondered if she felt anything. He had read a lot about the healing power of imagery and positive thinking, but he wasn't a fool, and he knew all the positive thinking in the world couldn't knit sundered nerve endings. But imagery was a different thing. Imagery was merely imagining. So as he lay there listening to her talk of this and that, he sometimes let his imagination run riot. He imagined that her wonderful hands were bringing back life and that small tendrils of healthy cord were growing and reaching out and meeting other small tendrils and that when they linked together even for seconds he could feel the sensation. A sensation of something unlike the deadness of paralysis. A feeling that wasn't quite a feeling at all.

Of course, that was playing games. He was adept at the game now. He played it all the time that Nancy Ryan was there. He could even play it and hold a conversation with her, saying, "Yes, yes, the baby is getting bigger and cuter every day. Yes, it won't be any time to Patsy's wedding. Yes, we'll miss her dreadfully – Sarah's parents will be lost without her."

"But they have their beautiful grandchild," Nancy would say, giving him an extra slap. He would smile and agree with her.

This day she was quieter than usual, and he found himself

thinking of Patsy and her impending wedding. He liked Rory O'Driscoll – he believed he was decent sort and would make her happy. Lying there he recalled all the times he had spent with her – getting to know this child and her mad impulsive ways, so aware of her flaring impatience when things didn't go her way. He had watched her grow from a skinny gangling kid, all legs and arms, into a lovely young woman. He smiled remembering her frustration at her first crop of pimples when she told him she looked like a leper and what was more she felt like leper and was glad. She'd enjoy living in quarantine anyway.

When the awkward young puppy was turning into a streamlined young woman, their friendship had remained unchanged. Alan had had experience with youngsters in the throes of a passionate crush. As a young teacher he had seen it: the discomfort, the blushes, the positive agony of embarrassment when he himself was the subject of a young pupil's passing pubescent agony. He had never noticed it with Patsy. Of course, the passing of time had seen them spending less time together, what with her studies, her growing involvement with her peer group, his engagement and the lengthy preparations for his marriage to Sarah. Then the accident. And the life he was leading now. It was confusing and unreal. Maybe he should have questioned her about who this married man was – and if he was right, maybe he could have guided her through the minefield of her emotions.

"Well, what do you think?" Alan turned his head and met Nancy Ryan's eyes. For a moment he thought she had been reading his thoughts.

"Think about what?" he asked. He sat up and swung his legs on to the floor. With the ease of constant practice, he swung himself into the wheelchair.

"Think about what's happening to you," she told him, her button brown eyes holding his. "There's a change and you know it. There's something happening inside. It's not your imagination any more. Things aren't dead any more. There's some feeling – I know by the very air around you that you feel it, too."

He felt his heart thump against his ribs and fear assailed him. For a timeless second he wanted to pretend he hadn't heard her, but there was no denying that this capable woman who had given him so much, and now meant so much to him, had stumbled across the possibility of an improvement in his condition. She was there – sitting on his bed, her eyes boring into his.

"Christ, Nancy, I'm afraid to think, let alone put it into words. Maybe something is happening. I'm just a gobshite that teaches – I wouldn't know."

She looked at him and not for the first time she was filled with love for this young man who had been robbed of so much. She loved him like she would have loved a son if God has seen fit to give her one. She sighed; maybe He had His own plans and this might have been one of them.

"You see, me boy, we can't go on like this if something is happening. You should be back up there in Dublin with the specialists. They have the up-to-date knowledge, all the latest devises on hand to monitor your condition."

He could see how troubled she was, and he knew she was right, but he couldn't face it yet. He couldn't build up his hopes, Sarah's hopes, everyone's hopes and go to Dublin only to be told that it was all in his mind. He looked at Nancy who stood there her arms folded, her eyes troubled and her mouth in a grim line of determination.

"A little more time, Nancy – I want a little more time. That's all," he told her.

"All right so. But at least tell me exactly what you are feeling."

"Sometimes, Nancy, I imagine things. I imagine heat and warmth instead of deadness. As if a small, a very small change is happening. But," he looked at her and his dark eyes were filled with purpose, "I'm not going to hope and fill myself with dreams of a miracle. Believe me, those doctors up there were so emphatic – no function below the waist. And," he added bitterly, "there hasn't been. But say – say there is a change and something is happening, I think it's probably happening because of you. If you're good enough to give me more time – and it's a lot to ask – I'll be grateful. Until there is something more definite than a sensation or a feeling, we'll say nothing. Madness to build Sarah's hopes up or indeed anyone's hopes. What about it, Nancy? Will you go along with me in this?"

"Of course, I will." She sounded positively irritable. "And, of course, I'll give you more time, you bloody well know that. Haven't I all the time in the world? Come into the kitchen now and we'll get a cup of tea. I could do with it."

They had to wait in Euston Station for the lift Rory had organised. Patsy had never seen as many people scurrying around in all her life. They looked like marching ants, walking in columns, crossing and criss-crossing, going hell-bent somewhere. The station was like a town: shops and flower sellers, policemen and restaurants and people standing up drinking from paper cups hurriedly and frenziedly before dropping them in disposal bins and rejoining the columns of rushing people.

Rory scanned the crowd impatiently. "The shagger said he'd be here. I thought the Brits might have taught the fellow about punctuality."

Patsy laughed. "We're only here ten minutes and you're already like a frenzied hen. Eventually you'll be running around like these." She pointed to the scurrying crowd.

"You're right. We'll get a cup of coffee and wait. When we live here I'll get myself a black coat, a bowler hat, an umbrella and a briefcase – would you like that?"

She laughed so heartily that she caught the attention of one of the bowler-hatted brigade who looked at her sourly, maybe wondering what on earth anyone could be laughing at on a cold, showery April day.

Halfway through their coffee, Rory spotted his friend standing by the newspaper stand looking around. He saw them and waved, and soon introductions were over and they were on their way to Islington. Rory's friend, Matt Devlin, who had been working in England for over a year now and was still quite excited about the experience, rattled away about life in England.

"Money galore but you work for it," he told them. "The Brits don't want any frilly talk – just put your head down, work your butt off and they'll make it worthwhile."

He turned round and spoke to Patsy, but she hardly knew what he said because she was so terrified that he'd hit the red bus in front of them. He laughed, "Cars are cheap here, but not that cheap – so don't worry."

"I'm not worried about cars – I'm worried about us."

"Don't. I'll mind ye. Anyway," he continued, "you'll like it here. Good scene – good crowd – never a dull moment. You'll like Jane, my woman – she'll show you the ropes."

"Are you married?" Patsy asked eagerly.

"Hell, no. I wouldn't rush into that like you two, but I'm as good as. Jane and I live together."

"Oh." Patsy hoped she didn't sound surprised. She added, "That's nice," for good measure.

Matt, looking in the mirror, could see her discomfort. "I know it's not done at home, but it is here. Sometimes I feel light years from holy Ireland. Here you live with your woman, and if it's as good as you'd want, you get married. If after a year it isn't, you go your way – no sweat. It's sensible, but if my mother knew she'd die. Anyway, tell me when is the big day?"

As they drove through the traffic, Rory told him all about their plans. With the wedding and the honeymoon behind them, they should be settled in Islington in the rented flat by the twentieth of June. Matt whistled when he heard that that there were a hundred and fifty guests going to the wedding. He then turned his attention to Rory, giving Patsy a chance to sit back and relax. They seemed to be talking in millions of pounds as Matt described the place where Rory would work. He spoke of expansion schemes, new housing estates, the high-rise complexes and the new hotels mushrooming all over the place.

"The bubble could burst, Rory, but right now we're coining it. So for you and that gorgeous young wan, it's raking-in time." Patsy was secretly pleased at being described as gorgeous. No one had ever called her gorgeous before.

Any preconceived notion that Patsy might have had of a London flat dissipated when she saw it. On the third floor of a large red-bricked, bay-windowed house in Islington, it was spacious but shabby, showing years of wear and tear from past tenants. However, it was bright and had a view of the road from the living room window. It consisted of a huge bedroom, a bathroom and a sitting room with a small kitchenette off it in what had probably been a pantry. The furniture was Victorian and dreary but the light pouring in from the windows more than compensated. Matt, who had succeeded in getting the flat, was pleased at her reaction.

"They believed in size in those days – not like now. Look at the plaster work on the ceiling and the intricate rose around the light. Imagine, Rory, paying a fellow to do that today. Anyway, I'll let you two poke around for a bit. I'll meet you in the pub at the corner at five. It's called the King's Head." He grinned at them. "Don't get up to too much mischief when I'm gone."

They could hear him clattering down the stairs, and when he was gone they were both silent. Looking around at what was to be their first home, Patsy was thinking, *So this is it. This is where I'll start my marriage and this is where I'll start my family and this is where I'll forget. This is where I'll wait for Rory to come home to tell me all the news and this is where I'll tell him of the happenings of the day. This is where my new life begins.*

Rory was the first to break the silence. "Well, Patsy Dunne, what do you think?"

"I think it's great. Bright, big and clean, and when I add my touches. . ." She laughed. "I often wonder what touches are – do you know? I'll have to find out."

"I'll tell you all about touches if you like," he laughed.

"Oh, shut up. Men – the nuns were right, only interested in the one thing."

She went over the window and looked down on the busy scene in the street below. The traffic was moving in a constant stream and she thought the red buses were far more cheerful than the green ones at home. A woman with a pram on the pavement below was wearing a silk sari, soft and billowing. She must be Indian or Pakistani. Emma had told her England was packed to the gills with all sorts of nationalities. Then she remembered with a jolt that they were staying in Emma's flat that night, and once again she was sorry that she had blurted out to Emma the reason why she was getting married.

I'm an absolute cretin, she told herself, *blathering away in a self-indulgent romp when I should have been thinking of Rory.*

"What's down there that has you daydreaming?" He had come up behind her and circled her with his arms. She turned around and kissed him and her kiss was tender. He pushed her gently on to the windowsill and went down on his knees, his head resting on her breast. "I can hear your heartbeat." His words were muffled.

"Maybe I'm having a heart attack," she giggled.

He didn't catch her mood, but standing up and taking her in his arms again, he nodded toward the bedroom. "I don't suppose we could have a practice run in now?"

"God, Rory O'Driscoll, I came over to see the place and now before you put the ring on my finger you want to jump on top of me in a bed without a single sheet. Look," she pushed him away, "if there's not another word out of you about bedding me before the wedding, I promise you'll be exhausted doing it after we're married."

He burst out laughing. "I'll sure hold you to that. That's

the kind of exhaustion I can understand. In the mean time we'd better get out there and see what kind of a place we're in and see what kind of a country we have on our hands."

After lunch she phoned Emma at her office to tell her that they had arrived, that she loved the flat, and that they were meeting people at five-thirty in the pub.

"Jesus, it's great you're here," Emma yelled. "Look, stay put in that pub until I get there. Then after a few jars, we'll have a bite to eat and I'll take you back to my place. It's the sofa for Rory, I'm afraid. Will he mind? Or are ye – you know – over the jumps, so to say?"

"He'll love the sofa," Patsy told her, "and we're not! God, I don't know what's happening to the young people at all, at all." She mimicked their mother's accent and they both laughed.

Patsy hung up the phone, suddenly feeling good that she was going to meet Emma. Her sister was so airy-fairy that in all probability she had utterly forgotten what Patsy had told her before.

They got to the King's Head at five-thirty and found it already crowded, noisy and smoke filled. Patsy had some notion that English pubs would be quite sedate, with a few of the bowler-hatted brigade having just one before catching a train and maybe a few moustached, retired RAF types reminiscing about times past. Matt Devlin waved them in and they were introduced to so many people that it was all quite confusing. Some of the fellows were from Ireland, obviously lured to London by the prospect of money. As far as she could make out, most of the girls were English. They were surprisingly pleasant and friendly, dispelling the notion that Patsy had harboured about cool, English-rose types.

She was introduced to Jane, Matt Devlin's girl, who seemed very different from the others. She had brown shoulder-length hair and hazel eyes, and her face was completely devoid of any make-up. Patsy found herself sitting beside her and Jane said quietly that she hoped that Patsy liked the flat that Matt had got for them. She and Matt lived a mere two streets away. Patsy couldn't suppress the questions that tumbled out. She wanted to know if she was long there. Did she work and was she from the area and did she know everyone in the crowd that surrounded them? Jane smiled and Patsy could see how pretty she was, the smile lighting up her eyes, so that the green flecks in their depths became more obvious.

"I heard the Irish are very curious and I do have experience of it from Matt. I have lived here for over a year. I'm from Sussex originally. I work with a firm of lawyers and the office is not far from here. Matt and I have been together about a year now."

Patsy glanced at Matt, who was laughing uproariously at something Rory was telling him. There were at least three girls enthralled, and yet the handsome, gregarious Matt was obviously very much in love with this quiet-spoken, unadorned girl. Patsy wondered how a girl could live with a fellow. What was the word – cohabit. She knew no one at home who did such a thing, no one in Waterford – no one in Tramore. Certainly girls admitted that they had made love (gone the whole way as they put it) but to actually live with a fellow! Patsy wondered how you started on that road. Did you pack your case and bring your things and did you hang up your clothes and make the bed with the new sheets you had just bought? Because there wouldn't be wedding presents, so she presumed you had to buy them. Or would you go hand in hand with your man and buy them together? Did you make your first meal a celebratory one and then gravitate towards the bed? Did you wake up the next morning awash with guilt like you would in Ireland, or did you wake up thrilled you had so much courage?

A shout from the edge of the crowd dispelled her thoughts. Then there was another shout from the door, this time as Emma came prancing in accompanied by a girl with spiky blonde hair. There were more introductions and greetings, and Patsy thought that this London was a very friendly place, full with bright people who seemed to live life to the full. Certainly they didn't appear to be knotted up with worries and problems like she seemed to have been swamped with for years.

Emma called her flat a pad. She shared it with Nicola, a Londoner, who had offered to stay with a friend overnight so that Emma could put them up. Nicola was a commercial artist who had put her stamp on the place. The walls were covered with brightly coloured prints and a few unframed pieces of linen. When Emma saw Patsy looking at them, she told her they were batiks and very very expensive to buy.

"God, I thought they were dish towels." Patsy sounded contrite at her ignorance.

Rory grinned at Emma's outraged expression. "I thought they were dish towels too."

Emma lifted her brown eyes to the bottle green ceiling. "I can see I have to educate you two to the ways of the big city." Then she burst out laughing and flopped down on the bed as she told them that at first she had thought that they were the nearest things to dish towels she had ever seen.

They stayed up till three in the morning, sitting in the small sitting room and talking. Emma was thrilled that they would be living a mere two stations away on the circle line. It would be great to have someone normal to visit.

"Sometimes you get tired of the London way – pretending you're world weary, sophisticated to the teeth and have experienced the lot."

"Well, well," Patsy exclaimed, "you're getting honest in your old age. I didn't think there was an iota wrong with your London life."

"Oh, shut up," Emma grinned. "Can't I make a little remark without you starting an argument. God, Rory, I pity you taking that one on." She sat on a bean bag with her arms around her black clad legs and asked all about the wedding.

"How many guests, what's Rory's cousin like, the guy who's going to be the best man?"

"A rich farmer," Rory told her, "and if you could lay your hands on that fellow you won't want again."

Emma retorted that she was all for riches, but farming was out. "The thought of slithering around in cows' shit wouldn't appeal."

"But the smell of cows' shit is the smell of money," Rory assured her. "Farmers' mattresses are stuffed with tenners, did you know that?"

Patsy was happy they were getting on so well. Before they fell asleep in the unfamiliar cramped bedroom, Emma murmured, "Hey, I like your Rory. He's a real guy. If you change your mind before the wedding, I'll have him.

"Okay," Patsy sounded sleepy, "that's a deal."

CHAPTER TWENTY-FOUR

"I THINK IT strange that a young man can spend so much of his free time pottering around in that old place." James Gillen sunk behind his paper, didn't comment. "Did you hear what I said?" She leaned over and flicked the back of the page with her forefinger.

"What's that?" He put down the paper and looked at her over the rim of his glasses, making an effort to suppress his irritation.

She nodded towards the wall where the faint strains of music could be heard. "You'd imagine a young man would have more to do on his evening off."

"He's on call, or did you forget that a doctor's work is never done – except when you get old and beat like I am."

"You're not that old and beat," Kit Gillen sniffed. "As for on call, who would dare to get sick in a heatwave like this?"

"You'll see. We'll have a few cases of sunburn, mark my words."

Suddenly the music stopped and seconds later their door-bell rang. Kit got up and whispered, "It has to be Conor – he must have heard us."

It was. He was standing on the steps in jeans and a faded T-shirt with a towel rolled up under his arm. "Kit, could I have a word with the boss?"

"Of course. Come in." He followed her into the conservatory and for a brief moment she was reminded of all the times their sons wanted something from their father."

"James, I was wondering could you stand in for an hour. This sticky heat is killing. I'd love to nip over to Sauleen for a dip – full tide about now."

"Of course, boy. I was only telling that woman there that the worst that can happen today is sunburn. Off with you, I'll hold the fort. Sauleen at full tide – I wouldn't mind it myself. Nothing like a swim in the oyster bed."

Conor parked his car at the top of the lane that led down to the beach. As he walked down the dry rutted path, there wasn't a breath of wind. An odd blackberry here and there reminded him that it was early August and that the long hot summer was drawing to a close. Turning the corner he was surprised to see that the golden beach was deserted, although he thought he saw someone out in the oyster bed. He could see from where he stood in the sand dunes that whoever it was was a strong swimmer, making excellent headway against the incoming tide. He tore off his clothes, thinking that the solitary swimmer wouldn't like the intrusion. The hard golden sand had retained the heat of the day but the straggling rivulets brought relief. Diving in he swam across the channel towards the oyster bed. The other swimmer reached the end where the oyster bed merged with the channel and where the tidal drag was considerable, then turned back and came towards him with a leisurely back stroke. He could make out the outline now and could plainly see that it was a woman. Shaking the sea water from his eyes, he saw that it was Sarah Beirne.

"Hi," he shouted. "What are you doing here at this time?"

"Hi," she answered, thrashing the water and smiling that brief familiar smile. She had no bathing cap on and her blond hair, now darkened with the water, was tied with a bit of twine. She answered his glance; "I found it as I ran across the beach, thought it would do the trick. I come here all the time. I was raised not too far from here – remember?"

Looking at her in the black swimsuit as she gently treaded water a mere few feet away, he cursed the notion that had brought him here.

"Look, as you are here," she said, "let's have a race. See those old wooden poles sticking out of the water at the far end of the bed? We call that the wreck. Over and back."

She was away in a flash, thrashing the water with a powerful crawl. Taking after her, he realised that he would have his work cut out to beat her. With his strong overarm he made it to the wooden poles merely seconds before her. Then turning back they were neck and neck, and neither was sure who got to the winning spot.

"I did," he shouted, "by a fifth of a second."

"Fifth of a second – what's that? I should have handicapped you. I was obviously tired, in the water an hour before you."

"True," he nodded, amazed at her mood, at the animation in her face – a face that was now slightly showing the cold. "We'd better go in or you'll catch a chill."

"Yeah, I suppose so." They waded in together and once again was sorry for the whim that had brought him to this spot. Her slim figure was never more desirable. The slinky swimsuit outlined her breasts, her narrow waist showing her shapely legs to perfection. Striding beside him she tugged at the bit of string and grimaced as she failed to untie the knot.

"Here, let me." He stood behind her, and as he started to undo the knot he was overcome with the such desire and such longing he knew she would notice. "I'm sorry, I can't do it."

"It's all right." Her tone was full of understanding as she broke into a run up to the dunes where her clothes were. A little later when he had dressed, he walked down and joined her. She was sitting on her towel dressed in shorts, a sleeveless blouse and canvas runners. Despite the fact that her face was devoid of make-up, her hair wet, her legs covered with fine sand, she had never seemed lovelier. Looking at her, he remembered the same body writhing in the pain of childbirth. He felt he knew her like few men would ever know their wives. To dispel his rising desire he plucked out a packet of cigarettes from his pocket and held out the packet, although he was aware that she didn't smoke. She surprised him by accepting one. He bent over and shielded the flame from a welcome small breeze. She put the cigarette between her lips and inhaled deeply, her blue eyes narrowed in concentration.

He laughed. "Don't kill yourself. I don't want to inflate a collapsed lung before I go."

She laughed then, and for a while it was normal: two swimmers who had met and who had raced and talked on a glorious evening toward the end of summer.

"How is Alan and how is my girl, Alannah?"

"Alannah is great, getting bigger every day. And the smiles and the laughs – she's made such a big difference. Alan is good – you know." She looked at him and he could see the questioning in her eyes. "You know," she repeated, "for three hours almost every day he still works out with Nancy. Conor, tell me, is it all a colossal waste of time? It is, isn't it? Nothing has changed. He tells me the physio and all the exercises are to prevent muscle wastage, and it has, he looks great."

Conor was silent as he looked towards the sand hills. In the fading light they looked almost blue and misty. Way up the long stretch of beach across the channel he could see the lights of Tramore twinkling and flashing as they came on one by one.

"He should go up and be assessed again." He looked at her. "There was something a bit inconclusive about his condition. Sometimes physio and exercises, particularly from someone like Nancy Ryan, can do immense good. I've heard of cases where neurological tissue can be regenerated to some extent. That only happens where the break in the spinal cord isn't total – where there is small nerve activity. But it is rare. I still think Alan should have an assessment and a total check-up."

She nodded in agreement, now very aware of his nearness in the empty silent world of sea, sand dunes and the great canopy of the fading summer sky. A silence hung between them which neither made an effort to break. Eventually she was the first to make a move. She stubbed out the half-smoked cigarette and stood up.

"I must go. Alan will be wondering."

Conor stood up and seemed to tower over her. Their eyes met.

"Sarah – I didn't want this. But now that we're here, tell me what to do?"

Suddenly she was in his arms and they clung to each other with a tearing hunger and an unstoppable passion. Then they were lying in the sand dunes and their hammering hearts made far more noise than the soaring, screeching gulls. His kisses covered her face, her neck, her whole body, filling her with such desire and need that they couldn't wait. Their union was rushed and frenzied, and yet she knew that if the dark, dangerous channel had overflowed and swamped the land it wouldn't have stopped their deep, demanding, fulfilling lovemaking. After it was over, they lay together and Conor was the first to break the silence.

"Don't feel too bad," he told her softly. She could hear the County Meath inflection in his accent. "It happened. It was inevitable." He drew her close as if to shield her from the small fitful breeze that had sprung up. "Did I ever tell you I play games? The day you were in labour, I pretended you were my wife and that the baby was mine. Imagine a cynical, grown-up medical man doing that."

She reached up and gently brushed the sand from his cheek, from his eyelashes. "You knew, didn't you?"

"Knew what." He held her gaze steadily but she didn't falter.

"That I wanted you desperately." He could hear the slight tremor in her voice. "But in the physical sense, only in the physical sense," she repeated as if repeating it would ensure that it was true.

"Only in the physical sense?"

"Please don't question me. You know too much already." She shook her head. Her hair had dried and she looked so familiar and so desirable that he wanted to take her again. He reached out and pulled her close. She shook her head and the fine sand went into her eyes, blinding her temporarily. She rubbed them impatiently, moving away from the circle of his arms.

"Conor, I would prefer to die." She got down on her knees and sitting on her heels started making little circles in the sand. He watched as she made them bigger and bigger. "Or maybe worse still – burn in hell for all eternity than Alan should ever ever find out what happened here tonight." She looked up and he couldn't see what was in her eyes because of the failing light. "I know what we've done was a desperate wrong and I should feel tainted and dirty, but I don't – I don't." Her voice broke, and he reached out, took her in his arms again. "I don't because if I said I did, I'd feel worse than a loose woman, I'd feel a hypocrite." She thought she heard him laugh then but wasn't sure. Looking up she peered into the twilight and could see the beach was still deserted. "I'll go first, just in case we meet anyone. The place is full of spies, did you know that?" She sounded like a child.

"No, I don't; I only know the one thing."

"What's that?" She was gathering up her towel and swim-suit as if she were indifferent to the answer.

"That I love you. I loved you from the very beginning. Do you know that?"

She leaned back on her heels, her clear blue eyes holding his. "I know, and it's wrong."

"I know that, too, but will I see you again?"

"You will. You know you will."

"You were a long time." Alan was sitting at the kitchen table working on a revised timetable for the school which would be opening in a few days' time.

"I was. It was wonderful – the water was so warm you could stay in it for ever. Tell me, did she wake up?"

"Yes, she kicked up a shindy. I think she's starting to teethe. I changed her and consoled her until she fell asleep. Eventually I got her back in her cot."

244

Looking at him sitting there, the light from the lamp highlighting his black hair which was now clearly touched with silver, Sarah was overpowered with guilt. It came and swamped her, filling her with self-disgust. It would have helped if he had savaged her about how long she had been; about the fact that he in his disabled state had had to take up his baby daughter and change her and be with her. It would have been easier if he had plainly shown naked envy that she was out and about, swimming in his favourite spot while he was tied to a bloody wheelchair.

Once over the long hot summer she had thoughtlessly suggested that they go to the beach. He had reminded her that his wheels wouldn't go too far in the soft sand. He had rather sarcastically pointed out that she mightn't like carrying a fairly heavy man. It hadn't been a pleasant exchange, but it had been normal under the circumstances. She would have liked some of the same anger now, but since Alannah's birth he had shown little bitterness. He adored the child and she was so happy and content to be with him. When he came in she gurgled and screamed with pure joy. When he put her on his knee she just sat there, her dark eyes glowing with contentment. He never seemed to mind when she woke up during the small hours to be fed, changed and comforted. He would swing out of the bed into his wheelchair, speed to the kitchen to feed her, burp her, change her with extraordinary efficiency, despite Sarah's protests that she would do it, pointing out that he had to be up for school.

> The tide was full at eight this evening, so after tea I told Alan I would like a swim. He didn't object. He rarely objects to anything I suggest lately and I wonder is this a good thing or a bad thing. He has changed a bit over the summer. Around the time Patsy got married and left. I think he misses her – I know I miss her desperately. Oh God, why am I writing all this? Is it to

keep me from putting down in this page what I must put down? A bit like, if you don't think about a problem, it might go away. Well, this problem I have won't go away. I went for the swim. It was strange to see the place so deserted. I thought that there might be a few like myself but no – not a soul. Then again the schools are opening soon and everyone is busy getting the kids back. Also farmers are harvesting and busy and the fishermen are on the lobsters over in Dunmore so maybe that explained it. See, I'm still writing away about stupid things because I obviously don't want to come to the point.

It was glorious in the oyster bed. Warm and yet refreshing and I swam and swam up and over and I felt I was the only person left in the whole world. Then Conor came and I couldn't believe it. The only person in the said whole world I wouldn't want. I wouldn't want him because I would want him. Why he picked my beach, my oyster bed, my part of the world when he had Tramore or the Guillomene or Newtown Cove at his front door. He swam out and we talked and we raced and wallowed in the coolness. Then we came in and we dressed and chatted and then we made love. I've written it fast to get it over with. I feel terrible – terrible, and yet there was nothing – nothing – nothing we could have done to prevent it. It was like something that was meant to happen. To stop it would have been like stopping the world turning on its axles, or stopping the incoming tide. Sitting here in this empty silent kitchen, I can't describe how bad I feel and yet – yet so strangely alive.

CHAPTER TWENTY-FIVE

FOR AT LEAST the first two months, Patsy felt as if her domicile in London were just a temporary thing. They would be home soon and they would regale everyone about London, like one would do after a holiday. But it wasn't like that; the days became weeks and the weeks became months and realisation came that this was where she lived now. The long heatwave ended, and during her many walks around Islington she saw that the trees were shedding their leaves and that it was now autumn.

She had only learned yesterday that she was six weeks pregnant. Rory had been so excited that he had opened a bottle of champagne the evening before and this very morning had insisted on giving her breakfast in bed. She had told him she really didn't need her breakfast in bed, she wasn't an invalid. As a matter of fact she had never felt better in her life. She hadn't a symptom in the world, not a pain or an ache, or nausea, or anything. She wouldn't have believed she was pregnant except that the test was positive. He had held her close and told her that he knew the minute he saw her that she was the most fertile bit of stuff he could find. That was the only reason he had married her. She had thrown him off the bed and they had tussled and fought like two children until he had sobered, saying that the horse-playing was over – that it mightn't be good for her. She told him, "Nonsense," that she wasn't going to change her life one little bit.

Glancing at her watch she saw that it was only three-thirty. She'd had another hour to kill before going back to the flat to prepare dinner. She decided she'd go the long way back and do a bit of shopping on the way. She passed the People's Park and then the long and never-ending avenue of red-bricked, bay-windowed houses known as Nelson's Place. There was a Catholic church at the corner and on a whim she went in. Inside it was dark and cool, with soaring ceilings, dark wooden seats and over the altar a large stained-glass window depicting Christ's ascension into heaven. She knelt at the back of the church and covering her face with her hands she tried to pray. The words of the Hail Mary slipped through her mind as she said the rosary – mantra-like, repetitive and relaxing. When she sat up in the pew she saw that there were only two other people there, both old, probably killing a few hours of their days by visiting the church. Suddenly feeling tired, even sleepy, she decided she'd do the same – just sit.

Relaxing in a quiet place with the muffled sound of traffic outside, the memories flooded back of the wedding and the excitement and hilarity of the day. Everyone, even her old school friends, told her she looked amazing, and when she got glimpses of herself in glass doors or hotel mirrors, she thought she looked fairly all right herself. It was a noisy, happy day, with Rory's father and his aunts looking so pleased that Patsy had told Rory during one of the many dances, "I think your aunts think I'll do."

"Oh, you'll do me all right," he had joked. She had trodden on his toe and he had yelped with exaggerated pain, and everyone had looked over smiling at the happy couple. Her parents and John O'Driscoll seemed to get on famously. Emma was a lovely bridesmaid, and Rory's friend, Tony, had eyes only for her. It was when her father hugged her sheepishly before they went away that she had tears. She had glimpsed Alan over her father's shoulder, and she was got so upset she didn't know if the tears were for him or because she was leaving everybody she knew and loved. When she came to Alan, she bent down in her flimsy dress and hugged him. His lips brushed her cheek and she felt then that it was all over. Any physical contact with this man from now on would be merely brotherly. She was married now and hopefully her obsession would end.

The first night was even fun. She had been apprehensive

that she would be nervous, or a frigid stick, or so inexperienced and green that she would be a disaster. It was none of these things. When it was over Rory held her and told her he loved her and she held him and told him she loved him, too.

Afterwards it got better. She filled her days with walks, with housework and with fixing the furniture this way and that way, adding the little touches she had earlier derided to make the unhomely place a little more welcoming. They already had many new friends, most of whom were associates of Rory's who often dropped in for a chat or a beer. She met their girlfriends at weekends and found them very pleasant, very different from her own friends back home, if anything too glamourous. She was beginning to understand how Emma had been carried away with the London scene. She was more drawn to Jane Campion, Matt Devlin's girlfriend, than to any of the others. The four of them had become quite close. Jane was different. There was something about her that seemed genuine and caring in this new world Patsy was learning to live with.

And now she was pregnant. She was glad she was pregnant. Marriage and children had been part of her plan; after all, she had told John O'Driscoll that he would have loads of grandchildren. She would get Rory to write to him soon and she would add a little bit and tell him all about the place and about the Indian couple who lived in the flat below them. The young wife and the baby girl had matching jewels in their noses. She would tell him how Rory joked that he would get her a nose emerald for Christmas and a tiny one for the baby if it was a girl. Maybe little titbits of news like that were the sort of things you missed when you lost your life's partner.

Glancing at her watch she saw that it was four o'clock, time to get back and prepare the dinner. When she stepped out into the golden autumn sunshine, the first person she encountered was a dark-haired young man bowling along in a wheelchair. They smiled briefly at each other, and as she turned round the corner she closed her eyes, praying that the brief encounter wouldn't unleash memories and longings that she fought every day to keep at bay.

"You're having a baby! That's brilliant – brilliant." Emma's voice was full of enthusiasm and excitement. "To think that my two sisters got there before me – even my kid sister. Did you tell the folks? They'll be thrilled, thrilled. Imagine a little kid with an English accent playing on Sauleen beach. Whew, that'll be something. Anyway," Emma said, dropping her voice, "I'll bet that all this excitement has completely put your foolish nonsense out of your mind. Bet I'm right?"

"You're right," Patsy laughed, crossing the fingers of her left hand as she always did when she told lies. "And I haven't told the folks yet. I'm writing tomorrow and I'll drop a line to Sarah and Rory's father. I think he's looking forward to this."

"It's great, Patsy, really." Emma dropped the gushing London pose and sounded more like the old Emma. "Tell Rory it's champagne all round in the pub next Saturday – he can forget his bitter."

She was gone and Patsy slowly put the phone back into the receiver. She looked around the shabby hall at the way the paper was loose at the seams on one side and at the worn pattern on the stair carpet. When she put her hand on the banister, there was a slight feeling of stickiness. At that moment it didn't come across as the perfect place to bring a baby up. But Rory had said, "This is merely the first rung. By the time we get to the top, we'll be flying, girl."

Walking up the stairs she smiled. Only last evening Rory looked at her, still finding it hard to absorb that she was pregnant so soon.

"Jaysus, Patsy," he shook his head in wonder, "I didn't think it would be that easy." He had put his arms around her waist then and swung her around in a wide circle. Her new fashionable clogs had fallen off with a considerable clatter.

"Put me down," she had insisted, "or the people below will think that the mad Irish are at it again."

The golden days of autumn had come to an end and today was a day of wind and rain. Looking at the leaves swirling down from the trees, Patsy realised that winter was a mere few weeks away. Sitting on the windowsill with her legs drawn up and her hands clasped around her knees, Patsy wondered what winter would be like in this city. Rory had told her there would be parties and dinner dances as the company had a high profile when it came to the social life of the staff.

"Hooleys galore," he had told her, "but there'll be no one singing 'The Patriot Game' or 'Danny Boy'."

"I'll give them 'Puppet On A String' to keep them happy, so."

"I don't give a damn if the Brits were happy or not," he declared. "I am and that's all that counts."

Looking at the swirling dance of the falling leaves, Patsy was glad Rory was happy. Was she happy? Was she content? When thoughts like that came into her head she ran them. She was adept at doing that. *Letters,* she thought, *I'll write all the letters today, to Mam and Dad, to Sarah and Alan.* The inner voice whispered, *That's really who you want to write to; you can't wait to get the pen in your hand.* She shook her head slightly, informing the inner whisper, "I'll write to Rory's father, too." She grinned when she heard her own voice. She was probably going a bit mad. Maybe that's what England and being on your own for hours on end did to you.

> Dear Mam and Dad,
>
> It's all wind and rain today – reminds me a bit of home. So, like a good girl I decided I'd write and tell you all the news. The flat is very big, if anything too big. It's a great Georgian house divided into flats. There's an Indian couple below

us and a nice woman about your age, Mam, above us. She goes out to work every day so we see little or nothing of her. Rory is flying in the job and keeps telling me it's the start of big things.

Now – now wait for it – wait for it – you're both going to be grandparents again. Now I know exactly what you're going to think: "Young impulsive Patsy going to have a baby of her own. She won't have a notion what to do with it. She'll probably leave it out in the rain." I don't think I'll be that bad and I presume knowledge comes with the package. Anyway, Rory is over the moon and I'm very happy about it. It won't be for ages – I should have been real cute and kept it under my hat for another few months, but I was never much good at keeping secrets. I think I'm two and a half months or thereabouts. So there – that's my big news.

I hope you're not too lonely, Mam – and I was delighted to hear that you have a little Yorkie pup. Emma told me that you were calling him Benjie after Benjie in the Riordans. It's great that she can make the odd sneaky phone call from her office and keep up to date. How is Sarah? How is that divine little scrap Alannah? How is Alan? The same I suppose. I'll finish now because I have heaps more letters to write. You put pen to paper and tell me EVERYTHING because I'm sorta bored during the days when Rory is working. The weekends are great though. I've met a lot of new people.

Love and best wishes,
Patsy

She found it hard writing to Sarah. The words got stuck and wouldn't flow as they would normally. She should be all excited, describing London, the flat, the way they met

Emma and her friends most weekends. She should search her mind for funny little stories about her new life, and then tell them she was pregnant. But it wasn't easy because of Alan. Sometimes just before falling asleep, her mind was full of him. Lying with her arms around Rory, listening to his steady breathing, Alan came back. She didn't think it wrong and sinful to do it then; someone had told her that the hazy, half-awake dreams before full sleep claimed you were due to lack of oxygen and that you were powerless to prevent what went through your mind.

She brought him back before his accident when he was physically perfect and strong and fun to be with. She brought him back when he was in the wheelchair and those dark eyes were full of shadows and yet his mouth was smiling as he tried to make the best of things. She brought him back when she impulsively kissed him the night she had sat at his feet, reading the poem to him. She brought back the admiration in his eyes the evening she had tried on the black dress. She knew all that remembering was wrong because of Rory and his love for her, but she only did it in the grey zone before sleep. She shook herself and decided that she'd better write the bloody letter.

She did, describing in colourful detail her new life, telling them about Rory's job, their neighbours and their new friends. She told them about Matt Devlin who lived with Jane Campion and hadn't a notion of getting married and there wasn't a worry on them that they were living in sin. Then she told them she was pregnant and that she'd be trundling a bump over at Christmas.

> Give my love to Alannah and I want a letter soon. The winter is closing in and a gale force ten is blowing, bringing back memories of the channel when it turns into a mad frenzy and our lovely oyster bed into a choppy heaving lake. God, amn't I dramatic with the descriptions? Here in England

they are so understated and unimaginative they'd simply say "a stiff one blowing then".

She wrote to Rory's father then, knowing that her news would give him enormous pleasure. She added the sort of titbits she thought he might like to read:

> So when we go home to Ireland you'll can show your grandchild how to fish in that great big lake outside your door. You'll show him what to take home and what to throw back. I always thought a fish was a fish. I never knew you had to be selective.

One week later the three replies came, all on the same day. When Patsy saw the white envelopes in stark contrast to the shabby carpet in the hall, she decided to forego her trip to the shop and go back to bed to read them. She felt cold and weak after a particularly bad bout of retching that morning, so bad in fact that Rory had wanted to stay at home. She told him not to be so silly.

She read the letter from Sarah first.

> Dear Patsy,
>
> It was great to hear from you. And it's absolutely great about the baby. As they say in these parts, you didn't lose much time. Rory must be thrilled. I know Mam and Dad are very happy for you – in fact Mam is over the moon – she can't wait to have a flock of grandchildren.
>
> Alannah is great. She's seven months now and has two teeth. She can sit up on her own and look around like an old curious woman. Alan adores her – and she adores him. When he comes in and she hears the whirr of his chair in the hall she goes berserk with happiness. Isn't it well I had her? Alan is well, very well, but things are much the same. Sometimes there's a terrible restlessness about him and I wish he'd freak out more and

shout and rant to the high heavens or scream a few fucks out the back door or something. God, Patsy, if Mam saw this letter she'd say that Sarah one is gone to the dogs. Maybe I am.

Anyway, the school numbers are up and that keeps Alan very busy, so that's a good thing. Incidentally, he told me to tell you that – now I must get it right – that he's happier than you'll ever know about the baby. He really means it. After we heard your news he kept saying, "Imagine Patsy with a baby. Incredible." I imagine Alan thought you'd stay a bit of a madcap for longer.

Conor McElroy comes over now and then. It's nice having him. Alan's parents come out a bit too. They just love to see the baby – I suppose they would. It makes up someway for what happened to Alan. By the way, tell Emma to write. Anything to cause a distraction in my life – and again, congrats – it's great.

Love, Sarah

P.S. Alan sends his love.

She lay there in the warmth of the wide old-fashioned mahogany bed and reread it. Her eyes devoured the P.S., and her knowledge that it was the usual routine scrawl at the end of the letter didn't take from the pleasure the words gave her. She reread his reaction to her news. "Happier than you'll ever know about the baby." *Yes*, she thought, *I can understand that he's happy. At least that troublesome young sister-in-law has a lot on her mind at last – no longer a head filled with fanciful notions. But Alan*, something inside cried, *they were more than that – I knew they were more than that. If they were only fanciful notions they would have gone away, lost in Rory's love for me – lost in the fact I'm going to have his child. But they're not, they're not, and I've tried – I've tried. God knows, I've gone to some lengths to bloody well rout you out of my mind.*

Dearest Patsy,

Dad and I were delighted to get your most welcome letter. We're thrilled with your wonderful news. I'm sure that you and Rory are thrilled also. Nothing cements a marriage like a little baby. Now take care of yourself – don't be lifting anything heavy. Get Rory to do all that sort of thing. It's very easy to lose a first baby, so be careful. You know what a tomboy you were, always jumping and tearing around the place. And remember Sarah nearly lost that baby – imagine what a heartbreak that would have been.

Well, let me think, have I any news? Dad and I are great. The house is so lonely since you all went, I can't believe it. Sometimes I think I will wake up and hear you all fighting about the things you used fight over. I don't know what I'd do if I hadn't Alannah. That baby gets more beautiful every day. She's so like her dad, so dark for such a young baby it's astonishing. Certainly no trace of a Dunne anywhere.

In a few weeks we'll all be looking forward to Christmas and the joy of having you, Emma and Rory home. I haven't much more news really. I met Doctor James yesterday and I told him your news – he simply couldn't believe it. He said it seemed only a couple of years since he delivered you. That's what happens when you get old – time flies. Doctor Conor McElroy visits Sarah and Alan a lot. It's great for Alan to have such a friend. And they tell me – the ladies in the ICA – that he's a wonderful doctor. They say he's never wrong in his diagnosis. Anyway, I won't ever leave Doctor James, but it's good that Sarah and Alan have befriended a brilliant young doctor.

Tell Emma to behave herself, and once again

be careful at least for the first four months. I'll start my novena to Saint Anne for you. Did you know that she's the patron saint of mothers? She always keeps an eye on expectant mothers and sees that everything goes well. Dad sends his love. By the way Benjie is a little dote. He follows me everywhere and I'm glad I got him.

God bless,
Love, Mam

Before her mother had posted the letter, her dad had decided to add a bit: "Patsy, congratulations to you and Rory. Mind yourself and don't get too carried away with the British way of life. Ireland is a better place for rearing children. Love, Dad."

Dear Patsy,

What great news to a retired fellow. When I got your letter I went to the pub and had a few balls of malt to celebrate the event. Tell that son of mine that it was good he lost no time. As for handing on my expertise on the art of angling, it will be a pleasure – an untold pleasure. If Rory's mother were alive she would have been over the moon with joy, but we must put these thoughts aside and be glad we have what we have. I would indeed love to see you around the Christmas – it can be lonely listening to the wind. Mind now – take care and tell Rory that I hope as the popular ballad goes that those London streets are indeed paved with gold.

Your overjoyed father-in-law,
John

"We must put these thought aside and be glad we have what we have." *Right,* she thought, *good advice.* Jumping out of the bed she felt the nausea rise like a bilious river and flew across the room, barely making the bathroom. As she knelt on the cold floor resting a forehead now covered with icy sweat on the toilet seat, she vowed for the umpteenth time that from now on she would do just that – be glad for what she had.

CHAPTER TWENTY-SIX

WHEN SARAH HAD worked in the bank before she was married, she used to hear whispers every day of people leading double lives, people who cheated on their married partners, people who had long-term affairs in a sort of sort of nudge-nudge, wink-wink world that sometimes left her astonished. She never thought for one fleeting second she would ever fall into that shadowy category herself. She was so much in love with Alan then that she couldn't comprehend such situations, and now it was happening to her.

Looking out the window at the familiar coastal fog that had clung tenaciously for days, guilt surrounded her like fog, cloying and choking. If Alannah weren't asleep, she would put her in her pram and tear down the country roads to try and escape it. But she couldn't escape any more than she could escape from her aching need for him.

They had managed to meet with subterfuge, lies and secrecy at least once a week since that fateful August evening. The approaching winter was a godsend. Alan's continuing acceptance of her need for long walks was another godsend. She always went down the lanes towards the sea, never up past the cottages or the schoolhouse, in case she'd meet someone. Conor was so careful he took to cruising down the steep lane with the engine of his car switched off until he reached the small clearing behind the tall trees.

The second time they made love was on a warm September night. They had driven down the long narrow lane above the dunes, so remote and little used that she could hear the bramble bushes scraping his car. When they ran down, hand in hand to the soft sand, their immediate need for each other was so frenzied and passionate that their union ended far too soon. Afterwards he had held her and apologised, saying that she was driving him so mad he was like a hungry adolescent. She had told him not to worry, that he was driving her mad, too.

The next time they met he told her they had to take precautions. He suggested the contraceptive pill. In fact he had brought the packet with him. Now, looking out the window at the fog, she remembered his advice: "Darling, you must take these – the instructions are inside. If there's anything you want to know, or are worried about, just ask your doctor. You know he loves you and you have him in the palm of your hand."

She had taken the packet hesitantly and then slipped it into her pocket. "This swallowing of a pill makes our affair sort of cold and calculated." Her gaze was unflinching and he could see she was troubled. "Men take no responsibility, just have the woman on the pill, and when the relationship dies, move on, give the next woman the pill and no repercussions."

"Christ, Sarah, how can you say such a thing? How?" He took her in his arms and kissed her roughly before going on. "It's because I love and care for you so much that we must take these precautions. In your case if, God forbid, anything happened, we would be destroyed because of Alan's situation. We were lucky to get away with it so far."

She could see the genuine hurt in his eyes, so she told him she was sorry. He didn't have to remind her she couldn't have any more babies – not for Alan and not for him. In the days that followed she read the instructions and swallowed the pill.

Sarah tried to analyse her feeling for Conor McElroy. Was her feeling more than sexual need and desire? Was she falling in love with this man who had come into her life at the most crucial time imaginable? Today looking out at the fog, she thought about the very first time she had seen him, the time she went into his office wondering if she was pregnant. The day up in the Dublin hospital when she met him in the corridor and he rushed her to the litter bin where she had gotten so sick. The routine visits before Alannah was born. The long terrible hours of her labour when he hadn't left her aide. His boyish jubilation when he hauled the baby out and handed it to her. The undesired conclusion was clear: Conor McElroy now played a bigger part in her life than Alan.

Suddenly Alannah started to cry a demanding loud cry as if something had interrupted her baby dreams. Sarah turned away from the fog-shrouded window, glad of the disruption that shattered the eerie silence and chased away her unthinkable idea of the importance of this illicit relationship.

Nancy Ryan, indifferent to the fog, felt that her old Morris Minor could make its own way to Alan's house. With her lips pursed, she drove along the country roads, wondering whether she should take Doctor James or indeed that young fellow Conor McElroy into her confidence. If she did she would be going back on her word to Alan, betraying a trust. She had never done that in her whole life, but she couldn't recall a situation similar to the one she was experiencing now. Alan Beirne's medical condition was changing. She couldn't absolutely say how; she just knew that there was some change. A simple x-ray would show what it was, but he was adamant that there would be no x-ray, no examination, no other opinion, until there was something more tangible to go on than a sensation and a slight movement in his left leg.

A farmer driving a tractor braked, hooting and glaring, and Nancy realised that she was so buried in her problem that she had drifted to the wrong side of the road. She disarmed him by smiling and waving, inwardly muttering that the bloody farmers were responsible for more accidents on the road than anyone else.

Alan was alone. Sarah and Alannah had gone to Waterford with her mother to do some Christmas shopping. "Imagine," he told Nancy, "Sarah's mother wants to have all her shopping done in November. I remember buying my parents and my grandmother their presents on Christmas Eve before the shops closed."

"Eileen Dunne plans ahead," Nancy agreed. "She likes to have everything ready weeks before. I bet she'll have her habit all ready and waiting at the end of the bed twenty years before she dies."

Alan's laugh was spontaneous. "I'll tell her what you said."

They were in the kitchen, where he was sitting at the table with the *Irish Press* opened in front of him. An unfamiliar strain had grown between them because of what she called his stubborn attitude. Over his shoulders she glanced at the headlines in the paper: "The IRA Shoots Two Off Duty Soldiers in Armagh", "Nixon Withdraws More Troops from Vietnam". Looking at him she nodded towards the page, "Isn't there fierce trouble everywhere?"

"Yeah, nothing new about that." He glanced up and could see she was troubled about something. "I can see you're like a divil? What's wrong?"

"You know well what's wrong. I'm concerned. You should go back to the doctor – back to the hospital in Dublin. I feel that despite everything I'm failing if you don't take my advice. There are signs that things are changing for you, Alan – you know that – but what's actually happening we don't know. How could we? I can't understand why you wouldn't want to know, why you're not rushing off to the hospital all excited. I think by now you must know I have your interests at heart. Haven't I shown that?"

Alan could see her deep concern written in every line of her face. He recalled all the endless hours of probing and massaging and pummelling, a service of love and dedication given freely.

"Please listen, Nancy," he said quietly. "You know how I feel about you. I haven't words to tell you deeply grateful I am for all the time you've given me – and I accept I'm a cranky enough bastard at times. There possibly is a change, and if there is it's due to you. I promise if it continues – if I

haven't reverted to the old familiar deadness by the spring
– I will be more than happy to get a second opinion. Until
then I would like to go on as we are, if you agree. If you
think I'm taking you for granted, I'm not. Christ, Nancy,
believe me when I say I'm not."

"All right, all right, of course I agree. God knows I'll be
the first to go off my head with celebration if you walk again,
but physio can only do so much. Sure, I'd give the sight from
my eyes if you stood there towering above me."

"And," he was smiling now, that rare smile that was warm
and genuine, "you'll be the first I'll ravage if I do more than
walk again."

She tut-tutted with impatience and tried to hide her grin.
"Alan Beirne, you're outrageous, so you are. I'm glad I
didn't know you when you were in the whole of your health.
Let's get started, but I promise, and I mean it," she shook
her finger an inch from his face, "only till the spring."

"All right, boss," he answered as he wheeled into the bedroom for another marathon of physiotherapy that might or
might not be giving him back a life.

CHAPTER TWENTY-SEVEN

LONDON WAS LIKE a fairyland. Patsy got the tube two or three times a week to go in to the middle of the city. She thought the lights and the window displays in the large shops absolutely enchanting. Sometimes she played little games with herself. She would rush just as much as the bowler-hatted brigade, tearing to the escalator as if she, too, had an important appointment with a high profile bank or the inner circle of a top financial centre. She even picked up some of the business jargon listening to the crowd that gathered in the King's Head where she and Rory went on Fridays evenings. She knew Jane Campion was a lawyer working in a financial centre and made the sort of money that, according to Rory, would make you drool at the mouth, but Jane never talked of her job or her work day. It sometimes seemed to Patsy that the most important thing in her life was Matt Devlin.

Despite the fact that Patsy was now five and a half months pregnant, her condition hardy showed. The early nausea had passed and she had such energy she could forget for days on end that she was pregnant. Today was such a day. She saw the tourist coach advertising the historic tour of London. Most of the people clamouring on to the coach looked like tourists, with a fair sprinkling of gabardine-coated Americans with the inevitable cameras slung across their wide midriffs, some noisy, talkative Germans and a young couple hand in hand who looked Irish and were possibly honeymooners. On an impulse she decided she'd do the historic tour. At least then she's know more about the city she lived in and would have something to talk about when she went home.

Alan would be interested, she thought as she paid the fare. He taught geography and maybe she could relate a few humorous anecdotes of her day touring in London. Alan again. She sighed despairingly as she sat down behind the young couple. *I won't think about anything like that today,* she told herself. *Today will be given to all things exciting and external with not a minute wasted on inner longings and memories that definitely should be blurring by now.*

Her wish was answered. She was entranced. After a half an hour she decided that it was the best pound she had ever spent. The coach swept through the thick traffic, sometimes so close to the red buses that she waited with bated breath for the grinding crash which never happened. The calm, cultured voice of the pretty courier described all the landmarks and famous places that were until then mere names inside the covers of the history books. The Tower of London looked grim and foreboding. Looking at it she recalled a film she had enjoyed so much, *Anne of the Thousand Days,* and wondered what the hapless Anne must have felt walking to the block. She was greatly relieved to hear it was now a museum where the crown jewels were kept. She looked in awe at Westminster, the Houses of Parliament and the famous bridge. Looking at the soaring spires and the wonder of the architecture, she wondered if the men who built such beauty had lived to see the finished work, or did their sons take over where they left off? She'd ask Rory – he might know – or Jane.

She looked up at the most famous timekeeper in the world, Big Ben. She thought it looked friendly and eternal, as if in ten thousand years it would still be there. But the most fascinating sight was Buckingham Palace. They were told they could alight to watch the Changing of the Guard ceremony in the palace courtyard. Looking at the jerky toy-like movement, and the total precision of the red-clad soldiers, she was so enthralled that she nudged the person standing beside her, saying, "Did you ever see the like of it in your life?" She was answered with a guttural flow of enthusiastic German from a large smiling lady.

She didn't think all that much of Number 10 Downing

Street. After all the great palaces and cathedrals, she thought it was pretty ordinary. The British should have done a bit better by their prime minister. At St Paul's the calm courier told them about the Great Fire of London in 1666, and how the King of England, Charles II, took part in the fire fighting. Patsy wondered, if Dublin were on fire, would Taoiseach Jack Lynch and his ministers battle the flames? She laughed at the thought of the gentle Jack with the quiet voice out there fighting a fire. She told herself that she had little or no control over her imagination – maybe that was her problem. When the tour was over she alighted from the coach feeling that now she knew far more about this city where so many Irish made a good living.

As she got the bus back to Islington, she wondered were the natives of the city, like natives of any city the world over, living out their days, taking things for granted, never bothering to see the famous places at their own front doors. She must ask Jane if she had ever done the London tour. Patsy herself had never been in Reginald's Tower in Waterford, built by the Danes in the tenth century, where the great Dane, Strongbow, married Aoife, the daughter of Art Mac Murchada. There and then she decided that if she had a girl she would call her Aoife, a beautiful Irish name. Aoife was also one of the legendary Children of Lir, and right now she couldn't think of anything lovelier.

"Well, what did you spend my hard-earned money on today?"

Rory, she had discovered, had a childish interest in Christmas. He liked to look at the presents. She had already purchased his father a well-presented book on all aspects of lakeshore fishing.

"You won't believe this, but I didn't even buy a Christmas card. I took myself off on a tour – it was great."

"A tour? What sort of tour?" He was wasn't all that surprised. If a notion took her somewhere, she would go.

"A coach tour of London. I know everything about this city now. I even know that King Charles himself fought the flames when it nearly burned to the ground on 1666. I saw Big Ben and the Tower of London and the Changing of the Guard outside Buckingham Palace – it was amazing. And by the way, I have something to tell you."

"What's that?" He was watching her animated face, the excitement in her eyes, the mobility of her full mouth, thinking that despite the lurching worry that at times kept him awake, he absolutely loved her.

"If we have a girl we're going to call her Aoife."

"Well, now, that's a funny notion you got. Won't your mother do her nut if it's not Eileen? What about all that stuff about a girl named after the wife's mother or a boy after the father's father. Or is it," he was laughing now, "the blooming other way round? Anyway, I like Aoife, although I'd say she had her hands full with Strongbow, like I have my hands full with Patsy."

Then they were laughing and she was in his arms, the tea forgotten, and he was telling her that she was his life and that she'd better not go on too many tours in case someone ran away with her.

"Run away with a pregnant lump?" she sighed.

"Never saw a pregnant lump so unlumpy. Are you sure there's a baby there at all?"

"I am sure. Isn't it doing the Irish jig at night?" He kissed her again, and then told her that she should meet Jane Campion for lunch. "She'll advise you where to shop to get those Christmas presents you want to excite the relations with at home."

"An idea – although I have Emma. Still, Emma throws money away. She's not a thrifty mother saving up for a house in Ireland when the bubble bursts. We will go back, Rory, won't we?" she asked almost casually, as if it hardly mattered whether they did or not.

"We will, love – we will."

She took Rory's advice and met Jane the following week during her lunch hour. Over a light lunch Jane suggested to her where to get the best value for her money, what undergound line to take for various shops, not to forget to visit Harrods even if she merely bought a handkerchief. "Just to see the most famous shop in London," Jane smiled. They agreed to meet later for dinner as the men in their lives were in Brighton on business.

An exhausted but happy Patsy got to the pub first. She put her laden bags under the table and ordered a glass of beer. Sipping it, she recalled the first time she had a beer shandy in the pub in Dún Laoghaire with Rory. Now sipping different beer in a different city, she told herself that love was a strange thing which manifested itself in many different ways. The love you felt for your parents was different from the love for your sisters. The love you felt for your friends was certainly a different kind of love again. She presumed the love you felt for your children was a bit like the way you'd love yourself, because they were part of you. The love she felt for Rory was a good love – that at least she knew. As the pub got noisier she didn't even try to analyse the love she felt for Alan Beirne. She only knew that it was a love that sadly wouldn't go away, wouldn't fade, wouldn't die while he lived on this planet.

She was glad when Jane arrived and suggested, "Patsy, I know a lovely little restaurant near here. Even at this hour it will be quiet. Will we go there? I'd like to treat you to dinner." Patsy agreed on condition that it would be her turn next.

Jane chose a small table in an alcove, and Patsy felt the tiredness seeping away as she settled down to enjoy the meal with her new friend. Between courses, Patsy found herself telling Jane all about Ireland and her life there, and about Sarah, and Alan. Jane listened with interest.

"Would it have made that much difference if she hadn't become pregnant?" Jane asked. "You tell me they are very much in love – was a child that important to their relationship?"

Patsy was astonished. "Jane, of course the baby was very important. It was more than important. In Ireland, having babies seems to be the prime function. If you are married six months and there's nothing doing, everyone would presume you were demented, tearing your hair out in clumps. When you're only married weeks, friends are asking, 'Is there anything doing?' The baby made all the difference, particularly in their case."

"And you and Rory? Is he excited it happened so fast? You've hardly had a chance to get to know each other, and you're so young, hardly more than a baby yourself. How will you cope with a baby in that flat? All those stairs and the lonely long day with just you and the baby cooped up."

"It won't be like that, Jane. I'm very happy with this baby. I wanted to get caught fast, as they put it at home. Rory is thrilled, everyone is thrilled – I'm very happy. Honestly, Jane, if you marry Matt . . ." She found herself blushing. If she told this calm London girl that it was called living in sin in Ireland, she would merely smile politely. "When you and Matt decide to marry, you'll probably love to have a baby," Patsy blundered on.

"I was pregnant," Jane said very quietly.

"You were?" Patsy failed to hide her absolute astonishment. "What happened? Did you miscarry? Sarah was threatened with a miscarriage – we were up the wall."

"No, it wasn't like that. I had the pregnancy terminated." Patsy look was so uncomprehending and puzzled that Jane tried to explain. "It was Matt's baby. He never knew. It was about the last thing he would want. Matt is like the wind – restless, wants to go here and there. He talks of our travelling the world together, but he never talks of our settling down in a rose covered cottage to live happily ever after. If I had gone on to have the baby, I believe I would have had his support, but he would have been devastated – I know."

"Terminated," Patsy repeated, still looking so shocked that Jane was sorry she had told her. After all, in Ireland, abortion was probably never even mentioned. Catholics even thought contraception a sin. Although Matt wasn't a practising Catholic any more, he sometimes told her that he was still a Catholic inside. It was a hard thing to throw off entirely. That's why she hadn't told him, despite the fact that he wouldn't want a baby. Instead of cementing their relationship, it might possibly have ended it. And yet there was this girl looking at her, so puzzled, so appalled, that she felt uncomfortable. For the first time she wasn't a hundred per cent sure. Maybe Matt Devlin, the attractive Irishman who had completely stolen her heart, would have been equally as appalled. Of course he would never know.

"I don't want you to tell Rory or anyone – please."

"Of course, I won't tell Rory or any other soul, but how can you be so sure about Matt's reaction? Maybe at first he would have been up the wall, but he would have accepted it – I think he would. Jane, I'm sorry I'm coming across like a horrified hen. I'm not a very sophisticated person really. I know nothing about what you've told me. I vaguely knew it went on, but like a bad thought you don't dwell on it."

Her blue eyes were filled with sadness for the attractive English girl who hadn't taken a chance, who had put her fear of losing her partner and maybe her career before motherhood. Patsy had never known anyone, had never even heard of anyone who had willfully terminated a pregnancy.

Jane put a hand on hers. "People lead different lives, Patsy. Live and let live."

Patsy thought it strange that Jane was comforting her instead of the other way round. Jane suggested a taxi to take them to Islington. They didn't talk in the taxi, but despite the revelation that had so upset Patsy, the silence that hung between them was comfortable.

That evening preparing for bed, looking at Matt lying waiting for her, Jane told him she had had dinner with Patsy O'Driscoll.

"Ah, Patsy, the young mother-to-be. How did it go?"

"Very well. She's good company. Told me all about her life in Ireland, about her family, a sister whose husband was in a car accident on their honeymoon and ended up paralysed. She put extraordinary emphasis on the fact the sister was pregnant before the accident and what a wonderful thing it was."

"It was, too," he murmured, his eyes roaming over her slim body as she stood there in her lilac silk slip.

"Why do you say that? Why do you Irish put such a store on children?"

"Ah, as my poor mother used say, there's no home but should have a baby." He was looking at her, his brown eyes filled with laughter, the dark shadow of stubble on his chin, his desire already showing.

"Perhaps we should have a baby then?" Her heart started to pound, wondering what his answer would be.

"No, my lovely Londoner – babies are not for us. We must set the world on fire first. Sure, come in here to me, will you, and we'll practise."

She got in beside him, and as he put his strong arms around her, she was relieved at his answer.

CHAPTER TWENTY-EIGHT

THE POSTMAN HANDED the book, addressed to Mr Alan Beirne, Principal, Carbarry National School, Co. Waterford, to Joe Doyle, the assistant teacher. Joe passed it on to Alan at the tea break.

"I see you're getting the dirty books posted to the school. Don't want the wife to know?" he joked.

The two men got on well, maintaining a united front when it came to the school. They could talk at length about the pupils: the scholarship hopefuls and the ones that remained so dense despite all their efforts. They talked about books, sports, the under-fourteen hurling team and its prospects in the school league games, and the disastrous football team that was going nowhere. The one thing they never talked about was Alan's disability. Although there were times when Joe Doyle had felt so sorry for Alan that he wondered how he could cope, just lately he noticed a sort of suppressed excitement about his superior. He was more cheerful, more like the old Alan Beirne he had known in Saint Patrick's college in Dublin.

"Spot on. I've taken to the dirty books," Alan smiled.

Later that evening when Alan was alone in the house, he opened the book. The title was stark in its simplicity: *Spinal Injuries*. His eyes scanned the pages, alighting here and there on what might be relevant to his particular situation. "Loss of neurologic function after a spinal injury can result briefly from concussion or more lastingly from suppression of the spinal cord due to contusion or hemorrhage. After a period of rest this is followed by spontaneous improvement but some slight residual disability may remain." *Doesn't apply to me – nothing slight about what's wrong with me*, he thought. "As in the brain, severed or degenerated nerve processes in the cord cannot recover, and damage is permanent. Any dysfunction remaining after a period of six months is likely to be permanent. Damage to the *cauda equina*" – *whatever the hell that is,* he thought – "anywhere in the lumbar or sacral spine may cause permanent impotence . . ." *God, only too well I know all about that.* ". . . and loss of sphincter control for bladder, bowel or both." *That's familiar, too.*

Though he read on, he bitterly wondered, *Why am I deluding myself when it's there in black and white?*

He placed the book down on his knees and, absurdly, thought that he felt the weight of it. Suddenly, without warning, his left leg jerked violently. There was no doubt; his leg had jerked so much that it had knocked the book on to the floor. He looked at it and saw that it had opened on the very chapter he had read. The word "may" jumped up at him: "may cause – may cause". Looking at the word until it blurred and danced, he wondered if it could mean hope, a hope for the miracle he wanted so desperately. God above, he wanted to walk, wanted to make love to his wife, wanted to play and romp with Alannah. Wanted to get back from the sidelines into a life that was swirling past him. Wanted to run, swim and horseplay with Patsy down in the oyster bed. Picking up the book he reminded himself that Patsy was a married woman now and soon to be a mother. *Sure sign of getting old,* he thought, *going back in time.* But his leg had jerked! The damn dead limb had jerked so hard that it had dislodged a heavy book.

He wouldn't tell Nancy, yet. Hearing Sarah's light footsteps on the gravel drive, he shoved the book amongst the school copies on the table. The time hadn't come to tell her any of the things that were filling him with a wild, desperate hope.

Emma decided she'd have a mad party before Christmas, "A breaking up sort of party before we go home," she told Patsy. "I'll have it in my flat – we'll invite everyone."

"What about food and drink?" Patsy asked. "That'll cost you a bomb."

"No, it won't. Over here, everyone brings a bottle or two – wine is the thing. Of course, I'll buy in some stuff, but it won't be like home with a mountain of food as if a war was coming. I think the famine did that to us – hoard up, the praties are going to rot. Nah, here it's different."

"But you'll still need food," Patsy insisted.

I'll get some of my friends to do plates of fiddily finger food and you can make me a few dozen sausage rolls. And a dozen bottles of Guinness for Rory and Matt." ·

"A few dozen sausage rolls, a few dozen bottles. God almighty, it's going to be a fair oul hooley," Patsy muttered, "for a place where food is only secondary."

The following Friday, Rory came home to see her red and flustered as she painstakingly brushed egg on to trays of sausage rolls. She looked at her efforts and sighed. "What do you think of them? They're all different sizes and they look pinched. Will they do the swinging Londoners?"

He put his arms, around her, noticing the large safety pin in the jeans now. "The said swinging Londoners aren't in our league when it comes to parties. Bet no one will be standing on the kitchen table at six in the morning singing 'The Bard of Armagh' to a lot of unconscious drunks lying on the floor."

"God, I hope not, Rory O'Driscoll. If you stand up on Emma's kitchen table yelling your head off singing republican songs, you'll make a show of us."

"I tell you what – I'll give 'em 'Kevin Barry'. 'Another martyr for old Ireland, another murder for the crown,'" he sang out of tune, his eyes full of mischief. "That'll sober them up."

"You must behave yourself, and that Matt Devlin, too. I'd say he's crazy when he gets drunk. Anyway, what'll I wear?"

He pulled her into his arms and kissed her flour-tipped nose. "Well, it's a safe bet to say you won't be wearing the black dress this year."

"No, I won't," she laughed, "and it's your fault. I don't

know why you gave a girl a black dress that cost a fortune and then banjaxed her so that she got no value from it."

As she turned away to put her sausage rolls into the oven, she recalled last Christmas: the black dress and the look in Alan's dark eyes, as if he'd seen her for the very first time. She slammed the oven door to shut out the memory. Too soon she would be back in close proximity to the man she wanted to forget.

It seemed almost miraculous that so many people could be crammed into Emma's flat. When Patsy and Rory got there, the music was blaring and the party was already in full swing. Emma whisked them both away, introducing them to hordes of young people. All the girls seemed to be called Samantha, Vicky, Sandy, Alicia, and all the guys seemed to be Jonathans, Cyrils, Cecils, Jeffreys and Duncans. Catching a glimpse of Matt Devlin with a pint glass of stout, she presumed that Jane was somewhere in the seething crowd. She was glad that she had taken Emma's advice and bought a jade green silk shirt to wear over new black maternity trousers. The day Emma had accompanied her to buy the trousers in Mothercare, she had muttered, "I hate the thought of maternity trousers with all that bloody elastic. Sarah never wore anything like that as far as I can remember."

"Of course, she did; you just weren't aware. You don't think she had a string of safety pins all the time, do you?"

"I don't know, maybe you're right."

"We don't really know much about Sarah any more. She never really told us how she felt about things. She was always a private sort of head anyway."

"Yeah, I know," Patsy agreed.

Next, Emma had brought her to a shop where the proprietor was Indian. "This place specialises in large floaty, gorgeous shirts in pure silk – perfect for you." Patsy had to admit that when it came to advice about clothes for a six months pregnant heap, Emma knew her stuff.

A black-haired fellow put a glass of wine into her hand and told her he was David. He told her that she was the tallest and the most striking looking chick in the room. She was totally taken aback and wondered was he mad. She told him she was a frumpy married woman as she gulped down the wine. He poured her out another glass and told her that her accent was amazing. The music blared and he grabbed her and they bopped round the floor, bumping into other boppers. He seemed to be talking because she could see his lips were moving, but since she couldn't hear a word he said, she just kept smiling like a gargoyle and nodding her head. When the music ended, he kissed her lightly on the lips and vanished into the throng.

She found herself beside Matt, who was on his second or third pint. Grinning at her, he leaned over and yelled into her ear, "That'll show 'em that the Catholic Irish mother-to-be knows how to enjoy herself." She told him to shut up and stop reminding her of her situation. Then the music started and he pulled her on to the floor. He held her so close for the slow number that she could feel the stubble of his chin against her forehead. He was very attractive, and she could understand why Jane was so much in love with him, but she was still shocked with the lengths Jane had gone to.

"A great party," she yelled, "but when are you going to give us the big day? You know, the marriage feast at Cana and what have you."

He laughed and his white teeth shone. "After I live, my young Patsy, after I live but before I'm old and grey."

"Don't leave it too late – kids don't want an old and grey dad."

"Hey now, just because you're a child mother-to-be, you want us all to join the club. Wouldn't suit me, I'm a real Kerry bachelor."

The rasping voice of Bob Dylan and "Blowing in the Wind" started. Rory came over with Jane, elegant in a knee-length cherry red dress, looking so well, so confident, that it was impossible to imagine that not so long ago she had done something sad, lonely and desperate to hang on to Matt. He was laughing, very drunk, very handsome, but to Patsy's way of thinking very unsuitable.

Then Emma shouted that the next dance would be an occasion of sin. Everyone laughed although most of them had no idea that they were laughing at an old dance hall joke in Ireland where once upon a time the priests had thundered against slow dancing from the altars. As she danced with Rory to "Smoke Gets in Your Eyes", he told her that she was the loveliest looking bird in the room and that he loved her – and again she felt comforted and good. There was another glass of wine and another, and when the food came out she saw she needn't have worried about the shape of her sausage rolls because everything disappeared off the plates as if by magic. A few bottle of brandy appeared, a present to Emma from someone named Jonathan who worked for a drinks company.

Hours after, with the thumping music turned low and the food consumed, the place seemed strewn with bodies. Emma sat in a corner with the fair, long-haired Jonathan. Her friends sprawled by cigarette strewn tables with their partners. One guy was getting so carried away with a girl with blonde straight hair to her waist that Patsy, who was pretty drunk and muzzy, thought he would make love to her there and then. Just when his hand was sliding up the length of her black glitzy tights, she reached out and poured a glass of beer slowly and solemnly over his head.

"Fuck!" he shouted and everyone laughed.

Matt Devlin drawled, "That'll soften his cough for him."

Then Jonathan shouted, "Well, then, this is an Irish party – what about an Irish song?"

Through a haze Patsy saw Rory jump up on the table to belt out "The Boys of Armagh". Matt got up beside him and they roared that, "It's a Long Long Way to Tipperary", and then there was bedlam as everyone tried to join in.

In the black taxi cab on the way home Patsy, slightly drunk and slightly sick, told Rory that it was a great party – she didn't think that Emma had it in her to throw such a party. But Rory didn't hear a word she said. He was fast asleep and snoring gently.

CHAPTER TWENTY-NINE

O N THE SAME Friday evening that Emma Dunne threw her Christmas party, her sister Sarah sat in the dark car at the end of a the lonely lane leading on to the far end of Sauleen Strand. She wore a thick sheepskin jacket and a head scarf covered her blonde hair. Removing her woollen gloves, she placed her hands on her lap. When she spoke her voice was little above a whisper. "I'm right, Conor, you know I am. It can't go on. Christmas is a week away and . . ."

"Don't, Sarah, don't."

"Please, let me finish. I spent all day rehearsing this so let me say it. I know in here, right inside me, that we must stop seeing each other. As I was trying to say, Christmas is a mere week away. The others will be home. And it is a religious time and . . . and . . . Oh God, Conor, this is wrong – this is a sin – and maybe a time like Christmas when people flock off to confession sort of shows it up."

He didn't answer immediately. In the confined dark of the car, they could hear the breakers crashing way out beyond the point. Across the channel beyond the sand hills, the lights of Tramore flickered and danced through the misty film on the car window. He reached over and opened the window an inch or two, letting the cold tangy sea air in.

"I know it's even more difficult for you than it is for me. You have Alan and Alannah. But Sarah, you just can't sit there and say we'll end it just like that. I love you. There's never time to tell you how much when you must always get back home and I must get back to the noble call."

"You're right, of course, I must always get back. I will always have to go back. If anything, that bears out what I'm saying. Don't you see how utterly hopeless this is? We can't expect to get away with this much longer. Someone out there will see us, if they haven't already, and then all hell will break loose. The crippled master's wife two-timing him with

279

the doctor. No, Conor, it can't go on. You have it all ahead of you. You'll meet someone else, and I'll simply get on with it."

"Get on with what?" he asked.

"My life. I have my child. I have my husband. He loves me."

"But he can't express it," he argued.

"Of course, he can – it isn't all about sex, for God's sake."

"At this age when you are both in your prime, the physical side is very very important. The friendship and companionship comes with the years."

"God, you sound like a dull doctor."

"Maybe that's all I am – a dull doctor."

"I wouldn't say that," Sarah relented. "I was over in my mother's the other day when she and Kit Gillen were making up parcels for the poor for Christmas, and Kit started talking about you and the difference you've made to their lives. How Doctor James is a new man since you came and how she loves to feel you next door in the flat – she said you made them feel like a family again. Then she went on to say how surprised she was that you hadn't a girlfriend yet. I listened and made a cup of coffee, and do you know what I felt, Conor McElroy – do you?"

"No, tell me."

"I felt smug – smug, mind you – because I knew why you hadn't a girlfriend, because you had me." Suddenly she started to cough, and though she tried to stop and gain some control she couldn't. Conor closed up the car window.

"You'll catch a cold in this bloody place. You're right, this can't go on. We should be together in comfort and heat. Do you know, Sarah, that we've never made love in a bed. Isn't that crazy?"

"It's more than crazy – it's wrong."

He didn't answer, just drew her into his arms and removed the scarf and gently bending back her head he kissed her long and tenderly.

"You'll catch my cold," she whispered.

"I don't care what I catch," he murmured, kissing her gently again, and then not so gently, and then passionately and desperately, only breaking off when she was wracked with another paroxysm of coughing. He was contrite then.

"Here I am a doctor and my woman going down with the flu." When her coughing had eased he felt her forehead, pushing back the thick damp hair.

"I think you have a temperature. When you go home, have a hot drink with two aspirin, then straight to bed or you'll be laid low for Christmas."

"Yes, doctor," she said huskily.

"I love you," he said, his grey eyes holding hers steadily.

"I love you, too," she whispered. The silence hung between them as if her admission put their relationship on a different, more frightening level. He broke it by turning on the ignition to take her back up from the sea.

Sarah saw her parents' car parked outside the cottage. Glancing at her watch she could make out it was nearly ten-thirty, later than usual, and she briefly wondered if she could say that she met someone and stopped for a chat. Her mother looked up sharply when she came in.

"Sarah, are you mad? Out on a frostily cold night like this. Wouldn't you be sensible and stay at your own fire? You'll get your death."

"I keep telling her that," Alan said. "She has cut her walks down to two a week to keep slim and trim."

"She's too slim and trim," her father added. "I prefer a woman with a bit of meat, and I'm lucky because that's what I have."

Eileen grimaced and Sarah started to cough a deep hacking cough.

"See, I told you," Eileen told her.

Alan immediately turned his chair and went into the kitchen for a glass of water. Sipping the water she avoided meeting his eyes because her own were blinded with scalding tears. From a distance she heard her mother saying, ". . . and Emma is giving a Christmas party tonight, a sort of farewell before they come home. It's hard to think Christmas will be on us any day."

"And then before we wink again the summer will be here," Tim Dunne added. His wife rattled off again, "I hope Patsy will mind herself and not go too wild at London parties now that she's the way she is and whatever."

A log fell out of the fire on to the hearth, bringing with it a shower of bright red sparks. Alan reached for the tongs to put it back. "I just can't believe that Patsy is going to be a mother. I still think she's a schoolgirl." A small smile was playing around his mouth, and Sarah was glad that thoughts of Patsy made him smile.

After her parents were gone she took the aspirin and, after checking Alannah, she went to bed before Alan. Alan brought her another glass of water when she started to cough again. She sat up and choked, "I think I'm getting the flu. I hope you don't get it; you don't want that as well as everything else." She could have bitten her tongue off. "I'm sorry," she muttered, her shivering body sliding down into the warmth.

"It's all right," he said quietly. For the second time that evening the thought of Alan brought tears to her eyes.

Eileen Dunne was filled with satisfaction that they were all around her again. It had seemed strange getting the spare room with the big double bed ready for Patsy and Rory. Only yesterday she had rooted out Patsy's favourite hot water bottle before she recalled that Patsy was married now and mightn't be needing it any more. There was only Emma left now, and the way things were going in all probably Emma would be married next year. But it was still great they were all coming home.

Patsy looked the very same, still slim and leggy with a big roomy sweater over black trousers. Her condition barely showed and yet she was gone six months. Eileen remembered when she was six months pregnant she had complained to her doctor that she was like an elephant. "Some women have more room than others," he had told her. She had accepted that and waddled around like a mountain before her girls were born.

After the initial greetings and hugs were over, Patsy looked around. "Hey, where's Sarah?" she asked.

"Dying," Alan told her. "She has flu and she's staying in bed hoping she'll shake it off before Christmas day. She's pretty bad – had Conor McElroy twice – on antibiotics – coughing non-stop. Anyway, I brought Alannah to see you. Won't we do?"

Oh dear God, she thought, *you'll do. You'll always do.* She laughed and said, "I suppose so." Alannah was sitting on the floor, her black glossy hair shining and the dark eyes filled with curiosity to know who all these people were. Patsy stooped down and swept her into their arms. "God, you're gorgeous – I'd die for you. Look, Rory, look at this glamour puss. Isn't she something?" Rory nodded in agreement as Patsy held the baby high and then dropped her and caught her, covering her laughing face with kisses.

"Here" Emma said, "I mightn't be in the pudding club, but give me a hold."

"Emma," her mother reprimanded. "I think that was very vulgar, opposite all the men," she fussed.

"Ah, Mam," Emma laughed, showing her white even teeth between her new almost black lipstick, "you're still so lovely and square." Patsy could see the pride on Alan's face as he looked at his little daughter.

At supper, amidst all the family chatter, Alan asked Rory about the employment situation in London.

"Great money now," Rory told him, "but it's boom time and it mightn't last. A few of the boys say there's another three years in it and then it'll be back home. With luck, for us a house near Lough Derg and hopefully a job for me in

Nenagh or Tipperary or Thurles. Have my eye on the County Council – a nice, safe, pensionable job to keep me and the ten children in bread."

Alan laughed, his dark glance taking in Patsy, who was animatedly talking to her mother. *She's like that,* he thought. *She can light up a room.* He was filled with gladness that she was home, even for a short stay. Alannah was nodding off as she lay propped up with cushions on the sofa. "Time to take her home and time to see my sick wife," he told them. Patsy propped the child on her knee and worked the tiny arms into the sleeves of her little jacket. They all went out with Alan to his car. His agility in getting from the wheelchair to the driving seat was practised now. With the baby in her chair in the back, smiling and waving, he was off down the drive. They stood against the backdrop of the brightly lit hall until the sound died away in the darkness.

"Isn't he looking great?" Emma volunteered. "He's so capable you'd completely forget he was crippled. Still, how will he manage with Sarah so sick?"

"He has Nancy Ryan staying until she's better," her mother told her. "She's still giving him physio. Sarah says the two of them are locked up in the bedroom for hours.

"God knows what goes on in there," her husband grinned taking the pipe out of his mouth.

"Men," Eileen muttered contemptuously. "You wouldn't mind, only she could be his mother."

"More like his grandmother," her husband said. Eileen ignored him as they trooped back into the house. She heard him say to Rory, "We'll let the women babble in the kitchen, Rory, while you and I have a little nightcap."

"Don't give him too many bad habits," Eileen snorted as she followed her two girls into the kitchen. It was like old times.

CHAPTER THIRTY

"WELL, IT'S OVER."

"What's over?"

"Christmas and all the panic stations that you women indulge in."

Patsy and Rory were was lying in the big brass bed in the dark beamed bedroom in his father's house. He had his hands behind his head as he watched Patsy getting ready for bed. She slipped her nightdress over her head and then eased out of her maternity jeans.

"Why didn't you take these off first and then put on the nightdress?"

"Because I hate seeing myself as a bumpy wreck."

"I love seeing you as a bumpy wreck. Think of it – our first Christmas and our last Christmas before we have a screaming brat."

"Well, that's a terrible thing to call our first baby. He or she won't be a screaming brat. It'll be a beautiful, quiet, serene child just like me."

"Serene," he laughed loudly.

"Shut up, you'll wake your father."

"No, I won't. That man never sleeps. He'll probably read the fishing book you gave him for half the night."

She slipped in beside him, telling him to warm her, that she was freezing. He drew her into his arms and they lay close together talking softly.

"Pity Sarah was so sick. She looked wretched."

"Yeah, I noticed," Rory agreed.

"I suppose if you had a bad bout of pneumonia it would be hard to look well, but I dunno. I don't think she's that happy, but she has Alan and that gorgeous child. Isn't she the spit of him?""

"Yeah, you'd think you cut the head off him."

She laughed. "A peculiar way to put it."

"That's the way they put it in this neck of the woods."

"What do you think of all the phone calls Emma got every night from Jonathan in London? He seems keen."

"And she's keen on him. You always know when a woman is in love; it's in the eyes."

"You're mad – and a total know-all into the bargain. Hmm . . . did you see it in my eyes?"

"Amn't I working on it?"

Lying close to him as he slept, Patsy was puzzled about his answer. Her heart started to pound. She had been bothered by palpitations since the start of her pregnancy. She blamed the brandy that John had given them after the lovely dinner he had prepared for their arrival. Then she felt the baby kick and, moving even closer to her husband, she vowed from the bottom of her heart that he would never ever know, not by word deed or stint, not at this side of the grave, that she had never loved him with the sort of love he deserved.

The next morning they could hear John down in the kitchen rattling pans and clattering plates and shouting at his dog, Shot, to sit down, telling him that he was the most impatient fecker in Tipp. When the delicious smell of bacon and sausages wafted up, Rory jumped out of the bed. "Come on. We might as well enjoy the fare – we won't get a smell like that in Islington."

Over the breakfast John O'Driscoll told her to eat for two to insure that his first-born grandchild would be a well-made child. She laughed and told him that was all old hat now.

"I wouldn't be too sure of that. That's the sort of thing you'd hear from those women's libbers – is that what they call themselves?"

"Yeah, and don't tell me, John O'Driscoll, you're one of those awful macho men who deride everything that they stand for. Up to now women in this country have had a rotten time. Look at Sarah; she had to leave her job in the bank when she got married. There are hundreds of girls who would like to continue work to help with the mortgage, get things for the house, even to save up for a holidays in the sun. What's so wrong with that?"

"Nothing, but young Patsy, if you're that way of thinking, how come you got married so young and threw away all chance of a career?"

"Because that's the way I wanted it."

"You're a woman after my own heart." He was still smiling as he turned to Rory. "Would you have a look at the roof near the gable end? A few slates came off in a recent gale. I put the ladder up there before you woke up."

"A fellow can't get a bit of a holiday without having to work," Rory grumbled

"And while you're up there, I'm taking this daughter-in-law of mine for a walk beside the lake." Before Patsy could open her mouth, he was shouting for Shot. When the retriever came bounding in the back door, John added, "I want you to get a bit of real fresh air into those lungs before you go back to the fleshpots of London."

"Have I any say in that?" Patsy asked.

"No, you haven't. Just wrap up well, wear your boots and be nice to an old man."

"You look fifty-five and you know it," she said dryly as she went up to the bedroom to get her boots and jacket.

Lough Derg was never lovelier. The vast stretch of water lay blue and glittering, the surface broken by a million white horses. The only sound breaking the stillness was the lapping of the waves against the shore. At the far side of the lake, the trees stood like black etchings against the winter sky. Shot, aware that his beloved owner carried no gun, had bounded off to create his own diversion. At a small jetty where a few boats were tied up, Patsy sat down gratefully on an old seat with faded and peeling paint.

"Amazing how I seem to be running out of steam."

John O'Driscoll took his pipe out of his pocket and sat down beside her, pushing the tobacco into the bowl of his pipe with his thumb. When he was puffing away contentedly, she asked, "How come you never married again? You've been alone all of ten, eleven years. Now you can tell me that I'm a nosy so-and-so."

He removed his pipe slowly

"You know, Patsy, real love can bring as much torment as happiness. When Ann was with me I was content; when she was anywhere else I wasn't. Now we could have a thousand disagreements – she was a fiery woman I'll tell you – but even in the throes of a row, I knew she was the only one for me. When she died it was like heart surgery without the anaesthetic; then when the shock eased I knew that half of me was gone. That's what the real thing is like. Of course, I went on for Rory – did my best for him – and I can't tell you how glad I am that he met you. So that's it, Patsy – when it's the real thing you don't bother again." He looked at her, his steely blue grey eyes holding hers for a minute. "But of course you know what the real thing is all about." *Oh I do – I do,* her thoughts spun, *and about the torment you talked about.*

"You'll be good to him, lass – that I know. Come on." He put his pipe between his strong teeth and helped her to her feet. "Enough of this profound lakeside chatting."

Removing the pipe again, he gave a piercing whistle which brought his dog bounding out of the undergrowth, its shiny black coat covered with bracken and withered leaves, a pink tongue hanging out and panting, its eyes looking at his master with adoration. As they walked up the driveway they could hear Rory hammering on the roof.

"Well, is it bad?" his father shouted.

"Bad enough. The lintel is a bit rotted and slates have slipped. That's where the rain came in." Rory clamoured down the ladder with speed and efficiency and gave Patsy a little kiss on the tip of her nose. "I suppose you know all the family secrets now?"

"No family secrets. Just a little chat." *They have a great relationship*, Patsy thought, *easy and relaxed with each other.*

"Dad, what I did will hold it for a bit, but I think you'll need a decent job done on it in the spring."

"Well, we'll have it all fixed and ready for the christening party. What do you think, young Patsy – a christening party beside Lough Derg?"

"Couldn't think of anything lovelier," she told him.

It was late on Sunday night when they got back to Carbarry. They were due to drive to Dún Laoghaire at dawn the next day to get the quarter to nine boat. Eileen Dunne fussed over them, obviously happy to see them back safe.

"Where's Emma?" Patsy asked.

"Out for a last fling," her father answered dryly. "After – after, mind you – a three hour phone call to London. Don't tell me I'm going to have an Englishman as a son-in-law."

"I hope he's a Catholic," Eileen added. "I wouldn't like any of my daughters to marry outside the Church."

"God, Mam, that's all old hat now," Patsy told her. "What about ecumenical thinking and Pope John and all that?"

"God be good to poor Pope John, I sometimes think that the poor man got carried away. I still wouldn't want Emma to marry a Protestant."

"An English Protestant at that," Rory laughed.

After a light supper, Patsy wondered if she should phone Sarah. "Now that she's on the phone, I wouldn't like to go without a phone call," she told her mother.

"You'll have to go through the postmistress, Mrs Machey. Sarah can't wait for a direct connection. The postmistress is a curious type, so don't say too much."

"How could I say too much? I only want to say goodbye." *Not to Sarah*, the inner voice whispered. *You want to say good-bye to Alan – just to hear his voice.*

Sure enough Mrs Machey in the local post office answered. "Who? Who's speaking, please? Oh yes, the young sister is it? Well, the master might be in bed and the missus

289

might be out walking, although she mightn't, what with being so sick and such. Sure, all we can do is try."

My God, Patsy thought in horror as she heard the phone ringing, *imagine telling sophisticated Jane Campion what it was like making a phone call in rural Ireland.*

"Hi," Patsy said, when Sarah answered the phone. "I was just ringing to say we're off."

"I'm glad you phoned. I was sorry to be such a miserable invalid over the Christmas."

"Couldn't be helped. How are you now?"

"Tired. I loathe this time of year. So flat after Christmas. At least the next bit of excitement will be your baby."

"Yeah, I can't believe it. How is Alannah?"

"Really great – nearly standing up. Alan is just foolish about her. Would you like to have a word with him?"

"I would. Bye, Sarah. Take care, okay? And kiss Alannah for me."

"I will, and you take care, too. Write and safe journey. Say goodbye to Rory for me."

Before Patsy heard Alan's voice, the same old weary longing assailed her, putting her poor overworked heart into overdrive again.

"Well, if it isn't Patsy. I was hoping you'd ring."

"Were you?"

"I was. I was even hoping that you and Rory might have gotten back earlier and visited this beleaguered male."

"You sound great. Anyway, we only got back a while ago and we're off in the morning at the crack of dawn. I just phoned to say goodbye.".

"I don't like goodbyes, young Patsy, but I suppose they're an inevitable part of life."

"Why does everyone call me young Patsy? I'm not young. I'm a big, heavy, pregnant married women that feels all of a hundred years old. So there – no more young bloody Patsys."

She could hear him laugh like he had laughed on a thousand days when they were together. She hadn't heard him laugh like that for so long. There was something in his voice: a vibrancy, a strength, something that had been noticeably absent.

"Goodbye, love," he said. "Give my regards to John Bull and take care now – seeing that you're a hundred-year-old pregnant married woman."

"Goodbye." She cleared her throat. "I mean *au revoir,* seeing that you hate goodbyes."

She put down the phone and wiped her tear-filled eyes impatiently with the back of her hand. When she went back into the sitting room, her father and Rory were talking about current affairs.

"Come over near the fire, love," her mother said, "you look cold and pale."

CHAPTER THIRTY-ONE

"**M**ISSUS BEIRNE, THERE's a phone call for you." Sarah was aware of the postmistress's burning curiosity. "Putting you through to Doctor McElroy now." She hadn't seen or heard of him since he had called when she was ill. It had been so impersonal then: his cold stethoscope on her clammy, perspiring chest, Alan and her mother, concerned at her rasping breath, Conor reassuring yet businesslike, writing a prescription for antibiotics.

"Hello, Sarah, Doctor McElroy here. I'm ringing with the results of your x-ray as promised. Nothing too major wrong. Drop over and we'll discuss it.

With her heart thumping but aware of the listening ear of the postmistress, Sarah replied, "Thanks, Doctor. I'm glad the result is all right. Do you want me to make an appointment now?"

"Could you make it seven-thirty this evening? I've had a cancellation."

"I'll be there. See you then." Then she heard the click of the phone and the kitchen was filled with silence.

She glanced at the clock: ten-thirty. She had nine hours to strengthen her resolve to finally end their relationship. The distraction of Christmas and Conor's break in County Meath had brought a welcome respite and time for her to think. Nothing he could say would dissuade her. As she walked into the bedroom to see if Alannah was awake, she was thinking again that their relationship had nowhere to go. It was doomed, hopeless from the very start. Sometimes in the quiet moments in the lonely backwater where she lived, she wondered what it would be like to walk out the door and go away with Conor. Even in her dreams she would break out in a cold clammy sweat thinking of the horror and the heartbreak she would leave behind.

The baby was still asleep. She examined the round face

292

with the tiny, well-formed mouth, the two dark crescents of black lashes, the dark hair, glossy and already curling. She wanted to pick her up and hold her close and closer still, hoping that she would get strength from the small warm body to end a situation that could only destroy the people she loved.

"Alan, I've now decided I'm ending these sessions. We can't go on. We shouldn't be here blundering along in ignorance in the heart of the country without a single facility."

"Nancy," he groaned, "how often have I to promise that if this whatever it is continues until Easter, I will go back. Sure, I owe it to you." They were in the bedroom, Alan sitting in the wheelchair with Nancy Ryan standing in front of him, frustrated and flushed.

"You're too stubborn, Alan Beirne, like most men. I can tell you I'm darn glad I never got married." He smile disarmed her but she refused to show it. "You know all the equipment and facilities they have in these places: parallel bars, a lot of new-fangled sophisticated machinery to strengthen the muscles, not to mention new techniques for monitoring."

"I'm well aware of all this, and I promise I will tell Conor McElroy everything, if what we think is progress continues. Providing you won't nag me to death in the mean time."

"All right," she sighed. "I'll offer it up. Now I want to know exactly what you feel?"

He didn't answer at first. He was afraid to put it into words, as if the whole thing might evaporate. Eventually he spoke.

"I feel things. Sensations, awareness, heat, cold. A slight pressure when Alannah is on my knees, pins and needles, terrible at times. I feel cramps, jerks. I'm trying to hide it from Sarah, from everyone. I don't, I emphasise *don't*, want to bring false hope to anyone."

"Think of how happy it would make Sarah. Think of your parents, Sarah's parents, your poor grandmother, all of them praying to high heaven." Her sigh was deep. "God knows I've met stubborn fellows in my day, but you take the biscuit." He nodded in agreement, knowing that once again he had got her to agree. "Get in there," she growled, "and I'll thump the bloody backside off you."

He rolled into the bed and she removed his shirt. She started to work silently and efficiently on the body she knew so well now. After half an hour her probing fingers moved down gradually to the lower lumbar region.

"Well, do you feel something?"

"Yes, something. Just a sensation of heat, a slight pressure."

She was silent as she helped him to turn over and sit on the side of the bed. Holding his hand in a vice-like grip, she looked at him, her face tight and stubborn, her mouth set in a thin grim line.

"All right, Master," she had never called him that before, "hold my hands tight. Place your feet squarely on the floor. Now when I say lift, try and lift; dig your feet into the ground. Try and put pressure on them. This," she glared at him, "will either kill or cure you."

He did exactly what she told him. He closed his eyes and, with a superhuman effort, tried to lift the lower part of his body. She could hear his laboured breathing as he dug his feet into the floor. Then there seemed to be some movement; then more; then a jerking of his right foot as he held on to her so hard she thought her hands would be crushed. *If they are*, she ruefully thought, *it will be in a good cause.* Then he eased himself off the bed and slowly and agonisingly drew up to a standing position. She could see that the effort had covered his face and chest with sweat. For a second he was there towering over her, swaying wildly before collapsing into her arms. She was prepared and squared her strong, stocky body for the impact.

As she held him in her arms, her breast was filled wit the thumping of his heart and her eyes with blinding tears. He collapsed back on to the bed, and she saw that his face was covered with tears, too – tears that ran down and mingled with the sweat that flowed in rivulets down his face.

When Sarah went into the waiting room, she saw that there was only one young man, no more that sixteen or seventeen, before her. His arm was in a sling and he had a dressing on his face.

"In the wars?" she asked, smiling.

"You could say that again," he smiled back. "Could be worse though; fell off the motor bike and hit a ditch. The mother said it was Saint Anthony that saved me. It happened on Tuesday – Saint Anthony's day. If it had happened on Wednesday I'd be dead, so she says anyway. But I think she has her wires crossed because I think he's only able to find things."

"My own mother thinks the world of him. Lights a candle every Tuesday. I'm a bit like you." Sarah agreed, "I only bother him when I lose things. What did you break anyway?"

"My arm in two places and a couple of ribs. The doctor put ten stitches in my face. He keeps telling me I'll have no scar, but I don't care if I do – might look good – might even attract the birds." He thought she must have been a beautiful bird in her day.

"I think you'd be better off without the scar."

There was a tap on the door and the young lad got up grinning, "See ya," and she was left alone with no distraction.

Conor looked tired, even pale, and she noticed that there were shadows under his eyes now. A small nerve throbbed at the side of his face.

"Hi," he said, his voice low, his grey eyes meeting hers then roaming all over her face then back to lock into her gaze. "Christ, how I've missed you." She didn't answer, merely licked her lips hoping for the strength she needed. She watched silently as he walked swiftly to the door and locked it. "You're the last." He switched off the light, "Just in case they'll still think I'm here." The room was in semi-darkness now, the only light the green-shaded desk lamp.

Then they were in each others arms and they clung to each other as if they were drowning. He kissed her and she tried to say something but she couldn't because she needed him so much. She returned his kisses and she felt his probing tongue and she was like water in his arms. He half carried her to the couch and she lay down with no protest, no arguments now, no words of protest that they should end this illicit affair. They made love, and he wanted it right for her and she wanted it right for him – and it was perfect, and when it was over she wondered how anything so good for two people could be so wrong. He had told her that he used to fantasise that she was his wife. Lying beside him, she knew what he meant. When she told him that she now felt he was her husband more than Alan ever was, he merely groaned as he held her closer than ever.

Later that night when Alannah was asleep and Alan had gone to bed, Sarah took down her new diary and wrote the first entry for January 1972:

> Today I spent too many hours trying to pluck up strength to end it all. I had to because I told myself there was nowhere we could go – hide – disappear. Sitting in the waiting room a woman waits until she's called. She goes in and she dies with longing. Then he locks the door and it's all over – all my resolve, all my argument – all my strength – because there is no argument – no strength – no anything but him. We make love and it's indescribable. Why am I not filled with guilt or remorse – or shame? I must be going mad – yes that must be the only explanation for what I'm at – I'm going stark raving mad.

After she finished she got up on her toes and pushed the new diary behind the old one in its hiding place safely out of sight. It was only then she remembered that she hadn't taken the pill; in fact she hadn't taken it since her bout of pneumonia. She wouldn't think of that until tomorrow. She slipped into the warm bed beside her sleeping husband, and for one heart-thumping moment she thought she felt his leg move. That was impossible – he was paralysed from the waist down. She thought she felt his leg jerk again. *More of it*, she thought. *There's no doubt I am going crazy.*

CHAPTER THIRTY-TWO

Patsy felt that January was the longest month she had ever lived through. Rory's company had sent him up to York for three weeks to do a survey on a site, and he was gone from Monday to Friday. He was concerned about leaving her on her own in the flat.

"Don't be silly," she told him. "I'm a big strong girl. And I won't be on my own. Haven't I the Indian couple below and the English woman above? Matt and Jane are practically around the corner, and Emma is only a hop on the underground away. I'll be fine. I'll read. I'll enjoy catching up on things. And I won't miss your nagging."

"Do I nag?"

"God, you're a fierce nag."

It was a rainy Sunday night and they were having a snack before retiring. Rory had plugged in the amber-shaded lamp they had got as a wedding present to make the place cosier. The overhead light showed up all the damp patches, the shabby wallpaper and the stained ceiling, and they liked sitting together in the pool of rosy light, shutting out the world.

He looked tired. Some of her friends had once compared him to Robert Redford. *His hair isn't as fair any more* – she presumed it was the lack of sunshine and the helmet he wore on the site – *but he does look a bit like him,* she thought, *with the square jaw and the ready way he smiles, not just a token smile but a smile that is meant.* His deep voice broke in on her musings.

"Do you know, there's something I'd like to know?"

"What would that be now?"

"Do you love me?"

"What a stupid question – of course, I love you. Would I be over here sandwiched in a flat with Indians below me and English women above me if I didn't love you?" She tapped her stomach. "Would I be expecting him if I didn't love you? That sort of thing annoys me."

But her heart had started to thump and she was glad of the rosy light because her stupid face had flushed.

"All right, I won't nag you any more."

It was appallingly lonely after he was gone. Everyone else seemed to have a purpose in life. When she went for the newspaper and the milk first thing in the morning, she rarely met anyone under fifty. The newspapers brought no joy. She read about the civil rights march in Derry ending in mayhem and bloodshed, with thirteen people gunned down in the streets on a snow-swept Bloody Sunday. She was so shocked that her eyes blurred with tears as she gazed at the priest, Father Daly, going ahead of the injured and dying waving a white handkerchief in surrender. Most of those killed were in their teens. She cried as she read, wondering what she was doing in England when the British soldiers were gunning down Irish people in Ireland.

That evening the diminutive Indian woman knocked at her door and said there was a phone call for her. She smiled her dark-eyed liquid smile. "Your husband, he want you on the phone. . ."

Patsy, taking in the bright coloured silk sari, the friendly smiling eyes, the sandalled feet, wondered how she could stand the biting cold.

"Look, I'm sorry that you had to come up all the stairs. We've looked for a phone in the flat, but they tell us we must join a long waiting list."

The girl, who seemed little more than a child, smiled again. "I do not mind. It is a pleasure." Then her eyes alighted on Patsy's abdomen, now encased in a very roomy smock-like shirt. "When is your baby coming? I do hope that it will bring joy."

"So do I," Patsy smiled, "and it's not due till the first week in April so the weather should be better."

They walked down the stairs together with Patsy feeling like Gulliver beside the petite Indian. When they came to the hall, she thanked her again. Rory was obviously phoning from a pub because she could hear music in the background.

"You've seen the television, the papers? Things are going to blow up in the North. The place is a shambles – thirteen people dead. Maybe I should take you home."

"Funny, after I read it I wondered what we were doing here, but it would be mad to run now. If all the Irish working in England were to flock home, the country would be jammed. No, Rory, you've a great job – you wouldn't earn half that at home. Don't think I haven't bawled over the people that were shot – I've cried down the rain, honestly I have – but your going home won't bring them back."

"Maybe you're right, but I don't like it. How are you, love, anyway?"

"I'm okay."

"How is my son?"

"Safe and sound away from harm's way."

"I love you. I'll be back on Friday to nag you."

"Okay, I can't wait." Looking in her purse she saw that she had enough coins to phone her mother.

"Patsy!" Her mother sounded surprised, even alarmed. "Are you all right? Are you minding yourself?"

"Of course, I'm all right, Mam. It's just that Rory is away, and it's just terrible about the North, and he just phoned me, and I was in the hall, and I thought I'd phone you for any news."

"Well, it's lovely to hear your voice. There's not much news except what happened in Derry. Everyone is upset about it. I just saw on the television that a huge crowed had gathered in Merrion Square in Dublin and they've burned down the British Embassy. Dad said it was a stupid thing to do as we'll have to pay for it in the rates, but at least no one was killed, thank God. You must miss Rory, and I hope you're minding yourself. It won't be long now."

"I'm fine, but I feel I've been like this since I was ten."

"You get like that at your stage, but it won't be long. I hope you're drinking lots of milk and eating porridge and taking your iron. Iron is essential."

Patsy tried to stifle a sigh. "I am, Mam, I am. How is Sarah?"

"I'm worried about that girl. She's not looking well at all. She's pale and thin and I don't think she ever recovered from that pneumonia. I told her to go to that nice Doctor Conor McElroy and get a good tonic. I hear from Emma quite a bit. I think she likes that Jonathan chap. It's still going on, the line, I mean."

"Oh, it is, and I think you're right, Mam. You'll have a Protestant son-in-law, what do you think about that?"

Before her mother could reply, Patsy's money ran out and she was cut off. Looking at the dead phone in her hand she was tempted to go back up the stairs for more money to phone Sarah, but she knew it wasn't Sarah she wanted to hear. As she stood in the icy hall, Rory flashed into her mind and his question, "Do you love me?" The only decent thing she could do was walk up the shadowy staircase and get on with her life.

Alan could stand for nearly a minute now. All the sensation was in the right leg, and the sensation was pure agony. As the numbness gave way, the cramping pain and the twisted cramp came and the pain was almost unbearable, but he didn't collapse into Nancy's arms any more. He would stand there swaying, holding her eyes, his own showing intense pain, yet pain mingled with wonder, hope and incredulity.

"When?" she would almost bark.

"Easter," he would say. "It's Lent now, so Easter isn't far around the corner. I can sack you then."

"And I'll be glad to be rid of you, I can tell you."

But, of course, she wouldn't. When the miracle of his first movement had happened, she was so overcome with joy for him that she didn't give herself a thought, but now her happiness for him was tinged with a selfish loneliness. Without him she simply wouldn't know what to do with herself. He had become almost everything: her son, her companion, her burning interest, and now nearly her reason for living. Today she asked him the sort of intimate questions they had avoided so far.

"Yes," he told her, "I can do without the catheter; and yes, my other bodily functions are under control." He laughed then and said, "I know what you're dying to know. It's not absolutely happening yet, but it will – and then you better be careful!"

"As sure as there's a God in his heaven, I don't know why I bother with you," she laughed gruffly, shaking her head. "Did Sarah notice anything? She must have noticed the very things you've told me about just now."

"No, Nancy. I'm keeping it a secret. I know you think I'm mad, but I want to surprise her. Some day when she comes in the door, I'll greet her standing – not a teetering, shaky wreck, but standing up straight – you know what I mean?" He sighed. "Actually, right now, Nancy, I'm worried about her."

"How? What are you worried about?"

"She's changed so much. It's as if she's living in a world of her own. She's so quiet at times – almost withdrawn."

"Maybe it's a delayed reaction to everything that happened. She could also be depressed after the pneumonia – or postnatal depression can affect a mother even months after a child's birth."

"That's why I want to surprise her."

"I hope you won't give her a heart attack," Nancy said disapprovingly.

CHAPTER THIRTY-THREE

MARCH CAME IN bringing cold icy winds that whistled and sighed, penetrating every corner of the flat. Rory bought yet more draught excluders, saying that it was crazy to be doing such jobs in the spring. "But," he muttered, "as my good mother used to say – 'March in like a lion out like a lamb.'" March also brought a letter from Sarah.

> Dear Patsy,
>
> I hope both you and Rory are on top of the world looking forward to the big day. Aware of your terrible curiousity, I'd better tell you why I'm writing. I would love to visit you for a week – thereabouts. Would that be okay?
>
> Alan, Mam and pretty nearly everyone tell me that I'm looking a wreck – they don't quite put it like that, but you get the gist. They think I need a break, so I thought of London – see my young sister and her husband and take in the sights. Nancy Ryan is taking care of Alannah. She practically lives here now and adores her. I think Mam is a bit jealous, but it seemed the best arrangement all round. Anyway, I'll phone next Sunday, so be in the draughty hall at eight o'clock and I'll give you all the details of my flight and arrival, etc.
>
> Regards to Rory,
> Love, Sarah

Patsy was overjoyed at the prospect of Sarah's visit, and she knew Rory would be also. He worried about her long empty days, asking was she bored out of her mind and was she sorry she married him? She would tell him of course not, so please shut up and not be bothering her, but at times she did find the long days interminable.

Rereading Sarah's letter, Patsy decided she'd go mad and give the flat a thorough cleaning. Matt and Jane had a comfortable sofa bed which they could borrow, and she would buy bunches and bunches of the daffodils which were on sale everywhere. She might even take Sarah on the tour and give her the feel of London. She wouldn't put on Emma's sophisticated London act, but she would show her that she was no longer the young impulsive one they thought she was. She couldn't wait to tell Rory.

"We'll take her to a show. What about *South Pacific* or *The Mousetrap* – the Agatha Christie one that's been running for years and years?"

"With all the hysterical running around you might have the baby at the play," he teased.

"Don't be silly. Jane Campion tells me I'm still 'tidy' – at home they'd say 'very respectable'. God, Rory," she laughed, "aren't we mad in Ireland, as if you wouldn't be respectable if you were big?" She was still laughing when he kissed her on the mouth.

"You're a bit mad, anyway, but I'm glad she's coming for your sake."

Sitting on the stairs with Rory's sheepskin jacket around her shoulders, Patsy jumped at the strident ring of the phone. Sarah sounded breathless, "I'll be flying into Gatwick and then I'll take the bus into the city and get a taxi to you. Okay?"

"Absolutely. If you're not doing it in style! Flying, mind you. No cold boat and train journeys and old buses for our Sarah." She thought Sarah might laugh, but Sarah hadn't much of a sense of humour. "I'll be here with the teapot in my hand and the welcome mat at the door. Emma is dying to see you, too, and show off her Jonathan. Take care. Safe journey."

Patsy loathed waiting. When she was a child waiting for exciting times like Christmas, birthdays, or summer holidays, or even waiting for awful things like the results of exams, all took such a toll on her limited patience that she drove everyone mad. Today waiting for Sarah had her on nail-biting edge. She flew around fixing things she had fixed a minute before. She looked at her many preparations with a satisfied eye: the fire blazing away in the old Victorian fireplace, the brasses shining, the daffodils smiling from an assortment of jugs and vases.

The sound of a car stopping in the street below had her flying to the window, but it was only the delivery van outside the local shop. Just as she was about to walk away she saw the black taxi stopping outside the door. Sarah must have enjoyed sweeping along in the big black cab. Smiling, she ran down the stairs and in seconds they were greeting each other with warm hugs, something they had never done in younger years. As they walked up the stairs, Patsy chatted non-stop to hide her shock at how awful Sarah looked. She was still beautiful, but she was now too thin, her cheekbones too defined, her blue eyes heavily shadowed.

"You're exhausted," Patsy fussed. "Just dump your bag. I'm sorry you'll have to sleep out here, but they tell me that sofa bed is very comfortable." She nodded ruefully at the borrowed sofa bed, but Sarah didn't appear to care. Patsy rushed on, "The bathroom is across the way and when you're good and ready we'll have a bite to eat and a bottle of wine. Emma's bad influence – your young sister has developed a *grá* for the wine. Then you can tell me all the news. You'd be amazed how savage for news you'd get in a place like this."

Sarah smiled but the smile didn't touch her eyes. *Maybe she's sick – really, terribly sick*, Patsy panicked. *Maybe she has TB or cancer.* But she couldn't ply her with questions yet

Sarah was so quiet during the meal that Patsy continued to prattle as she gulped down the wine that Sarah hardly touched. She babbled about Emma's boyfriend Jonathan and how the folks at home would have to get used to the idea that she was going to marry a real dyed-in-the-wool

Englishman, and the troubles in Derry and how Rory had actually got the notion they should go home. "I told him that the troubles were seven or eight hundred years old and that our going home before we intended to wouldn't make much difference." She even pointed to the bright sky and the scurrying clouds that filled the window saying, "Isn't it great that the spring is here. Remember Mam always referred to the cock's step when the days were lengthening?"

Sarah looked out the window and didn't comment. Finally, dragging her gaze back to her sister, Sarah said, "I'm in terrible trouble, Patsy. Terrible. And I shouldn't burden you – I know that – but there was absolutely nothing else I could do. I'm not here for a holiday; that was just to fob them off at home."

"God almighty, what's up? Are you sick? Are you dying?"

A ghost of a smile touched Sarah's eyes and then vanished like the sun behind an April cloud. "I wish I was. For me it's much worse – I'm pregnant."

"Pregnant! Pregnant!" Patsy shouted in her astonishment. "I can't believe it. I thought Alan was . . . was . . ."

Sarah didn't let her continue. "Alan isn't the father of this child."

"What?" Patsy almost choked. "What are you saying? What are you trying to tell me?"

"Alan isn't the father. The father doesn't know a thing about it." Patsy stared at her sister, her face registering such shock, such disbelief, that Sarah felt sorry to have burdened her sister at such a vulnerable time.

"Alan can't father any more children. To put it bluntly, he can't do it any more, and most people know that, too. So you see the position I'm in. Think of the shame and disgrace. Think of all the gossip where we live if word broke that the master's wife was having an affair. Jesus, I'm going crazy with the whole business. Don't think it didn't enter my head to go down to the oyster bed and go in and wait for the currents to sweep me away."

"Who is the father of your baby?" Patsy's voice was a hoarse whisper.

"Conor McElroy."

"Jesus, I knew. I knew he had a thing for you. I knew it." She was almost wailing now. "Jesus above, Sarah, how could you do it? How? How could you be so cheap and desperate to go off with him and you married to the most amazing guy in the world. How could you let him do that and . . ."

"And my poor husband crippled and tied to a wheelchair. Say it. That's what everyone else will say, so why not you," Sarah said bitterly.

Patsy stared blindly at her and then wept. The tears ran down her face in a scalding bitter stream. "You have no idea have you?" she sobbed.

"Idea of what?" Sarah was hardly listening.

"No idea of what Alan means to me. Have you the slightest idea of what he has always meant to me? Have you?" Her voice was a hoarse sob now. "Was there ever anything in your head only you? Were you so wrapped up in your own life that you couldn't see anyone else's pain?"

"Patsy, what on earth are you talking about?"

"I'll tell you what I'm talking about. I've loved Alan ever since I met him." Her sobs redoubled. "I've loved him with all my heart and soul. I'd bloody die for him."

Sarah looked at her distraught young sister. Her haggard face registered puzzled astonishment. "Alan . . . you're talking about Alan?"

"Yes," Patsy choked, "I'm talking about your Alan. God, I'm sick of it. If I was near the bloody oyster bed it's I who should walk in."

Sarah sat rigidly, staring at Patsy. Then she moved and Patsy could feel a comforting arm around her shoulder.

"I had no idea. God above, isn't life complicated enough without this? You're right," she was almost sobbing now. "Maybe I'm so wrapped up in myself that I don't see beyond myself. I had no idea. I knew you were great friends. He loved having you around. You brightened him up . . ."

"Thanks," Patsy sounded bitter. "I know he has no inkling. When I told him I was marrying Rory because I couldn't have who I wanted, because the fellow I wanted was married, he was shocked and tried to talk me out of it, but he didn't know I meant him. He put his arms around me, and afterwards when I went home, I clung on to the feel of his arms, wondering what it would be like to have him all for myself." She started to cry again and through the sobs she told Sarah, "So you see, marrying Rory was a way out. Just a way out."

"Don't say that – please don't say that or you'll believe it." Sarah's voice was barely above a whisper. "But I do know how hard it is to stop loving someone. I couldn't stop wanting Conor. Maybe I couldn't stop loving him. And I do still love Alan. I now firmly believe there are different kinds of loving."

"But mine," Patsy gulped brokenly, "is a wrong sort of loving."

A while later when they had come to some semblance of normality, Patsy wanted to know what she intended to do.

"I can't have this baby." Sarah's tone was dead. "I came over here hoping that you might know someone who had had an abortion."

"You can't be serious." Patsy's blue eyes showed the horror she felt. "You simply can't do this. We'll talk to Emma; we'll ask the Catholic priest for advice. We'll think of something else, you'll see."

"Oh, Patsy, don't you know that I've been thinking of nothing else day or night. There is no other solution. You know Alan's boss is the canon, and you know the power of the Holy Catholic Church in Ireland. This would destroy his career, and people would point to Alannah and say her mother was a tart. Not to mention what it would do to our Mam and Dad and Alan's parents, his grandmother – they've suffered enough seeing him the way he is."

Patsy could only see one face – Alan Beirne's – and imagine how he'd look if he stumbled across the truth: the dawning knowledge in his eyes, the grimness in his mouth and the heartbreak in his dark eyes. Worse still, he couldn't stride out of the house and escape like other men. He couldn't tear into the pub and get drunk. She hardly recognised her own voice, which seemed to come from far away: "Jane Campion. Jane Campion knows about these things."

"Will she help me?'

"Yes, she'll help you."

In the years that followed Patsy never forgot that March evening with Jane Campion sitting there dressed in a fashionable grey suit with the new midi length skirt, her customary unflurried self as she talked. Rory was uncharacteristically quiet. Sarah was pale and tense, yet her deep blue eyes filled with gratitude for this Londoner who seemed to be making it all so easy. Patsy, sitting still in the armchair, stared at the daffodils she had arranged only that morning. Their pale jaunty faces still smiled, but for her they no longer heralded a summer of promise. *Maybe it's a nightmare*, she thought. *Maybe I'll wake up and Rory will be sleeping the sleep of the dead beside me. I'll nudge him and tell him about this awful nightmare I had.*

But the hands on the mantlepiece clock moved on as Jane talked quietly. She would arrange the appointment through her brother who was the chief administrator of the clinic in Surrey. It was a mere two hours' drive away. Sarah would be interviewed and counselled about what lay ahead. It was only an overnight stay. It wouldn't be easy, but she would recover in time and life would go on.

Rory told her, "I'll drive you there, Sarah. It will be no problem. And listen to me, girl, you're not the first and you wont be the last to make a mistake." Sarah, who up to then had kept a tight rein on her feelings, suddenly burst out crying. Rory took one long stride over to her and, putting his strong arms around her, rocked her gently. Patsy felt a rush of emotion. *Sarah's right,* she thought, *there are different kinds of loving.*

The same night that plans were being made in a flat in the suburbs of London, Alan Beirne sat alone in his kitchen in Ireland. It was midnight and his baby daughter and Nancy Ryan had long since retired for the night. He had just finished setting the Easter exam papers, which now lay in a neat pile on the table. He felt strangely restless tonight. Maybe it was missing Sarah or maybe it was the beauty of the night. He could clearly see the light of the full moon shining through the window. At the end of the garden the sea was visible – glinting like a silver ribbon through the dark pile of the woods that ran down to Sauleen. How he had loved walking through the woods hand in hand with Sarah as they went down to the beach.

He remembered his plan, the one that Nancy had told him would be like something one read in a cheap novelette. No time like the present. Wheeling away from the table, he pulled the curtains closed just in case there might be a some lone passer-by out there in the moonlight. At the far end of the kitchen near the dresser, he breathed deeply, at the same time gripping the arm rests, digging his hands into the leather and tensing his muscles. Then taking a second deep breath, he tried to ease and lift his body out of the confines of the wheelchair as his mind sent a command to his lower limbs. When he reached a half crouching position, he gritted his teeth against the terrible knotting of his muscles. The sweat ran down his face and gathered on his neck. He felt the pressure of his feet on the floor, and through the pain he enjoyed feeling his feet touching solid ground again. Then, calling on any last ounce of strength, he drew himself up. This was the point at which he always depended on Nancy Ryan for support, but he was alone now, and he knew he had to do this alone. Standing rocking on his feet, trying to ignore the twisting agony of the cramping muscles, he was swamped with dizziness. As he blindly reached out and caught the corner of the dresser for balance, something fell. He closed his eyes, expecting a plate or the huge meat dish to clatter on to the floor, but it was a soft thud. Swaying, he glanced down and saw that it was some sort of notebook. With the last vestige of strength, he eased himself into the chair.

Nancy Ryan was right. The time had come to go back to the specialists in Dublin. He had said Easter, and Easter was almost here now. He sat still, waiting for the wild beating of his heart to subside and for his breathing to return to normal.

When it did, he bent down and picked up the small red-covered books. Flicking through the pages of the newest one, he saw that it was filled with Sarah's writing. It was a diary. He never knew that she kept one. It was wrong and intrusive to read someone else's diary, even more so that of someone as close to him as Sarah, but she had become so troubled and withdrawn lately. Maybe this would throw some light on why, maybe help him to understand her. He should have taken her into his confidence about the improvement in his condition, given her hope for their future together. He had been stupid with his boyish notion of surprising her. Sighing, he flicked through the diary. It fell open on the last entry.

Nancy Ryan woke up from what was becoming a rare occurrence at her age – a deep sleep. Some cry had woken her, perhaps the cry of a wounded animal outside in the night. She could see the room was filled with moonlight, its beams touching the small round face of the sleeping child. She waited, thinking she might hear the cry again. There was nothing but the stillness of the spring night.

CHAPTER THIRTY-FOUR

T HEY LEFT SHORTLY before seven in the morning. Sarah was pale-faced and silent, yet with an air of purposeful composure. *She's like someone going to the gallows,* Patsy thought, as she helped her on with her coat and straightened Rory's tie, little everyday gestures as if they were going off on an outing. Sarah hugged her and Rory briefly kissed her before leaving. After they were gone, Patsy stood there surrounded by a silence and her thoughts. There were footsteps and Rory came back in the door. Taking her in his arms, he whispered, "God, Patsy, don't look so distraught. All that lovely childish look is gone: I want it back. Sarah's news has levelled you, but it's not the end of the world. Everything will be okay and you and I will get on with our lives. Okay?"

"Okay," she whispered, and in the warm circle of his arms she thought her heart would break.

Sarah didn't talk much and Rory was glad. On this journey there was no place for small talk. It must have been hell for her, for both of them, not to be able to make love in the first year of their marriage when they were both so young. And so the good doctor, of all people, had stepped into the breach. Doctors were usually cute hoors, but obviously Conor McElroy had got it bad, so bad in fact that he had risked being struck off the register for having sexual relations with one of his patients. *What a bloody mess,* he thought. Then he thought of Patsy and how she had looked this morning, all the light gone from her face as if someone had turned a switch.

Sarah was saying something, a question about how long the journey would take. He was about to tell her when he heard the strident sound of a loud horn. In that split second he knew he was powerless. He saw a black car, whose driver had recklessly overtaken a truck at a bend, hurtling towards them. Even after the grinding, smashing impact his ears were still filled with the shrieking horn as if the hand that pressed it were now unable to move.

Emma looked around her in amazement, her gaze scanning the silent empty room. "Where's Rory? Where's Sarah? What's happened to the hearty reunion?" She looked at her younger sister, her brown eyes taking in the grave pallor, the red-rimmed eyes. "Jesus, look at you. You're like someone who's buried her six children. What's up?" Despite her curiosity she didn't even wait for an answer before she hurtled off in her customary way. "I wanted everyone to be happy on a day like this. I have the most amazing wonderful news. Jonathan and I are getting engaged. I wanted my sisters to be the first to know. I even splashed out on a bottle of champers and I find I'm in a morgue. What's wrong?"

Patsy patted the sofa beside her and Emma collapsed into it, still clutching her bottle of champagne.

"Everything is wrong," Patsy wailed. "Sarah didn't come for a holiday. She came for something terrible – so terrible – it just doesn't bear thinking about."

Emma looked round the spacious room, her eyes taking in all the preparations that Patsy had made for Sarah's visit. "What's wrong – tell me what's happened?"

"Sarah is gone down to Surrey: Rory is driving her to a clinic. She's gone for an abortion. She's pregnant and the baby isn't Alan's. Jesus, Mary and Joseph, how could she do it – how?"

It seemed a full minute before Emma could gasp, "What? Are you sure? Ah, you can't be. It just can't be true. Sarah, so in control – and so daft about Alan?"

Patsy told Emma the whole story, and she sadly watched the layer of London sophistication peel away as Emma digested the news.

Some time later as they sipped tea, Emma glanced ruefully at her bottle of champagne, muttering, "Certainly no time for champagne. And here I was thinking that we'd be wildly celebrating here, and then we'd go to the pub, and the three Dunne sisters would get well and truly locked. God, this is unbelievable. I wonder if she had brazened it out and had the baby, would Alan have pretended that a miracle had happened and he was the father of the child?" She didn't even wait for an answer but rushed on. "I know what happened. She was starved for sex. She was crazy about Alan, but after the accident he couldn't do what every guy holds dear, and that had to change him and she couldn't handle it."

"I don't think he was changed – he was the same Alan to me."

"But you weren't married to him. You weren't sleeping with him. You wouldn't know."

"No, I suppose I wouldn't know."

At ten pm the front doorbell rang. The door opened, and they could hear the sound of voices, one deep and gruff, one light and lilting.

"That's the Indian girl," Patsy whispered. "I wonder who's there? It can't be Rory because he has a key."

Footsteps got louder and stopped right outside her own door. Two policemen stood there, a younger one looking little more than a boy and a tired-looking older one, who cleared his throat and inquired if this was the home of one Rory O'Driscoll.

It was Patsy's turn to clear her throat.

"Yeah, this is where he lives and I'm his wife"

His grey eyes had a fatherly look as they swept over her, taking in her youth and her advanced state of pregnancy.

"Well, Missus, may we come in then?" he asked. Patsy, still wondering what on earth they might want, pointed to the sofa, asking them to sit down. They declined, the younger one standing straight and stiff like a ramrod, the older one looking a bit uncomfortable.

"I'm sorry to be the bearer of bad news, ma'am, but there's been a traffic accident outside Hinckley village. The driver had identification and the woman had an address in Ireland."

Patsy looked at Emma and shrugged, as if to say, *Why are they telling us this?* Then somewhere on the periphery of her mind, she heard that Rory O'Driscoll, her husband of less than a year, was badly injured and the woman with him had unfortunately been killed. Then things went out of focus, the two policemen and Emma faded, and through the enveloping pain, she heard the BBC newscaster announcing that Mrs Ghandi had a big majority in the Indian elections.

The room was full of light and white-coated people speaking softly. They told her that she was in hospital. She had collapsed and gone into what had seemed like premature labour, but the contractions had now stopped and she would carry her baby to full term. She looked around and saw Emma sitting near by and she wondered why Emma looked so downcast. Then she remembered the policeman.

CHAPTER THIRTY-FIVE

IT LOOKED AS if the whole population of Tramore, Carbarry and the outlying villages was attending the removal of the young and beautiful wife of the crippled schoolmaster. They waited in the cold March wind for the first glimpse of the hearse that was coming from Dublin airport. They stood on the grass verges, at the cross-roads, in their hundreds around the small church. Their conversations was muted. The God-fearing amongst them tried to quell the rumours that were rife in the place. Could it possibly be true at all, at all, that the shock to the master was so terrible that he actually walked again? And may God in his heaven forgive those who hinted that Sarah Beirne was straying, and had run off to England where the doctor was going to join her. Of course, there wasn't an ounce of truth in that, although Mary McLoughlin had seen her a few times walking the beach with him and once Annie O'Brien thought she saw them going in a car going down the boreen that lead to Sauleen. May Machey, the postmistress, stood there in the chilly wind, her lips firmly closed, her rosary slipping through her hands, and not even the bravest amongst the women of Carbarry had the nerve to approach her for some comment that might confirm the flimsy rumours that were rampant.

Then there was a hush and word spread that the hearse was coming. It came fast up the hill followed by the undertaker's black cars, stopped at the gates and slowly made its way in to the church grounds. Then the murmur of the crowd grew louder as they watched the coffin being removed and the people getting out of the cars. God above, wasn't the master walking, with a crutch? The Beirnes were there, even the poor grandmother, and all the Dunnes with the exception of the youngest one whose poor husband was in hospital in England.

In the packed church the priest spoke about the good qualities and the deep spiritual belief that the hallmark of this young woman who had been so cruelly and so suddenly taken from her husband and child. "But we have to accept God's will and try and understand that this world is a mere testing ground, a waiting period until we are called home to enjoy everlasting happiness in heaven."

When it was over, the people crowded around Sarah's family and relations, offering their sympathy. Afterwards they all agreed they had never ever seen such misery in a man's eyes as in the master's. Doctor McElroy was there with old Doctor James and his wife, and some of the more gossip-starved felt cheated that there wasn't an ounce of truth in the rumour that he had run off to England with Sarah Beirne.

Patsy was discharged from hospital when the doctors were sure that her baby was now going to stay put. Outside the hospital waiting for a taxi, she told Emma that they must rush and get to Ireland for Sarah's funeral.

"I must go, dammit. I can't just stay here. I have to be with Alan at this time." Emma looked at her troubled face and thought that her sister was well and truly unhinged.

"You know you can't do that," Emma said quietly. "Your top priority now is Rory. He's in intensive care and he is your husband. Sometimes you forget that."

Patsy looked at her blankly for a moment. Suddenly swamping waves of guilt enveloped her with the knowledge that she had forgotten her husband in the tragedy of Sarah's death and the thought of Alan, heartbroken and desolate. She ran her tongue over her dry lips.

"Rory. Of course – of course. Dear Jesus, Emma, I actually forgot him. Imagine, here I am on my last legs and I forgot my husband."

A taxi pulled up then and they clamoured in. As it pulled away, it was Emma's turn to rant. "God, isn't it an appalling nightmare? Sarah so young and everything to live for now dead, and that little baby she was expecting dead, too. If she hadn't met that bloody Conor McElroy she'd be alive. And on top of that you want to go home to Alan and leave Rory and he in bits in the hospital. God," she wailed, "isn't life an effing bitch?" Patsy was silent as she stared out the window at the slow moving traffic.

Three days after Sarah Beirne's funeral, Conor McElroy made a phone call to England to Peter Costelloe who had been in college with him. They had done their internship in the same hospital and when they finished Peter had been offered a partnership in a small practice in the south of England, not too far from Hinckley Woods. After the surprised but warm greeting, Peter had laughed, "I know you didn't phone me for the good of my health and I know you're not giving me back the fiver you owe me, so what do you want?"

"Help," Conor said quietly. He then went on to tell him about the accident. "They were both taken to hospital, the Regional in Islington, I think. He's still there. She died in the crash. I want you to find out anything you can, like, where they were going and how the accident happened. What exactly caused her death? The inquest will be months away, so I have to know."

"Was she your woman?"

There was a brief hesitation before Conor quietly told him, "Yes, she was very much my woman."

"I'm sorry. You intended getting married?"

"No. She was already married. It's a long, sad story, Peter, in fact a minefield of complications. If you could get me some information I would be grateful."

Three days later Peter Costelloe phoned him back. Sarah Beirne had been killed instantly. The post-mortem showed she had died from cerebral haemorrhage. It also showed that she was ten weeks pregnant. "I think she was on her way to have it terminated – that's what I gleaned. Not sure but maybe."

318

There was a long silence before Conor McElroy replied, "Thanks, Peter – I'm grateful."

"I'm sorry, Conor."

"I'm sorry, too."

He sat beside the phone, his heart hammering dully, his mind grappling with the enormity of what he had heard. He thought of their last meeting. She had recovered from the lung infection. They had driven away from the sea, away from the woods and taken the back road to Waterford. Three miles outside the city they parked on the grass verge. They could see the red glow from the city in the night sky. With a heavy heart he had taken her in his arms, kissing her, sinking his mouth into her glossy blonde hair.

"This is crazy," he had whispered. "We should be in there in some warm hotel, having dinner, drinking good wine, in amongst people, lights and life."

He had expected her to say what she had often said: that they should end their affair, that she must think of Alan and her child; that he must think of the dire consequences if it were found out he was having an affair with one of his patients. But she didn't. She had run her hand over his face and traced his mouth with her finger.

"If I were to ask you to come away with me – somewhere far where no one would ever hear of us again – would you come?"

He had taken her cold hand in his. "If you were to ask me, I would follow you to the ends of the earth. You know that. With you, Siberia would be heaven."

She had smiled then, that wide gamine smile that made her look so young. "Ah, sure, we can't go anywhere. I just wanted to know."

He never saw her again. Sitting there, the sheer physical pain of her loss was tearing him asunder. He felt he could reach out and touch her. He recalled the first time he ever saw her, fidgeting with the belt of her summer dress the day in his rooms and later striding along the corridor in the

319

National Rehab in Dublin before he rushed her to the bin, in the throes of labour her face and hair drenched with sweat. He could see her swimming in the oyster bed with her powerful overarm crawl, running back up the beach in her sleek black swimsuit, her hair tied with twine. And that time on her knees in the sand after they had made love, telling him that she would prefer to die and burn in hell than have Alan know about her betrayal.

He had to leave. He must give some explanation to the Gillens, and he would have to visit Alan Beirne. He owed these people that much.

When he knocked at the door he expected to hear Alan's familiar voice telling him to come in, but instead he heard footsteps.

Conor knew that shock having caused the cure was highly improbable, but whatever had wrought the miracle was to be welcomed, particularly at this terrible time. Alan nodded towards the kitchen and apprehensively Conor followed him in. Alan, who was now walking with the aid of a stick, sat down, his movements slow as if he were in some pain. There seemed a reluctance on the part of both of them to start the conversation. Conor scanned the bright kitchen, recalling that Nancy Ryan was now living there. Presumably she had gone somewhere for the evening. Sadly Sarah wasn't around either, but maybe her spirit was there, her spirit that might in some way help the two men who had loved her deeply.

Conor cleared his throat, feeling that he must break the silence. "I heard that you were," he nodded towards the wheelchair now folded near by, "out of that thing. My mother, who has great faith in the power of God and little faith in modern medicine, would say it was a miracle." He knew he was waffling, but he needed to gain time to have the courage to face this man he had destroyed. He had to get this meeting over with if there was ever to be a chance to return to some sort of normality. "Christ, Alan, this isn't easy, but I couldn't skulk off like a rat." He searched the ravaged face of the man who now sat opposite him. "I think you know what happened. We didn't mean it to happen; it was the last thing she wanted. She loved you, you see."

"I know."

"What can I say? I can't just say I'm sorry. I could be dramatic and say that I wish I was in that grave and she here with you." He was silent then, waiting for some outburst, some tirade of accusation and abuse, but there was nothing only the ticking of the clock and the gentle sound of the ash falling from the range. Alan just sat there with his elbows propped on the table, his hand covering his mouth, his black eyes boring into Conor's. In the years that followed, Conor McElroy often recalled the silence, the restraint, and something else. He didn't think it was hatred, but it certainly wasn't forgiveness. He stood up. "I'd better go, but you do understand I had to come."

"Yes, I understand."

"I will be leaving – maybe England or Scotland."

"I understand that, too."

Conor stood up aware that the other man wasn't anxious to prolong this unwanted meeting. Alan stood also, and Conor noticed that he had to grip the table to steady himself.

"I'm still a bit of a crock, but Nancy tells me by the summer I'll probably be able to dance a jig." Alan's eyes bored into Conor's. "None of us planned what happened. A chain of events was caused by an accident in Rome. If I tell you I understand what happened, you'll think I'm soft in the bloody head. Maybe I am. Goodbye, Conor. I won't see you again."

Later that night Conor McElroy went in to the Gillens. Looking at him, Kit went to pour him a substantial drink. He lifted the glass and words failed him as he looked at the two people who had become so close to him, two people who had welcomed him into their lives, their home, their world.

Gulping down the whiskey, he told them he was leaving, and he told them why. He didn't spare himself. He could see the unvarnished truth was shocking them, and when he finished he waited, for the second time that evening, for the torrent of recriminations and angry words that must surely come. They didn't. Maybe it was the air they breathed that made these people so accepting and tolerant at a time of crisis. Kit broke the ice.

"Thank you, Conor, for telling us. It would have broken our hearts if we had heard it from anyone else. Wherever you go and whatever you do, you will take my love and best wishes with you always. What you have told us is tragic, but you didn't come here to cause heartbreak. You came here a young man full of hope and promise."

James Gillen tapped his pipe audibly on his glass ashtray. "Aye," he growled, "I couldn't put it better myself. You're dear to us both and we'll miss you. And you'll get over this. You think that you won't, but you will."

Conor didn't answer and Kit could see that he was struggling for control. *He probably thinks tears are a terrible weakness,* Kit thought. *Pity that men feel like that. What might help is a good long cry.*

CHAPTER THIRTY-SIX

Rory's condition had stabilised, and although he hadn't regained consciousness, he was expected to soon. Until John O'Driscoll arrived, Patsy sat there alone till evening, when Emma and Jonathan came and stayed with her for a while, as well as Matt and Jane. When John O'Driscoll phoned to say he was coming over to stay, he told her that she needn't worry about accommodating him.

"I have too much money if anything, and I'll get myself fixed up. What's more, I'm not going back until after the birth of my grandchild." Patsy laughed for first time since Sarah's death.

John came and booked into a small guesthouse near the hospital. He found Patsy sitting alone, gazing ahead as if she were far away from the hospital with its antiseptic smells, its rhythmic drips, its bleeping monitors. He was filled with pity as he saw her pale face and the shadows under her blue eyes, her youthful slimness now a memory as she huddled in her final stages of pregnancy. He hugged her and told her to go home and rest, that he would take care of everything. Like a child ordered to leave the room, she went home and to bed, where she lay tossing and twisting, her imagination running riot. She imagined that she was at the funeral, trying to comfort Alan and ease his heartbreak. Did Alan know about Conor McElroy? Did her parents have any idea of what had happened? Her mother had thought that Sarah was coming over for a little holiday. Poor mothers, they knew so little of what went on in their children's lives. Conor McElroy must be out of his mind with heartbreak. After all, Sarah had told her that she couldn't stop seeing him – couldn't stop loving him. Different kinds of loving, she had said. Different kinds of loving.

It was all of two weeks more before Rory regained consciousness. Slow blurring hours followed when he tried to walk, to talk, to let them know he was alive. The doctors advised that he was to be kept in the dark about Sarah's death until he was stronger. A day came when she found him sitting in a chair near the window dressed in his jeans and sweater, the heavy bandages reduced to a dressing on his forehead, the bruising fading, the breathing easier. He was beginning to look so like his old self that she expected him to jump up and suggest doing something outlandish. Instead his eyes met hers and he quietly asked, "How did Sarah fare?"

"She fared worse than you."

"Did she lose the baby?"

"Yeah, she did."

"Strange the way things work out," he told her. "She'll have no guilt now. She'll be at peace."

"Yeah, she'll be at peace all right." Patsy crossed her fingers behind her back in the old childish way before she remembered that it wasn't a lie. Sarah was at peace now. Of course she hadn't received the last sacraments, but maybe she had time to mutter an act of contrition. God would surely forgive her her sins anyway because she had suffered so much. Patsy sat with her husband, trying to be bright and cheerful, make small talk, but her heart wasn't in it.

Three days later she told him Sarah was dead. His initial reaction was one of pure shock, then he took her hand in his. His hand wasn't the strong hand she knew so well; it was softer, thinner, and her eyes filled with tears as he tried to console her.

"Christ above, that's terrible. Sarah dead. Everything over – funeral, burial – while I was lying here like a bloody log. And Alan, how is he?"

"According to Emma, devastated. And you're not going to believe this: whether it was shock or the months and months of physio from Nancy Ryan, he can actually stand and walk with the aid of a crutch. Though my mother says Nancy is the best physiotherapist in the world, she now thinks that it's Sarah working a miracle from heaven. Isn't it ironic? He's recovering and she's dead."

Rory didn't answer immediately. He sat there looking at her with a musing sort of expression. "He's free now," he said.

She barely caught the words, almost as if he didn't want her to hear. "Who's free? What are you on about?"

"Alan is free and we know he's devastated now but time heals. And he's young and a good looking bloke, and according to you he's recovering, so who knows what's ahead for him.'

"No, it won't be like that. Alan was a one-woman man."

"How do you know?" She sat there, feeling her baby kick wildly inside her, and she longed for the other Rory: the breezy, accepting, devil-may-care Rory. But he seemed to be gone and the quiet grave fellow with the softer, thinner hands was sitting there instead. She hoped he wouldn't be gone for ever. Looking at him she realised that he was waiting for an answer.

"Because I know."

A week later he was discharged, and both Patsy and his father were astonished that he had made such progress in the brief ten days since he had regained consciousness. He was more like the old Rory, ebullient and positive, and he seemed to have put the shadows of Sarah's untimely death behind him. His father was a constant visitor to the flat, waiting all of three weeks before his first grandchild was born.

Patsy's labour pains started in the small hours, and Rory insisted on driving her to the hospital as soon as the pains were established. As they sped through the dark empty streets, he told her, "Now take it easy, Patsy Dunne. Do all that deep breathing stuff and don't panic."

"Who's panicking?" she gasped between pains.

"If you have it in the car," he bantered, "O'Driscoll here will tie all the knots and stuff and add midwifery to his abundant skills."

Three hours later she couldn't believe the pain could be so terrible. She gritted her teeth as it worsened, telling herself that so many people in her life had suffered that it was time she did, too. When her son eventually was born he was eight pounds of perfection – strong, sturdy, yelling lustily and the image of Rory. Rory was ecstatic. He put his arms around her and gazed with wonder at the baby cradled in her arms.

"Hey, you did it, Patsy Dunne – you did it." He looked at her his eyes filled with tenderness. "Remember, he's the first of ten." He brushed back her damp hair and kissed her on the mouth and the kiss felt good.

John O'Driscoll was equally ecstatic. He visited the hospital every day and spent hours gazing at the baby. He had insisted on buying drinks for the house in the pub that Rory, Matt and all the fellows from the job frequented. John O'Driscoll told Jane, "My cup of happiness would be overflowing if my wife, Mary, had lived to see this day." Jane felt isolated from these enthusiastic Irish who put such an extraordinary, almost inexplicable value on the birth of a child.

A month later the baby was christened. Tim and Eileen Dunne came over from Ireland and John O'Driscoll, who had gone home for a short stay, was back. All Rory's colleagues from the company were there, including Matt and Jane. Emma and Jonathan had also just returned from a few days in Ireland where they had celebrated a belated engagement. Rory got so carried away he invited the Indian couple and their little child from the flat below and Doreen Lawson, the pleasant English woman from the flat above them. They all accepted with alacrity. It was a joyous day when many of them tried to put the sorrow of the last few weeks behind them.

Tim Dunne raised his glass, saying that he was glad that such an intelligent-looking child would bear his name. "I think it's only right that an old Irish tradition is being carried on – the first son called after the bride's father, who undoubtedly deserves such an honour." There was laughter then, and Rory's father told them that this time next year they would all be gathered again, but hopefully in County Tipperary, where they would honour the next fellow by calling him John. Everyone toasted that and there was much laughter because it was that sort of day.

That evening when the guests had gone – Patsy's parents and John O'Driscoll to a nearby guest house and the young crowd to a local pub for the last roistering hour – Emma and Jonathan insisted on staying to help clean up the chaos.

"No," Rory told her, "there's no need. I'll do it all in the morning. I've got a few hours off."

"No, you won't," Patsy argued. "You're going hammer and tongs all day looking after everyone. Sit with Jonathan and relax – Emma and I will make a start. Anyway, I want to catch up with the news from that newly engaged sister of mine."

Rory seemed reluctant to relinquish the task before flopping back into the sofa and agreeing, "Fair enough. Jonathan will have one for the road and I'll keep him company."

Patsy watched as Emma took off her engagement ring, placed it carefully on the windowsill and slowly worked her hands into the new pair of rubber gloves she had found in the cupboard under the sink. Her heart thudded before she asked the simple question, "How is Alan?"

"Alan?"

"Yeah, Alan. You know I want to know all about him."

Emma, looking up from swishing the washing up liquid in the sink, was uncharacteristically slow with her answer. "He can walk now with the aid of a stick, but I suppose you know that. He was back in hospital recently and they told him he would recover completely. I think it's positively weird."

"How does he look?"

"Haggard and thinner and older. He looks so awful I wonder if he knows the truth about Sarah and Conor McElroy. You know rural Ireland – everything seeps out."

"I dunno. I hope not. And what about Conor McElroy, is he still there going around looking the innocent?"

"No, I don't think so. There was some talk of him coming over here to work. What a bloody sordid mess."

Patsy was silent as she picked up the glass. She watched the little coloured bubbles run around the rim, remembering the way she had abused Sarah for her unfaithfulness to Alan and the way Sarah had tried to explain her feelings for Conor. Emma was rattling away normally now. "And anyway, thank God, you got your act together. All that nonsense about Alan. It's well you got over all that."

"I didn't," Patsy said softly. Emma looked up from her sudsy task in astonishment.

"Of course you did. You must have. You and Rory have been through so much and now everything is fine. You have a beautiful baby and everything is fine," she repeated as if in doing so everything would indeed be fine.

"Don't I know all that? But I think if heaven was tossed in my lap, I wouldn't be able to get Alan out of my mind. You see he's there always. During the day. At night before I fall asleep. I can hear his voice in all my dreams. I'd be ashamed to tell you what goes through my head."

"You're fucking crazy. You'll have to see a psychiatrist, or better still maybe you should go over and get off with him, sleep with him – taste the forbidden fruit – get him out of your system once and for all."

They both looked up as they heard the rattle of glasses. Rory had come into the kitchen with a laden tray. His glance swept over both of them as he carefully placed the tray on the draining board.

CHAPTER THIRTY-SEVEN

T HREE WEEKS AFTER the baby's christening, Rory came home and told her that the company were sending a team out to the Middle East and a few of them had volunteered to go.

"We've been offered the sort of money that would be impossible to turn down. The stint in the gulf will last two years, and when we come home we should be up to our eyeballs in money. You don't pay tax out there and everything is dirt cheap. We get a free house and a company jeep, and when we come back we can build our own house. What do you think?"

Putting the baby back in his cot, she looked up at him in astonishment. "The Middle East, the gulf? They're on a different planet. They can't expect you to go to a place like that, just like that."

"They can, and maybe I want to go to a place like that. Sometimes," he sighed, "I mightn't even mind a different planet. Anyway, it's only when you're young you can do these things."

"Is Matt going? Will Jane give up her law practice and lope out after him like a good little girl?"

"No, maybe she won't. In fact, there's some question she won't, but they're not married with a child. Not, what do the call it these days, a family unit. Isn't that what we're supposed to be?"

"Rory, you know I can't go. I can't run off to the ends of the earth with a small baby and live in a desert. You know in your heart I can't."

"Of course you can. You're the one that's supposed to have an adventuresome streak. Remember all that stuff about backpacking all around the world? What happened to that girl? I don't seem to see her around any more." He sounded decidedly weary. In fact, it struck her that he had been decidedly tired and weary for a while now. She had been so busy with the baby she had been only barely aware. She looked at him, her blue eyes holding his.

"If I'm going anywhere, I'm going back home. I haven't been home for ages. I must let Mam and Dad see more of their grandson. I must see Alan and Alannah. Rory, I must go home."

Little Timothy started to cry then as if he knew the air was tension filled. Rory bent down and lifted him up, soothing him with a few tender words. With the baby's head cradled to his shoulder, he looked at her, his grey eyes cold and unblinking.

"So I go to Kuwait for two years and you go home to Ireland. Will you stay there the two years waiting until I return? Is that what you have in your mind, or have you some other devious plot somewhere inside your sick head?"

He bent down and put the child back in his pram. Straightening up he reached out and caught her roughly by the shoulders. She could feel the bruising strength of his fingers. "Why in the name of Christ can't you be honest with me? You want to see Alan Beirne. Don't deny it. Don't tell me I'm wrong because I don't want to bloody hear. I heard you and Emma talk about your sick obsession that night in the kitchen. Listen, I've waited – I've fucking waited – but no man will wait for ever. Will you ever fucking grow up?"

She had never seen him so angry, never seen his eyes so filled with fury. She tried to back away but he held her in a tight grip. She thought of lying and showering him with protestations, but her heart was suffocating her, making her breathing difficult. She was about to open her mouth but he reached over and placed his fingers against her lips.

"I repeat, don't say anything, because I'm sick of hearing things that have no meaning. I've known . . . Jesus, I've known how you felt about him. I knew from the very beginning. I've waited in the goddam wings hoping that this

330

would abate, but it didn't." He stared at her, his eyes ablaze with fury. "Maybe you should take your sister's advice and sleep with him. He'll be capable now from what I hear. As for me, I want you to know that the waiting is over."

There were frenzied preparations before the team went to the Middle East. During this busy time, Patsy and Rory rarely spoke to each other. Sometimes in the evenings when the curtain of silence closed in, she wanted to shatter the cloying thing and get back to the way they had been. But hadn't he warned her not to talk, not to try and explain, because he didn't want to hear. Though they slept in the same bed, they clung to their separate sides. She missed the warmth, the rapport. A few times she wanted to say, "You were right. It was only a childish obsession, a crazy, foolish thing. It's over, burnt out now." But she couldn't because she knew it wasn't.

The evening before their departure, Matt Devlin threw a farewell party. Rory told her coldly they were expected there and she was to get a babysitter. Emma stayed with Tim and they went to the party. It was a noisy, hilarious night with drink flowing like a river. Through the din she spoke to Jane Campion who told her that she wasn't going to join Matt.

"My career is here. My going out to a place like that would serve no purpose."

"But Matt must be devastated?"

"Maybe not as devastated as Rory. I believe you're returning to Ireland with the baby."

"God almighty, Jane, I don't know what I'm doing. Everything is so chaotic since Sarah was killed. Will you wait for Matt to come back?"

"Yes. I will wait for Matt to come back. It wouldn't be any good without him." Then Matt came over and told them they looked like two sad menopausal nuns and they both burst out laughing. Patsy realised that it was the first time she had laughed in weeks.

The farewell at the airport was strained and difficult. Before Rory left her he brushed his lips against her cheek. "I'll write to you at your mother's address." Then holding his son in his arms he covered the small sleeping face with kisses. Then he was gone, and loneliness swamped her.

With the tide out the lines of the oyster bed were defined, giving the impression of a sparkling oval swimming pool. Patsy thought she heard voices. Turning she saw a man tearing across the smooth golden sand with a boy chasing after him. There was a leggy, scraggy dog racing like the wind beside them. The racket they made disturbed the seagulls, who screeched their disapproval, rising like a silver cloud above them. She took the keys out of her jeans pocket and switched on the engine.

She had returned to Ireland two days earlier. When that morning, she had told her mother that she was going to drop over and see Alan, her mother had warned her that she'd find him changed.

"I don't think he'll ever get over Sarah, although he's a young man. They say time will heal, and it might – it might."

Patsy glanced at herself in the small mirror. She looked pale, her blue eyes were shadowed, and her cropped auburn hair blown and untidy. She glanced down at her faded jeans and the thonged sandals she had bought in the Indian shop on a bright spring day. Driving back along the dusty road she noticed with surprise that the blackberries were out. They glowed luscious and ripe on the hedgerows. Way down at the bottom of the hill she saw the cottage. Yes, she would call now. If she didn't it would be more difficult the next time. Her heart started to play up like it always played up when she was near him. She licked her lips in an effort to moisten them, but there was no relief. His car was parked in the gravel drive and the windows of the cottage were open to the lovely late summer's day. Her mother told her that Nancy Ryan was more or less living there now helping him with the housework and taking care of Alannah, but there was no sign of her Morris Minor.

Patsy slowed down and switched off the engine. She glanced at the closed, silent cottage and recalled the excitement when they had rented it. How happy they must have been, looking ahead to a lifetime of fulfilment. She didn't even want to think of the desolation and the heartbreak of the man who now lived behind the silent peaceful exterior. She knew now that she wasn't prepared to see him yet. No, her meeting with him would have to be later, when she was more in control. The sound of the engine spluttering into life woke her small son. With his demanding cries filling her ears, she drove slowly down the winding dusty road.

CHAPTER THIRTY-EIGHT

"WELL, DID YOU call to see Alan?" her mother asked. "I'm sure he was glad to see you. It's not easy for him there with a baby and only Nancy to keep him company."

"No, I didn't. I just drove over to Sauleen for a look. I went past the cottage with the intention of calling, but Timothy started to yell, so I decided I'd I call later. Maybe this evening."

"Go over this evening – he'll be glad to see you. He's changed, of course – not the same Alan at all. Then again we're all changed. Sure, I'll never get over Sarah . . ." Eileen tried unsuccessfully to hide the break in her voice.

"I know, Mam, I know." Patsy said gently. "We all miss her. We all loved her you know."

"It was strange, wasn't it, this drive they went on . . ." Patsy knew what was coming. Once again she would have to answer questions about what happened: where was Rory driving her? What was it about and why wasn't she with them?

"I told you, Mam," she explained patiently, the lies rolling with ease again. They had been told so often she now felt a semblance of truth in them. "Rory was going down to Surrey on business. He thought she would like to see that part of England. After all she was on a break that you all felt she needed. I didn't go along with them because I was on my last legs – pretty exhausted."

"Thank God, you didn't. At least I have that to be thankful for." Patsy was grateful for the loud cry as the baby woke demanding attention. She watched as her mother almost ran to pick him up, making soothing noises as she took him in her arms.

"Yes," she repeated as she gazed at her grandchild, "I have that to be thankful for. Now, Patsy, I'll give him his feed. You go in and have a rest. You look exhausted. I suppose the journey home and the worry of Rory going off to that awful desert has taken its toll. I can't understand why he wanted to go off to the ends of the earth so soon after the baby and Sarah and everything. There's no understanding people at all. But do go and see Alan tonight. He could do with a bit of company. Tonight is the ICA meeting, so Nancy won't be there."

She dabbled with the idea of wearing the black dress. She knew it would fit because if anything she had lost weight lately. She would stick a scarf inside the low neck to make it look a little more casual. She told herself she was a fool. A sophisticated dress that Rory had given for a drop-in visit to someone who lived in the heart of the country would be stupid. She settled for the green silk shirt she had worn for Emma's party, tucked into her jeans. She grabbed a cardigan in case she was cold.

The road she had travelled only hours earlier was almost deserted. There was a full harvest moon lighting the fields, the woods, the distant sea. She could see the cottage from way up the road. She felt a stab of memory as she passed the stile that Sarah had tripped over on that Christmas night. She stifled memory. She tried to scrub her mind clean as she approached the stone cottage. The light was on and Alan's car was parked in the short gravel drive. There was still no sign of Nancy Ryan's car – she was glad of that. Knocking at the door, she had never, ever, felt so nervous in her whole life. Neither had she ever knocked at the door before. Since Alan's accident the key was always in the lock, but it wasn't there now. She knocked again. She heard footsteps but wasn't sure they were his. Standing there with her heart thumping and her blood roaring in her ears, she wasn't sure of anything.

When he opened the door, he looked the same and he didn't look the same. He was standing and leaning on a stick. He looked older and there were lines etching the mouth that had passed the raking examination so long ago. There was slight touch of grey in his hair but his eyes were the same.

"Hi, I came over. I was around this morning but I didn't call – the baby was yelling and I came over now."

Her voice sounded completely alien to her ears and she was surprised that he sounded so normal and familiar.

"Good God, Patsy, come in. You're a sight for sore eyes."

She shakily followed him into the sitting room. She could see now that he walked with a slight limp. When he got to the sofa, he placed the walking stick near by. Turning around he opened his arms, enveloping her in a warm clasp. She went straight into them like a tossing boat arriving in a safe harbour. Encircled in the arms of a man she had loved almost all her adult life, thoughts tumbled through her head. Would he kiss her? Would it be on the mouth? Would it be brotherly on the cheek? Would it be a mere brush of his lips on her hair. He kissed her on the forehead and then held her away from him.

"God, it's great to see you." He dropped his arms and pointed to the chair.

She sat down and all the prepared things she felt she should say stuck solid somewhere inside her. She could only drum up five simple words: "I was so sorry, Alan."

He nodded, and now in the glow of the lamplight she could clearly see how changed and ravaged he looked. He didn't answer, but his dark eyes didn't stray from her face. In the silence she could hear voices in her head: Emma's lightly spoken, *"Why don't you go and sleep with him and get him out of your system."* Rory's bitter exclamation, *"He's free now. Why for God's sake don't you grow up?"* Sarah's soft voice saying, *"I didn't know – I had no idea, Patsy. I firmly believe there are different kinds of loving."*

With her head spinning she walked over and stood beside him and held out her hands, and he stood up taking her cold hands in his. She reached up and kissed him and there was nothing sisterly in her kiss. He held her then and, pulling her closer, kissed her, and there was nothing brotherly in his kiss. They kissed and it went on for so long that it seemed for ever.

When they broke apart her heart was hammering and she knew in her soul the feeling that swamped him was desire, too. She felt he needed her as desperately as she wanted him. His eyes, shadowed and almost black, held her eyes for so long she was weak and trembling with longing.

"I love you," she spoke like a child. "I've always loved you – but you know that."

He nodded and pulling her back into his arms, he whispered, "Don't, Patsy – please don't, for God's sake, please don't." Even as he spoke she could hear his thumping heart and feel the hardness of his body

"But I do. So many people know it now: Emma, Rory, even Sarah before the accident."

He rocked her in his arms, saying, "Please stop this foolishness, Patsy, for Christ's sake. There's enough harm done – we won't add to it."

She drew away, her blue eyes blazing into his. "You want me – you do just now. You feel something. I'm not a fool, Alan Beirne, I know you do." Calling him by his full name like she had called him in the old days made her sob, and the sob brought unwanted tears.

He led her to the sofa and firmly put her sitting down. She was glad of the reprieve away from his tortured eyes, away from his encircling arms – away from everything she wanted.

"Listen, Patsy – please listen."

She sat there looking at him, the tears impatiently wiped away now, leaving her face scrubbed clean. She was like a young child listening intently to her teacher. "You're right, Patsy. I felt something now. I wanted to take you in there," he nodded towards the bedroom, "and devour you." He closed his eyes and offered up a silent prayer that he wouldn't cause any more pain to this young woman who to him was little more than a child.

"The reason I lost control, Patsy, was for one blinding moment I thought you were Sarah. It's the eyes, you see.

337

They're just like hers. I felt I was drowning in them. You see, I won't be able to stop loving her, not for a long time – maybe not for ever." The room was full of silence then, a silence neither of them was prepared to break. A silence that seemed full of Sarah. Sarah so beautiful, so confident before her marriage. Sarah pregnant, restless and haunted after it. Patsy was the first to break it,

"You still love her even after what happened?"

"Yes. You see, I understood why it happened."

"Are you a saint altogether?" She sounded so hurt, so bitter, that it wrenched something inside him. "And Conor McElroy – I suppose Saint Alan will bloody forgive him, too?"

A brief smile touched his mouth and he momentarily looked like the old Alan. He was talking again and like a child at school she forced herself to listen.

"Yes, I do in a way. He was hurt, too. The whole thing was beyond our control. Fate – an act of God – call it what you like."

"And me? What about me? Is the way I feel fate, an act of God?"

He looked at her and she steeled herself not to melt ever again – ever again, not any more. He reached out and put his hand under her chin forcing her once again to meet his gaze.

"Listen, Patsy, you mean a great deal to me. I'll always want to know where you are and what you're at and that you're happy for the rest of your life. Do you realise you have so much: personality, looks, a good man, a beautiful son from what I hear? Be grateful, love, for all that. What does the Bible say – put away childish things."

She sat there and didn't interrupt as his voice flowed over her. He told her of the long slow process of his recovery. He told her how grateful he was to Nancy Ryan for her wonderful power of healing. He told her how he found out about Sarah and her involvement with Conor. Then he told

338

her that he and Alannah were going to Australia. A friend
he knew in college had encouraged him, and things were
already in motion. He knew it would cause pain to so many
– his parents, his grandmother, her own father and mother.
Nancy Ryan had asked him if she could go out there with
him, and he felt it was a great idea. He also felt most people
would understand why he was going.

When it was time to go he walked with her to the small
porch. She stood there beside him. Once again he drew her
into his arms gently and kissed her briefly on the mouth. She
pulled impatiently away and almost ran out the door. He
watched her go down the drive with her familiar long-legged,
purposeful stride, and he could see she was wiping her face
with her hand. He thought, *She will never really know how near
I was to taking her.* It would have been so easy, like the releas-
ing of a dam, because it had been so long – so desperately
long. When the sound of her car faded, he smiled as he
recalled her words – Saint Alan. Yes, he would miss her.
Wherever she went, he would miss her, and he would always
love her. Not the way she wanted, but with the sort of love
that transcended human need, human appetite and passion.

CHAPTER THIRTY-NINE

PATSY WAS GLAD her son was in a deep sleep. Glancing around the plane she could see many other passengers were sleeping, too. If anything she was relieved that her mind was sharp and clear, making it possible to relive the last few weeks.

The letter from Rory arrived three days after her traumatic and emotional visit to Alan. It didn't read like a letter from a loving husband, but rather more like a letter from a friend telling her what it was like to live in this small emirate on top of the Persian Gulf.

Dear Patsy,

I hope you're well and needless to say I hope my son is good, thriving and full of spark. The journey from London to Kuwait was fine. After a few brandies Matt and I slept most of the way.

There's fine airport in Kuwait and the city itself is a mind-boggling contradiction. The coast road is built on such a grandiose scale, with marble-fronted hotels, towers and monuments, that it leaves one utterly unprepared for the terrible shanties and the appalling, ramshackle dwellings outside the city. It was so hot getting off the plane it was like walking into a gas oven. The temperature is around 90 degrees as I write – but worse than that is the awful humidity. Matt and I went for a few swims and the sea was scalding hot – unlike your oyster bed, I'd say – and the sand was so hot you could hardly walk on the stuff.

The company has contracted to build three tower blocks of apartments not too far from the coast. One peculiar thing is that the Kuwait natives don't want to work – lazy feckers. I think I'm now working with five different nationalities: Palestinians, Koreans, Turks etc. Of course, it's the oil that makes it one of the richest little countries in the world. A Scottish architect gave the perfect description the other night. He said Kuwait is only an oil well covered with sand. Talking of sand, we get the most terrible sand storms. The sand is micro-fine and comes in everywhere – under windows, doors, cracks in the walls – you can't keep the stuff out. But in the evening sun, when the storm is abating, it makes the most peculiar golden patterns in the sky. Not as awesome though as the stars on a clear night over Sauleen. Remember?

As Patsy read she remembered and remembering brought a lump to her throat. She tried to swallow it because she was sick to death of lumps in her throat.

I think there are things you would like out here. There's a sense of friendship and a great social life. There's also the fact that parts of this country haven't changed in hundreds of years. Bedouins still sleep out in the desert and live in black tents. Before the oil wells the main business was fishing – it's interesting to see the dhows, the small currach-like crafts, going out every evening. A bit like the West of Ireland. I know my old man would find it very interesting – I'm definitely going to invite him out for a bit. By the way, so much is free and there's no income tax, no health charges, no school fees. There's even free transport for school kids, free lunches – free everything.

I'd better stop. Matt wants me to go over to a compound for a party – no Guinness sadly but we'll survive. Have you had a rethink at this stage about coming out? The company has already paid all the costs, and if you think you'd survive it here let me know and I'll send the tickets and all the information you need.

It might interest you to know that Jane Campion is coming out for a stay at Christmas, so maybe she misses Matt. Let me know and regards to everyone and a hundred kisses for that son of mine.

Rory.

Even though he had sent no love to her, and remembering the last few weeks they had spent together she didn't expect him to, she read the letter with a sense of purpose. One hour later a telegram was speedily dispatched. She put Timothy in his pram and told her mother she was going for a walk, went to the post office and sent it off: "Timmy and I will join you as soon as possible STOP Send on tickets STOP Will confirm date STOP Patsy STOP"

The following weeks were a frenzy of preparation with old school friends calling to say goodbye, and Rory's father coming to visit, telling her he'd be out to see them before you could say Jack Robinson. Her mother brought over Alannah to see the baby and Patsy marvelled at how fast she was developing and how bright and beautiful she was. Emma phoned her excitingly, wishing her all the best and whispering to her that she was glad she had finally got her head together. She also told her that she would have to return the following year for her and Jonathan's wedding.

Alan called the evening before she left. She was in the kitchen washing up after tea; her baby was in bed and her parents in the sitting room, her father no doubt reading the paper and her mother looking at her current favourite programme, "Poldark". He had come in the back door and stood there uncertainly, as if he weren't sure how she would react.

"Hi." Her greeting was warm and she hoped her smile was the sort of smile you give your brother-in-law. Her will-power was working to its limit trying to control every single thought, every single emotion. "They're in the sitting room. Come in and we'll join them. She's very low about my departure. God knows, she'll do her nut when she hears you're off."

Good girl, the inner voice whispered, *You're great. A lovely performance – nice and bright – perfect for the sister-in-law, the young companion of yesterday about to become the sane and normal wife going off to join her husband.*

"Right, I'd better show my face." She went ahead of him, wiping the suds on her jeans, staying a few paces away – staying calm, staying controlled.

They were glad to see him and they talked like they had in the old days, her father touching on current affairs and her mother pleased that he had called. Patsy, sitting on the sofa, studied him. She had read something somewhere about a lived-in face. She wondered was that how she'd describe his handsome face now? She glanced around the room and was glad that her mother had finally removed the wedding picture showing both Sarah and Alan on their wedding day: Sarah had looked so radiant, Alan so proud, so protective. There was just a faint outline where the picture had been.

When it was time for him to go, he stood up and, nodding towards Patsy, he said, "So she's off tomorrow."

"I know, I know, and I'll be dead after her and Timothy. But I know it's for the best. At least I have you and Alannah," Eileen said. Patsy's heart almost stopped and she was filled with pity for her mother. "See Alan out, Patsy, like a good girl," her mother asked.

They walked out of the warm room into the hall, out the front door and scrunched across the driveway to his car. They were silent. The only sound to break the stillness was a dog barking somewhere in the distance. Patsy glanced up and saw that the sky was dark and brooding with not a star to be seen.

"I wanted it to be starry on my last night. I like stars."

343

He followed her glance. "I know, I like stars, too. When you see them in their millions you feel unimportant somehow." He seemed reluctant to drag his gaze away from the sky to look at her. "Well, Patsy, this is it," he said finally. "It's time to say goodbye and safe journey."

It was so normal, so friendly, so everyday. Simple farewell words between herself and her brother-in-law. Then he put his arms around her and hugged her, briefly kissing her on the forehead. Remembering to keep every single screaming nerve inside her suppressed and controlled, she reached up and kissed him softly on the lips, telling herself that it was all right this time. This time she was kissing her closest and very best friend goodbye. She thought she heard a slight choking sound somewhere. It hadn't come from her, because in his proximity for the first time in her life she was in control. As he turned away and stooped to get into the car, the iron resolve inside her weakened. With a Herculean effort she held on to it, and as the car went down the drive a sob escaped her as she wildly tried to dismiss the thought that she would never see him again.

"Fasten your seat belts. We will be landing in approximately ten minutes in Kuwait airport."

Patsy was amazed that the baby had slept for so long. As she fastened the seat belt around both of them, he woke up his eyes startled and wide. She expected a demanding yell but it didn't come. He simply continued to gaze around curiously. She was suddenly filled with apprehension. Was she doing the right thing bringing such a small child out to a country she knew nothing about? Then there was Rory – a Rory that had become so different from the one she had known. She remembered his bitter words before she had left for Ireland and his letter with no mention of love. Maybe he only wanted her out there because of his son. She recalled how spontaneous and open he had always been: no hidden agendas, no secret world, no holding back. He had loved her despite her secret world, her holding back, even her failure to love him, to give completely.

The plane landed and as the passengers filed off, she went into a world that was suffocatingly hot and airless. The smiling hostess asked her if she needed help and she shook her head.

She saw him before he saw her and she could see that he looked different. His hair was so much fairer, obviously bleached from the sun. He looked bronzed and a bit older. When he saw her he waved, and when they met he dropped a casual kiss on her cheek. She couldn't read what was in his eyes because the sun was shining in her face. He immediately took the child from her arms, held him aloft and then dropped him a few inches before catching him and showering him with kisses.

"He looks great. You've done a good job with him, Patsy Dunne."

Maybe it was a good omen that he had called her Patsy Dunne like he did in the old days. Outside he opened the door of a sleek and unfamiliar car for her, put Timothy on her lap and went to empty the luggage trolley into the boot. She watched him in the mirror and despite the bronzed look he looked a bit strained and uncertain. As he was about to put the key in the ignition, she placed her hand over his, giving it a warm squeeze.

"Hi, Rory O'Driscoll," she whispered. "Great to see you." He looked at her and she could see the surprise on his face. She could see his eyes clearly now, eyes that were bluer than she remembered. Was it hope in their depths? She wasn't sure.

"Hi, it's great to see you, too." Then he had his arms around her and, careful to protect the child, he kissed her. The pressure of his lips on hers didn't just make her feel good like in the old days. She wasn't sure what the feeling was – was it longing? Was it arousal? Then he was looking at her again, his eyes clear and questioning.

"Tell me, because I want to know – and the truth this time – are all the ghosts routed?"

She held his gaze, her deep blue eyes steady and unwavering. "Yeah, I swear. They're routed. And nothing dramatic happened to rout them. Anyway, if they weren't, what on earth would I be doing here?"

He smiled then, the same old whimsical smile. "What indeed would you be doing here?"

As they drove from the airport into this strange new place, she felt the terrible tightness inside her ease. She wasn't sure what was replacing it. She hoped it was light, love and understanding. She glanced at her husband, her eyes noting the firm chin, the strong profile, the familiar hands on the wheel of the car.

"Well, will I really do this time?" She could hear something like jubilation in his tone.

"Yeah, there's nothing surer. You'll absolutely do this time."

Their eyes locked briefly and what he saw in hers seemed to satisfy him. As they drove on into this alien world, the unshakeable thought came to her that now – just now – her life was beginning.

FICTION
from
MOUNT EAGLE

KATHLEEN SHEEHAN O'CONNOR

By Shannon's Way

"Opening up Kathleen Sheehan O'Connor's latest novel is like taking the cork out of a bottle of bubbly and watching it fizz. It has that ebullience, that simple charm. . . The writing is limpid and free-flowing. It will keep you turning the pages with its pastoral romance. . . a refreshingly earthy read that captures the warp and weft of family life with gusto and bittersweet warmth." *Modern Woman*

"Even the River Shannon becomes an important character in this captivating novel." *RTE Guide*

"A page-turning story of the sixties, full of warmth and humour, heartbreak and tears." *Waterford News and Star*

"One of the most eminently readable and thoroughly absorbing books this year. Writing comes as naturally to Kathleen Sheehan O'Connor as breathing and it's this natural ability that has seen her top the bestsellers list with her novels." *Commuting Times*

ISBN 1 902011 11 2;
Mount Eagle original paperback £9.99

Nesta Tuomey

Like One of the Family

"This is a remarkable tale. Although the book is primarily a love story, its theme is one of sexual abuse compounded by tragedy. . . *Like One of the Family* is very readable in a style which is much better than average. It has all the ingredients of a bestseller." *Irish Examiner*

"*Like One of the Family* is a sensitive, powerfully written novel that will have you in tears one minute, smiling the next and in a state of shock the next. What you will not be is bored. This page-turner of a book is one you will not be able to put down once you have started it."
Commuting Times

ISBN 1 902011 12 2;
Mount Eagle original paperback £9.99

Lilian Roberts Finlay

Cassa

"Lilian Roberts Finlay has neatly married the faded gentility of 1950s Dublin with the brasher money conscious years of the '70s and '80s. . . An absorbing view." *IE Book Review*

"A romantic family saga related with elegant craft."
RTE Guide

ISBN 1 902011 07 4;
Mount Eagle original paperback £9.99